The Silenced Shooter

A Political Thriller
by
Braxton DeGarmo

Christen Haus Publishing

COPYRIGHT

Paperback and eBook Edition Publication Date: July, 2014
Paperback, 2nd Edition, July 2015 (new ISBN)

Paperback ISBN: 978-1-943509-12-6
eBook ISBN (mobi): 978-1-943509-04-1
eBook ISBN (epub): 978-1-943509-05-8

Cover design by Rocking Book Covers

For more information, go to **www.braxtondegarmo.com**

DEDICATION

This book is dedicated to all patriots, folks who believe in American Exceptionalism and our rule of law.

ACKNOWLEDGEMENTS

As in my previous books, I want to acknowledge and thank my dear wife, Paula, my awesome, multi-talented son, Braxton and my amazingly gifted daughter, Stacey, for their valuable assistance, whether it be proofreading skills, general help, or all around encouragement.

My thanks once again to my editor, Patrick LoBrutto, whose suggestions always improve the final result. And to Lenda Selph for her proofreading expertise.

I'd also like to acknowledge Det. Neil French, St. Louis County (Missouri) CSU, and Sgt. Scot Dunn and Det. Chris Ayres, of the Maryland Heights Police Department—for their insights and instruction on CSU procedure and police tactics. Likewise, a big thanks goes to Lisa Campbell, Asst. Director of the St. Louis County Crime Lab, who gave of her time to give me a tour of the lab and to answer questions about the lab and their techniques. Any errors in this story about CSU or police tactics are mine alone.

A special shout-out goes to Gordon Skelton, who provided me with the little known fact about car seat tags, and to Hank Phillippi Ryan, for her assistance in understanding the broadcast news industry. Also, Sharon Woods Hopkins and Bill Hopkins were great sources of information about federal prosecutors and search warrants. In addition, my thanks to Dr. Greg Clark,

Superintendant of North County Christian School, for access to the elementary school to take our cover photos.

Last, but not least, my thanks to contest winners: Leslie Fairley, Patricia Goymerac, Sheila West, Jim Collins, Mena Parson and Cindy Dye. They all earned cameo roles in the story, and their support as readers is greatly appreciated.

Prologue

An omen? Abdul Aleem Malik Fawaz exited the black government sedan and straightened the *kuffiyeh* covering his head as he glanced at the residence to his left. The building's planners had designed it first as the Presidential Palace, but budgetary constraints were common even in that day. He recalled his first visit there and how disappointingly small the building seemed compared to its reputation. This evening its façade glowed a dull orange, reflecting the brilliant sunset to the southwest and reminiscent of the desert sands. The effect made it seem even smaller.

The sun setting on that building. Was that an omen of what was to come for the country as well?

Today, he wore a charcoal gray suit rather than his customary *thobe* and *bisht,* robes appropriate for his role as a Senior Fellow. Today, he had an important meeting at the highest level. Today could possibly mark the beginning of a new era, the time for the emergence of a new world order ordained long ago. Yet, at no time had the pieces been in place to make that happen. Until today.

Fawaz accepted his briefcase from the driver and turned toward the main doors to the lobby of the building where his meeting was to take place. He entered the building and welcomed the warmth and the respite it provided from the frigid January day.

"Credentials please," requested the security officer

clothed in a dark blue, wool suit. The lapel mic and earpiece of his communication device were not obvious, unlike the bulge of a handgun inside his jacket.

For the second time, Fawaz presented his creds. At the gate, the car had undergone a thorough inspection. This time it would be his person, his travel mug, and briefcase, so he handed those items to the officer without a word. He'd been here often enough to know the routine.

The officer in turn lowered them behind his desk and ran them through the scanner Fawaz knew was there. The man glanced at the monitor before him and raised the case again to place it on top of the desk. He lifted the mug, opened the travel lid, and sniffed. Satisfied that its contents were innocuous, he handed it back to Fawaz and extended a white plastic tray toward him.

"The contents of your pockets, please."

Fawaz emptied his pockets to reveal only two items, his wallet and a chain holding two keys, one to his apartment and one to his office.

"Step over here, please."

Fawaz moved into the whole body scanner, similar to those used at some airports. The guard frowned.

"Please step back. What is in your coat pocket, sir?" He again extended the tray toward the Fellow.

Fawaz sighed. He'd forgotten the ornate, and expensive, pen his sister had given him to celebrate his promotion to Senior Fellow. He removed it from his jacket's inside pocket and placed it in the tray. A second officer appeared from a doorway behind the desk.

"So sorry, I forgot it was there."

The second officer inspected and scanned the items

in the tray, while Fawaz returned to the body scanner and successfully passed through. He reclaimed his personal items and without words, followed the second officer. They already knew whom he was to meet.

The guard ushered him directly into the office of Roberta Faris, an advisor on national security affairs. She was the third such advisor in her position and had the ear of their leader, but she was the first to embrace Islam openly. Her predecessors had been secularists, with no religious leanings, unless one viewed human secularism as a religion unto itself. She had been the one to recommend Fawaz for his promotion, and for that, he overlooked the fact of her gender.

"Abdul, it is good to see you again." She extended her hand, which he shook before taking the chair across from her where she motioned him to sit. In the past, she had relegated him to the wooden chair across the desk from her. Today, they sat as equals in an informal sitting area.

"I read your report, and Imam Mahdavi has confirmed your conclusions. Have you anything to add?"

Fawaz nodded. "Indeed, I do. There were names and locations I did not feel comfortable placing in writing."

"I understand. Please keep them to yourself right now."

He gave her a questioning look.

"I think you understand why I ask that."

He did. Plausible deniability. The United States' CIA had coined the phrase during the Kennedy administration, and it again became "popular" during the Iran-Contra affair of the 1980s. The concept rarely, if ever, worked, so he was surprised that Faris would even think to rely upon it.

Nevertheless, who was he to question a superior, someone who had direct influence on his career?

They discussed his written report, and he offered three distinct courses of action to initiate their response. All of them focused on the political aspects of the problem, as requested. It was, after all, an election year for the United States. The man they worked for was the consummate politician, who saw governing as a game of politics and himself as the ultimate competitor. To Fawaz, it appeared that the man's need to win superseded the needs of the people. Yet, that flaw, that lack of true leadership, fit perfectly with the goal of Islam, to make the world an Islamic state. The man's popularity polls had plummeted, and his standing among world leaders had become fodder for the European tabloids. The man was a classic narcissist, who continued to believe himself infallible. Yes, Allah could use him.

Ms. Faris nodded and looked thoughtful as he laid out his case and recommendations. At the end of his presentation, she stood, walked across the room, and proceeded to place his report in the shredder behind her desk. She turned back to him and said, "I expect you to remove all traces of this report as well. Shred any hard copies and wipe clean any electronic versions, as well as any correspondence pertaining to it."

Fawaz nodded. He had expected as much and would comply. Mostly. Direct order or not, he would make sure he had personal insurance. If he would somehow end up in a U.S. Federal Court, he would need leverage, and he knew these people well enough to know how rough they played. There were few places in the world where he could hide, and none of those locales were particularly hospitable or welcoming. He took a sip from his mug and with care, positioned it on the table beside him with the digital recorder's mic pointed toward Faris' chair.

Ms. Faris retrieved something from her desk and returned to the sitting area to join him. The envelope in her hand seemed thin.

"Your recommended options are all quite reasonable, but we have discussed a different course of action, in light of waning popularity polls. Here is what we would like you to do." She handed him a single sheet of paper from the envelope and watched as he read.

"I believe you have contact with people in Detroit and elsewhere who can accomplish this. Yes?"

Fawaz couldn't believe what he read. Were they really willing to take such a step?

He looked up at her and tried to read her eyes, only to see his own reflection in the ice.

"Y-yes, I have such contacts." He wanted to question her, but something held him back.

"Good. How soon can we expect it?"

He tried to think, but the potential ramifications of this plan flooded his brain. He struggled to pull his thoughts together.

"One month perhaps. It will require planning and perfect timing. I can give you a timetable, if you wish, after I've made contact with these people."

She shook her head. "That won't be necessary. In fact, the less we know the better. Just make sure it's completed before the spring primaries."

One

The groundhog had failed. Whether or not he had seen his shadow was irrelevant to the fact that Punxsutawney Phil had died during his long winter nap, and his handlers hadn't noticed until it was time to rouse him for his day in front of national television. They'd had no time to call up a replacement rodent while Buckeye Chuck and Canada's Wiarton Willie took the stage to provide conflicting forecasts.

Not that either prognostication made a difference to Fawaz. Detroit seemed stuck between the two, just as it was geographically between them and at the moment, was encountering a historic, and freak, storm. After the storm arrived from the north and dumped over a foot of snow on the area, an unexplained warm front from the south moved in to turn the precipitation to sleet that added over two inches of ice to already hazardous roadways. Roads were impassable. Trees, broken from the weight of the ice, made navigation of local roads like a maze, if you had chains for your tires and the raw nerve to venture outside. The ice had destroyed the power grid as well, taking out major substations and power lines in a one-two punch that would take weeks to replace.

Worse, information was hard to obtain. With no power, local radio and television stations operated on limited backup power with what seemed like an even more limited broadcast radii. The internet was intermittent at best, but totally gone at his current location. Powerless cell towers dumbed down the smartest of phones.

Fawaz stood at the window of the Islamic Foundation's office and stared at the bleak scenery. The hum of the mosque's backup power generators seemed distant, yet they had provided the electricity needed to keep the facility warm. Hundreds of followers had braved the storm, when it was first snow, to seek refuge there. For that, he was grateful. Why *he* was there was a different matter.

He turned his head as someone placed a hand on his shoulder. He had not heard anyone enter the office.

"Be at peace, brother. All will happen in Allah's timing."

Fawaz shook his head and turned to face the man. He gave a curt bow in respect to the imam.

"I did not hear you come in, Imam."

The older man gazed into Fawaz's eyes and furrowed his brow. "I suspect it is not the storm that truly bothers you."

Fawaz knew that to be true, but did he dare to confess his real concerns to the man? He did not want to appear weak before this man.

Imam Al-Bashara had founded the Islamic Foundation and this *masjid*, or mosque, and guided it to become one of the nation's largest. He, also, had served time in federal prison for directing money to Al-Queda, a mission he continued using much more discreet methods. Fortunately, the United States' current Justice Department turned a blind eye toward such activities these days as part of an administration that favored Islam while giving lip service to Christianity in order to appease the progressives who kept it in power.

He decided it would do no good to hide things from this man. "Imam, you are correct. Please understand. I am not a coward. I am willing to give up my life for Allah. It's just that I have finally attained a position of influence, and I do not believe I am destined to play such a direct role in the coming jihad. I can be much more effective in my role as a Senior Fellow and policy analyst. I do not understand why I have been tasked to take part in this."

The imam nodded. "I suspected as much. All I can say is that there must be some reason. Allah has something to teach you here. What that is, I cannot say."

Fawaz wanted to believe that, but he suspected he had been set up to become the scapegoat, the one who would take the blame in order to keep his superiors out of trouble. If so, the surprise might be theirs.

"I am also worried about the delay. We have a timetable to keep if we are to have maximum effect on our target. We are now a day late and are likely to remain held up by the weather for another two. More, if this bankrupt city's street department is unable to clear our way out."

The imam smiled. "I cannot control how much longer this storm will last, but I can assure you a safe road out. It pays to have brothers-in-Allah in positions of control in the public works office. I have been assured that you will have a direct road out of the ice as soon as feasible."

Fawaz returned the smile and gave the teacher a curt bow. "Thank you, Imam."

"No, thanks be to Allah," said the man in his habitual

reply.

A knock at the door caught both men's attention. One of the congregants bowed at the door, a fearful look on his face.

"Imam, you must come quickly. The ice has cracked the western half of the main dome. It looks like it may collapse at any time."

The imam's visage became stern. "Do not panic. Start moving people into the education wing. We can—"

Another man appeared. "Imam, part of the dome has just collapsed. We have injuries, and the cold has already dropped the temperature in the building. I don't think our generators can provide adequate power to compensate."

The imam took a deep breath in exasperation and rushed from the office.

Bradley Graham paced the small front office of his son's elementary school. During the middle of the night, he had awakened and felt an unease he was not accustomed to. That, of itself, would have made it difficult to return to sleep, but his mind became troubled over the safety of his family.

"Brad! To what do we owe this honor?" Principal Harris Burke emerged from his back office and extended his hand in greeting. Brad and Harris had been friends since college, and Brad had, on more than one occasion, used his contacts and influences to benefit the school.

"I'm sorry, Harris. I know this is an imposition, but Cara and I have decided to pull Mark from school and take him with us to Florida."

Harris gave him a quizzical look. "Oh? Decided to take a little side trip to certain amusement park, eh? I sure would, if I was headed to Orlando on business."

Brad smiled. He hadn't even considered that option, but maybe that diversion was just what he needed. *They* needed.

"Look, I know you ask for a week's notice, to give the teacher time to prepare any assignments, but, well ..." He paused and shifted to a whisper. "... I think God is warning me about his safety. I woke up about three a.m. with him on my heart and feeling very unsettled."

Harris gave a knowing smile. "Then, by all means, he should go with you."

The principal personally went to retrieve Mark from his third grade class on the second floor of the building, along with any homework assignments expected of the boy for the next four days. Brad appreciated the accommodation of both Harris and Mark's teacher, Leslie Fairley, who would have to drop everything to write out the upcoming obligations for the boy.

As he waited, his cell phone rang, with a distinctive tone assigned to but one person.

"Hi, dear."

"Any problems?" asked his wife, Cara.

"None. Have you packed?" This trip had been a surprise for her, too.

"Of course. Who do you think you're talking to?" She laughed.

Brad should have known better than to ask. His wife was the detail person. Organization personified. She had probably finished packing her bag and one for Mark before he'd even arrived at the school.

"And, since we're all going with you, I looked into admission to surrounding tourist options."

It was his turn to laugh. While his mind focused on his upcoming speech and half a dozen meetings to raise money for his U.S. Senate bid, she thought first and foremost about *them*, her family. No, he realized, an amusement park was not the 'Happiest Place.' Wherever they were together took that title.

"We'll see. That will depend on how the fundraising goes." He paused. "Look, we're running close. As soon as I have Mark, we'll head back for you. I'll call when we're a couple of minutes away and meet you at the garage."

"I expected as much. The bags are already by the garage door. See you soon."

He slipped his phone into the cell pocket of his jacket. "Dad?"

He turned to see Harris and Mark entering the office. Mark looked worried.

"Hey, big guy. Surprise! Hope you don't mind a short vacation to Florida." He tousled his son's sandy brown hair before grabbing the extra books and papers Harris had extended to him.

The boy's eyes widened. "All right!" He pumped his fist in the air.

Brad looked at his friend. "Thanks, Harris. I owe you one."

Harris huffed. "Not on your life. After everything you've done to help Northgate Christian Academy, we all owe you more than we could ever repay. Have a great, and successful, trip, Senator." Harris smiled.

As the father and son walked toward their car, the boy looked up at his dad. "Dad, why did he call you Senator? I thought the election's supposed to be in November."

Brad chuckled. "It is, Mark, it is. Mr. Burke was just being optimistic."

Mark crunched his brow for a moment. "Oh. I get it." He placed his arms out in front of his chest and pretended to hold something in both hands as he moved his torso up and down and around from right to left and back again.

Brad smiled but remained puzzled by Mark's actions. Finally, he asked, "What in the world are you doing?"

"Being optimistic."

"Huh?"

"Yeah, practicing for my favorite ride. I'm tall enough to ride it now." The boy kept up his strange movements as he now ran toward the car.

Brad laughed. He knew when he was outgunned.

As he climbed behind the wheel, he glanced at Mark in the backseat to make sure he was buckled in. Cara and Mark would be with him, where they would be as safe as he could possibly make them. Why did he still feel unsettled?

"Slow down, Muhab. We cannot afford to be stopped." This was the third time Fawaz had warned the man since their departure from Detroit.

Muhab eased up on the gas pedal and brought their speed down to three miles over the limit. They now blended in well with the traffic flow.

"Trust me. This speed will not make our trip that

much longer."

The driver gave Fawaz a steely gaze.

"That is not why I am annoyed."

"I do not care why you are annoyed," replied Fawaz. "We've been given a task to do, and I do not wish to fail before we even get there." Fawaz had no doubt that a police traffic stop would escalate to a full-fledged search, which would result in a one-way trip to jail.

"We won't," said Naji from the backseat where he and Sabir had been talking in hushed tones. "We are taking the fight to the heartland of the infidels. Allah is on our side. We will succeed."

Fawaz turned in his seat and looked at the younger man, unsure whether to praise him for his confidence or chide him for being impudent.

"Do not get overconfident, Naji. Did you not notice what we saw in Detroit?"

"Sure, snow and ice. It's winter." Sabir, sitting next to Naji, looked equally as smug.

Fawaz frowned.

"Do either of you believe in omens?"

Fawaz did. Perhaps it had been the influence of his grandmother. She had always credited this or that as a sign of things to come. She would have a premonition of some family tragedy or a feeling about something good soon to happen. Fawaz could remember as a child when she would boast of her accuracy, reminding everyone in the family when something happened, good or bad, that she had forewarned them of the event. He'd been in awe of her fortunetelling ability, her sixth sense. In adult hindsight, he now realized she'd only boasted when she'd been correct and had said nothing when she'd been wrong. Her batting average was more like .150, not good enough to put her in the major leagues, or to even warrant her own 1-900 psychic hotline. Still, her superstitions had rubbed off on him, despite his advanced degrees in public policy and mathematics.

"Don't you find it strange that the ice storm only hit parts of Detroit? The imam received reports of a dozen *masjids* damaged by the ice. We saw a number of them as we left. Did you see a single Christian church with damage?"

The four men sat in silence for several minutes. Muhab broke the ice. "Abdul has a point. There was no ice south of I-94. We could have left two days ago, on schedule. All we had to do was push the car a mile down Highway 39 until we reached ice-free road. Don't know if that's some kind of omen, but . . ."

Fawaz nodded.

Naji piped up. "The imam would just tell us that it was Allah's timing and not to worry."

Fawaz nodded at that, too. That is precisely what Imam Al-Bashara would say. Yet, as much as Fawaz wished to believe that, to have such a great level of faith, he couldn't help but see things as his grandmother would have seen them—as another omen.

Two

Amy Gibbs, RN, stood in the parking area of the large estate south of St. Louis, dressed to the nines in an expensive Givenchy evening gown, not her own, and Gianvito Rossi rhinestone peep-toe heeled sandals, also not hers. Covering her against the cold was Richard Nichols' LL Bean wool pea coat, handed to her by a redheaded police officer whom she thought looked familiar. Although it itched her bare shoulders, she appreciated its warmth.

All around her, members of the Jefferson County Sheriff's Office and the St. Louis Major Case Squad worked to search vehicles, identify women who had been held captive by human trafficker and the estate's owner, Darko Komarčić, and secure the mansion for an extensive search. Amy, too, had been his non-consenting "guest" prior to her rescue less than half an hour earlier by Richard Nichols, a current friend, and her thought-to-be-dead, once-upon-a-time boyfriend, Lynch Cully.

"Amy, you okay?" asked her father, Lt. Col. Andrew Gibbs, Ret.

"Dad? What in the world are you doing here?" She was flabbergasted to find her father walking in the midst of the controlled chaos.

"Are you kidding? You're my daughter. Do you think I'd let Richard risk his life by himself to get you? Hassle and I covered the outside for him, and believe me, I would have shot anyone who got in your way. No matter what the consequences."

She felt his arms surround her and relished the sense of security and the warmth of his love for her.

"Dad, Lynch is alive. He saved my life."

Her father's eyes widened. "Lynch? Cully?"

Before she could answer, she saw the paramedics wheeling Lynch out from the house toward their MedAir chopper. Several of the crew members came up to them and commented on being happy she was safe. How they knew what had happened to her was beyond comprehension, but she knew all too well that the MedAir rumor mill could rotate as fast as any of their chopper blades. At least there were no wisecracks about her outfit.

A moment later, Richard followed, and she watched as he approached his friends, Hassle and Clive. To Clive, he presented his hammer of Thor, one side collapsed and shattered. Crafted of Kevlar by Clive, she knew it had saved his life once, in Afghanistan. She wondered what had happened to it inside to destroy it.

After a couple of minutes of conversation, he broke free of his friends and stepped toward her. She excused herself from her father and approached Richard.

"Amy, I . . ." He paused. "I'm sorry. I honestly don't know how you got involved in this. I didn't have any—"

Amy put her finger on his lips to hush him. "I know you didn't. We're good. Really. My dad made a comment that sums it up. Folks need to take responsibility for their own actions and quit trying to blame others. You didn't make Darko kidnap me. He did it on his own, and he'll pay for it." She placed her hand on his arm. "Like I said, we're still good."

Together, they watched as the MedAir crew lifted Lynch's gurney aboard and secured it in place.

"Excuse me a moment," said Amy. Amy clutched the jacket across her chest and walked to the helicopter. She reached up to Lynch and took his hand. He looked down into her face, and she could see that somehow he'd changed. He'd been through some sort of ordeal. That was obvious. Yet, she couldn't fathom what had changed. He simply had.

"I'm really glad to see you. Shocked—but truly happy." She smiled and gazed into his eyes, not sure what she hoped to see.

"Amy." His voice was a bit raspy, and she could see him holding his chest as he tried to talk, trying to negate the pain of breathing caused by the bullet he had taken to the left upper chest. A bullet meant for her. "I'm sorry. I—"

She squeezed his hand. "That's okay. Take it easy. We'll talk later." She released his hand and nodded to the pilot and flight nurse. "Take good care of him." She knew they would. The paramedic climbed aboard and gave her two thumbs up.

As she walked back toward her father, she could hear the engines begin to whine and felt the rush of air from the blades as they began their escape from the earth. The old saying about helicopters filled her mind: "Helicopters don't fly. They make so much noise, the earth rejects them." Without needing to look, she could feel the aircraft lift off and ascend in a max power takeoff.

*   *   *

Had her rescue from Darko's estate really occurred two days earlier? Consumed with police statements for the past day and a half, she felt as if she remained a prisoner. Plus, Amy hadn't slept well, and when Richard called in midmorning to offer to pick her up and go to the hospital, she put him off. She felt so confused. And torn. Clearly, Lynch had been through something life changing. He would need her, and she would support him in any way she could. Yet, there was Richard. With Lynch thought dead and after much counseling, she had moved on, and Richard had shown himself worthy.

About eleven a.m. the phone rang, and she glanced at the Caller ID. Barnes Hospital? Her heart began to race. Had something bad happened? Had there been complications in surgery? Then she thought, *Maybe it's Lynch calling.*

"Hello?"

"Amy Gibbs?"

"Yes."

"This is Sarah Wade. We've met in the E.D."

Amy remembered the African-American female E.D. physician she'd met while flying a few patients into Barnes' McKnight Trauma and Emergency Center. Her name had been among a few that had filled the local news after taking down a white supremacy group with plans of racial cleansing almost a year earlier. In recalling that, she recalled the name of the police officer who had given her Richard's coat two days earlier, Sgt. Seamus O'Connor. He, too, had been instrumental in eliminating that threat.

"Doctor Wade, yes, I remember you. What can I do for

you?"

"Actually, it's what I'd like to do for you. I've arranged for the nurses to clear out all the visitors from Lynch Cully's room at lunchtime so you and those involved in the takedown of those human traffickers can see him. I hope that's okay."

Amy's indecision returned. She preferred seeing Lynch alone, to talk about what happened to him and, more importantly, what was happening with *them*. However, if Dr. Wade was going to such lengths to work out this group visit, perhaps that one-on-one time could wait.

"Thank you. I'll see about getting there around noon. That's really sweet of you."

She heard the doctor laugh on the other end. "Amy, that's the least I could do for everyone involved. I hope to see you there."

Amy hung up and called Richard.

"Hey, I was just about to call you," he said after answering his phone. "A Doctor Wade called a couple of minutes ago. She—"

"I just got off the phone with her," interrupted Amy. "I'd like to go there with you, if that's okay."

"Okay? I'd love it. I'll come get you."

Amy shook her head, even though she knew he couldn't see her. "No, no. I'll pick you up. Barnes is down by your place. Makes more sense for me to pick you up than for you to drive all the way out here." She looked at the clock, and then at her reflection in the mirror. "Forty-five minutes." She confirmed the address and hung up, before getting frantic about not being ready in time.

Fifty minutes later, she honked in front of the old home holding Richard's apartment. He appeared at the doorway within seconds, making her believe he'd been standing inside waiting for her. He climbed into the passenger's seat and leaned over to kiss her on the cheek. She felt awkward and almost backed away, but didn't.

"Hey, thanks for driving. I still don't know my way around town very well."

"As I said, made more sense for me to get you. "

He scrutinized her. "You okay?"

She looked at him. Such a difference between him and Lynch. She chastised herself for yet again comparing the two. However, now she realized she was going to have to, if she was ever going to make up her mind and end her confusion.

"Didn't sleep much last night, but otherwise, yeah, I'm okay."

He nodded. "Me neither." He looked at the buildings go by as she drove. "Amy, look, I'm, uh, glad Lynch is alive. I mean that. And I'm still really, really sorry I couldn't confide in you, and that you got messed up in that whole thing with Darko. I don't know how I can make that up to you. I just hope we can go on being friends."

Amy reached over and grasped his hand. "I told you the other day, we're good. I wasn't hurt. Hey, I even got to keep a $1,500 evening gown and $1,200 pair of to-die-for shoes. I think I've been compensated for my time."

She said that; yet the fact that she'd been kidnapped and almost drugged to become some pervert's sex slave still played like slow motion reruns in her brain. How would that play into her post-traumatic stress disorder? Her therapist expected to see her in two days.

And where in the world could she expect to wear that outfit? The MedAir Christmas party? Would she even *want* to wear that gown, with it being a reminder of the incident? Maybe eBay?

"Hey, do you think they'll let us stay long, or shoo us out after a brief visit?"

"I guess that will depend on Lynch."

"Yeah, I guess that's true."

"Why?"

He waggled his head a bit. "I guess I'm being a bit selfish, but the American Patriot Conservative Caucus started this morning in Orlando, and this guy, Brad Graham, from right here in St. Louis, is giving the keynote address at one o'clock local time. I've been following him since I arrived in town, and I'd like to hear him."

Amy nodded. She, too, had found Mr. Graham's political rise fascinating, and she certainly liked what she'd heard from him, and about him, so far. In fact, local news outlets had hinted at his making a major announcement of some sort. Now, she felt curious and eager to watch as well.

Three

❧✦✦❧

Fawaz paced as they awaited their fifth member, Usayd. Muhab, Naji, and Sabir sat on the motel beds cleaning and preparing their equipment one more time. They would make their noontime prayers, the *dhuhr*, at twelve-fourteen and depart. Their target would be back from lunch by then.

The other men looked drained, but then, a night of debauchery would do that. All of them knew there was a chance, a remote chance, that they might face death. Like their brethren who had taken down the Twin Towers, they spent the previous evening drinking and satisfying their carnal desires with prostitutes. Should they escape alive, they would make penance for their sins.

Fawaz would have no need. He had remained true to the Quran and would not need to pay for such fleshly deviance.

Yet, Fawaz wondered what such penance might consist of. The target was a soft target, one chosen to send a message, not start a war. He wondered, however, whether their wearing traditional garb might not do just that. No, this was not to be a suicide mission. He expected no reward of virgins in paradise. No, Fawaz did not expect any problems. Their biggest potential hurdle was all in the timing.

Current police tactics, based upon their Multiple Assault Counter Terrorism Action Capability, or MACTAC, training would have the first four responders move in immediately to engage them. In reality, while the first responder might arrive on the scene within minutes, the time required to assemble a team of four would likely be a minimum of five minutes. Adding in the time it would take for staff members to realize what was happening, call 9-1-1, explain the situation, and for the dispatcher to place the call for units to respond, they could add three more minutes. The first responders would come to the main door just as they would, leaving the perimeter open until a force of police could arrive to secure it. That gave them time to flee behind the building. Still, they had to get in, do their work, get out, and get away within less than ten minutes.

The men flinched at a knock on the door, and the room became quiet. Naji placed his finger on the trigger of his AK-74. With the Russian's recent adoption of the newer AK-12, thousands of surplus AK-74s became available throughout the Middle East, and hundreds had been "imported" into the U.S. The Kalashnikovs would be more for show than necessary to deal with their target. Still, they liked the assurance of protection that such firepower gave them.

Sabir peeked through the window curtains. "It is Usayd." He stepped to the door and opened it to their partner.

"Did you get what we need?" asked Fawaz.

The man nodded. "Of course. Did you doubt me?" He smiled. "A Ford Econoline work van. White. Automatic transmission, as requested. I found it in the parking lot at a large mall south of the city. The owner had a work badge for one of the department stores, so it should not be noticed as stolen until the end of his shift. We should be well on our way back to Detroit by then."

Fawaz looked at his watch. Time for prayer. He walked over to the corner of the room and took hold of his prayer rug, his *sajada*. Pointing the notch in the top toward Mecca, he prepared to perform *wudu*, the ritualistic washings necessary before prayer. The others followed suit.

By twelve forty-five, they had completed their prayers and petitions to Allah for success. A surge of energy flowed through the group.

"Allah will honor our prayer. I can feel his power," said Naji.

Fawaz suspected they felt an adrenaline rush that anticipated the task they were about to undertake. Yet, he would say nothing. Naji could be right. Allah most surely could use adrenaline for his purposes.

Each man placed his Kalashnikov into a duffle designed to hide it. They would leave the bags behind in the stolen van, so the men wore vinyl gloves to avoid fingerprints and reduce the risk of DNA transfer to the canvas. Fawaz took the keys to their vehicle from the nearby tabletop. He would be the getaway driver.

Usayd opened the door and glanced both ways outside the motel. The maid's cart was at the other end of the row, and no one else was visible. "It is clear."

Fawaz took their personal bags and loaded them into the back of their SUV. Having prepaid, he left the key to the room on the table while the others loaded into the stolen van. He closed the door to the room and approached

Usayd who now sat in the driver's seat.

"You are clear as to where I'll be waiting, right?"

Each man nodded and Fawaz watched as they unpacked the assault rifles and placed them on the floor. Each man's weapon was within immediate reach for fast egress when they arrived. Upon arrival at the building's parking lot, they would don their *kuffiyehs* and cover their faces before exiting the van.

As one o'clock approached, Richard nudged Amy. She gave him a subtle nod. With assistance, Lynch had moved from his hospital bed to the adjacent chair where he sat talking with Mike and Mary Southworth, new friends who had taken him in while he worked through his amnesia. They had turned on the television earlier for the local news and the top headlines had been about breaking the human trafficking ring and Lynch's return from the dead.

She eased past one of the myriad of get-well balloon bouquets and approached Lynch.

"Hey, if it's okay with you, Richard and I are going out to the waiting area for a while. We'd like to watch the keynote speech at the American Patriot Conservative Caucus. We'll be back when it's over."

Lynch grabbed her hand.

"Hey, will we get some time together? We need to talk."

She nodded. "Sure. How about tomorrow? I can come back in the morning, alone."

He smiled in return. "Okay. Why don't you watch it in here? I need to get caught up on local and national events anyway."

She laughed. "You might not want to. All everyone seems to talk about is how much of a failure the new federal healthcare act is."

Lynch reached toward the bedrail and retrieved the television control looped around it. "Here. I'll let you find it."

Amy began to switch through channels. None of the local network affiliates offered coverage. MSNBC and CNN, likewise, showed no indication they were covering the convention. *Surely, this is newsworthy*, she thought.

"What are you looking for?" asked Mike.

"The American Patriot thing, where Bradley Graham is speaking."

He chuckled. "Well, it's sure not going to be covered by the liberal mainstream media. If Fox News doesn't have it, then the internet is the only place you'll find coverage. Try channel 48."

Amy pressed the '4' and '8' to find the Fox News logo appear over a blank screen. A second later, Sean Hannity appeared onscreen.

"Welcome back. We're going live now to Orlando, Florida, where the keynote speech at the American Patriot Conservative Caucus is about to be given by Missouri's Bradley Graham. Graham is a state senator whose star has risen along with the growing popularity of the Tea Party movement, although he denies any involvement in any of that movement's chapters. He has already announced that he's running for the U.S. Senate, but there is uncertainty about his campaign, as neither the Republican nor Democratic Parties have claimed him or endorsed him.

There has been rampant speculation about this speech, and we understand . . . Wait. He's already at the podium and about to talk. We go to Orlando."

The scene cut to a stage brightly festooned in red, white, and blue with the American flag and the "Don't Tread on Me" flag of the Tea Party movement as bookends on the sides of the center stage.

Four

Brad Graham took a sip of water and looked out across the filled-to-capacity Orange County Convention Center. He took a deep breath and thought, *Okay, it's make it or break it time.*

"Ladies and gentlemen, members of the press, all 12 of you . . ." Laughter filled the hall along with catcalls against CNN, CBS, and NBC. ". . . and my fellow patriots across the country, we are here today for what many hope will be a defining moment for the conservative movement. For far too long, the progressives, the liberals, the globalists, or whichever term you like to use, have pushed and prodded to move our country toward their vision of a global community, a community where they are the elite class who knows all and can do no wrong while everyone else depends upon their kindness just to sustain a bleak life in service to the government."

Brad glanced at his notes on his tablet and decided to switch gears a bit.

"In order for them to succeed, they would have to remove their problem child in the world community. And that problem child is us, the United States of America. A country founded on God-given rights. A country unlike any the world had known before. A country where, and I quote, 'We hold these truths to be self-evident, that all men are created equal, that they are endowed by their Creator with certain unalienable Rights, that among these are Life,

Liberty and the pursuit of Happiness. That to secure these rights, Governments are instituted among Men, deriving their just powers from the consent of the governed, that whenever any Form of Government becomes destructive of these ends, it is the Right of the People to alter or to abolish it, and to institute new Government, laying its foundation on such principles and organizing its powers in such form, as to them shall seem most likely to affect their Safety and Happiness.' "

He paused to let those words sink in. Most people stopped reading the Declaration of Independence after the word 'happiness.' And sink in they did. Thunderous applause threatened the structure of the building itself as the crowd erupted to their feet. Five minutes later, he was able to continue.

"Our federal government has become such a *Form of Government.* No longer is it a 'government of the people, by the people, for the people,' as Lincoln stated in his Gettysburg Address.

"No, as Oscar Wilde stated in his essay, 'The Soul of Man Under Socialism':

Democracy means simply the bludgeoning
of the people by the people for the people.

That is what democracy means to the Progressives. They have created entitlements designed to make people dependent upon them. They have taken control of our healthcare with a bill nobody read. Well, somebody read it. They wrote it. They just didn't want *you* to read it before they could make it law. They seek to take away our right to self-protection—and I don't mean just our guns—and our right to self-govern. Democrat or Republican, it makes little difference. They have the same goal, and until the rise of the Tea Party, their arguments were simply for show while behind the scenes they created their Machiavellian schemes to . . ."

As the white van turned into the parking lot of the building, the three passengers donned their *kuffiyehs* and picked up their rifles. When the vehicle screeched to a stop in front of the main doors, Usayd donned his as well. Within seconds, they were out the doors and running toward the building 30 feet away.

Sabir reached the doorway first and pulled a can from his jacket pocket. He reached up and pointed the black spray paint toward the video camera a few feet overhead.

Naji pulled on the door. Locked, as expected. He pulled a small wad of putty-like material from his pocket and placed it over the lock. After sticking a short fuse into it, he lit the fuse and turned away. The charge went off, and the door flew open on its hinges.

One minute down.

Brad paused and took a sip of water. He looked into the cameras and continued. "We are *not* the villains portrayed by the liberal media. We are *not* extremists. We are *not* crazy, lazy, bigoted, mean-spirited, homophobic, anti-environmental, or any of the many terms used by the progressives to paint us as an enemy of this country. If they wish to seek an enemy, they need look only as far as a mirror. *We* are patriots, Americans who still believe in

American Exceptionalism. We are still the country everyone else wants to come to, despite every effort of the progressives to degrade us into European style socialism.

"But I don't want to belabor the multitude of faults, lies, and corruption of the current government. It's time to look ahead. It's time to let America know what conservatism really stands for. We believe in family, a work ethic, self-responsibility, individual freedom, the sanctity of life, and those God-given rights to life, liberty, and the pursuit of happiness. With regards to government, we believe in a constitutionally limited government that is fiscally responsible, as did our Founding Fathers. The progressives have burdened our future generations with trillions of dollars of debt. They have expanded government to a point where we have become a regulation nation. This has weighed down our businesses with expenses that do little more than line the pockets of lawyers and government bureaucracies, while costing Americans the jobs they need to support their families. And don't even get me started on how the Federal Healthcare Act has crippled our job market and resulted in a two-tier healthcare system. It's time to put that to an end."

Once again, the crowd stood to its feet and cheered.

Harris Burke watched his old friend deliver the speech of a lifetime. More than once, he pumped his fist in the air and said "Yes!" to statements made by Brad. His friend was nailing this speech. For the first time in years, he felt hope for his country.

Suddenly, he felt a shudder in the floor more than he heard a noise. *What was that?* he thought. He placed the video feed of the speech on pause and glanced up from his computer screen. He looked to the doorway security monitor and saw nothing, black. He called up the first inside monitor and saw a blur of motion along the right periphery. Something, or someone, appeared to move from the nearby stairwell into the second floor hallway. A metallic cylinder rushed across the screen. *Was that the barrel of a rifle?*

He started to bring up that monitor when he heard a scream from the area of the stairwell. Instinctively, he opened his center desk drawer and grabbed his 9mm Glock along with its magazine. In one fluid motion, he inserted it into the handgun and chambered a round.

In the outer office, his secretary had jumped to her feet and rushed toward his door. They nearly collided as he emerged.

"Call 9-1-1! Then lock the door behind me."

Her eyes widened at the sight of the handgun in his right hand. Fifteen seconds later, he ran from the office and bound up the stairwell. That's when the cacophony of automatic rifle fire filled the building and anguish filled his heart.

Brad raised his hand toward the crowd. "No longer can we depend upon a two-party system to bring balance to our federal government. The so-called moderate Republicans share a common goal with the Democrats. George H.W. Bush, in 1992, signed up our nation for U.N.

Agenda 21, without Congressional approval or oversight. Bill Clinton furthered that cause by signing presidential order #12858 to make it national policy. On New Year's Eve, 2011, another presidential order essentially nullified our Constitution's Bill of Rights, and subsequent administrations continue to give away our freedoms and remove our rights by furthering the progressive schedule of U.N. Agenda 21. What is that plan? Abortion on demand to help reduce our global population to a total of 500,000,000—a 93% reduction from its current population of six billion. Mandated vaccines containing cancer-causing and brain-paralyzing chemicals. Universal health care that will redistribute existing wealth and enrich those in power. The elimination of private property where single-family dwellings will be a footnote in history. Political brainwashing under the guise of mandatory public education and Common Core, which dumbs down our children rather than prepare them for college. There's more—and none of it is good. None of it puts people first. None of it empowers people to flourish, to use their creative abilities and to unleash their great social, economic, and spiritual potential. Instead, their policies seek to chain people to a life of servitude to the government."

Harris stopped at the second floor fire doors and took a deep breath. He had trained for this, but he could never have been prepared for it. Beneath his consciousness, he knew he was heading into harm's way, but he had no reservations about it. He had to protect his students first.

After a second deep breath, he prayed a quiet prayer for the children and for protection, and rushed through the doorway. Fifteen feet away, the hallways intersected and stretched in both directions. The noise echoed throughout the floor, making it difficult to know whether it came from his right, his left, or both. He instinctively turned right and what he saw astounded him. An average-sized male in a *kuffiyeh* stood firing into the doorway of a classroom.

Harris never believed this could happen in America, but there the man stood.

"*Allahu akbar!*" the man screamed and started toward the door.

Harris took a firing stance, as he'd been instructed to do, and fired. The surprised masked man reeled from the hit and his left arm went limp. Yet, he managed to turn and using his right hand began to spray the hallway with bullets. Harris fired again, not feeling the burn in his chest until a moment later. He watched the man fall, blood blossoming from his chest.

Harris glanced down to see the same from his body. His breath became short, and he felt his head swirl with lightheadedness. He managed to kneel on one knee before collapsing to the floor.

Brad took a sip of water and gazed across the hall. An ill feeling crept through him. Something bad was happening. Somewhere. But what? He tried to shake the feeling, but found himself saying a quick prayer before he could continue. He looked for his family and saw them seated safely in the first row. He continued.

"No longer should we tolerate the so-called *progressive* movement. We as Americans must retake control of our country before they destroy the final vestiges of our God-given rights. To do that, we must take control of our message. We must stay on point and stop letting the liberal media skew our words and divide us with semantics."

"So, to the point, this is what we, as conservatives and patriots, believe. We believe in family, first and foremost, with marriage defined as between a man and a woman, as God ordained it. We believe we have the right to protect our family, physically and emotionally. To that end we believe that the education of our children is of paramount importance and should be controlled locally, not by some burgeoning bureaucracy whose primary goal is to indoctrinate our children to their politically correct ways, their moronic Common Core."

He paused to allow the crowd time to respond and to still.

"We also believe in small, limited government. A responsive government that will not encroach on our families and our rights. A government designed to serve the people, not the other way around. The only way to achieve that is to regain control of Congress and the White House. Only then can we move toward true cuts in spending, shore up the economic foundations of our society, and make America and its ideals great again."

The center erupted once more into a boisterous standing ovation.

Leslie Fairley's day had a rocky start. Her oldest child rebelled at going to school, even though she knew he loved his classmates and their teacher. Her husband disagreed with her on how best to handle the situation, and that led to an argument. She had wanted to resolve their differences, but the late start already meant she'd be late getting to work.

By lunchtime, she'd managed to calm down multiple minor spats in her third grade classroom. However, after lunch it seemed as if the day would never come to an end.

She startled at the sound of firecrackers in the hallway.

"What in the world?"

As the door shattered, she realized the impossible was happening.

"Down children, down!" she screamed.

Before she could scramble behind her own desk, she made sure each child was on the floor behind his or her desk. The gunman was not a student, as she first worried. He wore one of those Arab headdresses. She couldn't recall what they called it. She couldn't even recall her parents' names, but the thought of never seeing them again crossed her mind.

Her breathing accelerated, and fear permeated her. She could feel the sweat in her armpits and moistness between her legs. For a brief second, she felt embarrassed. She had wet herself.

The gunman paused. She thought it odd. He appeared to be looking for someone. Yet, that delay gave her time to jump behind her desk. With trembling hands, she reached into the bottom right drawer and fumbled to find the handgun she never thought she'd be called upon to use. She'd gone through the training shortly after the State of Missouri approved the bill for teachers and school administrators to carry weapons in school. Never in her wildest imaginations had she envisioned needing such training.

She found the, the whatever it was—Smith & Wesson, maybe—and tried to recall its function. In training she'd done well. Yet now, under stress, she couldn't even remember what make of handgun she had. She kept the clip in place, recognizing that wasn't the smartest or safest move, but now she was glad she had because she knew she'd never manage to insert it in an emergency. Even *Scooby Doo* episodes scared her. What had made her think she'd be able to do something like this under duress? In fact, how in the world had she managed so far? Only by God's strength, she realized.

The man seemed confused, as if whoever he was looking for wasn't there. A look of anger crossed his face, and he raised his rifle. A spray of bullets began to pepper the room, and she ducked behind her desk.

She had no choice. She raised the handgun and pointed it over her desk toward the man. She pulled the trigger, but nothing happened. The safety! She'd forgotten the safety.

Her finger twitched as she sought the switch, or button, or whatever it was she needed to flip to make the weapon work. She felt the click, just a scatter of lead whizzed over her head. Once again, she raised the gun over her desk, toward the gunman, and blindly squeezed the trigger.

Brad could not shake the bad feeling he had, but he had to finish his speech. The country, his country, and his family had too much at stake to stop short now. He finished enumerating his points about abortion, marriage, self-responsibility, individual freedom, immigration, the economy, and jobs. He made his point about liberals wanting to *give* everyone a fish, while as conservatives they wished to *teach* people to fish.

"The question remains, how will we accomplish this?" He paused, knowing that the blockbuster announcement to come would shake the federal corridors of power. His mouth went dry at the thought, and he took another sip of water. "It is my honor and privilege to announce to you this afternoon, that for the past two months, we have been gathering signatures, signatures from the patriots of this country. And at this very moment across the country, men and women who want to see America thrive are presenting these petitions to the Secretaries of State in each of the 50 states, plus Puerto Rico and Guam."

The crowd hushed, and Brad could feel their sense of anticipation.

"What are these petitions? We have done what every political pundit on network news has said would never succeed. We announce the establishment of a new political party, the American Party."

At that moment, two young men appeared on stage. While one removed the "Don't Tread on Me" standard, the other placed a new one. The flag, in red, white, and blue held the image of a Minuteman, with the word "American" emblazoned across the top.

Before the crowd could react, Brad continued. "We must once again become Minutemen, called upon to free our country from tyranny. We have over 20 million signatures, and now we call on you to carry this message home. And from there, let's take our message straight to Washington!"

The crowd seemed stunned at first, but soon a crescendo of applause, foot stomping, and hollering rolled across the convention center. His message had hit home. They *would* make a difference, and make America great again.

The noise stopped, and Leslie heard only the cries and whimpering of her children. She expected the gunfire to erupt again, but it didn't, and she peered over the top of her desk.

The gunman lay crumpled on the floor. His vacant eyes could be seen above the scarf that hid his face. Leslie shook as she arose from her position. The man made no movement.

She rushed to the child nearest her. Although crying, she did not appear injured. Leslie stepped back to her desk and laid the gun on top. She then moved systematically from child to child. She found each emotionally distraught, yet miraculously unharmed. After inspecting the last young boy, she stood and glanced around her classroom.

What now? They had trained for this. She was supposed to lock the door and close any blinds. She was supposed to gather her children together at the furthest point from the door. She glanced at the door to see little more than cracked glass and splintered wood, the result of the man's kicking in the door. The entire room looked devastated. She thought of all the weeks of hard work at the end of summer, to decorate the walls, and now the last month's artwork of the students appeared destroyed. Desks sat in place, many splintered. Papers were shredded. Yet, the windows weren't shattered and not one child had suffered a physical injury. With a little cleaning, they could hold class here as soon as the police allowed them back in. *Thank you, Lord!* she thought.

The fleeting thought of how irrelevant her argument with her husband had been surprised her. Her wish to run into his arms did not. In the final assessment, though, she realized she had just witnessed God's protective power firsthand.

Five

꧁ ✦ ꧂

Fawaz had parked the SUV on a quiet cul-de-sac behind the school and ducked down to avoid attracting any attention. The street appeared quiet and empty of cars that might have filled it at any time before or after the usual workday's business hours. Their SUV fit right in with the remaining vehicles he had noticed on the road. The selection of this street had been perfect.

He glanced at his watch. Eight minutes had passed. Within the next two, he expected to see four men bounding through the yard to his right. He unlocked the doors and waited. He resisted the temptation to lower a window so that he might listen for them. Such an open window would seem out of place on such a cold day. Again, he reminded himself that they needed to blend in, not stand out.

A minute later, the echo of a gunshot rang out, but it was much too close. He sat up. *What has . . .?* The opening of the front passenger door interrupted his thoughts.

"Go! Go! Go!" Usayd screamed.

"The others!"

"They have entered Paradise. Go! Or we, too, will join them."

At that second, an older man, balding with a fringe of gray, ran from behind the home to their right, brandishing a shotgun. Fawaz stepped on the gas pedal and peeled away from the curb, leaving rubber and a puff of smoke behind.

"We must get another car," yelled Usayd. "The old man will describe this one to police."

Fawaz drove on, his mind racing ahead. *How could this have happened?*

Usayd pulled his smartphone from his pocket. "There is another mall northeast of here. As we leave this residential area, turn away from the highway. That road will lead us toward it. I will tell you where to turn." He called up his map app on the phone and allowed the GPS to place them on the map. "Yes. It is not far."

Sweat beaded up on Fawaz's forehead. This was not supposed to happen. This was to be a simple surgical strike with only one casualty, the kidnapping of one child.

"W-what happened, Usayd?"

"They were armed. The teachers and a man from the office had guns. You didn't tell us about that possibility. The others are dead because you overlooked that small detail." The disdain in his voice came through clearly.

Fawaz felt a pulse of fear run through him. Usayd was the type of man who would just as well save his own skin and leave Fawaz to the authorities, at best, or send him to eternity at worst. Sabir was his cousin, and Usayd might feel honor bound to avenge his death.

"Do not blame me, Usayd. Sabir, your cousin, had the task of determining possible resistance and such possibilities. If anyone is to blame for their deaths, it is him." Fawaz then recalled the gunshot he'd heard just before Usayd opened the door. "What was the gunshot I heard just before you arrived?"

Usayd appeared to calm down and contemplate the

question.

"I do not hold you to Sabir's death. That hangs on the old man's shoulders. We, Sabir and I, saw him working in his backyard as we ran toward you. He was looking toward the school, as if he had heard the gunfire, and must have seen us. By the time we got to the place where we jumped the fence, he showed up on his back patio with the shotgun. He shot Sabir as we ran through his yard. He had me in his sight as well. I don't know why he didn't shoot me, too."

Fawaz thought about that. *Another omen?*

"At the next intersection, turn right," said Usayd.

As they did, three police cars careened through the intersection heading toward the school. Fawaz watched them in his rearview mirror as they sped away and breathed a sigh of relief. They would have time to get away.

"The mall is on this road, about six miles ahead." Usayd pointed straight ahead as he said this.

Fawaz fought the urge to speed, to add distance between them and the school. As his heart rate calmed, and their speed with it, he began to think through the ramifications of what had happened. Three dead bodies. Three Muslim males. All possibly identifiable, despite their best efforts to hide those identities. Even if only one would be ID'd, that could lead authorities to Detroit and the names of his companions—and to Usayd. If the police somehow connected them to the mosque, the imam would deny them and halt his own activities until the scrutiny diminished. The teacher would not give up Fawaz to authorities. The sole loose end, the only man, who might identify Fawaz as part of the plot sat in the passenger seat next to him.

Fawaz had told the imam that he was no coward, but he also did not see himself as a killer. However, for the good of the coming *intifada*, his intelligence, his position, and his expertise placed him far above someone as common as Usayd.

Five minutes later, he turned into the sprawling parking lot of a nearly deserted shopping mall. Jamestown Mall, according to the sign. Two of its four anchor stores appeared closed. How many stores remained? He could only guess. More importantly, the lack of business resulted in a lack of cars as well.

Both men watched as a small, white Chevy Caprice, marked 'Security,' cruised the lot and disappeared around a curve.

"We must act quickly," said Usayd. "He will be back within minutes." The man turned in his seat and appeared to scan the lot. "We need an older car, one that requires a key, not a fob. Or another small truck." He continued to search the area. "There!" He pointed in the direction where the security car had vanished. "That silver Impala might work."

Fawaz eased toward the car and scrutinized the surroundings for observers. So far, the area seemed clear. He stopped an aisle away and Usayd slipped out.

"Stay here until I get it started. Then park next to it so we can quickly unload what we need from the SUV."

Fawaz nodded and watched the man walk casually toward the car. He, too, scanned the lot for a car and then took time to pull a rag from under the seat. He tucked the object that had been wrapped in the rag into his belt and began to wipe down the steering wheel, the seat around him, the passenger-side seat and door handle, and anything within reach that he recalled touching. As he finished, he noted that Usayd had already gained entry into the car, and seconds later, it began to vibrate. Usayd had succeeded. Fawaz pulled into the parking spot next to it, the one closer to the mall, where it could block from view their next actions.

He did not take time to turn off the vehicle and jumped from his seat. Usayd had already opened the SUV's wide, side door and had taken his munitions and thrown them onto the floor behind the front seats of the Impala.

"Quickly, we have little time," said Usayd.

Fawaz grabbed his personal duffle. But instead of tossing it into the car, he placed it on the ground.

As Usayd moved another load into the Impala and leaned into the back seat, Fawaz said, "Forgive me, Usayd." With that, he pulled the handgun from his belt, released the safety, and fired one shot into the back of Usayd's head. He wiped down the gun, threw it into the back of the SUV. He wiped down the SUV's door and its handles, along with the back door and its handles. Then he pulled a timed charge from his duffle, activated it, and tossed it into the SUV as well.

He picked up his duffle and walked away casually toward the main road. In the parking area closest to the road, he walked toward an older model Nissan Altima. As he neared, he pulled the key from his pocket and clicked it to unlock the door. Always have a failsafe, he had been told, feeling content that he had listened to his trainer.

Seconds later, he pulled away from the lot onto Old Jamestown Road. He glanced into the rearview mirror as the SUV erupted into a ball of flame.

Back on the main road, he pulled a disposable cell phone from under the seat and turned it on. A minute later, he hit a speed dial number and, mocking the 9/11 tragedy, said "It's time. Let's roll." He repeated the process two more times, smiled, and drove back toward the school.

Six

Officer 'Gordy' Wilkins sat in his Florissant P.D. patrol car and listened to the Code 1000 call. *Code 1000?* That meant everyone and his cousin in law enforcement was expected to respond. He asked for a repeat and received a confirmation. Code 1000. A mix of disbelief, fear, and anger filled him. He activated his patrol car's lights and siren, and floored the accelerator. Two minutes later, he screeched to a halt in front of the main door to Northgate Christian Academy's elementary school. Crying children and anxious teachers flooded from fire exits and ran to the farthest ends of the parking lot. Only the main door remained barren of activity.

He jumped from his car and retrieved his service weapon from its holster. He adjusted his body armor and stopped for the briefest moment. All he could hear was screaming and crying. He strained to hear more. No gunshots. He donned his helmet and double-checked his utility belt.

Weapon up, he moved first to an idling white van parked askew in front of the building. He cleared it quickly and left it running. Scanning the area, he then ran to the front door, which he found open, its latch and lock destroyed. He heard tires and looked back to see a second car stopping beside his. A faint sense of relief entered his mind. *Two more to go,* he thought. Within the minute, patrol cars from the neighboring communities of

Hazelwood and Ferguson arrived.

Seconds later, Officer Trevor Davis sidled up to him, followed in quick order by the two officers from the nearby departments. With his hand, Gordy signaled, '3 – 2 – 1' and they moved through the first door. A second, inner set of doors opened into the building while a wide set of stairs rose to their right toward the second floor. Gordy knew this building well. He'd attended school here when it was the St. Aloysius High School, before the archdiocese sold it to the current private school. He pointed to the first floor doors. He had decided they would sweep to the east first, clear that wing of the first floor, move up the stairwell at that end and work across the second floor to the west end. From there, they would go down, work back across the west wing of the first floor, and return to where they now stood.

Gordy perked up as a loud gunshot, like that of a rifle or shotgun, echoed from somewhere outside. Other responders would need to handle that one, as well as the north building, chapel, cafeteria, and gym. The 9-1-1 caller had mentioned the south building's second floor, and that was his primary responsibility.

The four men moved into the diamond formation, as they had trained, and worked systematically to clear the front office first. They found a woman, who identified herself as the secretary who had called 9-1-1, inside the principal's office. One of the officers escorted her out the main door and returned to the others.

With two men facing each direction in the hallway, the other two cleared each classroom along the hallway and a utility closet near the stairwell. Each room was empty, but they found one scared fourth grade girl sobbing in the closet. Officer Davis hurried her out the nearest fire door and returned to the others, who had cleared the stairwell.

"We have a dozen officers outside and TAC is gearing up. This fire exit is now covered and safe for extraction," Davis told them as they reformed at the top of the stairs. Gordy felt relief that the county's TAC, the Tactical Operations Unit, or local version of a SWAT team, was here.

On the second floor, the scene was stark. Two men, one with a *kuffiyeh* covering his head and face, lay unmoving on the floor, blood pooled around each body. The doorway to their left appeared shattered. With caution, they moved to a point in the hallway adjacent to that door. A third, shrouded male lay just inside the door. Gordy had point, while Davis covered him, and the others covered each direction in the hall. Expecting the worst, they entered the classroom and found the teacher and her students huddled together in the far back corner.

Gordy moved toward the body on the floor and kicked away the rifle that appeared to have dropped from the man's hands. An old Kalashnikov. The man showed no sign of life, but Gordy knelt by his side and checked his neck for a pulse. Nothing. The shooter was dead.

"Quickly, come with us," said Gordy. "Anyone hurt?"

"N-no," answered the teacher. "A-are they gone?"

Gordy cleared the handgun he found on the desk and secured it. He spoke into his shoulder radio, "Three dead on the second floor. Sending a class full of students and their teacher out the east fire doors."

Together they moved the youngsters and their guardian to the stairs. Two additional officers appeared at the base of the stairs. While one watched the first floor hall, the other motioned them to come ahead. Leaving the class in the protection of those officers, the foursome worked down the hallway, each classroom still full of children and accompanying staff. They set up a CCP, casualty collection point, in the hallway near the stairwell. Once they cleared a pair of rooms, they herded everyone down the stairs, single file, hands raised, as they had the first group.

As they came to the classrooms nearest the central stairs, Davis checked the second attacker's body. Dead. The adjacent classroom door appeared like the first. Inside, the students and their teacher remained safe, and he escorted them to the CCP.

Twenty feet away, Gordy bent down to check the third body. The man was obviously a staff member who had come to the aid of the students. Had he been the one to take down the nearest . . . what? Shooter? No, terrorist. That's the only way he could describe the shooter. The man on the floor moaned.

"Medics! We need medics! Caucasian male staff member on second floor, near central stairwell," he screamed into his shoulder radio.

Davis rushed to his side.

"C'mon. We gotta clear this floor before they can come up here."

With a life at stake, the four officers moved rapidly and began clearing the six classrooms of the west wing of the second floor. Each room was a replay of those on the east wing, but this time they established their CCP at the top of the west stairwell, to avoid passing the children by the wounded man and dead shooters.

As they cleared the second pair of classrooms, a young boy pointed to the man, and his eyes widened. "Principal Burke!" Suddenly every pair of eyes went to the body on the floor and crying resumed.

"Shhh!" said Davis. "C'mon, we need to get you all out of here before we can let the medics up here." With that, the students picked up their pace, and Gordy heard the teacher tell her charges to start praying for their principal.

With the final classroom cleared, Gordy returned to the wounded man while the others watched the hallways. They still had the backside of the building to clear, but right now, the wounded principal needed immediate attention.

"Front side, second floor clear. Scene secure. We need paramedics NOW!" he yelled into his radio. Gordy realized he'd never been one to pray, but the sense of respect he felt for this man overwhelmed him, and he, too, quietly asked for God's intervention. The man had come to the aid of his students and very possibly had saved the lives of every student in that one classroom, at the risk of his own life. Gordy realized he was standing above a man who took his Christian faith very seriously, a man willing to lay down his life for others.

Within seconds, he heard feet scrambling up the nearest stairwell. EMS surrounded the man, and Gordy watched as they cut away sleeves and pant legs and inserted IV lines into each arm and one leg. One paramedic knelt above the man's head and, with another medic securing the man's neck and gently positioning the head, inserted a breathing tube into the victim's airway. In less than 15 minutes, the man was bundled onto a stretcher. Gordy could hear the thrum of helicopter blades approaching. He envisioned the adjacent soccer field turned into a mass landing zone.

He escorted the paramedic crew to the stairwell, where other officers secured their exit. Through the windows he watched as the EMT-Ps took off at a jog with the stretcher toward the soccer field where the first helicopter had just landed. Gordy noticed two more hovering above, waiting to land as called upon. To the southwest, he saw the black form of the police helicopter zooming their way. Soon news choppers would also converge on the airspace, keeping the air traffic controllers at nearby Lambert Field on the alert.

He returned to his team, and they finished their sweep of the west side of the first floor. They prepared to sweep the north side of the building, but others had picked up that task, and they were called to the Command Center established in the parking lot. The parking lot had turned into a pulsar of writhing red and blue lights. He counted 16 squad cars from their city, neighboring departments, and the county, along with their police chief's car, six ambulances, and two fire trucks.

The fire fighters huddled in debate about their response. Hazmat, explosives, and live shooting were all among the concerns they had should they be directed into the building.

The county's TAC van sat off to the side, blocking a drive that curved behind the school toward the gymnasium and cafeteria. He had applied to join the county police so he could move up to the TAC team, but had heard only that he was on a waiting list. He wouldn't leave his current position until he had confirmation of being hired by the county.

A hand clapped him on the shoulder. He turned to see his police chief.

"Good job in there, Gordy," said Colonel Andrews. "That'll look good when an opening comes up on TAC, although I hate losing you to the county. Already lost one good officer to their CSU."

Gordy gave a faint smile, not wanting to appear too pleased under the circumstance. In fact, he would have preferred any opportunity other than a school shooting to prove his mettle.

Both men's radios crackled with news that the north building was clear. The TAC team would move next to the chapel, followed by the other outlying buildings. Gordy suspected all would be cleared quickly. Those buildings were not large, although they held a number of side rooms, offices, and storage rooms.

"Chief, I heard a rifle report just after we entered the building. It seemed to come from outside."

Andrews nodded. "Bad guys tried to escape past those homes over there."

He pointed to the subdivision to their north filled with small houses and traversed by several roads ending in cul-de-sacs. Each road emptied onto Florissant Road, a main thoroughfare through the area with access to the interstate one block away.

"We have guys over there, and they've secured the

secondary scene. What I'm hearing is a retired homeowner saw two hooded men running toward his place with automatic rifles in hand. He'd been working outside and heard what he thought were firecrackers coming from the school just before that. He ran inside and grabbed his shotgun. Said one of the men raised his weapon toward him after clearing the fence, so he shot him. That one's dead, but one got away, along with a driver in a dark blue Chrysler Town & Country. We got a partial plate number, and it's being tracked down."

"Chapel cleared!" came through the radio.

"All right," said his boss. "So, who showed up? Let's see." He looked at the officers standing with Gordy. "Hazelwood and Ferguson. Thanks guys." Underneath his breath he criticized another nearby department known for its high volume of speeding tickets and which failed to respond. He shook his head. "Okay, brief me on what happened."

Gordy laid out his report in detail, and stood by as each man in his team gave a similar debriefing. Throughout the process, Gordy couldn't help but reflect on the wounded principal. Gordy was a trained professional, someone who knew the risks of going into a situation like the one they faced, but Principal Burke was not. Trained or not, Gordy realized he had a lot to learn from a man like that.

Seven

Florissant P.D. had wasted no time in requesting Major Case Squad assistance on this case, and Sgt. Seamus O'Connor had once again been called up from his position with St. Louis Metro Police. Although there were over 20 participating departments and the Squad's manpower was to rotate through them, he seemed to get called for more than his share. It took him away from his daily workload, although he hadn't made up his mind as to whether or not that was a good thing.

At least he wasn't called upon as often as Lynch Cully. Cully could have been considered full-time, if such a position actually existed. They were all "volunteers," paid by their own departments while assigned to the MCS.

He eased up to the police barricade that had closed the western approach on Dunn Road just before the school's athletic field. A MedAir chopper bolted into the air in a max power takeoff and headed due south after clearing the trees and power lines. He assumed they would head for Barnes Hospital and the McKnight Trauma Center where his friend (neither of them could quite come to the point of calling the other a girlfriend or boyfriend) Sarah Wade, MD, stood by. No doubt she had received the medic's report and, as Chief Resident, had her team ready.

He rolled down his window and presented his credentials to the officer at the cordon. The man moved the traffic barrier and waved Seamus through.

"Thanks, but maybe I should just park out here." Looking ahead, Seamus saw that he might be able to advance maybe 20 feet farther before the sea of squad cars blocked his way.

"Up to you, Sergeant." The officer shrugged his shoulders as he spoke.

Seamus echoed the shrug and moved ahead 20 feet to park partially on the shoulder. From the look of the scene, he wouldn't need any special gear, but he doubled-checked his handgun and began walking along the road. As he turned into the parking lot's western entrance, he saw two more veterans of the Major Case Squad ambling toward the Command Center from the east. Paul Flannigan, who had been part of the MCS when Lynch Cully disappeared, waved.

A minute later, they converged on the Command Center. Florissant's Chief of Police, Colonel Wyatt Andrews, stood off to the side with four officers.

"Hey, O'Connor—"

Flannigan's greeting was interrupted by the nearby descent of another MedAir chopper. The three detectives looked in unison toward the soccer field. The noise abated as the bird powered down. The medic crew emerged and removed their helmets. Seamus saw Amy Gibbs and experienced a surreal moment. Had it been such a brief time since they had been together in Lynch Cully's hospital room? As with St. Louis' weather, 30 minutes could bring incredible change. He waved, and she returned the 'salute.'

"D'you know her?" asked Flannigan.

Seamus nodded. "We were together sitting at Cully's bedside half an hour ago."

"How's he doing?" The detective paused. "Still can't believe he's alive."

Seamus laughed. "Oh, he's alive alright." He waggled his head. "What I can't believe is that he says he had amnesia and *still* took down that human trafficking ring."

Seamus glanced skyward and noticed the medevac helicopters that had been circling the area when he arrived had departed and been replaced with local news choppers. He turned to see that Amy and her crew had settled into waiting inside their aircraft. Warmer there. He suspected they would remain onsite for a little while before getting a final release.

He also noticed officers moving their cars to allow two county CSU vans into the parking lot.

"I guess the scene is secure. CSU is moving in."

Flannigan shrugged. "Just got here myself, but from the way folks are moving around, I'd say you're right."

"O'Connor, Flannigan, Wexler!"

The three men turned to see the current head of the Major Case Squad, Captain Vincent Johnstone. The man stood in stark difference to the prior commander, Colonel Dandridge, "the Chief." Seamus shook his head at the thought of the Chief lying dead in the Jefferson County mansion of a vile human trafficker. The fact that he'd died saving Cully's life didn't come close to negating the fact that he'd been associated with those criminals in the first place. He hoped that Susan Prichard's inquiry into the matter would shed a kinder light on the man. The St. Charles detective certainly had her plate full with that investigation.

Seamus sighed. Where Dandridge used his intellect

and deduction to work through a crime, Johnstone liked brute force. Feet on the ground. No stone unturned. No hour too late and no day too long. Seamus wondered if the man had ever heard of technology, or a vacation.

"Wexler, there's a secondary crime scene over there." He waved toward the homes behind the school. "Locust Street. Take your car and drive around to it, so you don't muddle up the crime scene between here and there."

Johnstone looked back and forth between the two remaining men as Wexler hurried away. "Flannigan, tertiary crime scene at Jamestown Mall. Sounds like our fourth shooter. You take that one. O'Connor, you're here, with me."

Flannigan glanced at Seamus and gave him a subtle roll of the eyes. Seamus, on the other hand, felt like he was supposed to answer the captain with a crisp salute and a "Sir! Yes, sir!" For a brief moment, a sense of jealousy filled him. He'd give up the primary scene not to have to get stuck with Johnstone. Oh well.

A CSU detective walked up to them. A Nikon DSLR hung around her neck.

"O'Connor, Captain. I'm working the building to start. Kasey's got the white van. You know the drill. We'll work from the outside in."

Seamus replied, "Hey, Parson. Glad to see you on this one." Seamus had worked with Mena Parson before and knew the woman was thorough. "Let us know if you find anything, you know, out of the ordinary." Seamus stumbled on the last four words. How could anything in a school shooting be considered ordinary? "You know what I mean."

The CSU detective nodded. "Sad as it sounds, I do know what you mean." With that, she turned and headed to the far end of the parking lot, farther away from the building, to begin taking photos.

"Captain, I'm going to start interviewing the teachers and students."

Johnstone nodded and walked off toward the white Ford Econoline, where another CSU detective stood taking pictures. Seamus stood there and watched as the man walked away. Wasn't he going to help with the interviews? The CSUs would handle the evidence collection.

Seamus shrugged and turned toward the crowd of students and teachers huddling in the cold. Many were shivering. Many still cried. They needed to get these folks out of the cold or they'd have weather related casualties to deal with as well.

He diverted his walk and headed toward Colonel Andrews, who nodded in greeting as Seamus approached. They discussed the situation. The police chief talked with several officers and the head CSU, and informed Seamus of their decision.

Following the colonel's lead, Seamus and several officers from the local department began coordinating with the teachers. Each class was to line up in single file and walk along a designated path to the gymnasium, which had been cleared and appeared uninvolved in the event.

Seamus watched as the separate classes moved together under the watchful eyes of the local officers to that western side of the campus. He glanced toward the eastern edge of the building and saw Parson moving down the service drive. A moment later, the police helicopter descended to just above the treetops. Obviously, they had spotted something of interest. Seamus switched his radio to the 'Riot A' channel, a secure frequency that news reporters and scanner freaks couldn't monitor.

"Ten feet ahead and a foot or two to your right. It's losing heat quickly."

Seamus reasoned that the aircraft crew had used their FLIR to map out the escape route and spotted something. The police helicopter's Forward Looking InfraRed camera could not only spot a person's heat signature, it could follow the heat trail of footsteps across cold ground within a 20 to 30 minute window. The end of that time window fast approached.

He watched the CSU detective move slowly but deliberately to follow the aircrew's directions. The conversation on the encrypted frequency continued.

"You're on it. What is it?"

Parson replied, "A folded sheet of paper."

Seamus started walking toward Parson as the detective placed a numbered marker next to an object and took a series of photos. The helicopter rose several hundred feet into the air. By the time he reached the spot along the drive near the detective, Seamus noted that the item was bagged and labeled. Mena turned and saw him.

"Yeah, I figured the helicopter coming down would get your attention. Saves me from walking to you." She crossed the grass between them and handed Seamus an evidence bag. "You might want this when you do your interviews."

Seamus looked into the clear plastic bag to see a

standard sheet of white printer paper, folded into quarters. On one exposed face, there was a full color picture of a young boy.

"Must have been dropped by one of the shooters. It still held enough heat that the FLIR saw it. Bet the boy goes to school here, so you can have it to ask around, but make sure I don't leave without it."

Seamus scrutinized the image. "I think you'd win that bet. Thanks."

Parson glanced back toward where she picked up the paper and shook her head as she scanned the nearby fence line. "Now I've got to work this fence line, too. Every piece of litter will need to be photo'd, tagged, marked and collected. Might be a while before I get inside."

Seamus held up the bag. "Thanks for this. I'll be in the *warm* gym doing interviews."

"Yeah, yeah. Don't rub it in."

Seamus grinned. Despite the woman's grumbling, he knew Parson loved her work.

Seamus continued along the service drive behind the buildings and came to the gym. The last class filed through the doors as he approached. Inside, he found the bleachers pulled out, and each class sitting in a designated area. The younger children sat on mats on the main floor, and the older ones took the bleachers. A teacher sat with each group.

Despite the number of children in such a confined space, the place was remarkably quiet. Seamus likened it to the discipline he'd known growing up in the Catholic school system. Sister Michael came to mind, and he shivered at the memory. His mind shifted to the public schools, and he wondered if they could match the discipline under similar circumstances. But then, he hoped he'd never have to find out.

A small group of adults stood in the center aisle, at the base of the bleachers. Colonel Andrews stood with them. *The school administration, no doubt*, thought Seamus. He walked up to them, and Colonel Andrews introduced him to the group.

"I have a picture of a young boy I'd like to show you. Do you know who he is?" Seamus held up the evidence bag so that everyone in the group could see the image.

An older woman gasped, and the others all nodded or made some noise of recognition.

"That's Mark Graham, Bradley Graham's son."

Seamus felt a queasy wave of concern wash over him. He recognized Bradley Graham as a candidate for the U.S. Senate, as well as the owner of a major technology firm in the area. *A political target? Ransom? Or something else?* He didn't like the sudden wave of possibilities that surged through his head.

"Is he here? Which class is he in?"

"Oh no. His father pulled him from school yesterday to go to Orlando for the convention."

"He's a third grader. Mrs. Fairley's class. She's the one who shot one of the intruders. Poor dear. She's all upset."

As a group, they turned their heads in unison, and Seamus had no trouble picking out Mrs. Fairley. A woman, younger than Seamus anticipated, sat with a class of students to his left and held her head in her hands.

"Thank you, and please do not mention this picture to anyone. I don't know exactly where it came from, much less what it means, and we don't want needless speculation and rumors starting up. That could really hamper our investigation. Not to mention add to the risk for the Graham family."

After they nodded in acknowledgment, he asked them to stick around and headed toward the third grade class.

"Mrs. Fairley?"

The young woman looked up, and the intensity of her blue eyes struck him. She had amazing, no, mesmerizing eyes.

"Yes?"

"I'm Sergeant O'Connor, with the Major Case Squad. May I talk with you?"

"He's dead, isn't he?"

"Who?"

"The intruder, the shooter, the terrorist, whatever you want to call him."

"Yes, I've been told that he is."

Tears welled up in her eyes. Seamus understood. Everyone sees such a sanitized version of crime and killing in the media. Most never think it might happen to them. And when it does, they find it hard to come to grasp with the solemnity of taking another life. Seamus could see that such a reality might be more difficult for a Christian to accept, yet he could never believe that God would hold this against the woman who sought only to protect her kids.

"Ma'am, I need to hear what happened as you remember it."

She nodded. "Here, or do we need to go someplace else?"

Seamus thought about that for a moment. Ideally, he

would prefer to interview her away from the children, but that might be difficult. Before he could answer, she continued.

"There's the gym office, if it's not in use already. Someone else could watch over my class."

As he had entered the building, Seamus had seen another detective take a teacher into the office, so he knew that was tied up. The rest of the school was still to be processed by the CSU, so he couldn't go to a classroom or other office.

"The children will behave, if we need to talk here. Won't you children?" She said that more loudly and in such a commanding voice that Seamus knew *he'd* behave if *he* were her student. The thought, *Did she know Sister Michael?* crossed his mind.

"Okay, we'll do it right here," replied Seamus, as he pulled out his digital recorder from his pocket. As he dictated the date, time, and other pertinent information, several students inched in closer to their teacher and the others squeezed in beside and behind her.

"So, why don't you start at the beginning? What were you doing, and what did you notice first?"

Mrs. Fairley composed herself and began a detailed accounting of the event. Her recall under stress amazed Seamus, and from reading the body language of the students, not one of them disagreed with her. As she described the bullets flying around them, Seamus tried to envision the room as she saw it at the time. Personally, he would see it soon, after the CSU released it to them. Several of the girls started to sob at recalling the event. Even a few boys showed tears in their eyes. Yet, one boy in particular showed no fear, no emotion at all, over discussing the shooting. His reaction seemed out of place as Seamus glanced at the students collected around them.

"With all the bullets, you were quite brave to rise above the desk and take aim at the shooter," said Seamus.

"Brave?" She leaned closer to him and whispered, "I don't want the students to know, but I was so scared I peed my pants."

He nodded. "So, how did you manage to shoot the man?"

She shook her head. "Beats me. I just lifted the gun over the top of the desk, pointed it to where I thought he was, and pulled the trigger. Oh, first time I tried, I had forgotten the safety. It was the second time that I was able to fire."

"It was God," said the young boy who showed no concern. "He made the bullet hit the bad man."

"Jackson, shhhh."

Jackson was a bit pudgy and wore black-rimmed glasses. He had a mischievous air about him.

"But it was, Mrs. Fairley." The boy's whine took on a "you gotta believe me" tone.

Seamus raised his brow and looked at the boy. He didn't want to discourage the lad, so he asked, "How do you know that?"

" 'Cause I watched the whole thing."

"You watched it? You didn't have your head down like you were supposed to?" asked Mrs. Fairley. "Jackson, you know what we talked about in our drills."

"I know, Mrs. Fairley, but I wasn't scared or anything. I knew the bullets wouldn't hurt us, and they didn't, did they?"

"Jackson, you need to listen to your teachers. They've been taught how to protect you."

"I know, but Mr. Detective, sir, you'll see when you go to our room. We weren't in danger."

Seamus felt curious as to why the boy was so sure on his position.

"Why do you say that, Jackson?"

"Because two big angels protected us. I saw them. They were as tall as the ceiling, and their wings and hands kept the bullets from touching us. And one of them, when Mrs. Fairley's gun went off, he used his finger to move the bullet. Right between the bad guy's eyes." He let loose a big sigh. "Like I said, God made that bullet hit the bad man. He just used his angel to do it."

Several of the other boys snickered, but Mrs. Fairley gave them a stern look, and they quieted in an instant. Seamus knew that poor Jackson was going to take some heat after this was done.

"Mrs. Fairley, did the children see the man's body as you left the room?"

"Well, we all had to pass it to get out, but now that I think about it, I don't know where the bullet hit him. His face was covered with one of those Arab headdress things."

"A *kuffiyeh*?"

"Yes, that's what it's called. I don't think we could see his face at all. And I think all of us were pretty much focused on getting out, not on the body." She glanced at Jackson and then back to the detective. "You'll have to forgive Jackson, Sergeant. He's not a liar, but he is creative.

He writes the most entertaining stories in the entire class."

This time, several of the girls giggled, only to get the teacher's "look."

Seamus nodded and asked her to finish her story. Mrs. Fairley described hearing more gunshots from the hallway and then silence. Minutes later, the first policemen showed up and escorted them outside. After being frisked, they focused on staying warm since all of their coats had been left in the classroom.

Seamus started to ask about the Graham boy but decided against it after considering the whole class was there. Instead, he asked the entire class if they had anything different to say or anything to add. It appeared they all agreed with their teacher, although a couple of the boys gave Jackson playful punches on the shoulder. Yep, poor Jackson, was going to have it rough for days to come.

Seamus thanked them all and turned off the recorder he'd been using to record the interview. He stood and looked about for another teacher to interview when his radio crackled.

"Seamus, it's Mena. You might want to see this before they cart off the body. It's the third grade classroom where the shooter was killed. Second floor on the east side."

"On my way," he replied.

As he stepped outside, he noticed something odd. Not a single helicopter circled the area. The only major noise came from the interstate across the road. He knew the medevac helicopters had been released, but where were the news choppers? He jogged to the front of the main building and found his way to the third grade classroom.

"What's up?" he asked.

"Look around you. What do you see?"

Seamus didn't have to look hard to see shattered desks and papers scattered across the floor. He was surprised to see the windows intact. A glance at the walls revealed numerous bullet holes.

"The place is really shot up. I'm surprised the windows are intact."

Mena nodded. "Take a closer look. What kind of rifle does he have?"

"Not an expert, but it looks like an old Kalashnikov, maybe an AK-74?"

"Right. Now look at the holes in the walls."

Seamus focused on the nearest wall and found his second surprise. The bullets had stopped as soon as they had entered the wall.

"Yep, I see it in your expression. Those bullets not only should have passed through the wall, but they could have passed through two or three more before stopping. What else?"

Seamus felt a tingle along the back of his neck. Every bullet hole he checked showed the same thing, flattened lead slugs embedded in drywall. Some hadn't even passed through the inside layer of paper on the drywall. He glanced back at the shooter and the desks. Although many desks were destroyed, he saw a ring of spent ammunition and blunted bullets that encircled the shooter, as if someone had picked them all up and placed them along a circle ten feet around the shooter. No, it appeared as if some unknown barrier had protected the lower part of the room, the area where the students had taken refuge.

"What about the other room?"

"Haven't gotten to that one yet."

Seamus walked into the hall and two classrooms down to the doorway where the principal had stopped a shooter. The door and walls looked shattered, yet closer inspection revealed the same phenomenon. There were even a dozen slugs flattened against the door's window, but the glass remained unbroken.

Now, the hair on his whole body tingled and gooseflesh prickled his skin. He returned to the third grade class.

"Wait 'til you see the next classroom." He shook his head in bewilderment.

"Seamus, I can't explain how this happened. If you reduce the powder in the shell, or just use the primer, I can see the bullets not having the power to penetrate the wall. But, they'd still penetrate deeper than the paper, and they would certainly shatter the windows. And if that was the case, how do we explain the shattered desks? The techs are going to scratch their heads on this one."

Seamus consciously lowered his hand, which he'd begun to raise to scratch his own head. He couldn't explain what he saw, but a thought hit him as he returned the boy's photo back to Parson. "How did the shooter die?"

"The M.E. investigators couldn't tell right off. But when they removed the *kuffiyeh*, there was a single GSW, right between the guy's eyes."

Eight

Amy walked away from the helicopter at the Barnes Hospital helipad where the crew had picked her up following the Code 1000 call. She ducked into the closest bathroom and changed back to the clothing she had worn to visit Lynch. She tucked her flight suit back into her small duffle and prepared to return it to the trunk of her car. The adrenaline rush of the call had dissolved on the flight back, and now she wondered what to do. Technically, she was on medical leave following her kidnapping, but that ordeal had been an emotional one, a brief one at that, and no physical harm had occurred. She felt like she was on vacation, although somewhere in the back of her mind, she realized how close she'd come to becoming a sex slave.

Her thoughts returned to Lynch. She knew she had told him she'd be back tomorrow, but the emergency call had disrupted everything. She was there, in the hospital, with no immediate demands on her time. Richard had taken a cab back to his place. She decided to head back to Lynch's room. If the timing was poor, she could always return the next day as planned.

The hallway outside his door appeared quiet. The balloons and banner proclaiming "He's Alive" remained as they had been when she left. She stepped up to the door and listened. Silence. Was he sleeping? She knocked on the doorpost. No answer.

She knocked again and heard him say, "Come in." She

stepped into the room and saw his face light up in a smile.

"Hi. Didn't expect you back today." He held out his good hand to her.

She walked to the right side of the bed and scooted a chair up next to him.

"They had to bring me back because my car's here. So, I figured I'd stop back in." She paused. "If that's okay with you. If you need to sleep or something, I can come back. I do understand your needing your rest."

He laughed. "Yes, nurse." He reached over, took her hand, and gave it a squeeze. "So, what happened at the school?"

She briefed him on what little she knew, which wasn't much. "I saw Seamus from a distance. He can fill you in."

Silence commandeered the room. Amy felt awkward. Lynch had obviously gone through a major ordeal. Certainly a lot more than her being kidnapped and forced to play dress-up, which was how she chose to remember it.

He looked over at her. "You know, I vaguely remember eating Greek food at your place. Was that the last time we saw each other?"

Amy wracked her brain to think. Was that the last time? No. "Actually, we saw each other two more times. Once in the E.D. at Mercy when we brought Art Barklage in, and again when I took you flying to look for that bus. The one where you disappeared."

He looked over her shoulder and out the window. "I-I don't remember too much of that."

She gazed into his eyes and saw a difference.

Lynch went into his story of what had happened to

him. She wondered how many times he had told this story in the past 48 hours.

"Amy, I-I honestly didn't remember anything about you until less than two weeks ago. I saw a helicopter flying overhead, and your image came into my head. From that point, more and more memories began to flood my brain. Not just about you but about my parents and others, too." He paused. "I thought my memory was completely back, until now, when you mentioned flying together. The last I remember was eating Greek food together, but even that is fuzzy, and I'm not sure why we were together or what we talked about."

She could see the pain and confusion in his eyes, and her own emotions swirled. She knew she should respond but honestly didn't know how. How does one respond to someone recovering from amnesia, someone whose memories of his relationship with you didn't necessarily fit the reality of it?

Amy vacillated. Should she mention the problems they'd had? That he'd left her without so much as a goodbye and then wanted back into her life? Yes, that air still needed to clear, so she gave him the full story. As she did so, tears began to fill her eyes. Surprisingly, tears filled his as well.

"Amy, I am so . . . I'm sorry. I had a vague recollection that things weren't right between us, and now that you tell me all of this, I realize what a jerk I'd been and how much I must have hurt you. Yet, I also remember looking into a teaching position, so I could leave the police force and offer you a life like you deserve. I was going to surprise you after I got the position."

That revelation stunned Amy. Lynch had been looking to give up active police work for her?

Lynch continued. "Now, I'm not sure that position is still open for me. And . . ."

Amy still reeled from his disclosure, and immediately Richard came to mind. It took a moment for his unfinished sentence to hit her.

"And?" She didn't know if she should ask that or not.

"Amy, I don't know how to say this, but it's like we're starting all over."

Amy could see how he might think that, but that didn't erase her memories of what had happened. It wasn't 'starting over' for her. And there was Richard. They'd been dating for over two months.

"Lynch . . ." She hesitated, but she knew she had to be forthright. "Lynch, I thought, we *all* thought you were dead. Now? I don't know what to do, or say. I met someone a couple of months ago. He risked his life to save me, too. I . . ."

"Richard. I suspected there was more to the story than him being out to take down Darko."

Amy looked at him and scrunched her brow. Was he belittling her relationship with Richard? Maybe he hadn't changed after all.

"Oh? And what about Danijela? She seemed pretty cozy with you earlier today."

"Well, she saved *my* life. And I thought Darko kidnapped you *because* of Richard."

While that was true, Richard wasn't at fault.

"That was Darko's doing, not Richard's. He came to the estate to rescue *me*. You came to the estate to help

Danijela. You probably didn't even know I was there."

By his silence, she knew she was right.

"Amy, I'd like to start over."

"Well, that's what you said at the dinner you vaguely remember. It's oh so convenient for you to say that, when you have such little memory of our past relationship. However, I have a full recollection of that relationship and how you hurt me. And now that I've moved on, you suddenly come back from the dead and want to *start over*?"

Tears welled up in her eyes. She felt more confused.

Lynch hung his head.

"Amy, what can I say? I have changed. I . . . I . . ."

"What about Danijela? Before all of this, I had to compete with your job for your time and attention. Do I have to compete with Danijela now?"

Amy hadn't intended to make Danijela an issue, but somehow, in her mind, she knew that the woman had become one. Lynch furrowed his brow and frowned.

"Amy, coming back from the dead, as you put it, has been incredibly confusing for me. Do you have any idea what it's like to not even know who you are? I don't need to add to this stress. And what about Richard? Do I have to compete with him?"

Amy knew she had been the one to escalate the tension in the room. He was right. He didn't need the added stress. Yet, months of built-up frustration, worry, anguish, and more bubbled up to the surface. She'd been back with Lynch for no more than an hour, and already they were arguing. *Maybe* he had changed. He would have to prove it.

Moreover, she *had* changed. She could put their relationship into proper perspective now, thanks to all of her counseling sessions. Moreover, she really did like Richard.

"Yes. You will. I like Richard. He likes me. And if you want to start over, you'll just have to compete for *my* time and attention for a change."

"Well, I like Danijela, too. So, it goes both ways. But right now, I'm tired. I'd like to be alone."

Amy scrutinized his face. She had hurt him. She didn't like that thought, or the fact that the air which needed to be cleared was now smoggier than ever.

Lynch watched Amy exit the room and laid his head back into his pillow. What had just happened? All he wanted to do was have some time with her, get reacquainted, and make his intentions known. Had he hurt her so badly that his chances of reestablishing their friendship were nil? Maybe he needed to focus his attentions on Danijela. He could help her gain her citizenship here. He could help her with the education she desired. There was no 'starting over' with her.

He reflected on their conversation. He'd been honest and open. He thought he'd stated his desire clearly. Maybe to say they were starting over was unfair. Indeed, he realized that it *was* unfair, and that she was right. It would be impossible for her to begin fresh, as if nothing had ever happened.

He drifted off only to awaken some time later to the gentle prodding of the evening nurse.

"Do you need a pain pill?"

"I was sleeping."

"Yes, I know, but it's time for your pain pill, if you need one." She smiled sweetly.

"If I was in that much pain, would I have been able to sleep?"

She looked wounded.

"Are you going to wake me later for my sleeping pill, too?"

She stood upright and frowned. "Well, you don't have to get surly. I'm just doing my job."

She turned on her heels and marched from the room, no doubt to make some nasty comment on his chart. Lynch wondered how much longer he'd have to stay there. The pain was tolerable, as long as he didn't take too deep a breath, cough, laugh, or move too suddenly. Not to mention he still had a tube hanging out of his chest. He sighed.

Looking at the clock on the wall opposite his bed, he saw that the six o'clock news was about to start. So, he picked up the remote and switched channels to a local station. The pending winter storm warning topped the news, followed by another story on the "knock-out" game. He'd seen this on the news at the Southworth's home and could not understand the motivation behind the teens who did this. The teenager in this incident, however, caught more than he'd bargained for, a bullet to the heart from the victim's concealed weapon. No doubt, by tomorrow, the boy's family would be flooding the newscast with comments that he was a "good boy" and "never caused any trouble." 'He didn't deserve this,' an aunt will say. Perhaps not, but the victim didn't deserve being assaulted either.

Bored by the local events, Lynch flipped channels to find some national news. CNN carried more stories praising Nelson Mandela, who had recently died, as well as the latest on Democrats pushing for gun control.

Gun control?

That's when Lynch realized there'd been no mention of the school shooting that afternoon. He raced back to another local station and then another. Nothing. According to Amy, four gunmen had entered a local Christian school with automatic weapons, fired upon two classrooms before the principal shot one of the men, and two men fled the school. Why hadn't that been the top news story on every channel?

Lynch flipped back to CNN. A U.S. Senator, a New England Democrat, argued that teachers should not be allowed to have guns in school. School districts should have zero tolerance. Lynch shook his head.

He flipped to Fox News Channel as the anchorwoman came back from a commercial break.

"So, as we mentioned at the top of the hour, there's a culture war escalating in our country. The I.R.S. scandal has revealed that conservatives remain under attack by the current administration. The mainstream media remains fully complicit with these actions by ignoring the issue, or in some cases, by flagrantly attacking conservatives through its heavily biased reporters, as recently happened with a very personal attack on former Governor Sarah Palin. While that specific incident led to the resignation of that news anchor, many are disappointed that CNN failed to act by firing said news anchor."

"But tonight, I want to reveal a disturbing trend in this culture war. We're all aware of the ongoing attacks on Christmas, with school districts and municipalities across the country facing lawsuits for allowing Christmas decorations or manger scenes on public property. This past Christmas was no exception."

Lynch heard a knock at his door and turned to see Danijela standing there. She appeared to be alone. He motioned her in but signaled her to be quiet and to listen to the news report. She sat in the chair by his bedside and looked up to watch the newscast.

"Now, these same groups are taking their attacks further. A memorial cross atop a hill overlooking San Diego has been ordered to be dismantled by a federal judge. The cross has stood there for 60 years and is maintained by private donations, yet somehow its very presence on public land has been deemed as unconstitutional. In Colorado, an administrative judge has ordered a Christian baker to make a wedding cake for a gay couple, a task that goes against the baker's strong Christian beliefs. There are dozens of similar cases across the country, where the gay rights movement deliberately targets Christian business owners to force their agenda upon people of faith, despite many other bakers, florists, and photographers being available to them in their communities."

"These so-called progressives decry bullying, yet they have become the social bullies of our time." She paused. "They whine about diversity, yet won't accept the beliefs of others and expect everyone to conform to their ideas of society."

"This is bad enough, but now the attacks have turned violent, and again, the mainstream media ignores it. Last February, a Muslim man shot, then beheaded two Coptic Christians, and cut off their hands before burying the bodies at an uncle's rural property. You've heard about it, right? No, you probably didn't, despite the fact that the incident took place in New Jersey. New Jersey, people!"

"And today, a school shooting in St. Louis is all over the news. Right? Wrong! The initial reports we received have been confirmed. Four men, not students, wearing *kuffiyehs* and armed with automatic weapons entered a Christian school near St. Louis this afternoon. While the men attacked two classrooms, a teacher and the principal, armed with handguns, shot and killed two of the attackers. A third was shot and killed by a nearby homeowner. Miraculously, no students were injured, although the principal remains in critical condition in a local hospital."

"Where are the reporters? Where is the outrage? Where are the television broadcast vans parked outside the school? Where is the mainstream media? Silent. News helicopters disappeared before the crime scene unit even entered the building. And not a single television van can be seen outside the police cordon. Is it because the incident occurred at a Christian school, and the attackers appear to be Muslim? We'll let you be the judge. We will have more on this school attack as details become available."

Danijela's eyes widened. "What is this? Men attack Christian school? I not hear this on radio or TV."

Lynch fought to sit still. He needed to be there, on the Major Case Squad, working with O'Connor and the others. He couldn't stand being outside the loop.

"Do I have any clothes here?"

Danijela gave him a look. "For what reason you need clothes? You no like hospital fashion?"

Lynch returned the look.

"You not leaving," she continued. ". . . until doctor let you go. Beside, you got a tube in chest, and you not even on police force anymore. How you help?"

Lynch sighed and fell back into his pillow. She was correct. It would take more than his desire to be there to get him hooked into the investigation.

Danijela fidgeted in her chair. Lynch could tell she had something to say.

"Lynch, I come back to say to you I must go to courtroom tomorrow. Judge to decide if I stay or go. I-I want to stay. Here. With you."

"Go? Go where?"

"Back to home country."

Deported? Lynch had not anticipated that possibility. Suddenly he felt very alone. He had somehow alienated Amy, and now there was a risk that Danijela would be forced to leave the country. What had she done to deserve that? In light of the recently exposed fact that Homeland Security agents were actually bringing children into the country to their illegal alien parents, while Danijela had been a victim of human trafficking, this seemed extremely unfair.

He started to say something when she caught his attention.

"Hey, look." This time Danijela pointed to the TV.

Flashing across the bottom of the screen, the marquee read: "Breaking news. Apparent suicide car bomber drives up to Wisconsin Governor's Mansion. One state patrolman dead, one uninjured in blast. The State Patrol Dignitary Protection Unit has yet to identify the deceased officer."

Nine

Brad smiled as he watched Mark circling around the room, from the balcony overlooking the Maimea Volcano Pool to the door and back again. Following his speech and, what seemed to him, too few press interviews considering what they'd achieved, he and his family moved to the Hawaiian Resort at the park. Dinner had been remarkable, not just for the food, but for Mark's first encounter with life-sized cartoon characters.

As a ten-year-old, he vacillated between that ecstatic embrace of a child meeting a favorite character and still believing the fantasy, and the indifference of an older child who saw the character as simply an actor and no longer believed. Eventually, he had warmed up to the characters as they enticed him back to their make-believe world.

To have the innocence of childhood again. Brad closed his eyes and wondered if he might return to some make-believe world, but he could no longer pretend. He had become part of something much bigger than himself. How God would continue to use him was yet to be seen. People had had enough. They were beginning to see the progressive, "politically correct" monster for what it was. Attacks on Christian businesses often went under the radar, but the attack on America's favorite rednecks, the Robertson family, showed GLAAD and others to be the quacks they are. You didn't need a duck call to bring them out of the woods, just an expression of your Christian faith.

"C'mon, Dad!"

Brad opened his eyes and saw his son standing at his feet. The boy's vigor radiated like the heat of the sun. His small body seemed to send off ripples of energy. Too much sugar at dessert.

"C'mon what?"

"Let's go for a ride."

"But the rides aren't open until tomorrow morning."

"The monorail is. I saw it run by. Let's ride the monorail." Mark tugged at his father's shirttail.

If only science could harness the energy of youth as a renewable resource. Where did Mark find it? Brad felt ready to hit the sheets.

Brad sighed. "Sure. Why not?" He stood up and walked into the bedroom where Cara stood changing into pajamas after her shower. "We're going to ride the monorail. Want to come along?"

"What? Again? This will be the fourth time since we got here." She stood there toweling dry her hair. "I think I'll sit this one out and do some reading. Is that okay?"

"Sure. Be back soon."

She walked over and kissed him. "You're such a great dad. Did you know that?"

"Thanks." He shrugged.

"Something wrong?" she asked.

"I don't know. I've had this bad feeling since my speech. I haven't seen anything on the news. You?"

"Sorry, but I've been so busy with Mark, I've paid no attention to the news."

Brad nodded and sighed. "Off to the monorail."

He left the bedroom to find Mark with his shoes on

and ready to go. Brad smiled and shook his head as he pointed to the boy's shoes.

"Wrong feet again, Son."

Mark looked down and his shoulders sank.

"Oh."

Mark switched his shoes in quick order and, when finished, reached up for his dad's hand. Together they headed down the hall, descended the stairs, and walked outside toward the monorail. They passed the dining areas and gift shop, and bounded up the stairs to the second floor transportation station. A number of late diners passed them going to the dining rooms, and Brad kept a leery eye on everyone who passed.

The schedule showed that a train was due within the minute and, as promised, they could see the single light on the nose of the first car as it sped toward them. Passengers were few, and the rail schedule was now limited due to the hour, catering primarily to adults who visited the clubs scattered across the park's various properties. A handful of people emerged from the train as Brad and Mark waited to enter. Just as they crossed the threshold onto the car, he heard the scuffle of running feet coming their way. Instinctively, he placed himself between the door and Mark, but whoever it was wouldn't make it in time. As the doors closed and the train began to move, he saw two of his aides waving their arms as they yelled for him.

Too late. The train left the station with Brad's concern growing. What had happened to lead them to a late evening visit, much less to rush to the station trying to catch him? He reached for his cell phone only to find his pocket empty. In his rush to please Mark, he'd left it behind, and now he felt naked without it.

Fawaz had spent the afternoon doing menial tasks meant to kill time and nothing more. For a short while, he had parked across the highway from the school and watched events unfold. However, not wanting to be discovered, he found his way to a large, thriving shopping mall, The Galleria, and spent two hours strolling though it and many of its stores. He actually bought a few items, using cash, and enjoyed a dinner of soup, falafel, and pita bread at one of the eateries. Another restaurant enticed him to what was for him an uncommon treat, a dessert of raspberry-white chocolate cheesecake. He rarely indulged in sweets of any kind.

Throughout the afternoon, except for a few disruptions, his thoughts focused on the deaths of the four men and on how that unexpected turn might affect the ultimate plan he had been chosen to fulfill. Try as he might, he could not imagine any scenario that might link those men with him, or with those above him for whom such a disclosure would be truly scandalous.

Now, as the evening became late, he settled into a motel room, a half mile away from the school. He had official duties to carry out in the morning, although it would be long-distance by cell phone. He wished he could head home, but his handlers required his stay in St. Louis for a little while longer. No doubt to put some distance between themselves and him, and the events he had orchestrated, should something go awry and he be discovered.

He retrieved his Samsung tablet from his luggage and connected to the motel chain's Wi-Fi. Cautious that he was not on a secure channel, he surfed the major news sites for information on the events of the day. With the local school shooting conspicuously absent, he found reports of the other planned incidents, events he had triggered with his phone calls as he drove away from Jamestown Mall. These actions would begin their *intifada,* and before the election primaries in two weeks, life in these United States would become far from united.

He decided to turn in and stood to prepare for bed. As he entered the bathroom, his secure cell phone rang and he returned to the bedside table to answer it.

"Fawaz," he answered on the third ring.

"How did the day go?"

The voice on the other end was male and immediately recognizable. He had expected Ms. Faris, if anyone. Not a personal call from the Director himself. He knew the man by reputation only but had heard him speak on several occasions. His inflections and tone were unique. Fawaz felt both honored and intimidated at the same time.

Fawaz knew better than to brush aside any details and gave the man a detailed accounting of the day's events. Somehow, he sensed that the Director already knew everything he told him, that he was testing Fawaz. He had heard rumors that the man was clairvoyant, but in truth, he had the most sophisticated line of communications, and the deepest information network possible.

"I see. I'm sorry to hear we lost men we could count on, but their sacrifice will be honored. We will see that their families are compensated." He paused. "I have read your work, and I see that you would have approached our goal from a different angle."

Fawaz didn't know whether he should reply or not. The Director was correct in stating that Fawaz's plan was more subtle and would require more time. Fawaz also thought it provided a greater psychological advantage, and wasn't that a critical factor in creating terror? He decided to make his case, but the man did not give him time to do so.

"Your reasoning and considerations were sound. Yet, we have a need to speed up the timetable, so I chose to take our current path. The others concurred. If you stick with us, you, too, will be well compensated."

"Thank you, sir. You can count on me."

"Good. Now, I understand the day is not quite finished."

"Yes, sir. Any moment now, our plan in Honolulu should be completed."

There was dead air for a moment, and Fawaz thought they'd been disconnected.

"Ahh, actually, it just occurred. Thank you, Fawaz. For your dedication and service."

This time the connection ended. He grabbed the remote for the television and turned it on.

Fawaz's curiosity rose up. The man had said the event had *just* occurred. Was his communications system *that* good? How long would it take the media to catch wind of the situation?

As quickly as he could find the channel, he turned to Headline News. He watched a story about the status of efforts to create a free Palestinian state, followed by the latest on the massive winter storm that had delayed his own trip from Detroit. Hundreds of thousands remained without power across the northern tier of states from Wisconsin to Maine. Finally, after 15 minutes, the news anchor interrupted with an alert.

"We have a news bulletin just coming across the wires. A massive bomb blast has destroyed the U.S.S. Arizona Memorial at Pearl Harbor. We will have more for you as soon as we get new information."

Brad sat impatiently on the monorail waiting for the circuit to complete. After leaving the Hawaiian, he had hoped to hop off quickly at the stop at the eastern edge of the resort's property, only to see his son enjoying himself. He couldn't bring himself to shortchange the boy. He saw no choice but to complete the circle. He tried not to show his impatience, but Mark was an astute youngster.

"Dad, Mr. Eric and Mr. Stan looked like they needed to see you right away." His shoulders slumped, and he looked solemn.

"They did, didn't they?" He put his arm around his son, and they watched the lights of the main park rush toward them. They would pull into that station in a matter of moments.

As they pulled into the stop, a man who had boarded the monorail at the main transportation hub just east of the Hawaiian walked from his seat two cars away into the car with Brad and Mark. He had seen the man board and thought his clothing choice a bit odd. January in Orlando might warrant the occasional sweatshirt or jacket, but this guy was wearing a bulky down coat as if expecting an ice queen's magical touch to turn the park into an arctic wasteland. Now, as he sat nearby, Brad felt a stirring inside.

Just before the doors closed, Brad grabbed Mark's hand and said, "Let's get off here and see if they do fireworks tonight." He practically dragged the boy off the car, and as soon as they cleared the train, Mark began to protest. Brad ignored the complaints and watched the man rush toward the car's door only to be knocked backward by the monorail lurching forward.

A hundred yards beyond the station, the car exploded in a blinding orange flash. Both monorail tracks toppled and 15 seconds later, the train coming from the opposite direction flew off its track and careened to the earth, toppling onto its side near a beach at the northeast end of the lagoon.

Ten

Lynch had become the nursing staff's nightmare. First, he had refused his sleeping pill, and every nurse on the unit had taken her or his turn at trying to convince him he needed to sleep. And since he wasn't sleeping, his television had become the source of complaints by neighboring patients who wanted to sleep. The nurses' encouragement turned to cajoling to outright threats. Of course, he knew any such threats were hollow ones. Calling "the doctor" meant nothing. The doctor would simply shrug and say it was up to him as to whether he wanted the pill or not. And that was about as serious a threat as they could mount.

The doctor did, however, send his nurse practitioner in to ask him politely to decrease the volume on the TV. Lynch complied. He liked Sue, the nurse practitioner.

What Lynch really needed were basic supplies to check his theory. Paper and a pencil. A map of the U.S. Maybe something like a corkboard or piece of foam board. Some pins and string. Or a compass for drawing circles. He knew the nurses would be unable to help him there.

He also required a laptop. His old one was toast, at the hand of the psychopath who had almost killed him. His parents knew better than to buy him a new one. He would be persnickety about its features. Still, any basic laptop would fill his need at the moment.

Unable to supply him with anything more than the

paper and pencil, the nurses soon took to ignoring his call light—until he unplugged his monitor leads and made it appear he had just flat-lined. Unfazed, the charge nurse simply called the chaplain on duty and asked him to come give Lynch last rights.

Lynch knew when to quit.

Yet, he couldn't sleep. The marquee at the bottom of the screen screamed one news flash after another. At first, Lynch felt the same concern as he suspected most people would feel. What was the world coming to? Was there some event, some "anniversary" that had triggered such an onslaught of terrorist activity? Had the problems of Israel and some western European countries finally arrived on our shores? Why hadn't the government prevented these attacks? The President's approval ratings slid even further toward that of Congress.

But as the night wore on, he began to see something about the reports. A pattern perhaps. Mentally he couldn't quite see it. He was too tired to see it in his head. Yes, the nurses were correct. He needed his sleep, but he wouldn't be able to sleep now. And he didn't want to risk that some pill might chemically dissolve what his mind had partially assembled. This seemed more important. He needed to plot it out on paper, visualize it. He couldn't trust a freehand drawing because his scale would be way off. So, a map was necessary, not simply preferable. Mike Southworth could get him one, but they would be tied up assisting Danijela with her new set of legal issues. Maybe he could talk Amy into getting one for him, but they hadn't parted on the best of terms.

Seamus. He needed to get hold of O'Connor.

An hour after placing a call to the St. Louis Metropolitan Police dispatcher, he still hadn't received a return call. Dawn was about to break, and as he started to doze off, in that half sleep state, he saw himself in a parody of "Alice in Wonderland." Should he take the red pill to stay awake, or the blue pill to go to sleep?

Dawn broke as Brad exited the security vehicle and leaned back in to lift Mark off the seat and carry him to their suite. He, along with everyone else on the monorail platform, had been detained by security and questioned by the police. The Florida State Highway Patrol had been called in to investigate, and overnight, multiple federal agencies also arrived, invited and not.

Brad had been candid about his observations and belief that a suicide bomber had been involved. At first, his comments were taken as hysteria, but the discovery of a dead security officer led to a search of the parking lot near the main transportation hub where a bomb-sniffing dog found a car with explosives in the trunk.

What Brad didn't tell the authorities was that he had a growing concern that he'd been the target. He'd still be detained had he made that comment.

With Mark still asleep in his arms, he climbed the stairs at the Samoa and turned the corner toward their room to see a dozen people milling about in the hallway. As he neared the group, several turned and gasped at seeing them.

"Thank you, God," someone murmured.

Someone else ducked into the room, and a moment

later, Eric Lange, his aide, came rushing out.

"We thought you were dead. When Stan and I missed you on the platform, we came here, and as we waited with Cara, we saw the explosion through the glass doors."

"Didn't security call here? I asked them to call Cara to let her know we were okay."

Eric shook his head, and Brad's heart suddenly felt heavy at the thought of what Cara must have gone through. He handed his son to Eric and rushed into the room. The people from the hallway had filed back into the main room, so he barged through them to get to the bedroom. At the closed doorway, Stan McGonagle, his campaign manager, stopped him with a hand on his shoulder.

"She's been sedated."

Brad nodded and opened the door. His wife lay in the middle of the bed, spent tissues scattered around her and at the base of the bed. He sat next to her and wrapped his arms across her. He nuzzled her neck and kissed her on the cheek.

"We're okay, sweetheart. We're back. We're okay."

She stirred but did not awaken. He took a deep breath and looked about him. Despite the crowd outside that room, the quiet of the bedroom belied the chaos and noise that had swept across the entire amusement park universe. He stood, left the room, and found Mark on the couch where Eric had laid him. He picked up the boy and took him to the bed, laying him next to his mother. Should she awaken while Brad was absent from her side, she would see Mark and know that they were uninjured.

He walked back into the main room and saw that at

least half the crowd had dispersed. Those who remained were friends and campaign leaders, and all expressed their joy at his being safe. Several more filtered out the door after giving him their best wishes. Soon, only Eric, Stan, and Dominick Standish, the new American Party national chairman, remained in the front room.

The three men followed Brad's lead and sat down. However, Dominick stood back up and went over to the TV, turned it on, found a music channel and turned up the volume.

"Hey, that's a bit loud, isn't it?" Brad asked, trying to speak over the volume. "You'll wake up my family."

Dominick didn't turn it down. Instead, he went to the sliding doors to the balcony and closed them, followed by closing the curtains inside as well. By that point, Brad had had enough and went to turn down the TV himself. Dominick turned it back up and gave Brad a stern look.

"This won't take long," he said close to Brad's ear. "Humor me."

They sat down and Brad looked at each of them in turn. "Okay, so what's up? Why did you need me so urgently earlier, and why all the cloak and dagger now?" Half in jest, he added, "Is the room bugged? You've been watching too much TV."

Stan was the first to speak up. "It may be, but we suspect they're using a parabolic listening device on the windows."

Brad felt his jaw drop as the question, "What?" echoed through his mind.

Dominick continued, "That's right. I sent these two after you because we caught wind that you might have a target on your back. It appears you've made a lot of people mad, in both main parties. You've become the face of our new political party."

"Think about it, Brad. How did they know you were going to ride the monorail at that specific time?"

"And it also appears they knew about our announcement long before you made it," added Stan. "Have you seen the news?"

Brad took a deep breath and stared at both men. He would have dismissed their idea outright, had he not seen what happened on the monorail, and how he seemed to be the target of the bomber. Stan's question sank in, and he shook his head.

"There were close to a dozen terror attacks in our country today. A bombing at the Wisconsin Governor's Mansion. Several mall bombings. A major highway bridge destroyed. The destruction of the U.S.S. Arizona Memorial."

Brad sat back into the chair and pondered this. The governor's bombing he could understand. Unions throughout that state blamed him for "union busting" and their decreasing influence, and he'd been the target of bomb threats for months. Mall bombings and other attacks he had foreseen. How the U.S. had gone so long without one was more of a mystery. Why the U.S.S. Arizona? That one puzzled him.

He leaned forward and spoke, "We shouldn't be surprised about their knowing what we were up to. The endeavor was too big to go unnoticed. We'd always hoped they'd ignore us, like they have all previous efforts to start a new party. Like they do with the Libertarians. I guess our success registered with them because we cross a spectrum of people, and our numbers are huge for just starting out." He paused. "But why do you say I'm the face of the party? Just because I announced it? It's not like I'm running for president. And you're the party's national chairman, Dom. Not me."

The three men looked at each other, and Brad could read the hesitation on their faces, their reluctance. They hadn't told him everything.

"Okay, I know that look on each of your faces. What haven't you told me?"

Stan finally spoke up. "There was one other attack. Four Islamic gunmen attacked a school this afternoon. All four are dead, and miraculously not a single child was injured. The principal, however, is in critical condition after taking on one of the gunmen. Early evidence suggests they were looking for one child in particular. We don't know what their intent was for that child."

Brad had a sinking feeling in his gut. He already knew what still hadn't been said. He knew now why he'd felt that supernatural urgency to pull Mark from school. Tears welled up at the thought of his friend in intensive care.

He choked on his next words. "W-will Harris make it?"

Eleven

Seamus pulled into a parking slot reserved for police outside the Charles F. Knight Emergency and Trauma Center at Barnes Hospital, in the Central West End of St. Louis. The day shift would start soon, and Sarah would be there but, hopefully, not tied up yet. He also needed a good, as in strong, cup of coffee, and few coffee shops in the neighborhood could compare their product to the brew in the E.D., particularly if Sarah had a hand in making it.

He walked through the ambulance entrance and nodded to the clerk, who in turn, pointed him toward the doctors' work area. Pretty much all of the staff knew him now, even though he and Sarah had nothing formal going on between them. Despite having "dated" for almost a year now, neither had found the courage to tell their families. Nor did either push the other to do so. They understood the ramifications of a mixed racial relationship. They also had demanding jobs that each loved, and that easily became an excuse to limit their relationship.

He found Sarah sitting at a workstation, discussing a patient with one of the first-year residents. She nodded his way and gave him a raised index finger to say, "One minute." He knew better and went looking for that cup of coffee.

Five minutes later, she found him at the nurses' station where he was talking with the clerk and two nurses. As she neared, they yielded to her and resumed their duties.

"Tying up the staff, again?" she said with a smile on her face.

He glanced around to see if anyone was watching and gave her a quick kiss on the cheek.

"Needed a cup of coffee, and they obliged me. I was also getting the nitty-gritty on the school principal. Any word on how he's doing?"

"Last I heard, he did well through the surgery. I suspect he'll pull through just fine, but the next few days will be critical. It will take time before he's back on the job."

Seamus nodded. "I'm heading up to see him and thought I'd stop in to see Cully, too. He's evidently been trying to get hold of me since last night sometime. Wanna tag along and say 'Hi'?"

"I can't, but give him my greeting." She leaned into him and gave him a kiss on the lips, just as the clerk returned to the desk, followed by two paramedics, three nurses, and two doctors.

As the clerk raised her brow and smiled, he blushed.

The clerk laughed. "Got 'im to neon red this time, Doctor Wade."

Seamus blushed again at the comment and sighed. *Why does she always do that?* he wondered. Then he thought, *Why do I always do that?*

A few minutes later, he wandered onto the floor near Lynch's room. He overheard the nurses talking at their station and laughed quietly as he heard one night nurse complaining about their problem child down the hall. They could give him one guess, and he'd win the jackpot.

Obviously, *they* couldn't fulfill his need, so he called good ol' Seamus. That meant he had something that might be useful.

Seamus eased his head through the door to see Lynch curled up on the bed, his back toward the door. He knocked gently on the doorpost. Was he asleep? He knocked again, a bit louder.

"Heard you the first time, Shay."

"How—"

"Sarah's perfume. You must have stopped by the E.D. on your way here." Lynch rolled over onto his back, grabbed the bed control, and raised the head of his bed. Seamus turned his head toward his shoulder and sniffed, followed by checking the other shoulder. All he could smell was his coffee.

"I hear you've been the proverbial pain in the night shift's derriere." He grabbed a nearby chair and pulled it next to the bed before sitting down.

Lynch laughed. "Word travels fast. Were they talking about me in the E.D.?"

"Nope. Overheard a couple of comments as I passed the nurses' station down the hall."

"Sounds like a HIPAA violation to me. Should I call my lawyer?"

Seamus laughed. "No names were mentioned, but as soon as I heard the nurse say 'a pain in the gluteus,' I knew it had to be you. So, what's up?"

"Lying here all day, not being allowed to go home, that's what. But you know something, with little else to do, I spent yesterday afternoon as a news junkie, and you know what, there's something big going down. I just can't quite put my finger on it in my head, so I asked the nurses for some things to help. You know, visual aids."

"And let me guess, they couldn't help, so you kept buggin' them."

Lynch shrugged. "Well, maybe. A little."

"I heard something about wanting a map."

Lynch nodded. "I figure you were tied up with the school shooting, but did you see any of the news yesterday?"

Seamus shook his head. "Like you figured, I was up past midnight working on that one. In fact, I'll be heading back to it once I leave here. I actually came here to see if I could talk with the injured principal."

"Well, there were a dozen attacks of various kinds across the country yesterday, and something inside me keeps saying they're related. I sense there's a pattern there, but I can't quite see it mentally. I need a map of the country and either some push pins and string, or a compass to draw circles."

Seamus thought about that for a moment. "Umm, I'll see what I can do."

"What can you tell me about the school shooting?"

Seamus hesitated. Lynch wasn't an active officer, much less on the MCS. Would he get into trouble with the new MCS commander for discussing it with Cully?

Probably. That was all the motivation he needed to tell Cully everything they had, including young Jackson's story of angelic guardians and the condition of the two classrooms. Neither of those even fazed Cully.

"So, did you hear about any of the other incidents in the country?"

"I heard about the bomb at the Governor's Mansion in Wisconsin."

"That one just ended up being a disgruntled union member. I'm talking about the others."

Seamus had not and realized he needed to be more attuned to national events. Not every crime started and ended locally. He shook his head.

"There were a dozen incidents across the country, starting with the school here and ending with a bombing of the monorail at that Orlando amusement park. Ten dead and two dozen injured in the last one."

Lynch proceeded to share his list of events, as culled from the news stations. In order after the local shooting, they included a car bomb in downtown Tulsa, a bomb at the military recruiting center in Charleston, WV, a mall bombing in Memphis, TN, and the I-10 Bridge destroyed in Mobile, AL. These were followed by another car bomb in downtown Frankfurt, KY, a mall shooting in Charlotte, NC, a backpack bomb near the capitol building in Little Rock, AR, a foiled bombing of the Stillwater Dam in San Diego, CA, and another car bomb in Topeka, KS. He also mentioned the lack of news coverage of the local school shooting.

Seamus' eyes widened. He wracked his brain to see if there was anything special about yesterday's date. Nothing popped into his head. A sudden draft filled the room, and he had to push aside a "bouquet" of red balloons that suddenly collided with his head.

Lynch paused as Seamus battled the balloons. "I think they're all related. Except the Orlando bomber. That one seems an outlier. There was also a bomb at the U.S.S.

Arizona Memorial. I can't figure that one either."

"What?" That idea stunned Seamus. Maybe Cully's brain injury, like his gunshot wound, needed more time to heal, too. "How? I mean, if these were spread out across the country, how could they be related?"

"I haven't figured that out yet."

Again, the air moved inside the room causing a blue Mylar® balloon to drift between the two men. Lynch's eyes brightened, and a smile launched itself across his face.

"Of course, why didn't I see that at first? Must have been more fatigued than I admitted. Look, I need a map to confirm my hunch, but there seems to be one obvious factor. Except for the San Diego bombing, which was discovered and stopped before any damage, all of the other events took place in red states. Not a single attack in a blue state. Oh, Orlando is in a blue state, but again, it still smells of being an outlier."

Seamus nodded. He knew better than to squelch Lynch Cully's hunches. Cully's gut instincts had paid dividends time and time again in the past. The guy had been called a Wunderkind for his ability to see patterns where no one else could see a single connection.

"I'll find you a map. It might take me a little while. I still have to check on Principal Burke."

Lynch shrugged. "Fair enough. Thanks for your help, buddy." He paused. "Hey, who was the kid whose picture you found?"

"Mark Graham, son of Bradley Graham."

Lynch's eyes widened. "No kidding?" His brow furrowed. "Maybe that explains Orlando. I might be wrong about the red and blue state thing."

"What?" Seamus thought himself an astute detective, but there were times when Cully made him look like a rookie street cop. No, there were times when Cully made seasoned detectives look as if they'd never attended the police academy.

"Yeah. If they were after the Graham boy, then Bradley Graham and his new political party might be the real targets here. You need to find out if Graham was on that monorail. The news said he and his family had gone to the amusement park after the conservative caucus where he spoke. And then you need to see where the new political party has their offices in the cities I mentioned. Well, not all of them. The I-10 Bridge and Stillwater Dam might be red herrings, or something else. Oh, and the recruiting office. But the others, you need to check them out."

Seamus could see Cully's mind motoring ahead well above the speed limits. An image of John Travolta in his character, George Malley, in the 1996 movie, *Phenomenon,* flashed through his head. If Cully's brain injury now resulted in super intelligence and telekinesis, they'd never be able to "live" with him. Seamus made a quick survey of the room to make sure nothing was floating where it shouldn't be.

Amy picked up the phone on the third ring. She sat at home, "thanks" to her psychologist, Dr. Amanda Lange. She'd prefer working, but Amanda had insisted she take time off after her kidnapping, even though nothing had happened other than being kept against her will and forced to wear designer clothes. Amanda had expressed concern that Amy made light of the situation and that she chose to focus on the clothing as a way of subverting her fear and what had been a very real threat to her person. That concern had earned Amy another week off.

"Hi. Care to join me for breakfast?" asked Richard.

After her visit with Lynch, that question had an easy answer. "Sure. Can I meet you somewhere?"

"All depends. Are you prepared to leave right now, or do you need some time to get ready?"

"All I need to do is fix my hair and put on a coat. Where should I meet you?"

"How about your driveway?" With that Amy heard the toot of a car horn.

She peeked out the front window and smiled. "And if I hadn't been dressed and ready?"

"I'd drive around the block a few times and then honk."

She laughed. "I'll be out in a minute."

As she climbed into the car, she marveled again at his confidence and ability to surprise her. Lynch's only surprises had been to unceremoniously dump her and then beg to come back. Mentally, she chastised herself for continuing to compare the two.

She leaned over and kissed him on the cheek. "So, where to?"

"I've heard some good things about a place called La Bonne Bouchée, on Olive. Do you know it?"

Amy began to salivate at the suggestion. "I *love* La Bonne Bouchée. Their French pastries are to die for and breakfasts are fantastic."

"Great. We'll have to try it sometime. Today, I have enough cash for the dollar menu at McDonalds."

She sneered and punched him in the arm.

"Okay, okay. The Good Bite it is."

Amy gave him directions, and 20 minutes later, Amy had to pull Richard away from the bakery display to follow the hostess to their table. Both ordered coffee, black, and scrutinized the menu. They made small talk while waiting for her quiche and his frittata. Amy could sense a layer of tension underneath Richard's jovial banter.

As they neared the end of the delicious meal, Richard cleared his throat and said, "Amy, I asked you to breakfast to . . . well, to talk about something more serious."

He paused and appeared to gather his thoughts. He had this unusual air about him and an unexpected thought began to bother Amy. Was he going to *propose*? Despite nearly three months of dating, she didn't feel they knew each other well enough, or long enough, to take it anywhere close to that level. Or did they? *Oh Lord*, she thought. *Please, not yet. I'd have to say 'no', and I don't want to hurt him.*

"Well, um, as you know, I'm out of a job now. That was guaranteed when I helped put Darko behind bars, and the Feds confiscated his business. Oh, and killing his . . . um. Sorry, that's tacky."

Amy wanted to nod but restrained herself. To bring up the fact that he had killed the man's wife, albeit in self-defense, was in bad taste. True, but still nasty.

"I'm sorry. I don't know how else to say this, but I might have to leave town. I don't want to because I really,

really like you, and leaving would be hard."

Amy sat there, floored. This was a surprise she did not care for. As had happened so many times in the past, she had left Lynch on not so great terms. Something about him grated at her, despite her mental recognition that she should be supporting him, helping him move past the amnesia.

"The FBI was impressed with the way I handled myself and with my social media expertise. They offered me a position. Of course, I'd have to go through the Academy, and after that, I don't know where I'd be assigned. Would you ever consider leaving St. Louis? I mean, you know, if things work out between us."

Leave St. Louis? Her dad was here. Of course, he seemed to be moving ahead into a new relationship and wouldn't have to rely on her so much. Her remaining brothers were here, too, with their families. She loved her nieces and nephews. But, now that they were in school, she didn't see them all that often anymore. Leave St. Louis? She had no immediate answer.

"Richard, I-I don't know what to say. I like you, but we've just met. And my family is here. I-I can't answer that right now."

He reached across the table and placed his hand on top of hers.

"I don't expect a quick answer. I realize we're just getting to know each other, and it might go nowhere. But, I have your dad's permission to court you, even from Virginia, if that's where I go next. The next Academy class starts in a month, and I have to give them an answer soon. If something better comes up by then, I might give up that opportunity. But I have to admit, there was something neat about being undercover like that and helping to take down a bad guy here at home."

His words barely registered in her mind. He had asked *permission* from her father? What else had they talked of? Was her father signaling that he didn't need her help anymore? She didn't know what to think of that. And the fact that he'd asked her father in the first place seemed, well, somehow quaint but insulting at the same time. Didn't she have a say in the matter? Sure, some people still carried on such traditions. She simply didn't know such people, even in her circle of church friends.

Again, she found herself teetering on that familiar fence as she reflected on her most recent spat with Lynch. She couldn't forget how he'd treated her before his disappearance, but recognized that he had been correct in stating it would be like starting over. He had changed. And as these thoughts flowed through her mind, she sensed God telling her she needed to forgive. Could she?

Yet, more bothersome was the idea that Richard might leave.

Twelve

Brad awoke on the couch to the caress and kisses of his wife. After his team had left, he'd stretched out across the couch so as not to wake up Cara. He must have fallen asleep immediately.

He reached up and wrapped his arm around her, pulling her close to him and savoring her scent.

"Thank God you're alive! The thought of losing you both was too much to bear. I-I saw the monorail explode. It was horrible. I . . ." Tears formed in her eyes, as she appeared to relive that awful moment.

"God had his arms around us. I sensed something wrong and hurried off the train with Mark at the main park's station. I saw the bomber. He—"

He stopped there. He did not want to alarm her further by suggesting that he was the target. Yet, the more he thought about it, he had been, and if he was, she deserved to know. She had to be prepared.

Plus, she would learn of the attack at Northgate Christian Academy, of Harris Burke's injuries. Then, in short order, she would eventually hear the speculation that Mark had been the target of those terrorists.

He pushed her back so he could sit up and motioned for her to sit next to him. He took her hands as she did.

"Honey, you need to know something. I'm pretty sure I was the target of the monorail bombing. Dom and Stan agree."

Alarm rushed across her face. "How could that … how can you say that?"

"The bomber? He was in a different car until we arrived at the main park. There, he moved into our car. That's when I sensed something wrong. Then, as I rushed Mark off the car, he got up to follow, but the doors closed on him before he could get off. I saw the look on his face, anger, yet as if he'd failed, too. I'm pretty sure that had he managed to exit the car, the explosion would have occurred right then, on the platform, instead of the handful of seconds later, away from the station."

"No, that can't be right. You can't really believe that."

"There's more. Yesterday afternoon, four armed men invaded Northgate Christian. Harris was critically injured and is on life support at Barnes Hospital. All four men died, but they found something on the bodies of two of them." He took a deep breath. "They were carrying a picture of Mark. They were after our son."

With that revelation, she pushed away from him, stood, and rushed to the balcony doors. He saw tears streaming down her cheeks as he followed and engulfed her in his arms.

"Cara, I will never let anyone hurt our son. If it means dropping out of politics, I will do so," he whispered into her ear.

She turned and looked at him, her face aghast.

"No, don't you see? If you're the target, that's exactly what they want. For some reason, you, not just the new party but *you*, scare them. If you leave politics, they somehow win. That alone means you have to stay, but I think it also means they think you'll be elected."

He kissed her on the cheek and squeezed her tightly to his body. At that moment, he remembered Dominick's concern that someone was monitoring their room, and that sense of alarm rushed through him again. He pulled Cara away from the glass doors and onto the floor, just as the glass shattered where they had been standing two seconds earlier.

For the second time in 12 hours, Brad found himself talking with the Director of Security. The Threat Assessment Director and Special Investigations Manager, followed by the Senior Vice-President of Operations for the amusement park, soon joined them.

Brad restarted his story for the second time for the VP. As he related the events surrounding his trip on the monorail, he felt like he was trapped in a personal version of *Groundhog Day*, reliving the event for the sixth time, but the day never changed.

"After arriving back at our room at the Samoa, I discovered my wife had been sedated because she was so upset. She had seen the monorail explode and assumed Mark and I were on it. Your office had promised to call the room and never did, by the way." He addressed that last comment to the Director of Security.

"Sorry," said the Director. "Last night was a nightmare for us."

"For my family and me as well. As saddened as I am to say this, I think I was the target of the monorail bomber, and all those people died because of me. Well, not 'because of me,' but because someone without scruples or regard for life was willing to sacrifice them in order to kill me."

He continued by outlining his discussion with his campaign team.

"Anyway, after they left the room, I fell asleep on the couch, and my wife woke me up. She was obviously upset and had walked to the sliding glass doors to look out. I joined her there, and as we talked, I felt the same sense of alarm that I felt when I rushed our son from the monorail car at the platform. I pushed us away from the doors just before the glass shattered. We called Security, and while waiting, I found the bullet hole in the far wall. Someone tried to shoot me."

The VP spoke up. "I would be doubtful about your concern over being a target if there hadn't been the second attempt. You have real reason to worry and a real need for security."

"You think?" replied Brad. He sighed. "Sorry, I'm operating on two hours of sleep, and I'm worried about my family."

The Threat Assessment Manager fidgeted in his chair. His face had been cemented in a frown since Brad had started retelling his story.

"I'm sorry. I don't get this thing you say about having some negative vibe and jumping away from the window just in time. Seems perfectly timed to me."

"What?" That statement shocked Brad. Even the other men raised their brows.

"In my job, I have to look at all possibilities. Now, I'm not saying you're in on anything, but wouldn't this kind of thing generate all sorts of publicity and sympathy for you with the voters back home?"

"Did you really just say that?" Brad asked.

He stood and felt like punching the guy's lights out. Fortunately, politics had taught him restraint in a way his Bible studies never had. He looked at the other three men. Their faces showed they actually thought that a plausible idea.

"Do you really think we would blow up your monorail and kill over a dozen innocent people *just* for publicity? That's sick. There might be a lot of corrupt politicians out there, but even the worst, Chicago-style politicians that I know wouldn't stoop that low. Get real."

Brad brushed his fingers through his hair and shook his head. He took two steps away from his chair and turned back toward the men.

"Yesterday, my son's school was attacked by four masked gunmen. Not students. All four attackers were killed, and the principal, one of my best friends, was severely wounded. Did you hear about that?"

The men shook their heads and looked appropriately concerned.

"I didn't think so. The mainstream media, including your sister broadcasting company chose to ignore the story. We believe the reason they chose to ignore it was pure political correctness. The gunmen appear to be Muslim, and the school was a private Christian school. Also, two of the gunmen were killed because the staff was armed, as allowed by state law."

The VP got defensive. "Well, we can't speak for a sister company. We're only responsible for this one, and we have our guests to protect."

"I fully understand and appreciate that, but excuse me

if I don't trust you. The initial news reports about a bomb blowing up the monorail were, shall we say, *corrected* overnight to say it was a system malfunction. Is that how you protect your guests, with misinformation? Sounds more like the way to keep guests coming. Wouldn't want to scare them away with talk of mad bombers."

He crossed his arms and shook his head again.

"And frankly, you've failed. *My* family's vacation has been traumatic, and my son told me he had a nightmare about this place and cartoon characters trying to kill him. How would *that* sound as a press release? Your security and threat assessments sure didn't protect *us*."

The men looked at each other before the Director of Security spoke. "You're right. We failed you, your family, and two dozen other families. For that, I apologize. We are already looking into ways to prevent this from ever happening again."

The VP added, "All of your expenses here have been covered and refunds have been issued for any prior expenses, such as your multi-park passes. We also wish to cover the expenses of your travel here and back home, with passes and complimentary lodgings for any future date of your choosing."

"Thank you, but do you really think that will stop the lawsuits? I don't mean to imply I'm planning to sue you. I'm not, but the families of those who died won't settle for such peanuts. You had a better defense when the truth was out there. Your misinformation campaign will only add millions to your settlements. You do realize that, don't you?"

The VP nodded, and Brad saw that the man did indeed

understand. To these people, only money talked. What was ten, 20, even 50 million dollars compared to keeping the truth from the people and following a larger agenda?

Thirteen

Seamus had not been surprised to find Principal Burke still unable to communicate with them. The man remained sedated and still had a breathing tube with a mechanical ventilator assisting his breathing. The doctor told Seamus it would likely be another week before Burke might—he emphasized 'might'—be able to talk with him.

Lynch on the other hand was more than eager to talk with him. After locating and returning with a map of the country, plus some drawing tools, Seamus watched as Lynch fiddled with the map. As Lynch motored on, Seamus could barely get a word in, even edgewise in a six-point font.

"Hey, stick around for a minute. This won't take long. I've been contemplating those attacks I mentioned earlier and the fact that the four school shooters appeared to be Muslim."

Seamus started to confirm that they had not been identified yet, much less confirmed as Muslim, but Lynch kept going. He offered Seamus no point to insert his own comments.

"So, there was a pattern to the times of the attacks. If you start with the attack on the school here, the attacks occurred almost exactly 30 minutes apart. Thirty minutes, plus or minus five minutes, to be exact. And except for one, they all occurred in red states."

Seamus started to mention that Lynch had already

told him that. Again, Lynch continued his monologue.

"I wondered if there was more to the pattern than just timing. That's why I needed the map." He continued marking the map and exclaimed, "And I think I was right. Look at this."

He held the map at an angle for Seamus to see, but gave Seamus no time to respond.

"I've circled certain cities, using the mileage radius between Detroit and St. Louis and see? The cities attacked all fall along one of the circles I've marked. Now, you're probably thinking, why did I use these specific cities?"

Seamus found himself nodding. He had been thinking that. Now he thought again about John Travolta as George Malley. If the map started floating toward him, he was outta there.

"Follow me here. And if you think I'm off-base somewhere, let me know. If I was going to plan a series of terrorist attacks, would I use people who lived in the cities I wanted to attack? Not likely. I'd want to add as much confusion as possible, so I'd task people to attack another city. But I wouldn't want them to be so far away that the travel increased their chance of discovery. Right?"

Seamus finally had the opportunity to speak. "Okay."

Lynch drove on. "So, a day's drive, max. Right? An assumption, I know, but I'm making it anyway." He paused but only to take another deep breath. "Again, a day's drive. Get to the target city ahead of time. Strike your target and get away quickly, if your plan included a get-away, that is. An easy six- to eight-hour drive and you're home, protected by your compatriots around you. One gas stop at most."

"Sounds reas—"

"It is. Anyway, let's make the further assumption that these attacks are being done by fundamentalist Muslims out to bring terror to America. What's the largest base for Islam in the U.S.?"

Seamus shrugged and shook his head. He gave up on talking for the moment.

"Detroit. So, use Detroit as a base for the first attack. St. Louis. Eight hours away by car. Second largest Muslim population. Washington, DC. A red state city within that radius? Frankfort, KY. Actually, it's right on that circle, not within."

Seamus furrowed his brow. Frankfort was not the second attack, according to Lynch.

"You're right," Lynch continued. "Frankfort was not the next city, Tulsa was. Tulsa is on the circle surrounding Cedar Rapids, IA, and believe it or not, Cedar Rapids is the third largest Muslim center."

Seamus felt like wrapping his head in aluminum foil to keep Lynch from reading his mind.

"Whoever plotted this out tried to add another level of confusion. If you take the top ten centers for Islam in our country, and numbered them one through ten, the attacks followed a pattern following the odd numbered cities first and then going back to number two and following the even numbered cities."

Lynch sat back in his bed and smiled. Seamus waited for more words to follow. Lynch reached to his bedside table, picked up a sheet of paper and handed it to Seamus. It was the list of top Islamic centers. He looked at the circle around each city and saw a target city along it.

All except San Diego were in red states, just as Lynch had stated earlier. Other potential target cities lay along some of the circles, but they sat inside blue states. Concerning San Diego, it sat along the circle around San Francisco, and that circle crossed no other large metro areas. Plus, the Naval and Marine presence in the city would make it a logical target, especially its water supply during California's severe drought.

How in the world does Lynch see these things? wondered Seamus.

"I don't know how. I just do," answered Lynch to Seamus' thought.

Now things were getting weird.

"Oh, and two other things. Whoever thought this out is a very ordered individual and has a mathematical mind. He also thinks himself clever and somewhat superior. He figured his plan would seem random when, actually, it was far from it. He also didn't expect anyone to see his pattern. He probably has some obsessive-compulsive tendencies that keep him from doing anything totally random. Had he randomized his attacks, the connection with the Muslim community might have gone unnoticed."

"Second thing. Another connection with the Muslim population. The schedule works around Islamic prayer times in each location. I'm pretty sure you'll find Islam as a common thread between all the attackers, but I have a hunch there's someone else doing the weaving."

Seamus stood and gazed out the window. He wanted the "Easy Button" to push on this case, and Lynch kept adding "Hard," "Harder," and "Hardest" buttons to the line-up.

"Have you checked into the American Party theory for me?"

Seamus turned back to Lynch and shook his head. "No time, yet." He didn't want to think about the ramifications of that theory. That would be pressing the "Next to Impossible" button.

Fourteen

Lynch felt better than he had in days. Not just because his wound was healing and less painful, but because he felt useful. He remained restricted to the bed because of the chest tube extending from his left chest to the plastic bubbling thing on the floor next to his bed. At least the bubbling had nearly stopped. Once it did, they'd be able to remove that tube, and he'd have more freedom of movement.

Seamus had stepped out on a limb and "deputized" him, of sorts. He had provided Lynch with a cell phone and tablet computer, and had asked Lynch to make the calls to the police departments investigating the other incidents. Seamus would deal with the ramifications if MCS Commander Johnstone caught wind of it.

His very first call uplifted him.

"Tulsa PD, how may I help you?"

"My name is Lynch Cully, and I'm working with the St. Louis Major Case Squad on a case here. I'm hoping to touch base with the detective working the car bombing reported on the news yesterday."

"One minute."

After a brief interlude of 'elevator music,' a male voice came on the line.

"Detective Phillips."

"Good afternoon, Detective," said Lynch, who went on to explain who he was. "I have reason to believe your car bombing is related to an incident here, a school shooting."

"A school shooting? I didn't see anything on the news about another school shooting."

"Yeah, funny thing about that." Lynch gave the detective a synopsis of the incident.

"And *that* wasn't considered newsworthy? So, why do you think that's connected to our car bombing? That seems a mighty long stretch."

"Well, that's what I'm looking into. You're the first contact I've made, so I don't know what else to say right now. I do promise, however, that if I find the connection, I'll give you full details. Can I ask where the bomb exploded?"

"Sure, 2nd Street and Cincinnati Ave. Right across Cincinnati from City Hall. We're hoping it scared the City Council into increasing our budget." The man chuckled.

"What was across the street?"

"An old building. Been empty for a while, but we've heard that some politician or something is setting it up as a campaign office."

"The American Party?"

"Yeah, that was it. Some kind of Minuteman posters was in the windows."

"Anybody in the car? Suicide bomber?"

"Nope."

"Was the car registered and reported stolen in Cedar Rapids?"

"Hey, sure was. How'd you know that?"

"Like I said, we have a theory about how these incidents might be related. It's a little complicated to explain over the phone, but give me your email address, and I promise to send you more details as I get them."

"I'm looking forward to that. Got a number where I can reach you?"

Lynch gave the man his cell number and hung up. His second call, to Charleston, ended with a voicemail message for the lead detective on that mall shooting.

The mall bombing in Memphis yielded results similar to those in Tulsa. The bomb went off outside a new American Party office in the mall. No one was inside the office, but a dozen mall patrons had been injured, two critically. Eyewitnesses stated they saw a Middle Eastern-looking male, early to mid twenties, drop a backpack next to a trash receptacle and rush away. Two of them sounded an alarm, which was timely enough to spare over a dozen other people from injuries. Security video seemed to point to a car licensed in Illinois. Lynch suggested they narrow their search to Peoria.

By late afternoon, Lynch had culled enough information from other detectives to feel assured that his theory was correct. He had also stirred up a pot of interest by the other detectives. He felt they deserved to understand what he knew and his suspicion that something big was brewing. He used the laptop to produce a preliminary report. As he typed, a knock at the door interrupted his thoughts.

He looked up to see Mike Southworth. He looked past Mike, expecting to see Danijela with him. He felt disappointed that she wasn't with him.

"Hey, c'mon in."

Mike glanced around at the mess surrounding and on top of Lynch's bed. "Wow. Looks like you've been busy.

And you now have a laptop? What's up?"

"Is Danijela with you?"

Mike glanced away for a second. "She's with her family. They have to leave in a couple of days. So, what are you doing?"

Lynch sensed that Mike was withholding something from him, but he chose to answer Mike's questions first. Then he'd get his turn.

"I developed a theory about all of those terrorist incidents yesterday. Seamus got this stuff for me to look into it." He went on to explain his theory and the data he'd accumulated that day to support it.

"Well. You *have* been busy. Sounds to me like someone is stirring up a hornets' nest, and using it to mask his attacks on this new political party. But who?"

Lynch tried to shrug but found it too painful in his left side. He had no clue, and the list of potential suspects would be miles long.

"Every Democrat and Republican politician out there would have reason to squelch this party. How do you narrow it down?"

Mike made a face and waggled his head. "Maybe you need to look a little deeper."

Lynch furrowed his brow. "Huh?"

"Do you remember anything about conspiracy theories?"

Lynch thought for a moment but had to admit this was another thing he didn't fully remember. "Rings a bell, but no, my memory isn't back to 100%."

"Might never be," replied Mike. "Whenever someone suggests that some group or another is behind an event, and the suggestion seems, well, off-the-wall, that person is labeled by the so-called pundits as a conspiracy theory nut job. Example, the CIA was behind the assassination of President Kennedy. Or, the U.S. faked the landing on the moon on some sound stage in Hollywood. Or, that a New World Order controls the world through the central banks of the nations. Still a blank?"

Lynch thought about it. "Wait a minute. I'm recalling some names—The Trilateral Commission and the Council of Foreign Relations. But that's all I remember, the names."

"It's a start. There's also the Bilderberg Group. Almost all of our senior politicians are members of one or more of these groups."

"So, you're saying there may be some truth behind the conspiracy theories?"

Mike shrugged. "As someone once said, just because you're paranoid doesn't mean someone isn't out to get you. The quickest way to discredit someone is to label him a nut. So much effort has been spent on discrediting conspiracy theorists, the term itself is now considered derogatory and labels someone as crazy."

"You really think that?"

"I like to think myself open-minded, but there's a body of research that proves a small group of international elites, people with more money than we could imagine, pull the strings in Washington, Beijing, Moscow, and the European Union. Goldman Sachs is known for training its people for a global system and guess who the President filled his administration with? Goldman Sachs people. Guess who provides economic guidance to Russia and the Chinese?"

"I'll take a long shot here. Goldman Sachs."

Mike chuckled. "You catch on quickly. And the Trilateral Commission and Council on Foreign Relations are in the thick of it. Guys like Henry Kissinger and Zbigniew Brzezinski are members of both and are close advisors to the U.S. and Russian leadership. Maybe the powers behind the thrones of this world really did order the assassination of Kennedy. On June 4th, 1963, he signed Executive Order 11,110 that authorized the printing of 4.3 trillion dollars in United States Notes, with a return of the gold standard and a goal of dismantling the Federal Reserve System. A few months later, he was dead."

Lynch thought about that. Made sense, but like Mike, he would remain open. He preferred proof to speculation. After all, that had been the reason for all of his work that day.

Mike continued. "The Bible has a lot to say about all of this. First off, in Matthew 6:24, it says you can't serve two masters. You can't serve both God and wealth. The elites of this world are all about money and power. They have enough of both to manipulate the world's economies as well as world events with one goal in mind, to gain even more money and power. Second, the global system was foretold thousands of years ago. These people will succeed in establishing a global political, economic, and religious system, and it will be a time of terror and anguish because these oligarchs don't care about the people, just themselves."

Lynch had to ponder that comment as well. With billions of people on the planet, was it really possible for a small group to control *everything*? Something inside told him yes, it was. And if they controlled the governments of the world, they could manipulate the press, Hollywood, and more, in order to manipulate the people. Was our country *really* at odds with the Russians and Chinese? Or was that little more than deception to sway the hearts and minds of the people in each country?

Lynch's ability to see patterns could sometimes be a burden, as well as a blessing. If all these governments have a similar goal set by some group behind the scenes, then all of the political posturing, military threats, and more were nothing but subterfuge and manipulation by the globalists toward their goal of political and economic dominion. The same with terrorism. We had already given up many freedoms in the name of security from terrorism. Was this little more than a false sense of security, as a means to further the globalists' plan?

The two men talked for another hour until Mike checked his watch and said, "Whoa, it's later than I thought. I need to get home." He leaned forward in his chair and looked Lynch in the eye. "Hey, I came to let you know how Danijela's court hearing went."

Lynch had gotten so busy he'd forgotten that today was her "date" with the federal judge. From the look on Mike's face, Lynch felt a growing anxiety.

"First, let me update you about Ibrahim. The prosecutors have declined pressing any charges for his activities while employed by Darko, in light of his role in taking down that enterprise. However, he is going to be deported back to Bosnia because of those activities. He's being detained, and I don't know if you'll be able to see him one more time before they fly him home. They won't let me bring him here, and I'm not sure how much longer you'll be here."

That bothered Lynch. He understood the decisions, and, as an ex-police officer, he'd generally agree with them. However, Ibrahim was a changed man, as witnessed by his role in destroying Darko Komarčić's human trafficking and smuggling ring. Christianity had changed his life. He deserved a second chance, even though he would be competition for Danijela's affection.

The worst point, though, was that he'd turned on Darko, and Darko's associates in Eastern Europe would be on the lookout for Ibrahim. He needed to stay in the U.S. for his safety.

"Did his lawyer argue that he's a marked man if he's sent back to Bosnia? That's like sentencing him to death. Even his family might be out to kill him for abandoning Islam."

"Ibrahim wouldn't let him present that fact. He seems content to return home, and let the chips fall as they may. It's like his way of doing penance for his crimes." Mike frowned.

Lynch could see that streak in Ibrahim's makeup. He didn't agree with it, but he could see Ibrahim taking that stance.

"And Danijela?"

"The judge didn't grant her, or any of the other trafficking victims, asylum, saying there was no political persecution involved. He passed the buck to Immigration and Customs Enforcement, which, in turn, has only offered temporary visas until a full hearing can be held. Danijela's family has to return to Bosnia in two days, and Danijela is talking of returning with them and applying for an immigrant's visa from home."

"An immigrant's visa?"

"Yeah. That's different than a student visa or a short-term tourist's visa."

"I understand that. It's just that an immigrant's visa requires employment or family here, and she has neither."

Mike gave him a funny look at which Lynch remembered the other option for an immigrant visa, being engaged or married to a U.S. citizen. Was Danijela trying to force Lynch to, well, put up or shut up?

Fifteen

Seamus and Flannigan sat in the office with Captain Johnstone, listening to the man drone on about something or other. Seamus' thoughts swirled about the revelations of Lynch's findings, and he fidgeted in his chair, eager to head to the hospital for a full briefing. Lynch had only offered highlights over the phone.

The MCS commander picked up a photo of one of the dead men and waved it toward Flannigan.

"So, we're sure. We have this guy ID'd."

"Yes, sir. Muhab Abdelnour. CSU found personal items for four men in the SUV at Jamestown Mall. The only ID to survive was for this guy. "

"What about the address on it?"

"No good. It was an expired driver's license, ten years old from New York. I did call the precinct there and learned he had a rap sheet for petty larcenies, but folks there hadn't seen him in over five years. They thought he'd moved west, maybe Chicago."

Seamus doubted any Chicago connection, based on what Lynch had said. He wanted to say so but held his tongue.

"Any religious affiliations?"

"Oh yeah. Exactly what he looked like, Islamist. CSU found remnants of prayer rugs and the charred remains of a couple Qurans. Best we can determine he's not a local. I've inquired about him in Detroit, Chicago, and a couple of other larger cities with significant Muslim populations. Still waiting to hear back.

Seamus took the opportunity to speak up. "Focus on Detroit," said Seamus.

Johnstone perked up. "Oh?"

Seeing the look on the captain's face, Seamus now regretted his comment. He should have made it to Flannigan in private.

"Yes, sir. I, um ..."

How did he want to put this? Did he want to reveal his tasking of Lynch Cully now? Did he have any other choice? He had dug the hole he found himself in. Now, he hoped to build a ladder to climb out.

"I have a consultant, who, um ... well, he's working on a theory. I'm supposed to see him this evening for a more detailed report, but he has a theory about this shooting being tied to the other incidents around the country yesterday. From the brief he gave me over the phone, I think he's right."

"What?" Johnstone did not look happy. "First off, you know better than to divulge details to a third party. Second, we don't have a budget for consultants. That's why we have volunteers, like you. And third, how in the world could our shooting be linked to mall shootings and car bombings? Has Al Qaeda come to our shores? Really."

"Well, sir. I'll be able to lay all that out tomorrow for you, and I think the whole team should hear it."

"Really. The whole team. You want me to call in everybody from the important tasks they have, to hear some theory?"

"Yes, sir. This thing is bigger than you might think."

The captain eyed him closely, with knitted brow, and Seamus could feel the heat emanating from the man. He should have kept his mouth shut and talked with Flannigan afterwards. He made a mental note to keep his exuberance at bay when around the captain.

"Just who is this consultant?"

Seamus fidgeted in his chair again. He took a deep breath and said, "Lynch Cully."

The stern look on Johnstone's face never changed. He stood up from his desk and walked over to open the door. "Debra, call everyone on the team. Give 'em the heads up. Staff meeting at seven a.m. No excuses."

Seamus had a bounce in his step as he walked into Lynch's room. While he wished he had whatever it was that had placed Cully on a pedestal in Johnstone's office, he felt ebullient after Johnstone's praise for stepping outside the box to include the injured ex-detective. He didn't like the way the captain had stressed "ex-detective," but that hadn't mattered. The man obviously held Cully in high regard and had no reservations at all about using his talents, as long as no consultant's fee was required.

"You awake?" he whispered as he walked in. Lynch lay on his side facing away from the door, as he had the day before.

Lynch responded by moving onto his back but not without a grunt or two.

"Doesn't hurt as much on my right side. Not to mention, I can't really lie on my left side with this tube anyway."

"You okay?" Seamus pulled a chair up to the side of the bed.

Lynch nodded. "Will be. As soon as I get out of here."

He took a deep breath, and Seamus caught the wince on his face as he did so. Maybe his friend wanted his 'freedom' a little too soon.

Lynch pointed to the wide windowsill. "Grab those papers, will ya?"

Seamus obliged and watched Lynch reorganize the sizable stack. The man had amassed more material than Seamus had envisioned, assuming all of the papers in the stack contained the same amount of information as he saw on the first page. Lynch closed his eyes and remained silent. Seamus began to think he'd fallen asleep.

With his eyes still closed, Lynch said, "I'm right." He went on to explain what he'd learned about the incidents in Tulsa and Memphis. "I received a return call from Charleston PD, and the bombing there was reported as an attack on a military recruiting center, but it ends up the new American Party campaign headquarters had just moved in next door."

"Likewise for the bombings in Frankfurt, Little Rock, and Topeka. They all seemed like attacks on what appeared to be an obvious target, city hall, a recruiting center, a courthouse. However, in each case, this new political party was there—either a new campaign office about to open up or a party candidate's office. The police focused on the obvious, until I challenged them to rethink their theories."

"What about the I-10 Bridge and the dam?"

Lynch nodded and opened his eyes to look at Seamus.

"I can't be sure about them. I mean, about the motive behind those attacks. It's clear someone wants this new political party gone, and they're trying to intimidate the early organizers. But what if there's a deeper agenda here?"

Seamus felt inadequate for one of Cully's famous 'what if' sessions. Chief Dandridge had been known for keeping up with Lynch during such sessions, but few other detectives in the area could. Still, Seamus held his ground.

"Okay, so if there's a deeper agenda, what are we looking at?"

Lynch frowned at him as if saying, "That's not how this game is played."

"Follow my lead. Let's say the intent is simply to intimidate this new party, then why the other two attacks? Why Pearl Harbor? That still makes no sense. Why not make all of the attacks on campaign offices? Why do it now, when these offices are just being set up and no staff was present? Why not do it when they're fully staffed, and a bomb would inflict some real injuries."

Seamus saw how the game worked now. "They're just trying to intimidate without hurting anyone. Injuries would result in a much larger investigation and more press."

"Perhaps. So, why the outliers?"

"To mix things up and confuse anyone like you who might see the real intent and begin to investigate?"

"That would fit this scenario. They picked campaign offices near more likely targets, so confusion appears to be part of the plan. But, let's look at it from another angle. What if their real goal is to begin a campaign of terror by inflicting damage to our infrastructure?"

Seamus thought about that. The possibilities there began to emerge in his mind. "They might start with the attacks against the American Party so that if anyone does see a pattern, that's the obvious one. Everyone focuses on that and lets their guard down to other possibilities."

Lynch smiled. "Hey, you're catching on. They took the I-10 Bridge out. What if that was only a test run, to see how easy or hard it would be. There are 13 other interstate bridges crossing the Mississippi. They carry the vast majority of commercial traffic. What would happen if they took all of them down?"

Seamus shrugged. "Traffic would be rerouted to other bridges."

"True. There are about 125 other automobile bridges, and half of them are in Minnesota. Most are two lanes. The oldest bridge was built in 1856 and a lot are 50 years or older. I doubt they could handle the load, and most are highly inconvenient. The disruption to commerce would be catastrophic."

Seamus nodded and found himself wondering about other bridges. There were dozens of railroad bridges, too, and the rails carried more commercial products and raw materials than the trucking industry could. How could the states and local police even begin to cover all of them?

Lynch continued, "And what would happen if major metropolitan water supplies were taken down? We saw what just happened in West Virginia with a chemical spill that affected nine counties."

Seamus felt like he was attending a Terrorist 101 lecture, but he couldn't argue with Lynch. America's

NIMBY—not in my back yard—attitude left it ripe for attack.

135

Sixteen

Karolus Karling steepled his fingers and closed his eyes in thought. Less than an hour out of New York in his Lear 60, he contemplated his business plans and schedule. He sensed his destiny nearing, with the decision to speed up their timetable having been made.

"Sir?"

He looked up to see Francois, his aide, with a sheaf of papers and a glass of vintage Cabernet Sauvignon. He took the wine and sipped it before setting it into a secure holder. Then, he took the papers.

"Are the arrangements made?"

"*Oui, monsieur.* The staff awaits your arrival at the penthouse, and dinner is arranged at the 'Gordon Ramsay at the London.' Your first meeting tomorrow morning is at the U.N., with the Secretary General as requested. The Council members will join you for a luncheon at the Hilton Manhattan, and the business meeting will follow. The Bilderberg meeting is slated for the next morning, and I have confirmed that all members are already in New York. The meeting with the board of the IMF will start at one p.m., followed by dinner with the head of the World Bank. The third day starts with breakfast with Mr. Rockefeller, with the rest of the day dedicated to the Commission. The day after that holds your meetings with the boards at Goldman Sachs and J.P. Morgan Chase. Dinner that night will be with the Board of Governors of the Federal

Reserve. ”

This was a rare occasion in which the Trilateral Commission, Bilderbergs, and Council on Foreign Relations would all be meeting in the same city over the same three-day period. Yet, the occasion warranted it.

“Thank you. Well done, Francois.”

He took another sip of wine and settled back into his seat to read the papers. Most were accounts of the previous day’s incidents, along with advance copies of the editorials being prepared about gun control. He paid particular attention to a series of commentaries to be directed against guns in schools, even those possessed by staff members. He reread two of those editorials and summoned Francois. His aide appeared in seconds.

“Francois, please direct the editors over these two pieces to bring more attention to this principal’s actions and to stress that he’s at fault for his own injuries. Had he not been armed, he would not have been in a position to get shot. And have the local U.S. attorney look into whether or not he violated any federal laws.”

“Sir, I realize it’s not my position to comment, but wouldn’t that upset the liberals as well as the moderates? The principal was protecting children, after all.” Karolus twisted the 24-carat ring on his finger. Its double-headed eagle, with the number ‘33’ inside a triangle over its breast, now aligned with the digit. The banner in the eagle’s talons read, *“deus meumque jus”*—God and My Right.

“You are correct, Francois. It is not your position to comment.”

The Assembly had spent years, decades in some

cases, placing the right people in the right places of influence, awaiting this moment on the world stage. Magazine and newspaper editors, broadcast news editors and producers, morning show hosts and mainstream news anchors, corporate board members, and more, all moved into position like pieces on a chessboard. And he felt ready to move for checkmate.

Francois nodded, took the papers being extended toward him, and retreated toward his workstation.

"Oh, and has there been any interest in the condo?"

"The man turned back toward him. "*Non, monsieur.* However, we didn't expect any immediate interest, considering the economy and the price of the condo. I will let you know when there's been even the slightest interest."

Karolus nodded and returned to his paperwork. His 8,000-square-foot penthouse condo at the CitySpire building overlooked Central Park from the south. He loved the view of The Pond, the quaint Gapstock Bridge, and the Victorian Gardens Amusement Park. He'd had many pleasurable afternoons there, as well as at the nearby Central Park Zoo.

However, in his upcoming position he would need to move his accommodations to Rome, and the $100 million from the sale of his condo would go toward that goal. He would still need his condos in Washington and Paris, as well as Tokyo. They were, after all, the three regional seats of power of the Trilateral Commission.

Soon, the world would get to know him. He had a destiny to fulfill. A direct descendent of Charlemagne, the last emperor of Western Europe, Karolus had been groomed for leadership. Like his father and his father's father before him, The Assembly had educated and trained him, expecting their time to come to change the course of history. Now, it appeared that time was upon them. As the new Secretary General of the U.N., he would help usher in peace to the Mideast.

Seventeen

Fawaz glanced in the mirror and smiled. His Brooks Brothers suit fit him meticulously. Adding the fact that he had an athletic build, he looked as confident as he felt. He grabbed his Homeland Security credentials and slid them into the inner pocket of his coat. His first stop? The Florissant Police Department.

The five-minute drive seemed like seconds. He pulled off the main road and parked in a visitors slot outside the department's main entrance. His visit was unscheduled, yet he expected the police chief to be in.

He stepped up to the reception window and cleared his throat to get the attention of the woman sitting there. She turned toward him.

"May I help you?" she asked.

"I am Senior Fellow Abdul Fawaz, with Homeland Security. I need to speak with your police chief." He glanced at a piece of paper he pulled from his pocket. "Colonel Andrews." He already knew the man's name, but that simple act of having to refer to a listing made the chief appear less important.

"I'm sorry, sir, but the colonel is tied up and asked not to be disturbed. I can put you in touch with his secretary."

"Is he in the building? If so, I expect to talk with him. So please let him know I'm waiting. I am here on behalf of the Attorney General."

She glared at him but took his credentials and left the

desk. A moment later, she returned and told him, "One minute."

After two minutes, Fawaz became impatient. He folded his arms across his chest and began tapping the fingers of his right hand on his left arm. He thought he caught a glimpse of a smile on the woman behind the window. At five minutes, he realized this Colonel Andrews knew how to play the power trip game as well, and that Fawaz did not have the trump card he thought he had. At ten minutes, the nearby door opened, and another middle-aged woman appeared.

"Mr. Fawaz. This way, please."

She had butchered the pronunciation of his name like only some Ozark hillbilly could. He clenched his fist but smiled as she handed his credentials back to him. He longed to get back to civilized Washington, D.C.

At the chief's office suite, Colonel Andrews met him at the door to his private office and ushered him inside.

"Please, have a seat. Can we get you some coffee or tea? Perhaps just water."

Fawaz glanced at the only open seat, a wooden, straight-back chair. Two cushioned chairs remained filled with files and books. Fawaz shook his head and chose to remain standing.

"The DOJ received reports yesterday of a school shooting here. The Attorney General personally asked me to come here and investigate the facts of the shooting."

"I see. You couldn't get enough from the national news media?"

Fawaz frowned. From the man's tone and demeanor, he could tell there was no fondness for the federal government here and perhaps a true disdain for the media. The man was attempting to play him, and that could be a tragic mistake.

"We don't rely upon the news media for our investigations."

"Well, that's a mighty good thing, because in case you haven't noticed, the news media is totally ignoring this incident, and a lot of folks here are wondering why."

"I couldn't begin to tell you why," answered Fawaz, although he knew exactly why. The Assembly pulled its strings on the media as well as his bosses. "You would have to take that up with the networks. I'm here because the AG has two concerns. We've been told that the shooters appeared to be Muslim because of the way they dressed. We wish to make sure the Muslim faith is not disparaged in any way during this investigation. Second, while we recognize that the State of Missouri allows teachers and school staff to carry weapons, we don't agree with that position and will be closely checking the qualifications of those allowed to carry a gun and whether the use of said weapons violated the Constitutional rights of anyone involved."

Fawaz anticipated a stronger reaction, but the colonel's face remained emotion free.

"Anything else, Mr. Fawaz? We have an investigation to continue, and three more bodies to identify."

The last comment caught Fawaz off-guard, and he hoped his reaction had been as impassive as the colonel's. He could not afford even the slightest tell on his face. Yet, the fact that one body had been identified both mystified and worried Fawaz. The four men had been selected for their anonymity, as well as their skills.

"By the way, Mr. Fawaz, you won't have to worry about any rights violations if the victims prove to be illegal aliens, will you? Good day, Mr. Fawaz."

"I'm not finished, Colonel. I need everything you have so far on this matter. It's part of our investigation."

The colonel remained impassive. "Mr. Fawaz, when the Federal government does its job in securing our borders and shows itself to be a good faith partner with the states, then maybe I'll become a good faith partner with you. For right now, however, we're doing *our* investigation and will present our reports to the D.O.J. as required by law. You can do your investigation any way you wish, but my officers have already been informed not to cooperate with you."

"Colonel, are you obstructing a federal investigation?" Fawaz could feel his face reddening.

"Mr. Fawaz, we did some checking, and your position as a Senior Fellow is an analyst's position. You are not a sworn law enforcement agent. So, no, I'm not obstructing a lawful investigation, and you can go about analyzing your ass off, as far as I'm concerned. Again, good day, Mr. Fawaz. I have more important work to resume." He stepped toward the door and opened it for Fawaz.

"We're not done yet, Andrews."

"Yes. We are, Mr. Fawaz. And it's Colonel Andrews, thank you."

Fawaz took a deep breath and worked to contain his anger. He was a *Senior* Fellow, not some low level bureaucrat. He was not to be treated like this.

"If there is so much as a mention that these dead men

were Muslim *terrorists*, this department will face serious consequences."

"Mr. Fawaz, we will release only the truth. They were terrorists, in every definition of the word. And if they are discovered to have been Muslim, then they will be truthfully labeled as Muslim terrorists. As for their assumed rights, what about the rights of those students and teachers? Frankly, Mr. Fawaz, you make me sick. Coming in here to defend those scumbags out of some political correctness crap. Good day, Mr. Fawaz."

When Fawaz saw two armed officers standing outside the door, he knew better than to push this police chief any further. He had underestimated the man and overestimated the authority of his position. He would not make that mistake again.

Eighteen

Brad shook his head at the three armed men guarding his home but said nothing. After the events in Florida, he couldn't argue with Stan. Even though he was only a senatorial candidate, after the announcement of the American Party and its compassionate conservative platform, he had indeed become the face of the party. And a target.

Their car, parked in the long-term lot at Lambert International, had been vandalized. Local police had been called to protect their home and scared away intruders on at least two occasions. The turn of events worried Brad, yet together, he and Cara had agreed there was no turning back.

He glanced outside to the drive and watched a heavy black sedan pull up through the morning's mist and out of view. He walked through the house into the kitchen and from there to the garage where he hit the button for the door opener. Stan stood there with two more men.

Brad waved and said, "Give me a minute."

He rushed upstairs to Mark's bedroom where Cara helped their son prepare for school. Mark looked glum.

"Hey, you two, I hafta go." He ruffled his son's hair. "Ready to go back to school?"

"I guess. Wasn't much of a vacation." He pouted.

"Sorry, but I think you know why. And we also promised you a rain check, remember?"

Mark furrowed his brow. "But I don't wanna go when it's raining. Bummer."

Brad started to explain, but Cara interrupted. "I'll explain that to him again on the way to school. Stan's waiting for you."

Brad nodded. "Love you both." He leaned down to kiss Mark on top of the head, followed by a longer than usual kiss with Cara. "Please add my prayers during the vigil for Harris, will you?"

Cara nodded and returned to re-buttoning Mark's shirt. He had them out of order again. Brad sometimes worried about where his son's mind was. Shoes on the wrong feet. Misplaced buttons on his shirts. He didn't recall being so clumsy at dressing when he was in third grade. Still, the boy made excellent grades, was liked by his classmates, and could hold his own in discussions with most adults. Why should Brad worry about the kid's ability to get dressed?

Brad turned to look at them both one more time. Life had certainly taken an unpredicted twist.

He picked up his briefcase and left through the garage. He entered the back seat of the sedan to join his campaign manager.

"Where'd you get this car, the Secret Service?" He laughed. The car looked like something out of *Men in Black*. "Does it have a rocket booster? Or hidden guns?"

"Just the guns." Stan grinned. "Actually, it *is* bulletproof. Found it in Chicago and had it driven in."

Brad sunk down into his seat. "Do we really have to take it this far? You act like I'm running for president."

"Would you be up for that? Not too early to think

about it."

Brad stared at his friend. The man was serious.

"You're not kidding, are you?"

Stan shook his head. "Nope. Have you seen the polls and the financials?"

"No. Been busy putting out fires, as you know."

"The people in America have been waiting for us. They're so fed up with the government we have now, they're champing at the bit for something fresh—and we're it. The polls show moderates and conservatives alike flocking to our new party. And when you get liberals like New York's governor saying that pro-life, pro-Second Amendment, and anti-gay people aren't welcome in that state? Well, that's already produced announcements from a dozen medium-sized companies that they'll be relocating to friendlier states. Realtors there have noticed a sudden surge in properties being placed on the market. They're worried that real estate prices are going to plummet because of the glut of property up for sale."

Brad felt he should be surprised, but he wasn't. Everyone he knew griped about big government. They all talked about being tired of a small group of elites—bankers, businessmen, politicians, and more—dictating their beliefs and wanting to control everyone else. They wanted to see government once again become one "of the people, by the people, for the people," as he had quoted Lincoln just days earlier in his address in Orlando. The country needed term limits, and Brad would do what he could to initiate them, no matter which office he held.

"And our financials are incredible. The party has raised over 150 million dollars since the caucus. And what's so amazing is that most of that is coming from individuals, not businesses or PACs. It's still flowing in. We might double the amount by the end of the month."

Brad raised his brow. That *was* unbelievable. They had hoped to raise 20% of that amount before the spring primaries. Even that had been considered shooting for the stars.

"To get you back in the loop, we also have half a dozen senators and three dozen congressmen talking to us about switching to our new party. Two of those senators have already endorsed your candidacy. Also, two sitting governors have joined us."

Brad sat there, waiting for the bad news. With all of this positive spin, there had to be a negative side.

"So, that gets me back to you. We have polls showing that people liked what they saw of you in Florida. They're asking if you're planning on becoming the party's first presidential candidate. Dom is asking me the same thing."

Brad took a deep breath and gazed out the window in thought. In their planning discussions with Dominick and other party leaders, they had agreed that their primary focus would be on establishing the party and gaining a political beachhead in the state legislatures and Congress before ever tackling the big chair. Had things moved so quickly that they now looked to field a candidate in the 2016 election?

As he thought about it, maybe the time really was ripe for such an action. Hillary's Benghazi blunders, along with her past railcar loads of baggage, was dragging her further down in the polls. Yet, no Democratic challengers seemed eager to take her on and find themselves on her vindictive "enemies list" should she take the nomination. On the Republican side, the liberal media had piled onto Chris Christy over "Bridgegate" and complaints about Hurricane Sandy relief. Justified or not, they had succeeded in planting seeds of doubt in the public mind about the governor's suitability for the highest office. What was it Stan had just said? The people were eager to find something, or someone, fresh?

"Seriously, think about it. You have no political baggage, no skeletons in your closet, and no oddball relatives. The media fact finders will find themselves popping up in China trying to dig deep enough to find dirt on you." He paused. "Unless, you're hiding something from me."

"Nope, I'm as boring as anyone can get."

"I hope so. But also loyal, patriotic, honest, hard working, down-to-earth, and faithful. You'd get my vote." Stan grinned.

Brad chuckled and glanced out the window in time to see they'd missed the exit to his office.

"Hey, where're we headed? I thought we were going straight to the office."

"We're going to stop by Barnes first."

"The hospital? I thought Harris was still in critical condition."

"He is, but I thought you'd want to stop in, see his wife. And there's someone else I want you to meet."

"I talked with Rebecca yesterday afternoon." He paused as a thought hit him. "Hey, you're not planning some kind of photo op thing are you, 'cause I refuse to abuse my friendship with Harris that way. He's not some political prop. He's fighting to stay alive at this point."

Stan sighed. "I know. I have to be honest and admit that the thought did cross my mind. I am your campaign manager after all. But I knew you'd object, and even I would find that distasteful. We're stopping by to *help* him."

"Oh?" Brad found that comment curious. How would they be able to help Harris?

"Rebecca called me this morning and asked if you'd stop by. It appears that the U.S. Attorney has launched an investigation into whether or not Harris violated any federal law. She's also appalled that this incident isn't getting more press attention. She asked for our help."

Brad felt a righteous anger bubbling up within. His friend put his life on the line to protect his students, and the Feds have the audacity to portray *him* as a criminal? He would defend his friend's honor. There was no doubt about that.

Brad and Stan spent half an hour with Rebecca Burke, and Brad had taken time to pray with her over Harris. He came away impressed with her resolve to fight for her husband's good name and with her increasing disgust with the government. She stood behind Brad 100% and would support whatever he chose to do, knowing he would only do what was best for Harris.

"How long will it take to put together a press conference?" asked Brad.

"Actually, Dominick has one set up for noon. I'm sure he wouldn't mind sharing."

Brad nodded. "Good, because I'll be there."

Together they entered the elevator, and Stan pressed the button for a higher floor.

"Aren't we finished here?"

Stan answered, "The man I want you to meet is upstairs."

Brad found that curious. Were there offices above? He wondered just who this person might be.

A few minutes later, they entered a hallway, and Brad saw a room with a doorway festooned with balloons and a banner saying, "He's Alive!" Stan walked straight to that doorway and knocked on the doorpost.

A voice replied, "Come in."

Upon entering the room, Brad saw a younger man lying in the hospital bed with bandages swathed around his left shoulder and plastered to his left chest. A laptop and papers filled the bedside table.

"Brad, I'd like you to meet Lynch Cully. Lynch, this is Brad Graham."

Lynch's face lit up in recognition of the other and a smile ensued as Brad looked confused.

"Lynch Cully? I attended your memorial service. Wh-what happened?"

Stan stepped in to shake Lynch's hand as well. "You had left town for Orlando when the news broke." He gave Brad a short synopsis of Lynch's story and the human trafficking ring takedown.

Lynch commented on having watched Brad's speech, and the effect it had on those in his room at the time. "We all really liked the speech, by the way."

"Thanks."

"*I'd* vote for you for president. You ought to think

about it."

"Um, thanks, again." The comment stuck with Brad. Was God trying to tell him something?

"But it sounds like you experienced anything but amusement in Orlando," said Lynch. "Grab a couple of chairs. I have something to show you."

"Lynch contacted me earlier about a theory he has regarding those bombings two days ago. Dom was supposed to meet us here, too, but last minute details have stopped him."

Stan slid two nearby chairs up to the bed and offered the closest one to Brad. The two men sat down.

"Since I've been stuck to this bed for the last few days, I've had little to do but watch the news. I might have been more effective with a DVR, so I could record a couple stations at a time and review them later. However, some things still just kinda popped out at me."

Lynch winced as he moved to sit up straighter. "Sorry, they just pulled the tube out of my chest an hour ago. Smarts a bit." He used the bed control to raise the head of the bed.

"Anyway, something about the timing of the bombings and the local school shooting caught my attention, not to mention that your son seemed to be a target at that school." Lynch proceeded to show, in detail, his theory and findings. "I laid these out for the Major Case Squad yesterday, with Seamus O'Connor."

Brad appeared grave as he learned more and more. Stan had been forthright in the car about the positives of the campaign and American Party but had neglected the negatives. Now, Brad partly understood why.

He looked at Stan. "Did you know this earlier?"

Stan shook his head. "Only the theory about the American Party being the target of the attacks. These details are new to me, to all of us."

"If this is true, who's behind it?"

Lynch shrugged his right shoulder. "Don't know yet."

Stan continued. "We've made enemies of both major parties already. They expected us to whimper like the Libertarians, not gain the attention and favor of the grassroots from both their sides. I wouldn't put either one on a friends list. One or both could be behind this."

"It might go deeper than that," said Lynch.

Brad scrutinized the man's face, not liking the implications behind that statement but understanding its intent. He turned and gazed out the window. If what Lynch implied held even the slightest basis in fact, then a whole lot more was at stake than an election. Or even a political party.

He turned back to Lynch. "So, when do you get out of this place?"

Stan gave him a look of curiosity.

Lynch shook his head. "The sooner the better, but it might be a few more days. They have to make sure my lung stays inflated now that the chest tube is gone."

"And, I guess you're on medical leave from your police department for a while."

Stan gave him a knowing look and nodded.

Lynch huffed. "I guess, if you define 'a while' as permanent." He paused. "The department filled my slot while I was MIA, so I'm unemployed at this point. I was talking with the university, UMSL, about a teaching position, but this whole amnesia thing has thrown that off, too."

Brad smiled. "Come work for us. In light of what's happened, I need a chief of security, and we need someone who can find the root of this problem. And we'll make sure you have the leeway to investigate this whole thing."

"Excellent idea," added Stan. "If you've been able to ferret out this much from a hospital bed, I'd love to see what you come up with having all the tools on hand you need."

Lynch glanced back and forth between the two men. Brad thought he saw hesitation in Lynch's eyes.

Lynch spoke up. "You got yourself a security chief."

Nineteen

Amy paced just inside the door at Momo's Greek Tavern, too distracted to savor the aroma of roasting lamb or the many other mouth-watering smells wafting about her. Greek was her favorite ethnic food, but a stranger would never know that from the look on her face.

Richard had called her and said he needed to see her right away. He had suggested this restaurant and the lunch hour but never hinted as to why the urgency.

She checked her phone for the time. Only a minute had passed since her last check.

He'll be here any minute, she reassured herself. What she couldn't resolve in her mind was why she felt so anxious about the meeting. Had he taken the slot at the FBI Academy? Was he going to say goodbye? She realized she didn't want to see him leave. She wasn't ready to give up St. Louis and her family here to follow him there, but she didn't want him to go either. She was just now beginning to understand the depths of her feelings for him. Maybe the argument with Lynch had been meant to guide her.

"Are you sure you don't want to be seated?" asked the hostess, who had approached her for the third time. "We *can* direct the other person in your party to the table."

There was something about the way the young woman said it that spurred Amy to agree. She nodded. "Okay. That's fine."

The hostess directed her to a booth in the next room.

Amy glanced around and thought it a perfect spot, covered, with walls on three sides. If she started crying, no one would be disturbed.

The iced tea she'd ordered arrived, and she sipped at it absentmindedly. Lost in thought, she started at the sudden appearance of Richard next to the table.

"Hey, sorry I'm late. I got this really important phone call just as I was ready to leave."

Amy gave him a tenuous smile and nodded. "That's okay. I knew you'd call if something else had come up."

He shook his head. "Amy, I'd never do that to you. I'd have to be dead before I'd stand you up." He grinned.

She returned the smile, and as he removed his coat and tucked it on the bench opposite her, she noticed a cardboard box lying at his feet. She cocked her head to get a better look.

His grin became bigger. "Got a surprise this morning." He laughed and opened the top flaps of the container. "Ta dah!" He pulled out a brand new Hammer of Thor. "Clive made me a new one, with only one modification."

Amy laughed as relief flooded through her. He had called her to share this with her, nothing more. Now, the hammer meant as much to her as it did to him. The original hammer had saved his life twice, and that had taken on new significance for her.

"Look."

Amy glanced at the bottom surface where Richard pointed. "A cell phone? Why . . .?"

Richard pressed a speed dial button, and an instant later, ringing came from the box. He returned his attention to the box but stopped and turned back to her.

"Close your eyes."

"Uh-uh." The ringing continued, and they started to get stares from surrounding patrons.

"Close 'em. Or they might ask us to leave." He laughed. She closed her eyes, but she could hear him rustling in the box. The ringing stopped.

"Okay, open 'em."

Richard stood there with a matching hammer, but smaller and in pink, with a second cell phone built into the lower surface.

"He built one for you, too. And the phones only have one number built in, each to the other phone." He laughed again, as Amy's eyes lit up.

"Aww, how sweet. I have BFF bracelets and a couple of lockets. Macy gave me this friendship ring a few years ago." She held up her right hand to show it off. "But, I admit, I've never received a friendship hammer before. I'm truly touched." She gave those words a dramatic flair and struck a pose with her new gift.

She laughed out loud, and the more she thought about it, the more she couldn't control her laughter. That, in turn, got Richard laughing, and soon tears rolled from both of their eyes as they tried to control themselves.

She tried to talk but still found it difficult. The waitress had stopped by twice to take their order only to turn around without saying a word each time.

Amy finally got herself together enough to take a deep breath and say, "Please thank Clive for me."

Richard nodded and said, "Now, you realize you need a Norse name, too."

Amy blinked the remaining tears away. "Aaannnd, do

you have one in mind?"

"Freyja." He spelled the name.

"Freyja? Who the heck is Freyja?"

He blushed. "I'll let you look her up."

Amy grabbed her smartphone from her purse to do just that, but the waitress returned. After placing their orders, she pulled up her phone again.

"Hey, you can look it up later."

"No way, buster. I'm not leaving here without knowing who Freyja is."

A moment later, she blushed. Freyja was the Norse goddess of love, beauty, and sexuality, as well as a goddess of war. Her first reaction? She didn't know whether to hit Richard with the hammer or to change its cell phone number to a 900 number to make him pay. Yet, on second thought, she realized he had paid her an incredible compliment. Tough, sexy, and beautiful. She liked the fact that he saw her that way.

Over lunch, Richard updated her on Clive's new job, when he wasn't making self-defense hammers. The job offer had appeared just days after the press accounts of the role his craftsmanship had played in the Darko Komarčić case. Clive couldn't share much about it—on threat he'd have to kill anyone he told—but did mention he would make Q proud. He hadn't moved to England, so a position with MI-6 was out.

Nothing new sat on the horizon for any of the rest of Richard's band of brothers. Hassle, *and* his grandfather, sent their regards to Amy. Amy gave him a mock look of displeasure at his reminder about the General 'Ulcer' story. He smiled.

"Dessert?" he asked as they finished.

"No thanks. I'm stuffed."

"Well, I'm not passing up their baklava. I'll share."

As they waited for the treat, Amy gazed at Richard. The thought hit her that there was something else he wasn't telling her, and she began to worry again.

"So, was this *urgent* lunch date just an excuse to give me a hammer?" She grinned.

"Actually, no." He took the honey covered pastry from the waitress, placed it in the middle of the table, and poised his fork over it. "Bite?"

She waggled her head a bit and finally said, "Sure. Thanks." Within a few minutes she had devoured half of his dessert. "Oooo, that's good." She looked at him to realize he'd been sitting there watching her and hadn't yet taken a bite for himself.

"Must be. Do I get any?" He laughed.

She nodded and sat back, after pushing the plate to his side of the table.

After savoring his first bite, he said, "The hammers showed up this morning, *after* we made the date." He took another bite. "I wanted to see you right away because ..."

He took another bite and closed his eyes as he enjoyed it. He repeated the process, and she realized he was playing with her now.

"Because?"

He didn't answer and slowly finished the baklava.

"Again, your reason is ...?"

He laid down his fork, pushed aside the plate, and took her hands in his. His face lit up.

"I wanted you to be the first to know. I'm *not* leaving

town. I got a great job offer last night, so I'm here for the duration."

Amy felt giddy. "What? What's the job?"

"Dominick Standish has offered me the position of Director of Social Media and Marketing for the new American Party. I had an impromptu interview with him yesterday, showed him my resume, and he called after dinner with the offer. Since the party is based here to avoid being corrupted by beltway politics, I'm here to stay for a while."

"Congratulations. That's wonderful."

Richard paid the tab and placed the hammers in the box to avoid any stares as they left. They walked outside and stood on the sidewalk.

"Look, I want to find a place closer to the party headquarters. Would you help me look? I still don't know my way around town all that well."

"What about Mrs. Boyles and the apartment at her old house?"

"Well, her kids have been bugging her to sell and move closer to them, so she's been looking at assisted living apartments near where they live. She says she's ready for that. That beautiful old house is going on the market the first of the month."

"Why don't you buy it from her?"

Richard shrugged. "I thought about it for a moment, but it's not very convenient to where I'll be working, and, well, I don't know that I want to be saddled with a house right now, especially an old house. Plus," He paused. ". . . it's sure not close to you."

He took her in his arms and gazed into her eyes. Amy

felt the proverbial tingle from her head to her toes. As he leaned into her, she felt the warmth of his breath on her cheek. She closed the gap and met his lips with hers. That's when she realized that despite the entangled relationships of Norse mythology, she, Freyja, had fallen in love with Thor.

Twenty

"Next question . . ."

Brad watched from the back of the small crowd, unnoticed by the reporters in front of him. He didn't want to interrupt Dominick's press conference, but knew he'd get time at the end while everyone was still in attendance.

As he'd noted at previous American Party press events, the number of reporters was small. Yet, in comparison to the previous two such events, there was a 50% increase. If, in a month, they saw another 50% increase, they'd know the party was finally making some in-roads to the mainstream press channels.

"Yes, I've seen the new Republican stance on immigration. As compassionate conservatives, we can agree with much of what the GOP leaders proposed in their standards for immigration reform white paper. That standard needs to go a bit further, however."

"First and foremost, we must strengthen our border security to prevent further illegal intrusion into our country. Instead of leaving behind millions of dollars worth of military equipment for ungrateful governments in Iraq and Afghanistan, we would bring that hardware stateside for use by the border patrol, which we would double in size. We would authorize the use of armed drones to patrol areas too rugged for routine patrols. If you enter our country armed and prepared to fight, you will be treated as the armed invader that you are."

"For those already in the country, we would agree with the GOP leaders on a path to citizenship that includes background checks, the payment of fines and back taxes, the ability to speak English, the ability to support yourself and your family, and so on. However, we would also propose a period of civil service for all seeking citizenship. Four years of military service with an honorable discharge, or, if not fit for military service, four years of civil service in a program much like the old Civilian Conservation Corps to help rebuild our national and state parks."

Dom went on to outline more about their stance on immigration, followed by the party's platform on education. He highlighted how federal standards had consistently "dumbed-down" our education system. He condemned our placing 17th out of 34 countries ranked for global education quality, with a 26th place for math. Yet, only four countries spent more than our $115,000 per student annually for education. He called for the elimination of the Department of Education and the return of control to the states.

The half hour conference wound down, and Dom stated, "Ladies and gentlemen, before you go, Brad Graham would like a few minutes of your time. Trust me; this part might make your time here worthwhile compared to the stats and outlines I gave you."

Brad noticed several reporters look around. Their curiosity appeared obvious.

"Brad?"

Dom pointed to him in the back, and Brad worked his way to the microphones. He had calmed down a little since talking with Rebecca about Harris, and had taken time after meeting with Lynch Cully to make some notes.

"Good afternoon, folks. I think I know most all of you, but for those of you I've not met before, I'm Brad." He paused for a moment to consider how to start. "I asked Dom for some time because over the past few days a number of events have occurred that need to be brought to the public's attention, and you, the media in general, have been complacent in doing so. Maybe some of you have even been complicit in an effort to keep this from the public. If so, shame on you."

"Less than a week ago, four armed gunmen entered and attacked Northgate Christian Academy. Where has the press been? The principal of that school, a close friend of mine, was critically wounded defending our children. How many of you are following his progress and asking the public to support him? Now, the local U.S. Attorney is threatening him with federal gun charges, and where is the indignation in the press? Where is the support for a man who likely saved a dozen lives by his actions? Actions, by the way, which are legal under state law."

"Instead, it appears that collectively you have chosen to ignore this event. Why? I don't know, but it makes me angry. And as the word gets out, and it is, via social media, it makes more and more people angry. Soon, you will have no credibility at all, but that's your choice."

"Now, did I come here and ask for your time simply to berate you and try to shame you into action?" He paused and noticed several reporters beginning to pack up their gear. "Partly. But I also came here to let you know that a bigger story is emerging, and you're missing it. On the day of the school shooting, a dozen other incidents occurred across our country, mall shootings, bombings, and more. Despite initial reports, we have now identified that ten of those incidents had American Party campaign offices as their targets."

That got their attention. The first hand shot up.

"The American Party was never mentioned in the reports on those things."

"Exactly. And why? Because the offices were specifically chosen for their proximity to other seemingly more obvious targets. My new chief of security saw the pattern and has alerted local police departments, which now agree with us and are stepping up their investigations."

Another hand. "Do you know who's behind these attacks?"

"Not yet, but we have some strong leads, and with the cooperation of the other local police departments, we believe we will find out who is responsible."

"Was it the other parties? Are the D.N.C. and R.N.C. implicated?"

"Do you know anything more about the other incidents?"

"When will you have more information?"

Brad felt encouraged by the level of interest.

"Again, we don't know yet. And because there are active police investigations going on, we can't jump ahead of those investigations or interfere with them. We will be working with every department who asks for our help. For those interested, we can take your names and promise to get you more information as we're able to release it."

A hand from the back inched up. Brad didn't recognize the man.

"Why are *you* the one telling us this? Why aren't the police giving us this information? And isn't releasing this information now already a form of interference in those investigations?"

Brad expected this potential line of questions. He was ready with an answer.

"We have three reasons. First, I have a friend fighting for his life because he defended his students, and no one is defending him except his family, my family, and his school family. No one has publicly lauded him for the heroic action he took that day. Well, I am. Right now. To all of you here. Harris Burke is a hero, and I hope you'll echo that to all of your readers and viewers."

"Second, it was *our* people who found this link and are working to prove it, because it appears there's no such thing as a *real* investigative reporter anymore. You just rely on list servs for stories and scripts from other sources. I challenge *you* to search for the real story here."

He paused, blinking back tears at the memory of his family being targeted.

"The final reason I'm the one bringing this up is that I and my family were targets as well. My son was targeted at the school. The monorail incident that the park executives now claim to have been a system malfunction was a suicide bomber. I was there. I believe I was his main target, and the sick S-O-B had no regard for the other lives he took in his attempt to kill me. The next morning, my wife and I were the targets of a shooter, who missed but managed to take out the glass sliding door of our room at the Hawaiian Resort. They've made this personal, and I'm saying to you right now that I'm taking the fight back to them. Unlike our current President, who only gives lip service to justice, as with the Benghazi perpetrators, we *will* find who's responsible."

Brad knew the steel in his voice translated to his countenance. He also knew that the reporters present who knew him, knew he meant it.

He looked for the man who asked the question but did not see him. He tried to recall what the guy looked like, but he had been too hurried and angry to make a close observation.

"Thank you for listening and for your time."

He started to step away from the microphones, but one more hand shot up.

"Brad, you gonna run for president in '16?"

He heard a few chuckles in the group.

"Well, interesting question. Also unlike our current President who promised transparency but has the most closed administration in recent history, I *will* be transparent. That question was asked of me for the first time just this morning. Until then, I hadn't even considered it. Now, I am."

He grinned and a few cameras flashed.

"So, would I get any votes from this crowd?"

To his surprise, half a dozen hands went up.

Twenty-One

Karolus watched the replay of the St. Louis six o'clock news with dismay. Previously, word had been passed through The Assembly's channels that news accounts of that shooting were to be squelched. Selected news editors and producers were instructed to deem it a 'non-story' since no children were injured. They had no video of ambulances rushing from the scene, of helicopters being loaded with casualties. All in all, with all of the news available to report, they had no time to allot to it.

And they surely did not want to bring praise upon that foolhardy principal. They did not want to encourage other school staffs to take up arms, or other state legislatures to pass similar laws allowing school staffs to be armed. School shootings had been one of their best plays in terms of ratcheting up sentiment against guns. To their benefit, the mentally imbalanced were quite easy to manipulate by planting thoughts of grandeur and recognition for such actions.

Yet, the march toward elimination of privately-owned weapons in the United States proved to be a slow one. The need to step up the pace had become evident with the sudden and unexpected popularity of this grassroots political party, the American Party, with its silly Minuteman mascot.

Karolus disliked micromanaging, but this situation posed too serious a threat to delegate to someone else. He had his ways of controlling both the Democrat and Republican machines. Although taking slightly different routes, they both marched to the beat of his drum. This new party not only moved to a different beat, they marched in the opposite direction.

This new party had proven difficult to penetrate. He had his moles there, but nothing useful had yet come from those ranks.

In addition, the Party's decision to remain headquartered in the heartland of America kept them surrounded by conservative thinkers and those who called themselves patriots. The Senate majority leader had been correct in calling these people "domestic terrorists."

In Washington, the party leaders would have soon found themselves enmeshed in the local social scene, being influenced by more liberal ways, and enticed to accept a global perspective over those anachronistic nationalist views.

Perhaps they had overlooked a way to lure them to the beltway. He made a mental note to assign someone with that research task.

He replayed the newscast and made note of the reporter's name, as well as that of the producer who had allowed it to play. He hated that he had to take such an active role in this matter. Yet, this situation was on the verge of becoming a major stumbling block to his plans, to *their* plans.

He looked up at his aide and handed the tablet computer back to him. "Francois, work through the usual channels, but make sure this reporter and her producer are looking for new jobs by week's end. We cannot have such independent thinking."

The aide nodded. "*Oui, monsieur.* Our people at the station's parent company have already been alerted. They will be ready to act as soon as I call."

"Very good. Oh, and task Ricardo with finding some way to lure the American Party to move its headquarters to Washington."

Francois nodded and turned sharply on his heels. Karolus raised his hand.

"One more thing, Francois. Call Fawaz and have him initiate stage two. Inform him I'm not happy that his so-called *ingenious* plan was discovered so quickly. And tell him if he can't be more clever, we'll find someone who can deliver what we need."

"*Oui, monsieur. Immédiatement.*"

Karolus sat back and gazed out across Central Park. Perhaps Fawaz had been the wrong choice. Roberta Faris had seemed certain of her selection, and he *had* executed their plan regarding the attacks on the American Party without flaw. Yet, Graham still lived, and his family remained unharmed. As a result, he continued in the senatorial race where their unpublished polls showed him a staggering 21 points ahead of their own well-groomed incumbent. And now? Did a higher destiny call? Did the man feel he was ready for something bigger?

The reporter's question about running for higher office did not come as a surprise to Karolus as he reviewed the video. The show of hands did.

He picked up a nearby folder and again reviewed the dossier his people had created on Bradley Graham. He'd read it once before, but today its importance took on new meaning. Had they missed something, anything?

Bradley Graham had been raised by a single mother and worked his way through both private high school and college, graduating summa cum laude with a double major in software engineering and business management. He founded, developed, and ran a technology company that now employed just shy of a thousand people. He knew how to create jobs and work with people.

He had no skeletons in his closet, no twisted vices, or any other baggage to hinder a campaign. Not even a suggestive photo on social media. His lack of public office and government experience had become a positive in their polling. Of course, they would chip away at that 'positive,' hoping to negate it, but the trends also showed a growing distrust of government in its current state and a marked dislike of elitist politicians. Even their biggest hammer might not make a dent in that positive.

Karolus held on to one hope. That Graham's unwavering Christianity could be used against him. They had succeeded in turning public opinion against the Judeo-Christian perspective on homosexuality, while broadening that same opinion regarding what constitutes marriage. They had succeeded in their legal actions against Christian business owners who thought they could remain true to their faith.

Yes. That was Bradley Graham's Achilles heel. They would show him to be the bigot and extremist that all Christians were.

He pressed his intercom. "Francois, one more thing. Call the D.N.C, R.N.C. and Clinton campaign and make sure they put Bradley Graham on their radar. Advise them to begin to chip away at his religion. Meanwhile, get our pollsters to look closely at him, too. I want to see if he's a threat to our plans or not."

Fawaz had expected a phone call, but he hadn't expected one from the Director's office. He had gone to the press conference held by the American Party's chairman earlier that day. He had been killing time, waiting for the Florissant Police Department, or the Major Case Squad, to make a wrong move. So far, their actions had been those which one would anticipate early in an investigation.

However, he hadn't expected to learn that someone had already detected the pattern he had so carefully worked out. It had taken time to find American Party campaign headquarters adjacent to more obvious targets. And then to locate those within one day's drive of their organized cells. He had spent weeks creating their target list, often having to change targets because one campaign office or another did not go into an office space as planned. And yet, within two days, someone had seen through his subterfuge. And now, only four days later, the press had been briefed, and one eager reporter took up Bradley Graham's call.

He thought back on the recent call.

"Fawaz, the Director wishes to start phase two."

"But it's too soon."

"He must not think so. I believe he is more worried that the plan and the, shall I say, *action* cells we spent years putting into place will be discovered before you can finish."

"I don't know. There is a danger in moving so soon after the first attacks. Police, and even the public, will mobilize and unite against what they see as a war against them. Phase two, on the heels of phase one, will seem just that, like war has been declared. Plus, I will need to activate a new cell to replace the four men we lost. That will take time and my direct involvement. I cannot leave St. Louis at the moment."

There was dead air for a minute.

"I see. Very well, I shall inform the Director that you are unable to carry out his directions."

"No, no. Please. Don't do that. I will move on. I will initiate phase two as he wishes."

"Very good. Do not fail him."

No, Fawaz thought, *I cannot fail him.* Failure meant a sure and not-so-quick death where there would be no virgins awaiting him.

Fawaz considered his options. Yes, without doubt, he would launch the next wave of attacks, in the face of the risks. The Director was not a man to be crossed, despite his outward charisma and extroverted personality. He had seen the man in operation. Karolus Karling came across as a friend to all, with a quick wit and laugh to match.

The man could talk on any subject and was an undisputed expert on the Roman Empire, the history of the ancient Middle East, and its current events. Fawaz had heard him speak and saw that his grasp of the political situation there held no equal. Fawaz held no reservations that Karling would be the man of their time, the leader who could bring peace to the Middle East. And he, Fawaz, wished to be part of that history.

The man was also quite brilliant. Perhaps he foresaw a different outcome to moving so quickly.

Fawaz contemplated the situation. Of equal concern to the timing of their attacks on America, was the fact that someone had detected his plan and seen through the subterfuge. That person might be smart enough to see what's coming. That person had to be identified. That person had to be stopped.

Twenty-two

Colonel Andrews and Captain Johnstone, along with half a dozen detectives from both the Florissant Police Department and Major Case Squad, sat in the large conference room at the FPD. A large white board sat in the front of the room, holding photos and handwritten notes about the school shooting. They were already a week into the case and had little to show for it.

Andrews spoke first. "So, have we gotten anything new? This case board is still looking mighty sparse."

Paul Flannigan spoke first. "No, sir. Fingerprints on the shooters haven't come up with any new names."

Seamus saw the concern on the faces of the two chiefs. He felt the same way, as if they were treading water in the Niagara River, heading for the falls. Unless they could get a break in this case, more tragedy was going to befall someone, somewhere in the country. The other police departments around the country, working their respective cases, had made no progress either.

"Any word back from Chicago or Detroit on this Mudab guy?" asked Johnstone.

"It's Muhab, sir, Muhab Abdelnour, and so far, nothing. Folks at Chicago PD have nothing on the guy. Detroit PD keeps stalling. I get the impression they don't have the manpower to help us."

"Well, keep trying there. What about the vehicles?"

Another detective answered. "Well, the white van was stolen locally, and we've cleared the owner of that one. The lab couldn't find anything useful there, so it's been released back to the owner. The SUV at the mall was a GMC Yukon Denali. Plates on it were stolen locally, too. Its VIN identifiers were removed. Pros, they knew what they were doing."

"They got all the VIN markings? Engine and transmission numbers, all of them?"

"Yes, sir. Doorframe and left dash tags were taken out. Looks like the engine and transmission numbers were etched with acid, but the heat of the fire destroyed any chance of recovering them."

"The frame?"

"Same with the frame. GM gave our techs the info to hunt down all the hidden VINs. Either etched with acid or destroyed by the fire."

Seamus sat up, more attentive. "I thought I read something about one of the back seats having been blown out through the open side door."

The detective turned his way. "That's true. We have one largely intact seat."

"So, use the seat tag."

"What?"

"Yeah, the seat tag. I learned this from a guy who works for a seat manufacturer. All of the tags are computer linked to the VIN. They need that for potential recalls. If you've got a seat tag, you can get the VIN, the dealer who sold the car, the line of ownership, all of it."

Seamus watched the detective scratching notes into his pocket notebook as fast as Seamus spoke.

Colonel Andrews furrowed his brow. "Do the lab techs know this?"

"Guess not, sir, or they would have ID'd the car for us

by now."

There was silence in the room. Seamus could see both chiefs mentally cataloging this new bit of forensics.

Colonel Andrews spoke up. "Let's keep the facts about the VIN under our hats. That doesn't go beyond the eight of us. Got it?"

Everyone nodded. The captain spoke next.

"Okay, so what's it going to take to ID these thugs? We're not going to break this case until we have something on this Mudab guy or his buddies."

Seamus rolled his eyes, recalling it took the man four months to call him 'Shay-mus' and not 'See-mus.' He looked at Flannigan.

"Paul, who was the detective you contacted in Detroit?"

"A Detective Ahmad."

"Oh great!" groaned Johnstone.

Seamus didn't think himself politically correct by any stretch of the imagination, but he refused to lump people together based on their last name. He had learned long ago that when it came to religion, most people were lukewarm, which they equated to being a moderate.

Cultural Christians weren't that much different from Cultural Muslims. Their religious preferences evolved from what their parents practiced, and most knew little about what their respective religion truly taught. In the simplest sense, they sought a peaceful life filled with opportunity to succeed and provide for their families, not confrontation or a religious war.

Still, Seamus could see a detective protecting 'his own'—whether Muslim or Christian—if he agreed with the cause. It had happened before and would happen again. Corruption might be a strong word to use, but nevertheless, it fit and it plagued every police department, large and small.

"Sir, if they're stonewalling us, the fastest way to get some answers is to go there, personally. They can't ignore a person as easily as an email or phone call."

The two chiefs looked at each other. Seamus knew there'd be debate about funding a trip, which would end up coming out of Florissant's pocket. The MCS, after all, was a volunteer group with no budget of its own, other than donations to fund the executive director's office.

Col. Andrews responded, "You're probably right, O'Connor, but I won't authorize the funds without more to justify the expense. If we come up with IDs on the other three perps, or a vehicle ID that ties them to Detroit, then I can justify it."

The meeting ended after some additional discussion, and all of the detectives went on to their assigned tasks. Seamus walked up to Flannigan. He felt assured the detective was about to corral some techs at the county crime lab.

"Heading to the lab?"

Flannigan nodded. "I'm going to check on that car seat personally."

"Mind if I join you? I'd like to see this first-hand myself. I never had a need to before."

"Sure, but you might want to meet me at the lab. I've got a bunch of other things to do with the techs and will be there for a while."

That suited Seamus, who preferred using his own car,

too. Besides, Flannigan was a scary driver.

"Okay. Meet you there."

After arriving at the lab, they met with the technician and located the car's seat. Seamus scratched his head, puzzled, as he looked over the seat. The fabric looked brand new, without a single scuff mark. He furrowed his brow in curiosity. Nothing appeared to show that an explosion had violently expelled this seat from the SUV.

"Yeah, that caught our attention, too."

"What?" asked Seamus, surprised by the tech's comment.

"It looks brand new, like from a car in the dealer's showroom. Not a mark on it. Even more interesting . . . look at the bottom."

Seamus, now gloved, tipped the seat onto its back and looked at the structural supports. The bolts that connected the seat to the floor showed no stress at all.

"I would expect the bolts to be twisted or bent, something, but they're as straight as coming off the assembly line. Look at the welds."

Seamus saw that the welds were intact and three-inch squares from the SUV's floor had come with the seat, It looked as if someone had cut the squares from the metal floor, not that it was torn free by an explosion. It made no sense, but then, neither did the damage done to the classrooms.

Seamus started to upright the seat, but the tech stopped him.

"Wait a minute. Let me check the seat tag." The man jotted down some numbers. "Okay. Got it."

Seamus put the seat back upright. The tech motioned

them to follow him. On a nearby table, he had photos of the scene spread out.

Flannigan picked up one of the photos, followed by a second.

"You know, I was a bit confused at the scene when I saw the seat, but now, in retrospect and after seeing the lack of damage to the seat, it makes sense that none of this makes sense."

Seamus grinned. "C'mon, Paul, you're not making sense."

Flannigan rolled his eyes. "I know, 'cause none of this does. Look at the photos."

Seamus did so and saw the man's point of confusion right away. From the force of the explosion and resulting fire, they should not have found the seat where it was, much less sitting, as if untouched, in an upright position. It really did look as if "someone" had cut the seat free of the car and placed it on the asphalt. Again, Seamus reflected on the classroom and thought, *That "someone" wants us to crack this case.*

Ten minutes later, they had their car ID. An hour later, Detroit PD confirmed it had been reported stolen.

"Well, look at this," said Flannigan as he looked over the material faxed from the Motor City. "You don't think . . ."

Seamus took the papers and scanned them. Within the sheets was a copy of a photo taken from a security camera showing the man stealing the car—John Doe #2. Suspect believed to be one Sabir Ahmad.

Twenty-three

For the first time in nearly a week, Lynch climbed out of bed after lunch and went to look out the window. The overcast day did nothing to dampen his mood. The surgeon had stopped by and informed him that if his lung remained inflated and the next morning's follow-up chest X-ray showed no other concerns, he would be a free man, bound to the medical realm only by a few return visits to the doctor's office for wound checks and suture removal.

He turned at a knock at the door and saw Susan Prichard standing there.

"Hey, c'mon in. I didn't expect to see you this soon."

Susan smiled. "I didn't expect to finish up that human trafficking case so quickly, but we have. It's in the hands of the U.S. Attorney now."

Lynch pointed to a nearby chair, but she shook her head and declined.

"Thanks, but I really can't stay. I just wanted you to know what we learned about the Chief." Colonel Dandridge, former head of the MCS and "the Chief" to everyone who knew him, had been at Darko Komarčić's estate and implicated in the human trafficking ring. He had given his life for Lynch, a sacrifice stained by those allegations.

Lynch needed to know but feared what he was about to hear. He sat on the edge of the wide window sill and took a deep breath, ignoring the pain that it produced.

"When I went to the Chief's home, I found that he had a young housekeeper. She ended up being here illegally."

She paused as Lynch hung his head. The news he'd feared seemed to be reality.

"But . . ." she continued. "It appears he was not involved, and that he became a victim himself."

Lynch perked up.

"We interviewed the housekeeper, and I think we've pieced together what happened. When his wife died, he needed help at home. He reached out to a friend, who suggested a placement service. Ends up the 'friend' was on Komarčić's payroll and used the opportunity to snare the Chief. By the time he learned his new housekeeper was an illegal and a victim of trafficking, Komarčić had enough photos and video of the girl at the Chief's home and serving the Chief, that he essentially blackmailed the Chief into staying quiet."

"The Chief, to his credit, paid the girl a fair wage, placed it in a bank account for her, and promised her he would find a way to beat Komarčić so she could be free. I think that's why he was at that party that night."

Lynch felt a weight lifted off his shoulders. The Chief had been his mentor and had treated Lynch like the son he'd never had.

"The girl?"

"Immigration has her case, just like all the other women involved."

"And the so-called friend?"

She nodded. "You'll be hearing more about him, and about two dozen others, over the next week. Komarčić had an extensive network, and there are a number of police officers and politicians who are going to find themselves wards of the state for several years to come."

"Good. Thanks, Susan, for letting me know."

"Are you doing okay? I was a little surprised to walk in and find you up and about. "

Lynch gave her his right thumb up. "Home tomorrow, if all goes well." He paused. "Well, to my parents' home, anyway. Seems my condo was sold in my absence to avoid foreclosure. At least my folks remained hopeful and put my stuff in storage for my return. I just need to find a new place."

"I heard your slot at Ladue PD was filled."

"Yep, but I'll be busy. You're looking at the new chief of security for Brad Graham's campaign."

Susan smiled. "Need an assistant?"

They talked briefly, but the detective had to move along. Lynch returned to bed and the papers awaiting him there—campaign itineraries, background checks on top tier employees, and more.

His work was again interrupted. This time by the cell phone Seamus had provided. Seamus' number appeared on Caller ID.

"What's up?" he asked as he answered.

"Thought you'd want to know we have another body ID'd and a lead on the SUV." Seamus filled Lynch in on the latest details, including the puzzle of the car's seat.

In his mind, Lynch had little doubt "who" was behind that mystery. He chose not to pursue it.

"So, when are you headed to Detroit?"

"First of the week. Want to join us? I think I could swing it with Colonel Andrews."

"Thanks, but can't." Lynch told Seamus of his new position. "Officially no longer a cop, so you'll have to be careful what you share with me about open investigations."

"Not to worry. I'll still share 'cause I know you'll be discreet."

Lynch felt glad to know his comrade trusted him, but he also knew there would be things Seamus would not be able to tell him, despite what he just said. As long as such omissions didn't interfere with his new job, he had no problem with that.

"Thanks, Shay. Look forward to hearing about what you find in the Motor City."

The men hung up, and Lynch returned to his work. Ten minutes later, there was another knock at the door. He sighed in exasperation. He had work to do. But upon looking up, that work could wait.

Danijela stood in his doorway, but her smile seemed strained. He extended his hand toward her, and she walked over, took it, and sat on the bed next to him. He stacked the papers together and set them on the bedside stand.

"I'm happy to see you," he said. "Mike seemed to imply we might not get that chance."

Danijela flashed that wan smile again. "I, too, am happy."

Lynch sensed he didn't want to hear what she was about to say. He had several questions he'd wanted to ask her. Now, he hesitated.

She squeezed his hand. "Mike and Mary sit downstair with my family. They must go back to Bosnia in morning.

Tomorrow."

Lynch swallowed hard. "And you?"

"I-I have decide to go with them." Tears welled up in her eyes. She clasped his hand with both hands now.

Lynch looked down toward the floor. His heart followed his gaze and landed in his stomach.

"I see," he replied. Why couldn't he say something more?

"I want stay, but . . . well, is complicate. Much has happen at home. My family need me, and I miss them."

"Are you sure? I will help you, if you want to stay." He sought to tell her that he *wanted* her to stay, but the words stuck in his larynx.

"I know." She leaned forward and kissed him on the cheek. "But, I have decide. My family need me."

Lynch nodded. He didn't want her to go, but he also didn't want to make things harder for her—especially when he didn't know what might happen between them. His thoughts briefly flashed to Amy. He didn't know what might happen there, either. Yet, that seemed less important now.

"Will I see you again? I might get out of here tomorrow."

Danijela shook her head. "Our plane leave five in morning. Bright early."

Lynch forced himself to appear positive, despite feeling quite the opposite.

"I will miss you. I hope you'll find a way to come back for a visit at least."

He saw her searching his eyes, seeking something more from him. *Was* there something more, something he hadn't found himself?

She shrugged. The chance of her returning was slim once she returned home. He knew that.

"Good-bye, Lynch. My Jusuf. Thank you for save me. I will always . . ." She choked up. ". . . always love you." With that, she kissed him fully on the lips, tears in her eyes, jumped up from the bed, and rushed from the room.

Lynch lay there, unmoving, for the next ten minutes. A shroud of loneliness enveloped him, and the emotion caught him off-guard. He picked up the phone to dial Amy. They needed to talk. He needed to clear the air with her.

As the call connected, another interruption entered the room.

"Hello?"

"Amy, it's Lynch. Would you hold for a second? A nurse just came in the room."

Lynch heard no reply but addressed the nurse. He hadn't seen this woman before, but her name tag appeared legit. She held a syringe in one hand.

"Hey, what's up? I'm on the phone."

"Just something the doctor ordered." She reached for his IV tubing, inserted the needle into a hub, pinched off the flow, and slowly pushed the fluid into the tubing before Lynch could question her. "All done. Bye."

"Amy?" Lynch returned the phone to his ear.

"Lynch?"

"A-Amy? A-are y-you . . . help. . ." The last word emerged as a whisper.

Twenty-four

After a day on the phones talking with supporters, reporters, and media distorters, Brad felt a bit like Doctor Seuss. Or rather, a victim of the *Cat in the Hat*. The more Eric and Stan tried to adjust his schedule, the more he felt as if he was trying to stay on that big red ball, balancing everything in the campaign on top of his umbrella. Pretty soon, that fish would be out of its bowl and floundering on the floor.

"Brad, your office called. They have papers you have to sign if you want to finalize the deal with Walmart."

He nodded. At the moment, he didn't need another distraction, but he couldn't ignore the multi-million dollar deal they'd negotiated with the retail chain. He'd be able to add 200 new jobs in his company, not that such news would offset the cries from the left about his new ties to the evil Arkansas corporation.

As the afternoon ended, Brad stopped by his corporate office to sign that contract. He walked through the building, stopping a dozen times to talk with employees, as was his habit. The sixth such stop caught his attention.

The graphics team in the marketing division tried to hide what they were doing as they caught wind of his approach. They weren't fast enough.

"Hey, what's up? You folks look like four-year-olds who just got caught by mom with your hands in the cookie jar." He laughed. "What's that, Cindy?"

He pointed to a stack of what appeared to be two-by-three-foot posters that one artist, Cindy Dye, was in the hurried process of stashing under a table as he walked in.

Cindy was a dyed-in-the-wool Carolina Blue-blood. Pun intended. The fact that she rooted for the wrong team in the Atlantic Coast Conference didn't minimize her talent. She had a way with colors that extended from her work there to her "hobby" of hybridizing daylilies.

Her face flushed at the question. She did indeed look as if she'd been caught red-handed.

"Oh, that? Nothing, Brad. Really, just a little project we've been working on. Probably won't go anywhere. You don't need—"

He laughed. "The lady doth protest too much, methinks."

"Shakespeare, right?"

He grinned. "Well, it sure wasn't Dean Smith or Roy Williams yelling at a Duke cheerleader." He pointed to the stack. "Care to show me what those are?"

Cindy gave him a wry smile. "Nope."

The others also shook their heads, or echoed her comment. Brad knew they wouldn't be doing anything illegal, immoral, or even distasteful, so he almost passed off the group's behavior. Yet, his curiosity got the better of him, so he walked over to the pile and pulled off the top one.

As he flipped it over, he saw his smiling face and the words, "Brad Graham for President! Bold, fresh, the right man for the job." He could see Cindy's touch in the coloring.

The second one read, "Brad Graham for President! A non-politician looking out for you!"

He looked up at the group and raised his brow.

"Really?"

Now, all four of them blushed. Cindy shrugged.

"Might say we've been fantasizing a little. Still haven't come up with the right catch phrase."

Brad pulled the entire stack up onto the nearest open table. He laid them on their sides and thumbed through them. He couldn't argue with her comment. Nothing jumped out at him either. "Too wordy."

One of the two men jumped in. "See. I told you we gotta keep it short and sweet. Like 'bold and fresh,' or 'fighting for you.' "

The others piped in with ideas. Brad watched the exchange and chuckled. Excellent artists? Yes. Copy writers? Not so much, although he did like the 'fighting for you' phrase. He turned to leave the room and let them continue their bantering. As he made it to the door, Cindy spoke up, and he turned back.

"Wait a minute, boss. You didn't tell us to get back to work or to try something else. Does that mean—"

Brad raised his hand to stop her, but he said nothing and left the area to continue his rounds. From behind him, he heard her say, "Hey, he is, he's actually thinking about it. C'mon, let's get busy."

He smiled, and this time, he did turn back and comment. "How about, 'Let's take back America'?"

Smiling, he resumed his walk before he could hear their reply. Was God telling him something? This was the third time today that someone or some group had encouraged him to consider the high office. Although he realized he was taking the scripture out of context, it still came to mind. "Every fact is to be confirmed by the testimony of two or three witnesses."

Brad arrived home to find more than the usual strange cars in the drive. The security detail was there but so was Stan, plus two other cars he didn't recognize.

Cara met him in the kitchen as he entered their home.

"Stan brought two people to talk with you. He introduced them to me, and I recognized one of them, that female TV reporter with the unbelievably long eyelashes. She must use that Latisse® stuff. They're amazing. Anyway, the guy is the station's general manager. Stan didn't say what they wanted."

Brad furrowed his brow. What was this about? And why were they in his home?

"Dinner?"

"I already fed Mark. He's finished his homework, so I'm letting him play a video game upstairs. Dinner can hold, so we can eat after they leave."

"Thanks. Drinks?"

"I've already provided them with iced tea and sodas. I'll bring you some tea."

He kissed her on the cheek and left the room. Was he about to get knocked off the red ball and see that fish flapping on his living room carpet? He found the trio there, making small talk.

"Oh good, you're home," said Stan. The three rose to meet him. "I apologize for coming to the house, unannounced, but I think you'll want to hear this. I believe you know Sheila West."

Brad nodded and took the woman's extended hand to shake it.

"Sheila, good to see you. Thank you for your, shall I say, polite coverage of my campaign."

Brad studied her face. He had often wondered about her personal politics. Unlike some local reporters whose reports bordered on hostile, she had always kept her reporting on him civil, with a hint of favor trying to poke through. She had been one of the few reporters to show up faithfully at every one of his press conferences. In fact, as he thought about it, she had raised her hand at the previous day's conference. Now, he felt a sense of expectation.

"And this is Jim Collins, the station's general manager."

Brad shook his hand as well. He was not accustomed to meeting with the bosses of the regional media outlets. Something was up.

"Pleased to meet you," said Brad.

Cara arrived with iced tea for Brad and offered the others refills, which they declined.

"Brad, I think you're going to find this interesting, but I'll let them take it from here," said Stan. "Jim?"

"Brad, first off, I want you to know that Sheila and I both are rooting for you."

Brad raised his brow.

"I know, hard to believe that. And maybe harder to believe two media types are actually admitting they have a political bent, especially toward the conservative. But that's kinda why we're here." He paused and took a sip of soda. "Not everyone at the station agrees with our stand, but we're behind you. We don't discuss it, and we have to be careful how we show it."

"Something strange is going on, and I can't put a finger on it. In 40-plus years in this business, I've never had corporate tell us how to do our business. They talk about meeting financial goals, stuff like any business, but never about how to report. Recently, I've caught wind of someone in corporate, at least I think it's from corporate, discussing events with our news editor. And what I'm hearing is that this someone is trying to spin events a certain way and influence the news editor."

Sheila perked up. "I'm with Jim. Eighteen years in broadcast journalism and I've never heard of someone trying to squash a worthwhile story. It's a competitive business, and if we don't cover a newsworthy event, someone else will."

"But," she continued, "in our production meetings, the news editor keeps downplaying the school shooting. He says it's uninteresting, since no kids were injured. Like a home invasion where the intruder gets shot. It happens more often than people know, but they only get covered if there's some angle, like the homeowner being elderly. Boring, by the way, is the kiss of death for a story, or not fitting our viewer demographics."

Jim spoke. "As for Harris Burke, he calls it a process story. That is, nothing's happening right now, but if he dies or when he leaves the hospital, then that event might warrant a short clip."

Jim's cell phone buzzed, but he ignored it. Whoever

was calling persisted and called again. He looked at the Caller ID. "Sorry, I need to take this."

Sheila stepped in. "I know from the press conference the other day that you're upset by the lack of coverage of recent events. Jim and I are, too. As are several others at our station and others we know. We talk. We know what's going on, but this is what's happening, at our station anyway."

Brad knew the limits of broadcast news. A half-hour newscast amounted to ten minutes of real news after subtracting time for commercials, weather, and sports. Many stories got ten to 15 seconds, while big stories might get two minutes. By the next newscast, a hundred new stories had flooded in across the AP, list servs, and internet.

"I was able to talk our producer, Art Franklin, into overriding the news editor with my story about your friend using a 'Hometown Hero' approach, but we won't be able to keep it up."

She took a sip of tea and looked directly at Brad. Cara was right. She did have amazing eyelashes. He would never have paid attention to them if his wife hadn't said something.

"There's something else weird going on. The FCC has never interfered with or gotten involved in how stations report the news. Word leaked out today that they're preparing to launch what they call their 'Multi-Market Study of Critical Information Needs,' which will let them go into every broadcast news room, every newspaper, every radio news room, even internet sites. They call it voluntary, but really? Who's going to turn them down if it might be a black mark on your station's license renewal? Needless to say, the collective press is up in arms over this. Talk about a threat to the free press."

Jim returned to the room and looked upset. He shook his head in disgust. "Never in my career . . ."

He sat down and hung his head for a minute before looking up. He took a deep breath and appeared to be composing himself.

"As I started to say, never in my career have I seen stuff—interference, micro-managing, political correctness, whatever you want to call it—like I'm seeing now. I tell you, you're right, Brad. There's a bigger story here, but it's going to take a miracle to ferret out the truth."

He looked toward Sheila. "We need to talk."

She gave him a quizzical look. "Oh?"

"Outside, on the way out."

Brad saw Sheila blanch and felt his own stomach go sour due to how Jim said those words.

Sheila took a deep breath. "Is it personal?" He nodded. "Something the public will know about anyway?" Jim nodded again. "Then, just spill it. I don't want to wait."

Brad gave her high marks for her fortitude, but he wasn't sure he wanted to be present for her bad news. And this was going to be bad news. That much was clear.

"I mentioned micromanaging. That was corporate, you and Art have been fired, and I've been offered early retirement. Or, I should say, I've been *granted* early retirement."

Twenty-five

Amy's breath left her as she heard a slow release of air escape from Lynch's mouth over the phone. She had heard that sound too many times to count and knew she had but seconds to get help. Could she get that help in time?

She clicked off her smartphone and fumbled to look up the number for the Barnes Hospital switchboard.

"C'mon, c'mon," she said, her own breathing picking up as her anxiety mounted. This was taking too long.

Then she remembered the call from Doctor Wade several days earlier. She moved to her call log and found the call. A dial-back should take her to either the E.D. main desk or the hospital switchboard. Her nervous fingers managed to make the call.

"Barnes Hospital."

"Oh, thank God. Quick please, the 6500 floor nursing station. A patient there is in trouble. I was—"

"One moment, please."

The delay in the connection wore on . . . and on.

"Sixty-five hundred. How may—"

"Quick, Lynch Cully, in oh-five, is in trouble. I was on the phone with him when he stopped breathing."

"Hey! Somebody check oh-five!"

Amy could hear people scrambling. A moment later, in the distance she heard, "Somebody get the crash cart!"

Amy sank into her chair. She had already become an

emotional frazzle trying to decide how best to tell him their relationship was over. She'd fought to control herself when he called, but then ... that terrible sound of the body relaxing so totally its air escapes in a slow, long sigh.

She tried to recall every little thing she heard. He'd mentioned a nurse coming into the room, and she remembered the woman saying, "... something the doctor ordered." There was a pause, and then the woman said, "All done, bye."

The time delay. Had she given him a pill? Amy didn't think so. Nothing had been said, like "take this." Plus, the effect was immediate. No pill worked that fast. She envisioned herself at the bedside. Something IV. The timing was right in line for administering something into Lynch's IV line. From the immediate effect, she suspected a paralytic. Maybe succinylcholine, the curare of poison darts. It affected the type of muscle found in the arms, legs, and torso—the muscles used to breathe. 'Suxx' could paralyze him that quickly, and it was common on every floor, in every crash cart, to rapidly paralyze someone in need of an orotracheal, or breathing, tube.

Were they in time? The effect of the drug had been immediate and brain damage would kick in within minutes. The simple act of bagging him, using that simple breathing device to force air into his lungs, would be enough to save him until the effect of the drug wore off. *If* it was succinylcholine. Amy's mind raced, trying to think through the other potential drugs, even poisons, which might have been used.

She waited on the phone for what seemed like forever, again. And then someone hung up the phone.

"What? Say that again!" Seamus couldn't believe what he heard. "Be there as fast as I can."

Seamus ran from his home to his car parked in the alleyway pullout behind his home. Living near the Botanical Gardens had its advantages, and this time one of those advantages was being less than five minutes away from the Barnes-Jewish Hospital complex.

He pulled into a "Police Only" parking slot at the E.D. lot and buzzed into the department. As he rushed past the nursing station, one of Sarah's friends and colleagues, Dr. Ricardo Alvarez, tried to catch him.

"Sarah's not on duty, and we don't have—"

Seamus stopped long enough to shake his hand and answer. "I know. I've got to get to sixty-five hundred." As he moved on, he continued, "Someone tried to kill Lynch Cully."

The elevators took so long he began to wonder if they were out of order. As he waited for a car, a crowd formed to join him, and he saw them stopping at every floor. He debated pulling out his badge and commandeering the car, but realized that people on each floor would have pressed the 'Up' button, and he was likely to stop at every floor even if he was alone. What he needed was a fireman's key to take control of the car. Like that would ever happen.

The drive to the hospital took less time than his trip to the sixth floor. As the door opened, he politely pushed forward and ran toward the ward where Cully recuperated. The banners and balloons remained undisturbed about his door. The crash cart sat outside the room, and as he neared, a nurse emerged, smiling.

Seamus took a deep breath and relaxed. A doctor that he recognized by face came through the doorway as he stepped up to it.

"He'll be fine, but I hope he's not getting close to the last of his nine lives."

Seamus nodded and said, "Thanks."

He walked into the room to see Cully looking pale, but alert and breathing. The heart monitor showed a healthy, regular beat—as best he could recall from Sarah's attempts to educate him on such things.

"Hey, what are you doing here?"

Seamus applied a fake smile, trying to lighten the mood, and replied, "Amy called me."

Lynch nodded. "Good thing I had just called her when this went down. Had I not been on the phone, or if it had been someone else, I might not be here. Thank God, she had the experience to know what was happening."

"What *did* happen?"

Lynch proceeded to tell Seamus about the 'nurse' coming in and putting something into his IV line. "Not that I believe in reincarnation, but remind me not to come back as some rabbit in Borneo, if that's what curare-tipped darts do to them. Man, talk about a scary sensation. All of sudden, your muscles just stop working. You're still awake. You can still feel your heart beating, but you can't breathe. You don't even have time to take a deep breath to hold, not that you *could* hold it." He finished his story, telling about the staff running in and helping him breathe while they figured out what happened.

"What about the nurse?"

"Security's scanning video and personnel records. My buddies at the 9th District have been called in. With God's help, we'll get her."

Seamus nodded. "Yeah, but she's just the tip of the iceberg. I was thinking about this on my way here. Why you? A grudge? Someone wanting revenge for one of your past cases?"

Lynch took a deep breath and looked appreciative of the fact that he could. He shrugged and again had that thankful look. "Can't rule that out, but what if it has nothing to do with the past?"

Seamus pondered that. "You mean the current cases, or incidents? What if whoever planned those didn't like his plans being discovered so soon?"

"Yep. What if he has something new planned and wants to reduce his chances of discovery again?"

"Okay, but how would he know you were the one who figured him out?"

"Exactly." Lynch smiled. "Hey, you're getting pretty good at this game. So, how would he know I'm the one who figured him out? "

The ramification of what Lynch just said hit Seamus like a solid punch. There were two possibilities. Only two groups knew of Cully's role in this—the MCS and Brad Graham's inner circle. Either the schemer was actually in town and had some connection with the MCS, or Graham's campaign had been infiltrated.

Twenty-six

Seamus sat in Captain Johnstone's office with Flannigan early that next morning. He'd been selected to join a Florissant detective for the trip to Detroit, and they'd be leaving within the hour. However, before that departure, Seamus felt the need to brief the MCS commander on what had happened to Cully. He also handpicked Flannigan to sit in on the conversation, knowing the man was not only loyal but considered Cully a good friend.

"So, is Metro or hospital security any closer to ID'ing this so-called nurse?"

Seamus shook his head. "That path is going nowhere. Cully was able to give them a first name, the one he saw on the nametag, and records came up with over a dozen employees with that name. But when they showed pictures to Cully, not one of them was the woman. And like many nurses, she wore gloves in his room, so we have no prints on the tubing."

Flannigan spoke up. "So, we need to focus on who might be behind it."

"You got it, Paul. We don't want to step on any toes at Metro. I work with those guys. But, Cully's our friend, and if there's a leak here on the MCS, we're in a better position than Metro to spot it."

Both men nodded.

"I'll put the clamps on folks, in general. Let them know

there appears to be a leak in the ranks. That sensitive information got out and they're to speak to *no one* about what we're working on." Johnstone paused. "I'll let Andrews know, too. He can tighten down on his folks in Florissant."

Flannigan furrowed his brow. "But seriously, who knew about Cully in the first place? As far as I know, there were only a few of us who knew about his role in this."

"A few of us here on the MCS. What about Florissant?" asked Seamus.

"Just the colonel," replied Johnstone. "I asked him to keep that info to himself. So, it has to be the Graham camp. In fact, as I think about it, he mentioned in that press conference that it was his people who found the pattern." Johnstone looked as if he'd convinced himself that the campaign people were responsible.

"But he didn't mention Cully."

Flannigan nodded. "Okay, so while you're gone, I'll have a talk with Graham and his manager."

Seamus had been surprised at the airport to find that Florissant was sending Detective Pat Goymerac with him to Detroit. She was an experienced officer. He had no qualms with her capabilities. The surprise came in the fact that her department would spring for two motel rooms.

But then, as he thought about it, he realized *he* was the outlier here. If they were expecting to save that rooming expense they would have selected two *female* detectives. As sexist as it might be, two male detectives would get individual rooms, but two females would be expected to share.

The shuttle arrived at the Budget Car Rental facility, and Goymerac dealt with the paperwork. At the car, she asked, "You want to drive?"

Seamus replied, "Feel free. You're footin' the bill." He smiled.

"Good, 'cause I like to drive. I just didn't want to bruise anyone's ego." She returned the smile.

Seamus wasn't offended. He knew a lot of male-female partnerships where the male officer insisted on driving. It *was* an ego thing. He also knew some male-female partnerships where the woman drove, as if it was some sign of showing she was a good as the guys.

"Not going to hurt my feelings," he said. "Besides, I like being chauffeured around."

She rolled her eyes. "I just figured with you being Famous Seamus and all, you'd want first dibs on driving."

Seamus laughed. "Naw, that's why I have paid assistants. And don't get upset when all the reporters talk to me and ignore you."

He waited for her comeback. She obviously could hold her own in their male-dominated profession. They would get along just fine.

"And don't you be surprised when they realize you have a beautiful partner and all turn their cameras on me."

Yes, they'd get along fine on this trip.

At the Detroit Police Department downtown, they waited half an hour only to be told the investigator they needed to talk with worked out of the 10th Precinct on

Livernois Ave, off I-96. They made their way to that station and waited.

After a wait that made them seem as if they were being ignored, a slim, African-American man in a rumpled suit approached them.

"I am Detective Ahmad." He extended his hand.

"Good morning. I'm Detective Goymerac, and this is Detective O'Connor, from our Major Case Squad. The MCS is assisting us on this case. Thanks for seeing us."

The investigator looked them both over carefully. "Sorry to keep you waiting. We're short staffed, and I caught a case that held me up with some things." He pointed toward a hallway. "Please. Come with me."

He showed them to a conference room and offered them a choice of coffee or water. "You might want to stick with the bottled water, in my opinion."

They sat at the table, and Pat produced a file, which she opened up. She spread a collection of photos across the table.

"As I mentioned on the phone, we found your stolen SUV. It was used in an attempted school shooting in which all four gunmen were killed." She showed him the photo of the burned out vehicle. "We traced the Denali to Detroit through its VIN, and your department confirmed it as stolen. Thanks to the security video you sent, we were able to identify this man, Sabir Ahmad, as one of the shooters."

She pushed the photo of Sabir Ahmad toward the detective. For a brief second, Seamus thought he saw recognition in the man's eyes.

"We also have positive ID on this man, Muhab Abdelnour." She slid his photo forward, followed by the last two. "However, we still have two John Does. We're hoping you can help us ID them."

Seamus saw that same flash of possible recognition. What was the man holding back?

The detective picked up each photo and appeared to scrutinize them, shaking his head subtly in the process. After the last photo, he released a gentle sigh.

"I do not recognize any of them personally. Our records on Sabir Ahmad—no relation, by the way—show he's been picked up on several occasions for petty larcenies, but his activities seemed to escalate. He was suspected in one prior car theft, one week before the Denali. Maybe that first one was practice."

Seamus didn't believe the man. He showed some common tells as he spoke that suggested he lied about not recognizing the men. From those slight shifts in body language, Seamus suspected he knew at least two of them.

"I can put these others into the system and see if we can help you." He picked up the photos. "May I take these?"

"Certainly, they're for you," replied Pat.

Seamus spoke up. "What more can you tell us about Sabir Ahmad?"

The man looked uncertain. "What do you mean?"

"Well, you have arrest records. Don't you have more? Addresses, names of family members or other contacts, any group affiliations."

Ahmad hesitated with his answer. "Oh, yes. Of course. The address we have is old. No one there knew him. We were unable to contact his listed next-of-kin." He stood. "Let me get those for you. Back in a minute."

Just moments later, he returned. "There was

something new in the system this time. It appears Sabir Ahmad has been attending one of our larger mosques." He handed Seamus a Post-it® listing the mosque's name and address. "However, I wouldn't advise going out there to ask questions by yourselves, even armed." He paused. "We're really shorthanded, but if you give me a day, I'll see if I can arrange to take you there."

Seamus again looked at the two names on the note. One of a *masjid* and the other, The Islamic Foundation of North America, along with a common address. He made a mental note to check with a friend at the FBI about this group.

Detective Ahmad stood next to them. "Here's the other information I mentioned, the old contacts and so on. I'll let you know if we ID those other two men, and if I can be of any other help, please let me know."

"Thank you," said Pat. "And we'll let you know if we find anything significant."

An hour later, they, too, had struck out at the addresses provided. Neither officer felt surprise that Sabir Ahmad had provided a fake address. The next-of-kin might not exist either.

They attempted to find a phone listing for the relative. They even checked with the county registrar's office for property listed under either name. That also went nowhere.

Seamus decided to see what Goymerac was made of. "Up for an adventure?"

She'd evidently been waiting for him to ask. She

smiled and said, "Sure, never been inside a mosque. Do they let women inside?"

She raised a good question. Seamus didn't have the answer.

"If not, then it's going to be a *grand* adventure, isn't it?"

They had no trouble finding the mosque. Once they arrived in the general neighborhood, its domes rose above everything else except a few nearby church steeples. Seamus noticed that at least two of the domes were covered by blue tarps. He wondered how extensive the damage was underneath and how it happened.

They parked outside what appeared to be the entrance to the business office of the Islamic Foundation. Seamus regretted leaving his Arabic-English dictionary at home. "How do you want to handle this?" asked Pat.

Seamus thought about that for a moment.

"Well, after being warned against coming here, I don't think it would be healthy to get aggressive. Let's just play it like we're here to pass on bad news and our condolences. No references to the shooting. Just follow my lead."

Goymerac rolled her eyes at the last comment. "You sure you don't want me to give it a woman's touch?"

Seamus answered by exiting the car. Together they entered the office, to find a young woman at the reception desk, her head covered by a scarf.

"Good afternoon. My name is Seamus O'Connor and this is Patricia Goymerac. We were sent here by Detective Ahmad at the 10th Precinct. Is your imam available for a few minutes? It's about one of your members."

Pat added, "We're so sorry to interrupt like this, but we represent the Kutis Funeral Homes in St. Louis, and we're trying to arrange for the proper funeral for a Sabir Ahmad. We didn't realize he was Muslim, and we don't have much time if we're to follow your religion's traditional rites for him."

Seamus about choked and resisted the temptation to give her "the look." He quickly played along and hoped he looked somewhat like a funeral director. Eh, probably not.

"That's correct. It took time to get us this far, and we have been unable to reach any next-of-kin."

The young woman looked suitably upset. She recognized the name, without saying so. She picked up the phone and dialed an internal number, only four digits. Seamus understood nothing she said. So much for needing a dual language dictionary. He wouldn't even know where to look in it.

"Imam Al-Bashara will be with you in a moment." She reached under her desk and handed Goymerac a scarf.

The detective looked hesitant, and Seamus could understand. How many and whose heads had that scarf been on before today?

Without missing a beat, she thanked the young woman and covered her head. Seamus gave her credit for knowing what to do, but then again, she'd been the one to question whether they'd even let her into the building.

Five minutes later, a man of medium build in elegant robes entered through a doorway behind the desk.

"I am Imam Al-Bashara. What is this about one of our members?"

"Thank you, sir, for your time. We're sorry to inform

you that one of your members, a Sabir Ahmad, is deceased. We're trying to arrange for the care of his remains."

"Sabir Ahmad? I'm sorry, that name is not familiar."

Goymerac was prepared. She opened her purse and retrieved the man's picture. She handed this to the cleric.

Seamus had to give the man credit. He covered his reaction well.

"Again, he does not look familiar."

Pat looked genuinely concerned. "Oh my. Well, that puts us in a delicate place, doesn't it, Seamus?"

Seamus gave a quick flick of his brow and nodded. Where was she going with this?

"You see, Imam Al-Bashara, this man and three of his friends died in St. Louis. Our funeral home was contracted by the city to locate relatives and deal with their remains. If that's not possible, they will hold the bodies up to a month in the morgue, and then they will authorize cremation. We have no control over that."

The imam sputtered. "No, no. That is not acceptable. We do not cremate our deceased."

"I understand that, sir, but if we can't validate the men's religion through family, we can't verify that they are even Muslim, and the city's hands are tied by law."

Imam Al-Bashara looked flustered, and that surprised Seamus. His initial impression of the man was that he never got upset, always kept calm.

"I will ask around of the other *masjids*. Do you know any of the other men's names?"

"Only one, sir," added Seamus. "Muhab Abdelnour."

At this, the young woman at the desk lowered her head, rose, gave them all a gentle bow, and rushed from the room.

"Thank you," said the imam. He had regained his cool. "Again, I will ask around. Now, if you'll excuse me."

"Thank you for your time, sir. We'll be at the Quality Inn & Suites tonight." The detective bent over the reception desk and wrote down her name and O'Connor's on a "While you were out. . ." note sheet and handed it to the imam. "If you find anything, please have someone call."

She placed the scarf on the desk and turned around to leave. Seamus followed.

Once inside the car she turned to look at him. "Well?"

He laughed. "So much for following my lead, but that worked for me."

"The imam knew both names, but he covered himself well. I think he was truly shocked to learn they were all dead."

"I agree. Now that we've shaken the tree, we'll see what falls out, but I suspect we're going to get more from the receptionist than the imam."

"You caught that, did you? You're pretty observant, for a guy." She started the car and began to pull away. "I'd say she not only knows both men, but she has some relationship to Abdelnour. I'd put money on it."

They checked back in with the 10th Precinct to find Ahmad absent and no messages waiting for them. It was getting dark and Seamus' gut grumbled. On the way back to the airport, Pat pulled off the interstate and into the lot of LongHorn Steakhouse. They enjoyed a nice meal, on Florissant PD's tab, and resumed their drive to the Quality

Inn.

As they entered the lobby, a young woman, her head covered with a *hijab*, rose from a nearby chair. She looked around the room and approached them. Seamus saw that her hand was inside her purse and became alert, placing his own hand on his holstered gun. He unsnapped the strap, prepared for anything.

The woman came closer and withdrew her hand. In it was a photo. She looked up into their faces.

"You are from St. Louis?"

Pat answered. "Yes."

Seamus thought the woman looked familiar. On second glance, he realized that while she wasn't the receptionist, she was related. A sister, perhaps.

"May w-we talk?" Tears formed in her eyes.

"We can go to my room," replied Pat.

"No. I . . . I am not sure that would be appropriate."

The young woman looked at them both as if they were a couple.

"It would be. We have separate rooms, but . . ." She glanced around. "There. Let's go in there." Pat pointed toward the breakfast room. The place was empty and had doors that closed it off from the hallway when not in use. Once inside, they sat at a table along the far wall.

The woman placed the photo on the table. Seamus saw that it was a picture of a living, smiling Muhab Abdelnour. He glanced at the woman's face to see that she looked emotionally devastated.

Pat spoke up. "I'm Pat and this is Seamus. We're actually police officers from St. Louis."

The woman swallowed hard. "My cousin, she

suspected as much. T-the imam, as well." She took a deep breath. "I am Miriam. My husband w-was Muhab." Tears began to flow.

At first, Pat looked hurt that her ruse had been obvious, but she took Miriam's hand to comfort her.

"Did you know what your husband was up to?"

Miriam quickly shook her head. "N-no. I still don't." she glanced around. "I suspected they were going to do something illegal, a robbery or something. His friends had been arrested for that before. W-what d-did he do?" Her lip quivered.

Pat took a different tact. "Tell us about Muhab."

"Muhab was a good man, sweet, gentle. We looked forward to having a family, living the American Dream. Then, the economy went bad. He lost his job. We had to apply for welfare and ask for help from the mosque. Even then, we went hungry many months."

She paused and took a deep breath. "After we started receiving help from the mosque, they started to ask him to do things for them. Sometimes he would tell me what he was doing, but as time went on, he stopped telling me. He changed. He started talking in more radical terms. His friends changed. He started hanging around Sabir and Naji and Usayd. I do not know their last names."

"On the good side, we had money for rent and groceries, and an occasional night out. But, he treated me differently. I became 'property,' like so many women in our families' home countries. We fought more, and he sometimes got physical."

"Then, one day, he gets a call from the mosque. An important man is coming and needs four men for a job in another city. Suddenly, Muhab is talking like a terrorist. Jihad. Intifada. Infidels. He scared me, and I left to stay with my cousin. And then, he was gone. I did not know where, until my cousin told me of your visit."

"Is he really dead?" She looked at Pat with that all-important question in her eyes, *Were you telling the imam the truth?*

Pat nodded. "I'm sorry, but yes. They all are."

"How?"

Pat hesitated. Seamus would have, too. Was it better to know the whole truth, or to remember mainly the good times?

"Are you sure you want to know?"

Miriam nodded. "Yes. I want to know."

"The five men attacked a Christian elementary school. They were shot in the process."

Miriam hung her head and sobbed. A couple of minutes later, she regained her composure. "Y-you said five men attacked. My cousin said four men died. You have already identified two of them, Sabir and . . . M-Muhab. Who are the others?"

Pat opened her purse and pulled some folded papers from inside. She opened them and handed two of them to Miriam. Seamus noticed that she withheld Muhab's photo. There was no point in showing Miriam his face in death.

Miriam pointed to each photo and gave the names: Usayd and Naji.

"What about the fifth man? Is he dead, too?"

Together, Pat and Seamus shook their heads.

"He is the one responsible. I will hold him to account for Muhab's death." There was steely tone to her voice.

"What can you tell us about him?" asked Seamus, hoping for a name.

"Very little. I never heard his name. All I know is that he is an important man. Oh, and he came from the east somewhere. New York, maybe. Or Washington. That's all I know."

Twenty-seven

Fawaz took the call from Imam Al-Bashara earlier in the day and received the news that two St. Louis police detectives were at the mosque asking about Sabir and Muhab. This was not a good development.

That they'd gotten so far so quickly indicated two things. One, he'd underestimated the capabilities of these Midwestern police departments. Two, they could have the other names soon as well. He prayed to Allah that Naji and Usayd had used burner phones as instructed and not phones listed in their own names. Yes, in hindsight, he should have made sure of that before ever placing a call to either man.

Although he used a disposable phone as well, and had paid cash for it, the retrieval of either man's phone could become the starting point for finding his phone number. It would stand out within their call records. With phone number in hand, the police could ultimately find store security video that might reveal his purchase and give them a face to go with the phone.

Similarly, his phone's call records could lead them to their jihad cell groups in a dozen cities. Such a discovery would lead to his disappearance. Forced and permanent.

However, any further potential problems ended now. As he drove across a bridge over the Missouri River, he slowed and tossed his phone into the water. He felt sure it had cleared the guardrail but glanced into his rearview mirror to make sure it hadn't landed on the bridge. As he thought, it was gone.

A few minutes later, he spied a Walmart on the south side of the highway and pulled into the lot. In short order, he had a new flip phone, with 100 minutes of prepaid calling.

As he drove back toward his motel, he placed another dozen calls, each with the same terse message— السماح للجسور نصفق مع الرعد –Arabic for 'let the bridges rumble with thunder.'

Economic chaos would soon also rumble across the country. With east-west commerce reduced to a crawl, prices would skyrocket, and the securities markets would plummet. The Assembly would soon have a world primed for its global currency and governance. Along with its centuries-old hold on the Vatican, they would finally have their *Novo Ordo Seclorum*, their New World Order.

As he sat in the motel parking lot, he decided to make one additional call. Bradley Graham would not escape this time.

Amy paced the lobby of Barnes Hospital, her heart racing and her mouth dry. The elevator arrived faster than she expected, and her tachycardia accelerated toward needing cardioversion—shock therapy—to bring it back to normal. Yet, she could delay this task no longer.

She'd heard through friends at the hospital that her guess had been correct. Someone had tried to kill Lynch with succinylcholine, but her call had been timely enough to save him. For that, she felt grateful.

However, her visit now was likely to destroy him.

The episode had resulted in his discharge being delayed an additional day. That worked to her benefit as she now prepared to meet him on neutral ground. She didn't think she'd be able to pull it off had she needed to tell him at his parents' home.

She stepped off the elevator and stopped. Could she do this? She didn't want to hurt him, as much as he'd hurt her over a year earlier. And she knew how much support he needed now, after the horrific events he'd suffered. Events to which the previous day's attempt on his life only added.

In a flash, she realized how much easier it would be to turn around, go home, and simply abandon him. Not return his calls. Ignore his emails. Go out of her way not to cross paths. Move, if she had to. To take the route he had taken with her.

In that moment, she developed an understanding of what he must have felt then. Yet, no, she couldn't do that. She would not leave him on such terms. She was not that kind of person.

Amy took a deep breath and resumed her walk toward his room. As she neared, she found a laugh emerge from within as she saw that someone had used a marker on the banner over his door to add the word "STILL" at an angle between "HE'S" and "ALIVE!"

She stopped long enough outside the door to get serious . . . and determined. As soon as she entered the door, his face lit up in a smile.

"Amy! My guardian angel."

He sat in the chair beside the bed but arose and

pointed to it for her as he climbed back onto the bed.

"H-how are you doing?"

"Fine. Thanks to you. I hate to think what might have happened if I'd not been on the phone with you."

She sat down and he reached for her hand, but she scooted the chair just a little farther away, out of easy reach. Her move did not go unnoticed.

"Thank you." His tone was a bit more somber.

She smiled, but it felt forced so she stopped.

"I guess we're even now. You saved me at Darko's."

He shrugged his right shoulder.

"So, really. You're okay?"

He nodded. "Scared the you-know-what out of me. But I'm good. I guess my brain's a bit more resistant to low oxygen levels now."

He grinned, but to Amy, that, too, looked as forced as her own smile. She knew he referred to the anoxia chamber of Matthew Koettering, aka 'The L.A. Rapist.' Lynch had stumbled into it and almost died on that case, only to fight his way back through months of amnesia.

"And, um, how's Danijela? Is she—"

"She went back to Bosnia with her family. They left this morning." His eyes lowered.

Suddenly, Amy's 'chore' became harder. In the back of her mind, she had anticipated Danijela helping Lynch, continuing to support him as she had during his amnesia. Now, she realized Lynch would be left alone, with just family and a few friends for that support.

"I see. Sorry."

"I'm happy to see you, Amy."

He said that with a tone of hope in the words. What

was it he expected her to say?

Amy straightened up in the chair. It was now or . . . No, it was now. No later.

"Lynch, I've been thinking about our last conversation, and I . . ." She paused and took a deep breath. "Well, I've been thinking a lot about where things were before you disappeared, and what's happened since you came back. I'm sorry, but I don't see our relationship starting over . . . as much as you'd like it to."

He made no reply but simply gazed at her. His face appeared crestfallen. In a sense, she found it unbearable.

After an interminable silence, he finally said, "Richard?"

"Yes," she whispered. She stood and touched his hand. "I hope we can remain friends, and I wish you all the best, but there is nothing more than that for us."

Silence again greeted her comment. And it reminded her of the shortcomings in their previous relationship. Had he been able to express his feelings more openly, had he not placed his work first, had he . . . No, despite his comments about changing, he hadn't. Not really. Not as far as she could see.

"Bye, Lynch." She leaned forward, kissed him on the forehead, and rushed from the room.

"Thanks, Eric. Did you get those estimates from Theisen Media for the commercial spots?"

"Not yet. I did put another call in for them, though. Need anything else right now? Or something to eat? I'm heading out for some lunch."

Brad looked up from his desk to his aide, debating. "Where're you headed?"

"Just the Bread Company."

"Yeah, sounds good." Cara would lecture him if she knew. "I'd like a smokehouse turkey Panini. Tell you what, get someone to help and check with everyone who's here. Lunch for everyone is on me. You still have the credit card?"

Eric grinned. "Sure do. Thanks, boss."

"Oh, and get half a dozen extras. Just in case."

Brad noticed a lighter spring to the young man's step as he left the office. Until recently, the funds for such a morale booster were scant. Their latest financials produced no concerns for feeding the volunteers now. That was the least his campaign could do.

Stan popped into the office, followed by Dominick. They made themselves at home and sat down. Brad made a couple of quick notes in the margin of the speech in front of him, put down his pen, and sat back.

"So, did you get my email?" He looked at Dom.

"I did."

Stan nodded. "Me, too. You know, when we talked about campaigning on a platform about job creation, I didn't expect you to create them all by yourself." Both men laughed.

Brad grinned. "I know. But it's a perfect fit, don't you think? I mean, we can use them, can't we?"

Both men waggled their heads noncommittally.

"Well, make up your minds. They just walked in the front door and are heading this way."

Dom held up both hands in front of him.

"Sure, I think they could be a good fit, but they might not be interested. It'd be a big switch for them."

Brad nodded. "It's a big switch for a guy like Lynch Cully, too, but he jumped on board. People are fed up with the federal government and want real change. They—"

There was a knock at the doorpost. All three men stood as Jim Collins and Sheila West stopped at the doorway and Jim knocked.

"Hey, thanks for coming in. You two doing okay?" Brad asked. "Have you had lunch? We're getting food from the Bread Company."

Brad pulled a couple of extra chairs into the room. The two broadcasters gave questioning glances at each other.

"Okay, Brad, why are we being buttered up? We don't even work at the station anymore. We can't offer you anything."

Brad sat on the edge of his old wooden desk and folded his arms across his chest.

"Can I ask you both a question?"

Jim and Sheila nodded.

"Do you believe God is still in control, and that He works things out in ways we could never expect?"

Sheila nodded right away, while Jim looked more skeptical.

Brad continued, "Well, I do, which I'm sure is no surprise to either of you. When you got word at my home about being fired, I felt awful. I mean, that happened because you stepped out on a limb to do something I asked you to do. But yesterday morning, I felt like God was saying, 'Don't feel badly. My hand is upon that, and I'm making them available to you.' "

Brad gave that a moment to sink in. Sheila looked pensive, while Jim remained skeptical.

"I guess what I'm trying to say is that we want you both to come on board with us. Jim, we'd like you to be Director of Communications for the new party, and Sheila, you'd have the same role in my campaign. You'd be working closely together. We need people with a deep knowledge of the industry who can help us make the right media choices, help shape our image, direct us away from landmines, and so on."

"I know this is a big switch for you. You've always tried to remain apolitical and now, all of a sudden, you'll be as political as it can get. But you know this business and how the liberal press will try to trip us up, maybe even try to sabotage our campaigns."

Stan spoke up. "When Brad brought this idea up with us, I thought he was just feeling guilty. Yet, the more I think about it, I have to agree. You'd be invaluable to us."

"So, no pressure. If you want time to think about it, that's fine. Any thoughts, questions?" asked Dom.

Jim pursed his lips and grunted. "I probably should take time to think about this, and discuss it with my wife. For me, it'd be an interesting switch, and since they've officially retired me, I'm not likely to work anywhere else at this point."

He looked at Sheila. "But, Sheila, you need to consider what Brad just said. If you take this position, you'll be marked for life. The mainstream newsrooms will never see past your affiliation with the Graham campaign. They might never forgive you, except Fox."

Sheila laughed and put her hand on Jim's shoulder. "Thanks, *Dad*. Still looking out for me. Brad, I'm game. I don't need to think about it, and I know my husband will support me on this. He was already wondering what it'd be like to work for your campaign. I do have one question though."

Brad looked at Stan, gave him a thumb up, and looked back at the ex-reporter. "Shoot."

"When you're elected president, can I be your press secretary?"

Brad laughed, and both Stan and Dom shook their heads, like saying '*I can't believe she actually asked that.*'

"I don't want to make a promise I can't keep, so let's just say we'll discuss it, *if* that scenario ever happens."

Stan looked at Sheila and said, "Come with me and we'll talk details."

Brad added, "Tomorrow morning, ten a.m., we're having a staff meeting. This'll be the first time we'll have all of our new chiefs meet and discuss plans. I look forward to introducing you to everyone."

Dom walked up to Jim. "How long do you need? Should I call you next week, or do you want to call me?"

"I won't need that long." He smiled. "Just give me time to run it past the missus."

Dom handed him a business card. "Call me then. We'll be meeting tomorrow as well. In fact, we'll all be meeting with Brad's folks at ten a.m. to start, and then heading upstairs to discuss party specific strategies."

The men shook hands, and Dom turned to Brad to give him a wink.

"Great. I'll see you all tomorrow at ten a.m.," said Brad

as he returned behind his desk and said a quiet prayer of thanks to God for making this happen. Yes, he saw God's hand undeniably on his campaign. Even Lynch Cully's situation the night before had all the markings of God's grace flowing about him. Was it a coincidence that he had called Amy Gibbs just before the attack? For Christians, there was no such thing as a coincidence.

Twenty-eight

൚◆◆ൟ

"Carson, we have your room ready. I even pulled some of your clothes out of storage, and we can get anything else you might need from there. If you need a space for work, you can take over one of the spare bedrooms. We rarely use them anymore."

Nancy Cully fawned over her son, and Lynch already had had enough. He hated it when she used his first name. *Nobody* used his real name, except her, but he'd given up years ago trying to convince her to use 'Lynch.' Still, Carson was his grandfather's name and his dad's name . . . and his name only on paper. He held no delight in being 'the third.'

Lynch had fought hard to return to life as 'Lynch.' He would need to find a suitable place of his own ASAP, if he wanted that life to continue.

Yet, he didn't want to *be* as alone as he felt. Danijela was gone. Amy would be a friend and nothing more. He knew how that would work out. Perhaps, he needed to be 'Carson' for a while, just as he'd been 'Jusuf' for Danijela.

"Thanks, Mom. I'll need to gauge that need later. Right now, I need to get cleaned up and dressed for work. I'm expected at the meeting at ten." He stooped down to pet their Golden Lab, Rufus. "Hey, Ruf, old buddy. Remember me?" The dog obviously did, as his tail threatened seismic destruction of the nearby furniture.

"Oh, and thank Dad for helping me get out of there

early. Barnes usually doesn't move so quickly with discharges. By the way, I don't know when I'll get back home tonight."

His mom leaned up to kiss him on the cheek, having made the mistake earlier of trying to hug him. His shoulder wasn't ready for that.

"Well, dinner is at seven, as usual. And I'll have a place set for you, just in case." She practically squealed in delight. "It is *so good* to have you *home!*"

Lynch didn't want to admit it, but it felt good to be home, too.

Thirty minutes later, Lynch was dressed appropriately and repositioned the sling on his left arm for comfort. His parents had retrieved his car after his disappearance and had kept it parked at their home. Lynch was surprised that it started right up. His father must have had someone work on it.

He slid the shoulder portion of his seatbelt behind his back, backed out of the drive, and headed for work. The drive from his parents' Town and Country home to the four-story office building where he'd have his office took 15 minutes. At least he was going against traffic and not delayed by having to crawl *with* it.

The building housed both the Graham campaign in the storefront spaces of the first floor and the American Party headquarters on the second and third floors. One of his first suggestions would be to move the campaign office. Its location made it vulnerable, and considering recent events, a single attack could damage both.

He ran a little late but still would be there on time. He got stuck behind a grey GMC Savana cargo van whose driver appeared lost. That driver drove slowly past the turn into the building's parking lot, enabling Lynch to make his turn and pull into a slot across from the campaign office with just a few minutes to spare.

As he looked back toward the street, he saw that van make a sudden U-turn, its tires screeching, and accelerate back toward their building. Even to the uninitiated, the van's movement would seem suspicious. To Lynch, the intent was obvious. The driver could make the turn with minimal slowing, accelerate again, and plow deep into the glass-fronted building. With a cargo of fertilizer and the proper igniter, half the building would be gone before anyone could be alerted.

Without hesitation, Lynch restarted his car, put it in reverse, and burned rubber to get the traction he needed to move quickly. Backwards, he sped into the entry lane, blocked the path for any incoming vehicle, threw the car into park, and bolted from the driver's seat just as the truck made the turn into the lane and headed for his car.

He ran for cover, expecting the van to ram his car and try to move it aside. Instead, the van stopped, and the driver opened his door. "Hey, buddy, what the . . ." He let loose a string of expletives.

Lynch eased back his way, his right hand on his weapon. He had to remind himself that even though he held a valid conceal-carry permit, he wasn't a police officer anymore. He couldn't just brandish his weapon and flash his badge.

As he neared the driver's door, the guy started swearing again but made no move to assert himself.

"What's in the back?"

"Who's asking?" He started to swear again but caught himself short.

Lynch wanted his badge back, to show him who was asking. Not having that authority would take some getting used to.

"I'm chief of security for occupants of this building. We've had some threats and your actions seemed suspicious."

The man pursed his lips, mulled over that comment, and shrugged. "Yeah. I guess I can see that, in this day and age. Sorry." He paused. "Copiers. I got two copiers, one for the American Party, and, uh, one for some campaign office."

"Can I take a look?" Lynch still kept his hand near his gun.

"Sure. Boss offered me a bonus to get them delivered by ten. Guess I'm missin' that deadline."

Lynch eased around to the back of the van and peered through the window. Copiers.

He chastised himself but only briefly. His instincts were still good, just a little rusty. He could just as easily have been right.

He walked back to the driver's door. "Okay. I'll move my car. And I'll make sure your paperwork shows a timely delivery."

"Hey, thanks. Sorry for the scare."

Lynch nodded and walked back to his car. As he put it into gear he saw that he now held up a handful of cars. *Yep, we need to move this office. Maybe both*, he thought. *Definitely too vulnerable here.*

"Hey, you must be Lynch Cully." A young man about

his own age walked toward him and extended his hand as Lynch walked into the offices. "I'm Eric. Eric Lange. Brad's aide and chief go-fer. Welcome." They shook hands. "So, what was that about? Outside. I saw what you did."

"Nice to meet you, Eric. Um, maybe I'm just a bit zealous for my first day. Thought we were about to be attacked."

Eric raised his brow and glanced behind Lynch. Lynch turned to see the delivery guy wheel in a copier.

"Hey, I told the guy I'd help him out. Could you time stamp the delivery for just before ten? He would have made it if I hadn't stopped him."

Eric shrugged. "Sure." He then walked over to the man. "You can leave it here and we'll put it in place. We don't have the location cleared out quite yet. Oh, and you can leave the second one down here, too. They'll come get it from here. Save you the hassle."

"Sure. Thanks. Be right back with the second one."

Eric turned back to Lynch. "Everyone's in the conference room. Back there, to the left. I'll show you your office after the meeting."

Lynch walked toward the back. He saw what had to be Brad's glass-walled office in the immediate back, with a view of the doors. A hallway extended off to the left. He followed it toward the commotion.

"Lynch, welcome!" Brad extended his hand as he walked up to him.

Stan followed Eric into the room and approached the two. Off toward the far corner, he saw the back of a man who seemed familiar and to his left was a news reporter he'd seen on TV before.

"You sure you're ready for this?" asked Stan.

"You bet. My other choice is to become a couch potato at my parents' house. What do you think?"

"Hey, he's already thwarted a truck bomber," added Eric as he joined the group.

At Brad's questioning look, Eric told them what had happened in the parking lot. Lynch offered a wan smile and a sigh in return. "Guess my gut feelings are a bit out of sorts."

Stan laughed. "We'd rather it be out of sorts than nonexistent."

Brad clapped his hands and got the group's attention. When the man across the room turned around, Lynch saw that it was Richard Nichols. Forget being out of sorts. This time his gut churned, but he couldn't resent the guy. Lynch had screwed up his relationship with Amy over a year ago and then disappeared. Still, it might be hard to work with the guy, knowing he'd won Amy's heart.

After a round of introductions, he felt a bit of relief to know that Richard would be working upstairs, for the AP. He saw the same sense of relief cross Richard's face when he was introduced.

He listened to Brad and Dominick present how the AP could help the Graham campaign and what their limits would be, despite being in the same building. They then outlined other ways the two offices could legally interact.

"Above all else, we *must* be above board. We can't afford even the *slightest* appearance of illegality or inappropriateness. We are going to represent a new wave of public service. Questions?"

Lynch used that opportunity to raise his hand.

"Lynch?"

"Do you think it wise to be in the same building? I mean, what if that delivery truck had been a bomber, he could have taken out both groups at once. It's my advice that one group move, and I suspect it's easier to move a single campaign than a whole party headquarters."

Brad looked contemplative and paused before answering. "Dom and his folks need to get going, so let's give them a moment to head upstairs and you and I can discuss this."

As Dom, Richard and the rest of the AP group left the room, Brad looked at his campaign staff and said, "Eric has some paperwork for each of you. Take a minute to review it and we'll be right back."

Brad walked with Lynch back to the front volunteer area.

"One of the reasons we're here is that I own the building, but your point is well taken. In fact, we've discussed it before, in light of your discovery of the other attacks on party offices. Come with me for a moment. Let me get your opinion."

He started to point outside, mentioning the possible addition of concrete barriers that could prevent a truck or car driving into the building. Something else caught Lynch's attention.

"Do you hear that?"

Brad gave a subtle shrug. "Someone's cell phone."

Lynch quickly scanned the front. No phones on anyone's desk. In fact, the place was empty of volunteers, and in his mind, no one in the conference room would have left their phone out here. He took a step closer and realized the second set of tones came from the first copier ... a copier that remained unplugged.

He pushed Brad back into the hallway and to the floor. "Everyone! Get down! Now!"

After a flash of confusion in the room, he saw that they had all done as he said. Only then did he throw himself to the floor . . . just as a flash of flame and concussive air rushed over them. Drywall tore apart. The glass windows of Brad's office shattered into deadly shards. Tables from the front room flew against the back wall and onto the steel studs of the wall, now opened up and exposed, to their right. Ceiling tiles came crashing down around them and dust filled the air. Almost immediately, the automatic sprinkler system spurted to life, although ruptures in the pipes poured water into the front room.

Twenty-nine

Fawaz paced the motel room, wishing to return to Washington, to his own apartment. Yet, his task held him here. He fretted that those above him continued to refuse him permission to return. He knew they had concerns about creating any apparent connection with the events he orchestrated on their behalf and the Washington power base. As such, they wanted him outside the capital as he directed their activities.

He also realized that he alone was that connection. Had he been played? He knew he was expendable. No one was irreplaceable, not even the President. As with Kennedy when he moved to act against The Assembly's ambitions, a single bullet could produce the needed change in power and put a member of that brotherhood into office.

Fawaz's personal cell phone buzzed. He hesitated to answer. Only those above him had that number, and he hadn't relished the last call he'd received, from this same number. Sweat formed beads upon his forehead as he answered.

"I am calling for a status report. The Director wants an update."

Fawaz felt a brief sense of relief. Had the caller *been* the Director again, the report would have been much more difficult to provide. Something about the man made it seem impossible to mislead him, intentionally or not.

"Four bridges are down. The rest are pending."

"Pending when?"

Fawaz wanted to stall. Their plan had been to focus on the Union Pacific and BNSF Railroads which owned 17 of the 31 rail bridges over the Mississippi. Most of these bridges facilitated moving freight through Chicago, the nation's busiest rail gateway.

"Hopefully, six more tonight and the remainder within two days."

"Hopefully?"

"Yes, hopefully. As soon as the first bridge went down, the companies and state governments moved in to secure the rest. We lost six more men while taking down the other three."

There was silence on the opposite end. Fawaz realized he didn't even know who was talking with him. He double-checked the number of the caller. Whoever it was, he had called from the Director's number.

"Who am I talking with?"

"I will inform the Director." The caller hung up.

Fawaz closed his eyes for a moment. Forget his apartment in D.C. He needed a sunny beach in the Caribbean somewhere. However, he knew he had nowhere he could run, no place to hide. If he failed, they would find him no matter where he might try to fade into the local scene.

Out of habit, he found himself scanning the room to make sure he was alone and felt embarrassed at doing so. Yet, he knew what The Assembly was capable of doing. Putting his room under surveillance was not beyond them. He checked behind the mirror and framed pictures, and scrutinized the smoke alarm for anything unusual.

Satisfied that he was safe, he grabbed his suitcase from the closet and plopped it on the bed. After opening it, he removed the clothing that remained inside and felt for the right place in the upper right corner of the lining. Finding it, he slid his finger underneath and found the release to the hidden pocket within.

He took a deep breath, slid open the pocket, and retrieved a manila envelope. Inside the packet lay his 'insurance.' He made sure the papers and CDs were all there and replaced them inside the envelope. He unscrewed the lid of his travel mug and removed the digital recorder that had been so skillfully installed inside the double layer of the lid. This, too, he now placed within the envelope.

Then he debated how to handle it. He considered placing it under the mattress. Should something happen to him while he was there, the county's CSU would likely find it. Yet, he realized they might not be the first ones to check the motel room. The odds lay in favor of the CSU finding a tossed room.

He would need to mail it. But to whom?

Karolus stood at the entrance to the Executive Chamber and addressed his audience, the 33 members of The Assembly. They had convened at the House of the Temple in Washington, D.C., at his request and with the concurrence of the Grand Commander of the Mother Council of the World, who was also one of them. He gazed across the room, past the central display and its Bible, to the Grand Commander and his deputies seated on their raised platform between two columns. To his right and left sat The Assembly's members.

He raised his eyes toward the ornate ceiling, with its now-covered skylight and the Freemason symbols deliberately placed in the corners around its base. He cherished the moment.

"Brothers, friends, we are here to witness the most historic event for mankind since the eve of history itself. For centuries, from Nimrod through Solomon's masons to Emperor Constantine . . . through the Knights Templar, the Illuminati, and other societies before ours . . . and now, to us, we have carried the ancient mysteries forward, guarding them until the time was right."

He paused and began to walk around the room, looking at his colleagues individually, face-to-face.

"That time has come. The past 50 years have been spent cultivating the United Nations to become the governing body of the world, *our* governing body. It has taken time to place the right people into positions of power, but we have succeeded.

"Similarly, it has required time to bring down the United States as *the* dominant power in the world. A superpower, as our brothers in the press like to call it. Through our federally mandated education programs, we have, to use a popular term, 'dumbed down' society so that there are few independent thinkers to challenge us. We have marginalized the Christians who still believe that book we display in the middle of the room for show."

Karolus was just warming up. He felt energized.

"Through two middle eastern wars, we have

eliminated or reeducated those able-bodied young men who could have become our fiercest resistance. More importantly, those wars took the country into deep debt, made the people tire of conflict, and provided fodder to distract the populace from noticing their presidents implementing our policies, the policies of UN Agenda 21, by executive order."

Karolus had circled the room once and now stood in the middle, next to the pedestal on which a Bible lay. He picked up the Bible and held it to his chest as he continued to speak, slowly revolving to address the entire room.

"As the time drew near, we picked a man whose narcissistic traits played well into our plan. We renamed him to match a sixth-century prophecy, by Muhammad's son-in-law no less, Ali ibn Ali-Talib, which spoke of a western leader who would rule the most powerful military of the world prior to the coming of the Muslim Mahdi. As our 'blessing of Hussein,' 'he is with us.' "

"We groomed him. We brought him out of nowhere to lead this nation. We staged his major speeches, such as his Berlin speech in front of the *Siegessäule*, and his inauguration on a stage made in the likeness of our Great Altar of Zeus. We chartered him to further bankrupt this nation and enabled that charter through an unworkable national healthcare system and insolvent economic policies. And now? . . . Now we are on the brink of removing the United States as an obstacle to our plan.

"As I speak, events are taking place in this country that will further cripple the economy. Just before entering the chamber, I received word that four railroad bridges across the Mississippi have been irreparably damaged. By tonight, six more will be gone. The inability to move freight by rail from one end of the country to the other will cause prices to soar. The markets will panic. We will see the great wealth of this nation dissolve, and with it, the global economy will collapse."

With the slight ripple of applause meeting his ears, he paused. He motioned for quiet.

"And we will pick up the pieces. Within the week, I will be selected as the new Secretary General of the U.N., where in due time I will announce the U.N.'s control of world governments as the answer to failed nationalist governments across the globe.

"As we started in the economic agreements between Russia and China in 2010 that eliminated the dollar as their reserve currency, we will cancel the Bretton Woods agreement to establish *our* global currency as the world's new reserve currency. Those bank notes have awaited us in warehouses across the globe for a decade.

"Our brethren at the Vatican will assume international control of Jerusalem, and we have assurances from our Muslim brethren that they will comply with our international regime. The peoples of the world will rejoice at the peace we bring to the Middle East and the stability we offer the entire world. We are on the doorstep of our *Novo Urdo Seclorum.*"

The members stood as one and applauded. Several men broke decorum and whistled.

His comrades surrounded him, extending their hands toward him, patting him on the shoulder. He basked in their positive energy.

Thirty

Lynch rolled onto his back, holding his sports coat as a filter over his mouth with his right hand. Dust still swirled about, but the failing sprinkler system had reduced the debris in the air significantly before losing all pressure. His left shoulder and chest felt nothing like it had after taking the bullet, but he longed for one of his hydrocodone tablets. Next time, he needed to remember which side to fall onto and which side to protect. *What am I thinking? Next time?* he thought.

Dropping his coat from his mouth, he took a deep breath. Despite the pain, he felt his lungs fill, entirely. Still, he knew he would need to go to the E.D. and get checked out. He wasn't so macho to think he should tough it out, when he had a better than even chance of having reopened his wounds.

He sat up and looked about. Bodies moved in the conference room. Through the open wall, he saw Eric using a portable extinguisher on several small fires.

"Looks like your gut was working just fine."

He looked to his right to see Brad standing next to him, extending his hand to help Lynch to his feet.

"You okay?"

Lynch nodded. "I think so. Anybody hurt?"

"Not down here, thanks to you. Stan's heading upstairs to see how they fared." He looked at Lynch's left shoulder. "You sure you're okay? Looks like you're bleeding."

"I'll be fine. But don't get me wrong, I plan to get checked in the E.D. I don't need something worse happening to put me back in the hospital."

He followed Brad to the front room, although with the drywall down and some of the wall studs blown apart, he felt hard-pressed to define a "front" room. The place looked like one big, debris-filled cavern. The ceiling, and subsequently the floor above where the copier had sat, yawned open. Actually, it looked more like the Hulk had jumped through it, ripping it apart.

Distant sirens filled the air, flowing in through the gaping wounds of the building's exterior as freely as the cold air. Lynch soon noticed the first pulsating lights, as police and fire units converged in chorus on the scene.

Together, the men walked outside and moved away from the building. The fire battalion chief ran up to them.

"Paramedics are on the way. I'll get one of my EMTs." The man looked back toward the nearest truck. "Hogan! Over here!"

Lynch protested. "We're fine. You guys need to check the office next door and the floors above."

The chief gave him a funny look and pointed to his shoulder. The EMT ran up, carrying his first response kit.

"Hogan, check him over and get him to the paramedics when they arrive."

"Look, it's an old wound. Not from the explosion."

Lynch tried to wave him off, but the technician would not take 'no' for an answer. Within a couple of minutes, he had a pressure dressing on the wound, and Lynch had to admit the dressing was a pretty good job.

"Here comes Stan," said Brad.

The look on the campaign manager's face was grim. The man fought to control his emotions.

"Stan?"

"Dom's dead. Two others, secretaries I think, are dead as well. Three appear critically hurt. The others have just minor wounds."

The EMT overheard the comment and bolted toward his chief. After a brief word, the man sprinted toward the building. Two ambulances appeared on the street and were waved forward by the battalion chief as they entered the parking lot.

"Richard Nichols?" asked Lynch. He prayed that Richard was okay, not wanting to see Amy go through another loss.

"Minor wounds. He was using his military training to help the others."

Lynch smiled. If Amy hadn't been between them, they might have become friends. Maybe in time, when the awkwardness of it all disappeared, they still would be. Yet, as he thought back to his last encounter with Amy, he realized that she might no longer be an issue after all. Danijela had filled his thoughts more and more. If only she wasn't leaving. . .

"He's a good man."

Brad produced a weak, brief smile. "I'm glad to hear you say that."

"Why?"

"You don't think we hired you without vetting you both, do you? We know all about your relationship with Amy Gibbs, and what happened in your absence."

Lynch started to protest, but Brad cut him short.

"We're not taking sides. And we're not judging. Your personal relationships are yours to deal with, unless they interfere with your job or might reflect badly on our campaign. If that were to happen, you and I will be having a discussion about it."

Lynch nodded.

"Your jobs won't intersect much, but when they do, I hope you can work together."

"I think we can, but I'll be honest, it might be awkward for a while."

"Awkward we can deal with."

Brad placed his hand on Lynch's good shoulder for a moment and left with Stan to walk to the waiting ambulances. Lynch could wait. From Stan's report, there were people who needed those ambulances much more than he did at the moment.

He walked to his car and recovered his prescription bottle of hydrocodone from the compartment between his front seats. He discovered a half-full bottle of water on the back floor and wondered how long it had sat there. Was it safe to drink?

He decided against risking drinking it and followed his boss toward the ambulances, which now numbered five. They'd have some bottled water. Moments later, with water in hand, he popped the pain killer into his mouth, swallowed it with a swig of water, and chased it with the remainder in the bottle.

"How many lives do you think you have left?"

The words came from behind him, but he smiled. He knew that voice.

"As many as it takes to get this S-O-B. It's become personal now."

Seamus sidled up next him, leaning against the ambulance.

"Aren't you supposed to be out catching whoever is behind this?"

"Yeah, but I needed to see how my old friend is doing. Besides, I figure all I need to do is hang you up as bait, and we'll catch him, or them."

Lynch wasn't up to the banter, but he appreciated Seamus' attempt to lighten things. For three people in that building, they were too late.

"Is Sarah working right now?"

Seamus nodded. " 'Til six tonight."

"Good. Can you drive me there and talk her into checking me over? I don't need to tie up one of these ambulances."

"Sure, but if you're up to it, why don't you give your statement to the good sergeant here first. I'll let her know we're coming." He nodded to the Chesterfield police sergeant who had just approached them. "Sergeant Tucker, nice to see you again."

"O'Connor. So, I finally get to meet Lynch Cully." The plainclothes officer extended his hand to Lynch. "Kerry Tucker. Great to meet you."

"You, too." Lynch shook hands with the detective.

"You up for this? Looks like you could use some medical care."

Lynch nodded and followed the officer to his car. Half an hour later, he emerged from the detective's car and found Seamus sitting in the driver's seat of Lynch's car. He had the seat leaned back as far as he could and seemed to be napping. Yet, as Lynch approached, the window eased downward, and Seamus opened one eye to look at him.

"Flannigan needed my car, so I hope you don't mind using yours. Give me the keys and hop in."

Forty-five minutes later, after some clandestine movement within the Barnes' E.D. and a chest X-ray that the bean counters and radiologists would never know of, Lynch was declared fit.

"Well, maybe fit-for-duty isn't the right terminology, but at least you don't appear to have any new damage, and your lung is still inflated."

"Thanks, Sarah. I owe you one," said Lynch as he donned his coat.

"Yeah, well, just watch Shay's back and we'll be even. Now, regarding you, you know what to watch for, right?"

Lynch nodded. "Don't worry, I'm not that stoic. Shortness of breath. Bleeding. I'll get help."

Sarah escorted Lynch back to the ambulance entrance, gave him a gentle hug, and turned back inside. Lynch found Seamus waiting in his car, keeping it from being towed from the "Police Vehicle Only" slot.

"Let's go," said Lynch as he climbed into the passenger seat.

"Do I look like a chauffeur? Anyway, we're staying put. There was an attempt on the MacArthur rail bridge. One dead, one wounded. He's on his way here. And he had a cell phone on him. Time to work some magic."

Lynch smiled. Maybe this would be the break they needed.

Thirty-one

Amy walked from her small home "office," a spare bedroom furnished with a desk and reading chair, to the kitchen for a second cup of tea. She felt guilty sitting at home, but then, she hadn't done this much reading in years. She realized how much she enjoyed it and decided to read more during her down time.

It had been almost two weeks since she'd been kidnapped by that vile man, Darko Komarčić. She had argued with the MedAir bosses that she didn't *need* time off, and her therapist had released her two days earlier. Still, her boss had insisted and her forced vacation, her medical leave, extended through the end of the week.

The good news, though, was she'd been cleared to return to flight duty. At first, it would be a 50-50 split in her time because they still needed a training 'officer', and she had done such a good job in the position.

Maybe too good. She had come to appreciate sleeping in her own bed every night and having normal hours. Perhaps the 50-50 split would be a great compromise.

As she turned back toward her office, cup of tea in hand, the phone rang. *Richard?* she hoped.

The Caller ID read "Mercy." It might as well have read, "Macy."

"Hey, girlfriend, have you been listening to the news?"

"Good morning to you, too, Macy. And no, I've been reading."

"Well, you better turn it on. There was a bomb at the American Party Headquarters. We're going to get the first casualties in the next couple a minutes. Bye."

Amy's heart plunged to her gut as the phone line clicked dead.

She ran to her living room and grabbed the remote. Seconds later, she found a local station that had broken into the usual morning drivel to cover the breaking story. Behind the reporter she could see the devastated building with emergency response vehicles lining the parking lot.

The reporter's words flew past her ears as she focused on the scene. She wanted to see Richard walking among the people there. Where was he? "C'mon, I want to see Richard," she spoke to the empty room.

The reporter's words, "three reported dead," registered in her brain. Tears began to well up.

"Lynch?" she said, again out loud. What was he doing there? It was definitely him, left arm in a sling. He had just gotten out of a police car. She didn't recognize the man getting out of the driver's side but assumed him to be a detective because of the regular clothes he wore.

Lynch disappeared behind the reporter's head but emerged on the other side and stopped at another car, his car. Someone else was in the driver's seat, and after a moment, Lynch walked around the car and got into the passenger's seat. As the car left the scene, she returned her focus to the scene behind the reporter. Still no sign of Richard, but what were her chances of seeing him in the chaos?

Should I call Lynch? she wondered. She wanted to, badly. She realized how unfair that would be, to call him only to ask if he knew whether Richard was injured, or . . .

She didn't want to consider that option. A thought hit her, and she ran to her office to get her cell phone. She scrolled through her contact list to the S's, but no "Seamus." Maybe she had him listed under his last name. Her finger trembled as she tried to scroll back up the alphabet. No "O'Connor" listed.

She fumbled her way through the whole contact list, but saw no one else on the MCS who might know what was happening. She wracked her brain for a name to call.

She returned her scrutiny to the television screen, but the image had moved to a different angle. She saw no helicopters, and in that urban setting, their competition would likely get that call, if needed. She didn't know anyone on the ground crews there.

Amidst her anxiety, she realized she hadn't even tried Richard's number. Duh? What had made her such an emotional basket case that she hadn't tried the simplest route first?

She dialed. The call went straight to voice mail. Now her anxiety ratcheted up two notches. "Call me. Please," were the only words she could manage to say in way of a message.

She fought the desire to go to the scene. She'd be too late to help and she'd never get near it anyway. The police would have cordoned off the area and diverted all road traffic. All she could do was watch the TV. Maybe the other stations were on scene now, too. She began channel-surfing, hoping for a glimpse.

Seamus and Lynch sat in the doctor's area of the E.D. waiting for the wounded terrorist. Sarah occasionally stopped through to check on them, but she was busy with patients and the residents on her service.

While there, Seamus received a second call, briefing him on the situation and his role as assigned to the MCS. Being a city detective in the first place, his department had jurisdiction since the guy had been discovered trying to plant a bomb on one of the bridge piers on the Missouri side of the river, within the St. Louis city limits.

"Should be here any minute," he said to Lynch, before explaining to him the details of the incident. He knew he could get reprimanded for the same, but he'd already told Lynch he'd keep him in the loop. Besides, he knew how to manipulate a phone and check its call registers better than anyone Seamus knew.

Seamus saw Sarah from a distance and hopped up to talk to her. He caught her before she could go into another room.

"Hey, this guy the police shot. When he comes in, I need his cell phone. That's all. We won't get in the way."

"Cell phone. Got it." Her head perked up and turned toward the ambulance entrance. "Looks like he's here. Hey, how about dinner tonight?"

Seamus nodded. "If I can. Call me as you go off duty. Thanks."

He returned to his seat and waited. Five minutes later, a nurse walked up to them.

"Sergeant O'Connor, here. Doctor Wade said you needed this." She extended her gloved hand, holding a bloody cell phone, toward him. Her other hand held a pair of gloves, which he quickly donned before taking the phone.

"What kind of phone is it?" asked Lynch.

"LG." He paused to open the phone. "Looks like a 221C." He flipped it over and inspected the back before attempting the power button. "Tracfone, I think."

"Typical burn phone. Prepaid minutes, easy to get in any town. Just go to your local Walmart or Dollar General. Ten to one it's government subsidized."

"Great. Not only do we pay for mosques overseas that teach radical Islam and hatred for our country, now we're subsidizing their communications while they attack us here."

"Yeah, ain't America great?" Lynch looked around for a pair of gloves and found a box on an adjacent desk. He gloved up and Seamus handed him the phone.

Lynch pressed the power button. Nothing happened. "Dead?"

Lynch frowned. "Maybe." He pulled the back off to inspect the battery, pulled the battery out to clean its connections, and sighed. He held it up for Seamus to see. "Or maybe not. No SIM card. We're getting nothing from this phone unless the perp has the card in his pocket."

Seamus took a deep breath in exasperation and stood. As he started to head toward the trauma bay where he saw the paramedics take the guy, he saw Sarah heading toward him.

"You might want to see this," she said.

She directed them toward a computer with a large vertical screen. A moment later, a chest X-ray appeared on the monitor. Even Seamus had no problem seeing what she was about to point out. She pointed to a dense white rectangle just below the guy's ribs.

"We did this portable chest X-ray to check his lungs and saw this." She pointed toward the obvious. "It looks like . . ."

"A SIM card." Seamus and Lynch said it simultaneously.

"Yeah. The size. The cut-off corner. It's in his stomach."

"How in the world did he manage to swallow that? Wouldn't it get stuck going down?" asked Seamus.

"You would think, but you'd be surprised what we find on X-ray at times. And obviously, he swallowed it."

"That settles that," said Lynch.

"What?" asked Seamus.

"You're not getting anything off that card. The stomach acid's gonna make sure of that."

Seamus' shoulders sagged. "Great. The perfect way to destroy a SIM card."

"If you've got the stomach for it," added Lynch.

Amy jumped at the ring of her phone. Maybe Richard was calling. Caller ID revealed "Mercy" and the same number.

"Macy! What can you tell me?"

"I'm not sure what she might tell you, but *I'm* calling to let you know I'm okay."

Amy began to cry, tears of relief. Richard sat on the other end of the line and a weight lifted off her shoulders.

"The explosion toasted our landlines and my cell

phone, or I would have called earlier."

"Oh, Richard. You're okay. I was—"

"Yeah, mostly. Had to get a few stitches, but . . ." His voice dwindled away.

Amy could sense his sadness. He seemed much farther away than the 25 miles that currently separated them.

"My new boss was killed, along with two secretaries. Dominick leaves behind a wife and three teenaged kids. Both women were married and had kids, too." He paused. "This . . . this is the legacy of a government that only gives lip service to protecting our borders."

Amy shared his sorrow. Her brother, Chad, had died in Afghanistan, and Richard had lost friends while serving there. And for what? The Afghan leadership now turned its back on America and criticized us openly. The administration's lack of spine portrayed America as weak, and now they planned to gut our military in the name of protecting their cherished entitlement programs.

"Look, I can't tie up their phone any longer. I have to get a new phone and run a couple other errands, but can I pick you up around five? I need to see you. And I want to take you out to dinner."

His choice of words did not go unnoticed. He *needed* to see her. Just what did he mean by that?

Seamus flashed his credentials at the cordon, and the uniformed officer let them pass. The fire trucks were gone, as were the ambulances, but five CSU vans filled the lot, along with marked and unmarked police vehicles.

Lynch didn't expect to see anyone from the campaign there, and he was correct in that thinking. He pulled out his cell phone and called Brad Graham directly.

"Brad, it's Lynch."

"Lynch, this isn't a good time. I-I'm with Dominick's family." Brad's voice was just above a whisper.

"I won't keep you. Just wanted you to know we're, *I'm* back on the scene. If you want to give me a call later, I'll tell you what we've found, if anything. Do I need to secure anything in the office?"

"No. Stan took care of that. I'll call later. Gotta go." The line clicked dead.

Lynch followed Seamus toward the building. A uniformed officer from the Chesterfield Police—a white shirt wearing the rank of captain—stopped them from coming farther. "Sorry, crime scene, no civilians. You'll have to clear the area."

Seamus flashed his creds again. "Captain, I'm Seamus O'Connor and this is Lynch Cully. I believe Captain Johnstone talked with you, or maybe it was your chief, about a possible tie to the school shooting we're still investigating."

The captain extended his hand toward Lynch, ignoring Seamus for the moment.

"So, you're Lynch Cully. Pleased to meet you. Man, you sure surprised us all coming back from the dead like that."

Lynch shook his hand. "Yeah, well, um, thanks. I, um, I'm actually the new chief of security for the Graham campaign. I sure didn't anticipate this on my first morning at work."

"I wouldn't have either. Too bad about the people

upstairs."

Seamus tried to reinsert himself into the conversation, making Lynch stifle a small smile.

"Captain, Lynch was on site when this happened. Detective Tucker has his formal statement. Look, we're not here to step on anyone's toes—"

"Does it look like that's our concern?" the captain interrupted. "We do our own crime scene investigations in Chesterfield, but we know when we can use some help." He waved at the five CSU vans, only two of which were his. "Go ahead, make yourselves useful. Every eyeball on the scene improves our chance of finding something helpful."

"Thanks, Captain."

The two resumed their walk to the building. As they arrived at what used to be the door, a county CSU appeared. "You stalking me, O'Connor?"

Seamus smiled. "Hey, Mena. So, they dragged you in from first precinct, eh?"

She shrugged. "You know how it goes. We work where they tell us to work."

"Got anything?"

"We were told the bomb came delivered inside a copier, so we're trying to find pieces of it, plus anything identifiable as a bomb part. It's slow going. Who's the handsome one with you?"

Lynch felt awkward. He'd never had another police officer call him handsome. Seemed strange somehow.

"Mena, this is Lynch Cully. Lynch, Mena Parson."

She extended her hand.

"I was here when it went off. A cell phone triggered it."

"That's what we were told. Hey, where exactly was it in the room?"

Lynch stepped over the damaged threshold into the gaping maw of the building. A pile of rubble sat in the location where the copier had been.

"Right there." He pointed to the spot.

"Okay, confirms what we thought. All of that debris is from the second floor. We're sifting through it for evidence. The Chesterfield guys are working the perimeter and moving toward the center."

"Need some help?"

"As long as you know what you're doing. I don't have time to spend splainin' procedures to you." Her index finger started shaking in splainin' mode and Lynch laughed.

"No splainin' needed, ma'am."

Lynch walked back toward where he and Brad had stood when he first heard the cell phone ring. He closed his eyes and tried to recall exactly what he saw. He had seen no cell phone and the sound came through as muffled. The copier had been a commercial grade machine, which meant at least four paper trays. By his estimate, explosives packed into such a space would have been enough to explain the damage.

The opening for the trays had been toward Brad's office, meaning the greatest force would have been directed that way. The phone would have been close to the opening as well. A phone buried deeper inside the machine might not have received a signal. In addition, the copier would have focused the charge in that direction, if even briefly, before being ripped apart. In his mind, he could see the blast.

"Mena, I know you need to work the whole room, but I think the focus of the charge came this way." He stood where the door to Brad's office once existed. "Even though pieces of the copier will be all over the place, you're more likely to find remains of the actual device in this direction."

She walked over to him and listened as he explained his reasoning. She nodded as he finished.

"You know, you could be handy to have around."

She flashed him a smile. Now he definitely felt strange. A police officer was coming on to him. Was she into handcuffs? She looked the type. He shook that thought clear from his head.

She eased through the debris into Brad's office, her eyes scrutinizing the floor and the desk. She stopped and turned back.

"Hey, John, bring some markers and a camera."

Her colleague from the front room complied, and she laid out a series of markers on the floor, followed by photographs. After that, she bagged and numbered the items she'd found on the floor and worked toward the desk.

"Looks like pieces of pipe and plastic embedded in the wood of the desk, along with glass from the interior windows of the office. John, did you guys get pictures of this?"

"Chesterfield said they did the photo canvas."

"Eh. Better be safe." She took more pictures and moved around behind the desk. "Looks like anything above the desk would have been shredded. But anyone getting behind the desk in time would have been protected. It's almost clean back here."

Lynch saw that Brad's desk chair had been blown over by the blast. As the CSU detective had mentioned, that portion of the chair rising above the desktop appeared minced. He doubted Brad would have had time to duck behind the desk.

After a picture, CSU Parson uprighted the chair and began to probe the shredded top third. Squarely in the middle, where Brad's head would have been, she pointed to a rent in the leather.

"I'll be. What are the odds?"

She spread the torn material and took a picture. Then she inserted two fingers into the hole and pulled out a small rectangular lump of plastic. A portion of a cell phone, and as she turned it over, the SIM card.

Lynch looked skyward and mouthed the words, "Thank you, thank you, thank you." He noticed Seamus make the sign of the cross over his chest.

"Any chance you can rush that through the lab? We *really need* the call log from that chip. We think this case is related to all the recent bombings across the country."

"Really?"

Lynch gave her the two-minute version of his theory and earlier findings.

"I'll see what we can do, but a call from the MCS commander and any other bigwig you can find to add pressure will help." She paused. "Our lab geeks shouldn't have any trouble checking out the SIM card, but once we figure out which carrier served it, we'll have to subpoena for records. That could take a while. Under the circumstances of its discovery, I don't think we'll have any problem getting a judge to sign off. That's how it works."

He did remember how "it works" and he knew who to call. "Can you get it to Mike Jurgesmeyer at the computer lab?"

She looked surprised. With a sense of mystery in her voice, she said, "You know him? He's like a ghost. We hear about stuff he does, but no one ever sees him. It's legend that he lives in a supercomputer grotto of his own design and feeds off the electrical charges all around him."

He gave her a quizzical look. Mike had been an introvert but not a hermit.

She waggled her splainin' finger and laughed. "Just kidding. Sure, I can get it to Mike."

Lynch looked at Seamus and rolled his eyes. He stood and glanced back at the outer room. It appeared the charge had been directed right at Brad, but thankfully, Brad hadn't been in his office and had survived. And by yet another divine miracle, the potential key to finding this guy had survived as well, saved by the very chair the killer had expected his victim to be sitting in.

Something nagged at Lynch. How did someone know which way to direct the charge? Or had they simply expected the overall explosion to accomplish their task? The delivery guy sure didn't seem like assassin material, or even an educated accomplice. Not to mention that the campaign expected the copiers. They could trace that order easily enough, along with the delivery order.

Someone had to have known about the copier being on order. That same someone had to have expected that Brad would be in the office. Even more incriminating, that someone must have known that the entire upper echelon would be there.

A few dollars into someone's pocket could make him look the other way when the rigged machine was switched for the real one. And why was the delivery guy offered a bonus for delivery by ten? Who offered that money? When was the switch made? Lynch suspected this part of the case would be easily cracked open. Someone would be going to jail for a long time as an accomplice to murder.

But that didn't answer his first question about directing the charge. Had the delivery guy positioned the machine, or had Eric moved it after the delivery man left for the second machine? Suddenly the question of being an inside job filled Lynch's mind. Yet, he couldn't incriminate Eric without evidence. Maybe someone else moved the machine after Brad walked Lynch to the conference room. Lynch tried hard to recall the chain of events as he had witnessed them.

Thirty-two

✸

Amy fretted over her outfit. Yes, Richard had told her the dress code would be "nice," as in wear something nice, but not fancy. Definitely not jeans. Was she too dressy?

The doorbell rang and she rushed to answer but then hesitated. *No, don't seem too eager*, she thought.

The open door revealed Richard holding a bouquet of cut flowers—tulips, Peruvian lilies, daisies, roses, and carnations. She found that an unusual combination, but it worked. She thought back to the first time he'd brought her flowers. That night had ended poorly. Actually, worse than poorly. Maybe these were meant as a "do-over" of that night.

"They're beautiful. C'mon in and let me get those in water before we leave."

"I'm glad you like them. Anything I can do?"

She shook her head. "It'll just take a minute."

Richard followed her to the kitchen where she located a vase, added water, and placed the stems into it. She could re-cut and arrange them later.

"There." She turned toward him and gave a little bounce up on her toes and back down, smiling. "Okay, then. I'm ready. My coat's by the front door."

Forty-five minutes later, Richard parked his car in downtown St. Louis and fed the meter to cover their time before free parking kicked in. He escorted Amy down the street, and as they turned the corner, Amy started to laugh.

"What in the world are we doing here? This is the last place I expected you to take me."

They stood in front of the Bridge Tap House & Wine Bar. Only a few months earlier, he and his Army pals had tried to pick up Amy and her nursing pals. That hadn't ended well either.

"Yes, well, should I get my emergency poncho from the car?"

Amy blushed. On their first meeting, here, she had tossed her drink into his face.

"Um, I don't think that's necessary. Is . . . is this where we press the 'do-over' button?"

He gave her a coy look and said, "You might say that."

He opened the door for her and they walked in. Surprisingly, the place was less than half full.

"Gee, guess we won't have to wait for a seat."

"Guess not." He gave a second's pause. "Well, it is Thursday. Maybe folks are waiting 'til tomorrow night."

Amy gave a subtle shrug of her shoulders. "True. And it's a little early for this crowd. I'm sure the crowd will pick up."

Richard picked the table where she had doused him, smirked, and laughed as he pulled out her chair. They chatted over drinks, followed by dinner. Richard gave her a synopsis of what had happened earlier that morning.

"The memorial service for Dominick is Saturday. Would you be able to go with me?"

"Sure. And to the services for the others if you'd like. Just give me enough notice to arrange things at work if I have to."

Richard looked solemn and nodded. In the silence of

the moment, Amy realized the crowd hadn't increased but had actually thinned out. They sat alone on the loft and only a few tables below held diners.

Richard took her hand.

"Richard—"

"Amy—"

They both laughed. She said, "Go ahead."

"Amy, I brought you here because this is where we met, even if under, um, less than auspicious circumstances. You mentioned a 'do-over' button. Well, I'd like to think of it as a 'new start' button."

As he stood up and went down to one knee next to her, Amy lost her breath.

"Amy, this morning made me realize how fleeting life can be, and I don't want to miss a momentary chance, or watch another day of my life or a single minute go by, without spending it with you."

As he pulled a ring box from his pocket, tears flooded Amy's eyes. She'd often fantasized how this moment of her life might occur. Every imagination underestimated the depth of her feelings right then.

"Will you marry me?"

Amy leaned forward to caress Richard's face and gaze into his eyes.

"Yes."

She leaned forward and kissed him with a passion she never knew she could feel. After lingering with their foreheads together, she felt him shift to one side and lift his arm. Surprised, she drew back to see that he'd raised his hand with a thumbs up.

A moment later, the front doors flew open and in

marched her father and Macy blowing noisemakers. Richard's friends, Clive and Hassle, along with her brothers and their wives, and dozens of extended family members and friends followed and joined in the joyous mayhem.

In surprise, she jumped to her feet to acknowledge them and give them the "customary" ring finger salute, to show off her ring. As she did, she knocked the table a bit too hard and the half-full pitcher of beer sitting there doused Richard across the front, covering his shirt and pants.

Thirty-three

Fawaz read the report with anger roiling up within. Despite voicing his concern earlier about labeling the school shooting as a Muslim terrorist action, the local police department had done just that. The individuals involved were not named, and lacking any other details, they were described as Muslim men in both a preliminary report to the FBI and a news release to the local and regional press.

He stood and paced within the motel room. He had his instructions, to suppress reports that highlight such Muslim activity. The Committee on American-Islamic Relations and Islamic Institute of North America had spent much time, effort, and money cultivating a benign image of Islam in America, while raising money for fundamentalist groups overseas and organizing cells within America, such as the ones Fawaz had called upon to attack America's infrastructure.

The national news organizations yielded to these organizations' threats and complaints out of political correctness and their leftist leanings. The support of the press in creating public opinion was crucial.

Yet, an increasingly vocal number of reporters began to stray. A school shooting by alleged Muslim terrorists would strike the heart of even the most liberal individual. Reports such as the one he held in his hand had to be suppressed. *Not* to do so increased the risk of adding to the roster of noncompliant journalists.

Fawaz wiped away the sweat beading up on his brow. He was unaccustomed to the levels of stress he now felt. He needed to perform his job and do it well. Yet, he felt as if he was in the middle of a frozen lake with the ice cracking and breaking apart all around him.

He stared at the television, its muted screen displaying CNN, and wondered about that ice storm which had delayed him at the beginning. He had lectured the others about omens. Now, it seemed, he needed to pay closer attention, for his own good.

The image of a fallen train trestle appeared above the newscaster's shoulder. He clicked off the "mute" function.

"Yesterday's attack on our country saw the destruction of five railroad bridges across the Mississippi. Fortunately, state and local authorities in Minnesota, Wisconsin, Iowa, and Missouri thwarted similar attacks on several bridges in their states. The total number of attacks has not been released, but the Department of Homeland Security has labeled the attacks as the work of homegrown terrorists."

"Our nation's freight rail system carries over 40% of our commercial goods, such as cars, produce, coal, lumber, and more. This disruption in service will cause delays and higher prices, and this spate of recent terror attacks has not gone unnoticed by the markets. The Dow Jones Industrials opened 128 points lower, while the S&P has lost ten points."

That was not enough. The attacks should have removed the busiest rail bridges from service and caused a massive slide in the markets, not unlike those in the fall of 2008. With local and state police units on alert, he would have to select new targets.

Again, he paced.

While this failure was not his fault, it would not go unnoticed. He had to act quickly and decisively. Economic disruption would no longer suffice.

Yet, he would need to think through the idea forming in his mind. He could not act rashly without increasing his personal risk.

He stopped pacing and inspected his appearance in the mirror. At the moment, he needed to pay a visit to a certain police chief and "request" a rewording of this report.

"Not going to happen, Mr. Fawaz," said Colonel Andrews. "The report says it like it is, and will stay that way."

"You realize that this is racial profiling and the Department of Justice can sanction your department. Not to mention the potential lawsuits you'll face from the ACLU, Committee on American-Islamic Relations, and more. They could bankrupt your city."

"Bull crap." The police chief shook his head. "Do you actually believe I don't know what the DOJ can and cannot do, Mr. Fawaz? Their policy clearly allows for the investigation into terrorist activities, which this attack was."

"As for threat of lawsuits, is the Department of Homeland Security now in bed with the ACLU and your Muslim lobbyists? I bet the American people would love to know more about that."

Fawaz had to change tack. The colonel had called his bluff. In truth, the DOJ could withhold federal grants to obstinate departments like this, but the policy had been written broadly to make sure its own hands would not be tied regarding terrorist activities. The risk in doing so had been that they alone would not be the only ones who could define an event as "terrorist" related.

"No, sir, we are not tied closely to any group."

The police chief rolled his eyes. He was gaining no advantage with this policeman.

"Well, if we get sued, we'll find out for sure, won't we?"

"I have no control over that. All I can say is that other departments in your position have avoided trouble by refusing to racially profile."

The chief stared at Fawaz, as if trying to read his mind.

"Mr. Fawaz, we have no need to back down. We can prove our standing."

"Oh? I thought the vehicle's VIN numbers were destroyed and you had only identified one man."

Fawaz knew this to be untrue, but that information had come from Imam Al-Bashara, and he could not reveal that. He hoped to use this to pull out more details from the police chief, details the imam did not know.

The man hesitated before answering, a pause that did not go unnoticed by Fawaz. Fawaz only knew that Sabir had been identified as well and they had traced both men to Detroit. He wasn't sure *how* that had been accomplished and fished for that answer as well.

"We ID'd that one shooter by a driver's license found

at the site. Not all of the vehicle's tracking numbers were gone and through that we were able to track down the identified shooter's residence and ID *all* of his fellow terrorists. We've even been to their mosque."

The colonel paused again, watching Fawaz closely. Despite knowing this, Fawaz felt his heart rate accelerate and hoped this reaction wasn't obvious. As a faithful Muslim, he never played cards, but he knew what a "tell" was.

"We also know there's a fifth man." That pause came again. "We're closing in on his identity."

Fawaz struggled to maintain his composure.

"Yep, Mr. Fawaz. We can support our claim that this attack was by Muslim terrorists against a Christian elementary school, and we'll be releasing a formal statement to the press within a couple of days . . ."

His eyes gleamed with satisfaction. Fawaz fought hard not to strike that smug look from the man's face.

". . . along with our report to the FBI. Where are you staying? I'll make sure you get a copy."

Fawaz took a slow deep breath to calm down. Did the man already know that *he* was the fifth man? Did he suspect? He needed to keep his wits collected and respond as an employee of Homeland Security, not as a man under suspicion. He would give the man no reason to suspect anything further.

"Yes, thank you. I wish to see that as soon as you have it prepared. I'm staying at the Hampton Inn near the school itself. However, I believe my superiors expect me to return to Washington by the first of the week. If the report isn't completed by then, please send it to me at my office." He fished around for his wallet in his coat pocket.

"I have your card, sir. I'm sure you'll be among the first to know."

Fawaz didn't like the way the man said that. Again resisting the instinct to fight back or run, he acknowledged the comment and stood to his feet.

"Colonel Andrews, I hope you'll reconsider, and I anticipate seeing the next report."

With that, he turned and left the department. That he was escorted outside also sent alarm through his brain. He needed to act, and act quickly, so he could leave for Washington as he had stated.

As he neared his car, the burn phone in his briefcase began to buzz. He recognized the number and thought, *How in the world did the Director get this number?*

"U.N. Secretary General Retires" announced the headlines. The story gave mixed reviews to the departing bureaucrat, but that was of no concern to Karolus. The two men had different assignments, if that was the appropriate word.

Karolus finished the article and returned to his work. He had to complete his first address to that international body, to be followed by a major press conference in which he would further push for acceptance of Agenda 21 and lay out his own program for peace in the Middle East.

"Sir?"

He looked up to see Francois holding out a sheaf of papers.

"The information you requested."

His aide handed him the papers.

"Thank you, Francois."

The man began to turn away but hesitated and faced his employer.

"Sir, I was thinking. Soon you're going to be swamped with work. Would you like to delegate this to someone else?"

Karolus had already considered this. The matter would be settled soon enough.

"No, that's alright, Francois. I'll finish this."

"Yes, sir. Oh, and one other thing, His Holiness has asked for some time with you. There have been some snags in the assumption of control of the Old City. The Israeli Prime Minister has again balked and insists on the status quo."

Karolus contemplated that turn of events. He was not surprised, but that would not be acceptable. Within his plan, the Vatican would take control of Jerusalem's Old City as an international zone with full ecumenical access. Within a short time, they would be able to eliminate fundamentalist claims to the area from all sides and prove their point that only an ecumenical approach would bring peace.

"Yes. Please let them know that we will come to the Vatican on my way to Geneva. Set up the needed time and give it priority. Thank you, Francois."

He turned his attention to the papers now in his hand. Only five bridges. State and local police had been alerted by the bombing of the I-10 bridges earlier and placed guards on the interstate and rail bridges. Ten men were dead and one captured alive, which could prove problematic . . . for Fawaz.

Karolus stared out the penthouse window. They had avoided going after the electric grid because, despite its vulnerability, they wanted to reboot the economy as quickly as possible after assuming global control. He remained hesitant to attack the power infrastructure.

The last few sheets in the stack comprised the preliminary report from Missouri about the botched school shooting. Fawaz had failed to intimidate that police chief, and from the word he received privately, there was little chance he would succeed for the final report. That department's detectives had already identified the men and the mosque. Fawaz now became a liability, but before using him as a scapegoat, he had one more task for the man.

"Francois!"

He waited for his aide to appear.

"Where is Fawaz at the moment?"

"A moment, sir." Francois left the room, only to reappear a minute later. "He is outside the Florissant, Missouri, police station."

"Please get him on the phone for me."

Fawaz pulled his phone from his pocket and answered, with some trepidation.

"Yes, sir?"

"The bridges still stand."

"Yes, sir, I am aware of this. We had speculated on just such a scenario and recognized we had no way to compensate. We do not have an army able to overpower a police presence and cannot afford to lose the very men we need for the next phase."

"Yes, that was understood. You are aware that the four dead school shooters have all been identified, yes?"

"Yes, sir. I just learned that within the past half an hour. What would you like me to do?"

"Initiate phase three. The President and Homeland Security are in the loop and prepared to capitalize on the events."

With that, the Director hung up on him. Fawaz hung his head. He had hoped it would not come to this. Many fellow Muslims were likely to die. Was he prepared for what now seemed inevitable? He would need to offer fervent prayer to Allah that he might still be found useful. Otherwise, he, too, would be among those to die.

The problem as he saw it was that while others would die as martyrs, he would be sacrificed by those above him. This fact he saw as unfair and unrighteous . . . and worthy of retribution.

Thirty-four

Lynch pulled into the lot of the St. Louis County Computer Forensics Lab only to discover an empty building. Even the signage was missing, although the scar of a previous rectangular sign could be seen on the wall near the main door. He glanced around, certain he had the right place. He'd spent time here with Mike Jurgesmeyer as they tried to find the L.A. Rapist prior to Lynch's "accident" and battle with amnesia.

He exited his car and walked up to the building. The last time he'd been there, a camera using facial recognition had opened the door for him. Now, substantial locks held the door tight. He looked for a notice, anything, to suggest where the lab had gone.

As he returned to his car, his cell rang. The Caller ID revealed Brad on the line.

"Cully," Lynch answered.

"Lynch, sorry it's taken me so long to get back with you. This has not been a . . ."

Lynch waited for his boss to continue but replied when no further words came.

"Brad, no explanation needed. Anything I can do for you?"

"I think you're working on that. Find who did this. Other than that, well, the campaign's on hold right now, and I don't see anything more that you can do. But thanks. Discover anything yet?"

"Yeah, someone stole the county's computer forensics lab."

Brad chuckled and sounded like he needed the catharsis.

"The county opened a new nine million dollar crime lab at the county police headquarters while you were out of commission. I heard they quadrupled their size, so maybe they moved the computer lab there."

"That might also account for why the number I thought I remembered for the chief tech there wasn't any good. Thanks." Lynch paused as he heard Brad speak to someone in the background. "If the phone remnants are any good, we might have a big lead on who did this. If not, well . . . Anyway, I hope to find out today. But, actually, I wanted to talk with you about something else."

Lynch carefully explained his concerns about the bomb's placement and Eric's possible role in things. Brad didn't say anything when he finished, but the dead air didn't faze Lynch. He knew Brad would need a moment to digest what he'd said and consider his response.

A minute later, Brad replied, "Lynch, I hear your concern, and I won't disregard it, but I've known Eric for over a decade. I-I find it hard to fathom he could have been part of this."

"I understand that. I just can't ignore the possibility. Whoever is behind these attacks is well-funded and has access to a small army, not just terrorists but informants and others, too. Money doesn't always talk, sometimes it screams."

"He's in the other room. Should I ask him anything?"

"No. I'd like to interview him later. Body language can

be more revealing than the words spoken sometime."

"True. Just let me know when and I'll make it happen. Anything else?"

"No, sir. I guess I'll head to Clayton and see if I can locate Mike at the lab."

Lynch heard a voice in the background with Brad again.

"Here's the phone number. Might save you some running around," replied Brad. "Call me when you've finished."

"Yes, sir. Thanks."

After two more calls and a series of relays, Lynch finally found Mike Jurgesmeyer, at home. Ten minutes later, he knocked on the guy's front door. Mike answered on the second knock. He looked as Lynch remembered him, tall, athletic and fit, with that silken, long ponytail that made some women jealous. Not exactly the stereotypical computer geek.

"Hey, a ghost from the past."

"What? No facial recognition at the front door?"

The two men shook hands, and Mike reached out for a man hug, catching Lynch unprepared. The discomfort passed.

"Budget cuts."

"Huh?"

"Budget cuts. No facial recognition system and no lab. They opened this fancy new crime lab, gobs of space, but since they ran something like a million plus over budget, they cut out my lab. They laid off my technicians and gave me an eight-by-ten room. Do you believe that?" He paused. "Oh, hey, c'mon in. We don't need to stand here on the stoop."

Lynch entered the front room and thought he'd been transported to the NSA spymaster center. He gazed across consoles holding half a dozen computers controlling close to 20 monitors. He couldn't tell what each monitor showed but knew that most of them showed scenes that were not in St. Louis. Mena Parson's comment about Mike living inside a supercomputer and feeding off its currents passed through his mind.

"I got that SIM card this morning. It's downstairs. When I protested the closet they gave me at the lab, they gave me permission to set up a 'satellite' shop here at home. Officially, I still have my closet at the crime lab, but mostly I work from here. Now I'm trying to get them to help defray my electric bill." He grinned. "Like that will ever happen."

He led Lynch to the basement, where Lynch thought he'd stepped back into the old forensics lab. Grounded worktables, storage shelves, tools, and more filled the space.

"It's over here." Mike walked to the nearest table. "I didn't expect you to stop by, so I've already scanned it through the reader. I was just getting ready to print out the data. Give me a second."

Lynch gazed at the equipment. He recalled working with such tools, but their operation eluded him. Another glitch in his memory.

"Do you mind if I play with this a bit? I'm trying to remember how to do it."

Mike stayed his hands as they reached for the SIM card reader.

"Not this card. But, you can try it on an old card."

Lynch flushed. Mike was right in stopping him. He was no longer a police officer, for one thing. Had he accidentally erased that card, he'd be in big trouble.

Mike pulled two sheets of paper from the nearby printer.

"I don't know if I'm supposed to give you a copy or not, but here it is. You didn't get it from me."

Lynch looked over the printout. The phone had been a government-sponsored disposable. As expected, there had been no outgoing calls or text messages. It had received, however, half a dozen incoming calls, all from the same number.

"Yeah, I know your next question. C'mon back upstairs." Mike led Lynch back to the front room and proceeded to sit down in the rolling desk chair surrounded by his screens. "You didn't see me do this, either." He rolled to a keyboard to his left. "As soon as I saw it this morning, I plugged that number into a program that I will disavow owning if anyone ever asks. *Capish*?"

Mike looked serious.

"I mean it, Lynch. If we didn't go way back and if I didn't trust you with my life, you would not be seeing this. Heck, by showing you this, I *am* trusting you with my life."

Lynch had never seen the easy-going, lighthearted, hippy throwback Mike Jurgesmeyer look so determined.

"What program?" The secret was safe with him.

Mike nodded.

"Right before you knocked, I got a hit on that number and guess what, the phone is right here in St. Louis. North County is closest I could localize it because it was on the move. There was a brief conversation in one incoming call, and then it broadcasted a single text message to a dozen different numbers before it was turned off."

Mike rolled the mouse to direct his cursor over a button and clicked. The text message appeared on the screen.

"The virgins await you. *Allahu Akbar*!"

Mike looked up at him. "Yeah, virgins means martyrs. This doesn't look good."

Lynch nodded. Twelve text messages meant a minimum of 12 martyrs. There might be more, all fanatical and suicidal, but 12 was symbolic. Just as there were the 12 tribes of Israel, there were 12 princes of Islam.

"Has the phone been used since?"

"Nope."

"What about the conversation?"

Mike hesitated. "It lasted just seconds, but . . . this is the part you really, really gotta keep secret."

Lynch crossed his heart.

"Okay, I haven't listened to it yet, but here's the conversation."

Lynch's eyes bugged out. His old friend had NSA-like capabilities?

"Umm, before you do that, are you sure we should? I mean, like wow, I didn't expect this."

"Yeah, well, I'm not the only one who can do this, and some of the others aren't exactly law-abiding citizens. Far as I know, only the NSA has the supercomputers and storage to record *everyone's* phone calls. I can only monitor a few numbers at a time, numbers I have to plug in. It's not like I could screen every call in St. Louis for buzz words."

Lynch sighed. He fully understood Mike's concerns now.

"Okay, let's hear it."

Lynch didn't recognize the voices, but one was obviously the boss and he had a stern, but cultured, tone with the hint of a foreign accent. As the "boss" spoke what would be the last sentence of the conversation, both men's jaws dropped.

"Oh crap," whispered Mike. "Pardon my French, but we are so dead if they find out we heard this." Mike's usual tan seemed to puddle on the floor as he blanched.

The President? Homeland Security? Lynch couldn't believe he'd just heard that they were actually involved. Well, aware and complicit, more than involved perhaps, but that was bad enough. His thoughts returned to his conversation with Mike Southworth about conspiracy theories.

How had he put it? Just because they label you a nut-job conspiracy theorist, doesn't mean there isn't a conspiracy.

Yet, who was doing the talking? Who pulled those strings? More importantly, who could he tell and how could they stop this?

Thirty-five

Seamus took the call from Colonel Andrews and headed north to Florissant to meet with the police chief. The man had refused to discuss whatever he had on the phone, and that made Seamus curious.

Seamus walked into the department, and the chief met him at the door to his administrative offices. He looked angry. That piqued Seamus' interest further.

"Come in. Have a seat." He turned toward his secretary and said, "Hold my calls. I don't want to be disturbed."

Seamus raised his brow at that. The man had something serious on his mind. Or had the MCS missed something vital and was Seamus about to become the scapegoat?

"I've been thinking about the report you and Pat Goymerac put together. I know we have names, but have you folks found anything specifically tying them to that mosque or that imam?"

Seamus pondered the question. Not the query itself but why the chief was asking. He already knew that answer. There had to be something else on the man's mind.

"Um, no, sir. Do *you* have something we need to look into?"

Colonel Andrews looked thoughtful for a moment, and then the anger returned to his visage.

"Maybe. That squirrelly Muslim apologist from Homeland Security came by first thing this morning. He'd apparently received a copy of our prelim report to DHS and wasn't happy with some of our, um, terminology, you might say. Started threatening legal action by various Islamic groups."

"Always a possibility, sir. The courts seem to rule on their behalf more often than not these days, so they'll jump at the chance to make waves knowing they'll get press, if nothing else."

"Yeah, yeah. That doesn't concern me. What I found interesting was that when I told the guy we could back up our claims, he got a little fidgety. He's got a tell. He probably doesn't even know about it, but when he gets nervous, his right eye twitches. Doesn't happen when he's just plain upset or angry."

The chief sat back a little in his chair. "So, I thought I'd test him a bit. I told him we had traced the shooters back to a mosque in Detroit and had their names. He'd be learning that soon enough anyway. Man, did his eye set off seismic tremors with that. And when I stated we were closing in on the fifth man, the twitch kept going."

"But we aren't any closer to the fifth man."

"You and I know that. He doesn't. Anyway, all of a sudden this thought hit me. This guy already knows who it is."

"Why would he hold that back?"

"Because I think *he's* the fifth man."

Seamus raised his brow in surprise. That would be a scandal of incredible proportions. Maybe even treasonous proportions. How high would such a plot go?

"Do you have reason to suspect him? I mean, the man is an analyst with Homeland Security. Not much surprises me anymore, but that goes, well—"

"He knew about the VIN numbers being eradicated and that we'd ID'd one shooter."

Seamus thought about that. The one shooter being identified had leaked out. Might the facts about the VIN have leaked as well?

"Could that fact about the VIN numbers have leaked?"

"Well, it's not been in any written report, and if you remember, I told the eight of us at that meeting to keep it close to the vest. My folks haven't talked. Anyone on the MCS?"

Seamus shook his head. "No, sir. You said to keep it under our hats, and I can't imagine Flannigan or Johnstone speaking of it, especially under the circumstances." Seamus felt a bit nervous. He had told Lynch, but he trusted Lynch. "Are you sure about your people?"

"Nothing's 100%, but I trust my folks to follow protocol, not to mention orders. You were with Goymerac in Detroit. Nothing was said there, right?"

"Yes, sir. I mean, no, sir. Nothing was said."

Seamus knew that Flannigan wouldn't divulge that info. Captain Johnstone would have nothing to do with this Fawaz character. After seeing Pat Goymerac in action in Detroit, he held no worries about her. But the other FPD detectives he didn't know well. He would have to rely on the colonel's knowledge and instincts there.

"So, where do we go from here?"

The police chief frowned. "Well, I was hoping you could help me figure that out. I can put someone on him while he's staying at the motel near the school. But I don't have resources to track him if he goes back to Washington."

Seamus thought about it. Without involving the Feds , they were indeed limited. Their only recourse would be to get a legal tap on his cell phone, one that followed him home when he left. He discussed it with Colonel Andrews.

"Okay, I'll get someone to watch him. You see if you can use the MCS to get us that tap."

"I'll need to clear that with Captain Johnstone, but under the circumstance, I don't think he'll object. I think he'd drool over the chance to get something on that guy."

The colonel smiled and nodded. "Good. Keep me in the loop."

Seamus stood and they shook hands. On the way out the door, he pulled his cell phone from his pocket and called the MCS commander. Seamus chuckled to himself. All he had to say was that Fawaz was now a suspect, without offering details, and the captain agreed. Obviously, the Senior Analyst from Homeland Security had made an impression on the commander . . . of the wrong kind.

Johnstone had even offered up a name, a U.S. Attorney he thought would be sympathetic. Seamus hoped she would be more than understanding. It would take a long shot to get the warrant on Colonel Andrews' gut feeling and Fawaz acting squirrelly, as the chief had put it.

He placed the call and was offered an immediate appointment, as soon as he could get to the Federal Court Building. Fifteen minutes later, he stood in Assistant U.S. Attorney Thrin's office, where she stood up from her desk and offered her hand.

"Sgt. O'Connor, I don't think I've had the honor of meeting you before, although your reputation precedes you."

The thin Afro-American woman standing before him reminded him of Sarah, although about ten years older. Like Sarah, she seemed confident and intelligent, which she'd have to be to gain the position she held.

"Ma'am, thank you. It's an honor for me as well."

"Please, have a seat." She pointed to a chair opposite her at her desk. "I understand you have an urgent matter."

"Yes, ma'am, we need a warrant to tap a cell phone." He went on to explain more details about the case. "We have an individual we think might be involved. He's a Senior Analyst with the Department of Homeland Security."

He watched her mouth drop for just a second before regaining her composure.

"You think someone from DHS is involved in this school shooting, and that's based on his knowing what, one fact about the case that you think has been kept highly privileged?"

"It's more than that. The timing of his arrival in town, his size and hair coloring match a man seen on surveillance cameras at the mall where the burning SUV and one shooter were found. His behavior in general." He paused, trying to find more straws to grasp. "Look, I know it's circumstantial, but we're not going to be able to prove any deeper involvement without the phone tap."

"I can't go to a judge with this."

"Please. We have him under surveillance now, but he

says he's heading back to Washington on Monday. Once he's there, we lose him. We don't have the manpower to deal with the police or him there."

She sat back into her chair and stared at him.

"Okay. I-I'll run it by Judge Hopkins. Sometimes the old coot surprises me. But don't get your hopes up. He'll stick with the law. No compromises."

She picked up her phone and made a call. Seamus was aware she had called the judge's office, but his mind fled elsewhere. If push came to shove, could he get his hands on a cell scanner? Sure, but anything he picked up would be inadmissible. And he could get into big trouble, but that had happened before and he'd survived. Well, maybe a federal phone tapping charge was a league above his previous antics. Still . . .

His thoughts were interrupted.

"The judge will be in his office on recess in 15 minutes. I can see him then. Why don't you stop back here in half an hour?"

Seamus left the office, unsure how to kill time. He thought about a quick visit to Sarah at the E.D., but that would take too long. He found himself descending in the elevator and meandering into the lobby. His cell phone rang, and Caller ID revealed Lynch on the other end.

"Shay, we need to talk. Right away. Where are you?"

"I'm at the Federal Court Building. We have a lead on the fifth man. I'm waiting for a judge's decision for a phone tap."

"Yeah, about that. We *need* to talk STAT. Not over a phone, any phone. And don't discuss it with anyone else on your phone either."

“What?”

“I will say again. We *need* to talk. Now. In person.”

“Okay. Um, I can’t leave here for another 30 minutes. Where should we meet?”

“I’ll be waiting for you in the park, Aloe Plaza, across from Union Station.”

Lynch hung up without further explanation, leaving Seamus playing the “what if” game on his own. He walked outside to find a cold drizzle had set in over the city. He didn’t envy Lynch waiting outside for him.

At the 30-minute mark, he returned to the attorney’s office, where she waited for him.

“Judge Hopkins says no. You need more to go on before he’ll snoop on someone from DHS.”

Thirty-six

Lynch wasn't hard to spot in Aloe Park. He alone stood outside in the cold rain. No sooner had Seamus walked up to him, Lynch grabbed his elbow and led him back toward Union Station.

"C'mon. I'm buying you a draught at Maggie O'Brien's." They headed past the station to the restaurant across the street.

"I'm on duty."

"Trust me. You'll need it. Plus, what I have to tell you is best said in a crowded room." He leaned toward Seamus' ear and whispered. "They could be listening to us right now."

"They?"

"Shhhh."

Seamus began to think his friend had lost more than his memory a few months back. But then, recalling all of the strange, even miraculous, events surrounding this case, *anything* might have triggered this behavior.

Inside Maggie O'Brien's the lunch crowd had started. The buzz of conversation filled the room, making the many televisions seem to be on mute.

"Back here," said Lynch. "I stopped in earlier and had them reserve me a table."

Seamus followed Lynch toward the back of the restaurant where an empty table looked conspicuous beyond the crowd at the bar. Lynch took a seat where he could watch the front door. Seamus had never seen him look nervous, ever. Today, he fidgeted like someone had covered his seat with stinging nettle.

The waitress descended upon them as soon as they sat down, carrying two Guinness draughts. Lynch had meant it when he said the drink was on him. They ordered food, and as soon as the waitress left, Lynch leaned toward him.

"Shay, we are *sooo* into something big. We have *got* to be extra careful."

Seamus furrowed his brow and gave Lynch a questioning look.

"I can't say where I got this info, but I can vouch for the guy's integrity and, well, patriotism. He's not one to hunt snipes or fly off investigating conspiracy theories, but we stumbled onto a doozie here."

"Lynch, you sound crazy. Is your head okay?"

Lynch frowned. "Yeah, I'm fine. Look, the SIM card from the bomb revealed one phone number. I, uh, took that number, and a guy I know, well, he did his thing with it and recorded a brief conversation followed by the broadcast of a text message to 12 other phones." He slid a piece of paper from his coat, opened it, and slid it over in front of Seamus.

Seamus read the words and felt his gut growl. The words were clear. Only martyrs could expect virgins in paradise. His mouth dropped and the look on his face must have been obvious to his friend.

"A minimum of a dozen martyrs have been set loose on the country. They're starting a war," said Lynch. "Down at the bottom is the list of numbers. You need to trace those phones and alert those communities. Of course, the attacks could occur anywhere, at anytime, but with the numbers, maybe we can head off some of these folks."

Seamus needed to return to Judge Hopkins personally. But then, what could he tell the man? That they had gotten this info from an unknown hacker performing an illegal phone tap? No, that was a five-gallon bucket of snakes he didn't want to open.

Yet, as Lynch had just said, they could find out where the phones were registered, or at least sold, and alert those police departments. Where might things travel from there? Only God knew. After all, the first shooters had driven in from Detroit. These "martyrs" could strike anywhere.

Seamus' mind raced, formulating a list of actions to take. When Lynch spoke up again, the words didn't register at first.

Lynch poked his hand on the table. "I said, there's more. Pay attention."

Seamus looked up to see Lynch pulling his phone from his coat.

"I told you we have a recorded conversation. It lasts less than a minute, but you need to hear it."

Lynch flipped through the apps on his phone and handed it to Seamus. Seamus saw that he had accessed an audio clip, so he hit the play button and held it to his ear. A minute later, he replayed it. No, he hadn't misheard it the first time. He felt his face blanch, as if his pasty white complexion could get paler. He mumbled something Gaelic under his breath.

"See? This is something waaayyy beyond us, Shay. I

mean, who would believe us to begin with, and how can we use this information that wasn't exactly legally obtained? Who do we talk to about this? Everyone in the federal system would have to be suspect until we cleared them."

Seamus nodded. The information they now had was dangerous and potentially destabilizing for the country. He had friends who'd begun stockpiling weapons and ammo, expressed fear and distrust of the government, and made contingency plans for a social meltdown. He'd thought them nuts. Now, they were about to be proven correct.

"Any thoughts on who was speaking?"

Lynch shook his head. "None, but the one guy, the leader, has to be well placed if he's in a position to talk with our pr—" He changed to a whisper. ". . . our leaders. I can tell you the one guy, the guy in possession of the phone, was in North County when the call came through, but he was on the move so his position couldn't be pinpointed."

A gnawing worry struck him "What . . . what time was that?"

"Early. Between eight and nine is all I have."

That info hit Seamus like a sandbag to the solar plexus. He had just provided crucial information to a federal U.S. Attorney and judge, people he didn't personally know and couldn't vouch for.

"Lynch, tell me, what's been your experience with U.S. Attorneys?"

"What do you mean?"

"If you needed a warrant from a federal judge and

went through one of the prosecutors to get it. What's been your experience?"

"You'd better have a slam dunk case, and not waste their time. They expect the police to make the case."

Seamus sighed and repeated that Gaelic phrase under his breath. Had he just given up their fifth man to the wrong people?

Seamus went on to explain to Lynch that they suspected Fawaz, a DHS Senior Analyst, of being the fifth man. In light of the recorded conversation, Seamus was willing to bet his house on that now.

Lynch surprised him by turning his attention to a nearby television. Seamus followed his gaze toward the TV to see a Headline News reporter speaking in front of the United Nations building.

Lynch jumped to his feet and rushed to the bar. He called over the nearest barkeep.

"You guys have DVRs on any of these? I need to hear the beginning of that news report."

The barkeep shook her head. "Sorry."

"Can you turn that TV's volume up?"

She nodded and shrugged, and grabbed a remote from behind the bar. Pointing it toward the television in question, she raised the volume until people started to complain.

Lynch walked closer to the unit. Seamus stood and followed.

"What's up?"

"The beginning of this segment on the United Nations. A man's voice caught my attention."

Seamus gave him a questioning look. "How could you

even hear it? Over all this din, I can't even tell the sound is on."

"Don't know. I just did." He raised his hand to keep Seamus from responding. "Look. Listen."

The reporter continued. "Yesterday's resignation of Secretary General Ban Ki-Moon from the United Nations caught many people by surprise. Even more surprising, however, has been the quick announcement of his replacement. Little is publicly known about Karolus Karling, yet those in the higher echelons had nothing but praise for his selection. We expect we will learn more about this man, who has already promised a sweeping plan for peace in the Middle East. Let's move back inside for more of his acceptance speech."

The scene moved to the great hall of the General Assembly. At the podium stood a tall, slender man with a full head of jet-black hair. He appeared athletic, poised, and confident.

Lynch rushed back to the bar and grabbed the remote from the unsuspecting barkeep. He returned to his spot and pushed the volume higher, shushing those around him who began to complain. When one man stood and assumed a threatening position, Seamus intervened and flashed his badge. The man backed off.

"Just give us a minute," he said to those around them.

"And so, ladies and gentlemen of the General Assembly, the time has come for a new world order. One in which peace comes to the Middle East, and the United States, Russia, and China no longer feel the need to flex their nationalistic muscle. . ."

Lynch quieted the television and returned the remote

to the bar. Seamus reclaimed their table and as Lynch
again sat across from him, they stared silently at each
other. They needed no more proof. The new leader of the
U.N. was the man on the recording.

Thirty-seven

Amy had walked into work just before lunchtime, not expecting to do anything. After all, her forced "medical leave" didn't end for two more days. She wanted to share her good news, but more importantly, she wanted to talk with her boss about the future, now that she was to be married. She had found Craig Sheehan a reasonable man in the past and had no expectation of his being otherwise now.

She arrived at the COO's office and, seeing him at his desk, knocked on the doorpost. He looked up and smiled.

"Amy! Good to see you, but you aren't due back until Monday."

She smiled back and walked into the office. "I know, but I wanted to talk with you."

"Oh?" His face transformed into a visage of concern. "Is something wrong? I thought Doctor Lange had released you for full duty."

"Oh no, nothing like that." She smiled and waved her left ring finger in front of him.

A smile captured his face and a laugh emerged from his mouth as he stood up and walked around the desk. "Hey, congratulations!" He seemed intent on a congratulatory hug, but stopped and extended an awkward hand toward her. She knew he was a "hugger", but that would have been equally awkward for her, so she accepted his hand.

"Do I know the lucky guy? And does he know how truly lucky he is?"

He pointed to one of the chairs in front of his desk and then took the other himself, rather than return to his seat behind the desk. Amy sat down.

"Richard. Richard Nichols."

Craig nodded in understanding, although to Amy's knowledge, the two men had never met.

"I've heard he's a good man. I read about what he did to get that Darko character. Sounds like you're an equally lucky lady."

"I am." She thought about Richard's close call with the bomb the previous morning and quivered at the thought of just *how* lucky she was. "He took me out for dinner last night and surprised me. He even arranged for a party afterwards."

Craig chuckled. "Must have been pretty confident about your answer. I shook in my boots when I asked my wife. I was sure she'd turn me down." He paused and turned a bit in the chair to face her more fully. "So . . ." He put his fingers to his temples and closed his eyes, like some sideshow mind reader. "I sense you want to talk to me about your job here."

She laughed as he resumed his normal posture.

"Yes."

"I figured as much. I've been down this road before. You're hoping for a normal life as a newlywed and don't want to be spending nights away from Richard."

Amy nodded.

"Well, Amy, right now you're fortunate that we have need for you full-time in the training position."

"Thank you, but actually, I don't want to give up flying totally, and I don't want my skills to get rusty. Is it possible to balance the two?"

"Hey, we can balance it anyway you like . . . once the training manuals are revamped and the audit is over. Right now, I need you just where you are. Is that okay?"

She waggled her head as if saying "I guess so, but . . ."

"Look, I'd like you to become our permanent training officer. We could have you fly special cases and maybe call on you for last minute substitutions, if that's alright with you."

"Special cases?"

"Sure. Like that long distance transfer we did a few months back from Farmington to Nashville. I had a special crew from here fly the patient to Memphis where we had another team ready to fly her the rest of the way. We don't like to pull a team out from their call area for those cases."

Amy thought about that. She liked that idea, although transfers wouldn't involve anyone with acute injuries, she would be able to keep up her trauma skills by flying as a substitute. She liked this idea.

She extended her hand to Craig. "It's a deal."

He smiled and shook her hand. "Fantastic. I'll let the board know we have a full-time training officer again. Oh, and you do know that you'll have to travel on occasion to give classes at our other regional centers, right?"

"Yes, I know that. I get my own helicopter for those trips . . . right?" The inflection in her voice matched that in his statement-turned-question.

He laughed. "Actually . . . it's almost like that. We try to coordinate a visit from the head honchos at the same time, so everyone flies in together. You're usually home in time for dinner."

He stood and she followed suit.

"So, when do I get to meet Richard?"

"Soon. I promise to bring him around. He's . . ." She started to say "really busy right now" but didn't want to get into why. ". . . been asking me to show him around here. He wants a ride sometime, too."

"I'm sure that could be arranged.

Lynch and Seamus left the restaurant with no clear guidance. What they had discovered was so monumentally huge, they felt overwhelmed by it. How could they combat it? And if they "fought," would they have any chance of winning? Unlikely. Yet, to admit defeat was not in either man's nature.

Lynch did know one man he could trust. Fifteen minutes later he drove through "downtown" Ferguson and into the tree-lined neighborhood of century-old homes. He pulled into the Southworth's driveway and hoped Mike was home.

"Lynch, it's good to see you," said Mary as she answered the bell and met him at the door. "Come in. I'll get Mike from his shop."

"That's okay. I can head out there, if that's okay."

"Sure. You know the way."

Lynch walked through the restored 1904 home and felt amazed it had only been several weeks since he'd called this "home." He still felt at peace here.

He walked through the kitchen and out the back door.

Mike's shop filled the home's original carriage house, a detached structure that sat in the backyard overlooking their sunken patio from the east side and garden pond, complete with waterfall, to the south. Lynch walked along the brick walkway, under the vine-covered pergola and into the shop.

Mike looked up as Lynch opened the door and a smile lit up his face. He powered down his table saw, flipped off the dust collector, and removed his hearing protection.

"Lynch, to what do we owe this honor?"

Lynch took a deep breath and replied, "You might not consider it an honor after you hear what I have to say."

Mike's brow lifted. "Oh? Want a beer?"

Lynch shook his head. He'd downed a second draught at the restaurant after hearing the newscast. He didn't need to risk a DWI pullover by continuing to drink, as much as he wanted another one.

Mike pulled out the shop's two stools and offered one to him. "This okay, or do you want to go inside the house?"

"This is fine."

Lynch had decided to turn to Mike because he valued the man's Godly perspective. Lynch had seen the man's faith in action and wanted to have that kind of belief and trust. He had become "born again" in this home, and Mike had become his mentor. And for something so huge, Lynch realized only God could help.

He proceeded to tell Mike what he and Seamus had come across. Mike's face became more and more serious as Lynch progressed with his report.

As Lynch finished, Mike sat silent for a moment and then replied, "So, it really *is* about to happen." The man shook his head as if trying to come to grips with whatever thoughts he had at the moment.

"What is?"

"Lynch, I've mentioned the word eschatology to you before, right?"

Lynch nodded. "Yes. It has to do with the Bible's prophecies about what's called 'the end times.' "

"That's right. A lot of Bible scholars over the centuries have put a lot of time into postulating when that time was coming and what it would be like. The Bible says we're not to know the day and hour of Christ's return, and date setting has always ended up badly for those who try it. But . . ."

Mike paused, pursing his lips.

"The Bible also says we're to be aware of the season. That is, seeing the events around us that should make us look for the Lord's return. I think that's what we're about to witness. A turn of events that will lead to Christ's return."

Mike moved into teaching mode and for the next ten minutes gave Lynch a synopsis, as he saw it, of "the end times." The coming one-world government, economy, and religion as revealed by the book of Revelation. How the recent events in the Ukraine might lead to a strengthening of Iran's world position, which could embolden them, along with other Muslim nations, to strike out at Israel and fulfill the prophecies of Ezekiel, chapters 38 and 39. The pros of "the rapture," an event where God's people would be removed from the earth, as well as its cons, that the idea was based loosely on only a few scriptures. And that, like Noah, God's people might be called to go *through* the rough times, not be "airlifted" away.

Lynch had no problem absorbing what Mike told him. And as his friend spoke, he began to see the world from a different pair of eyes.

"Do you know what happens next week?" asked Mike.

Lynch shook his head.

"We'll see the beginning of a lunar tetrad."

"Huh?"

"April 15th, Passover, will give us a full lunar eclipse, a blood moon. It is the first of four lunar eclipses, all blood moons, and all occurring on Jewish holidays. In-between the lunar eclipses this year and again next year, we'll also have full solar eclipses. This won't happen again on the Jewish holidays for hundreds of years."

"Okay."

"The Book of Joel tells us 'the sun will be turned into darkness and the moon into blood before the great and awesome day of the Lord comes.' God told us He put the sun, moon, and stars in the heavens as signs for us. It's not a coincidence that these signs in the heavens are coming at a time when mankind seems about to make its global society a reality. I'm not trying to set a date, and I can't tell you what's about to happen, but I don't think it'll be pretty. We need, more than ever, to focus on Christ and follow Him."

Lynch at once felt both a burden and lightness. The information he possessed seemed to weigh him down. Yet, his recent choice to accept Christ gave him hope.

"So, what do we do? Shouldn't we alert people about what might happen? If we're really dealing with a dozen or more suicide bombers, hundreds, maybe thousands of people might die. It could start a literal war against Muslims in this nation and that would take down our country."

Mike looked pensive and didn't respond right away.

"I can't speak for anyone else, but I have my opinions. I don't think the power behind this really cares. Fundamentalism in any form is a threat to the ecumenical, all-paths-lead-to-God religion they want the world to believe. As for civil unrest and a possible war here, that might be just what they want. That would enable them to declare martial law, which in turn would let them take guns from private owners, confiscate property, take over banks, and more. All in the name of peace, while seeking to consolidate their power and dictatorial rule."

A year ago, Lynch would have seen that comment as crazy. Now, he saw it making sense.

"So again, I get back to my question, what do we do?"

Mike sighed.

"It might not do any good. It might even precipitate events faster, but I've always believed a good offense is the best defense."

Thirty-eight

Seamus drove straight to the Hampton Inn, where Fawaz had told Colonel Andrews he was staying. He wanted to confront the man but knew that would only cause trouble and not help him reach his goal of indicting the man.

He drove once around the building, looking for the police department's stakeout. No one. All of the cars in the parking lot were empty. As he sat idling near the empty outdoor pool, his cell phone rang.

"O'Connor, next door, at Meyer's Barn."

He chuckled. He'd recognize Pat Goymerac's voice anytime and anywhere after their stint together in Detroit. He looked up and saw the car. She wiggled her fingers in reply.

He drove out of the lot and into the adjacent one. Along the east side, next to the motel, the lot held five parking slots, and the detective's car occupied one of them. He parked behind her and joined her in her car.

"Nice view, but what if he leaves on the other side of the building?"

"We'll adjust. Right now, his car is parked right there, third from the right. If he leaves, we can follow without seeming so apparent. If he returns and parks on the other side, we'll use the bank's lot, or Arby's."

"Ahh, and if he leaves by the road in back?"

"We have a secondary at Arby's or Starbucks."

"I thought Andrews tasked only one car."

"Yeah, well, we want this guy. We got some reservists to volunteer during the day."

"Well, I really want this guy more than you can believe. I learned some things today. Things that I'm not free to divulge yet. And if this guy is who we think he is, this case will take on a whole new dimension."

Goymerac gave him a funny look.

"Sorry, guess I shouldn't have said anything, but this guy *is* crucial to more than one case. I wish I had an opportunity to talk with him."

"That could be arranged."

Seamus thought about that. "Not officially. I just want to hear what he sounds like."

"That could be arranged, too. The clerk says he takes off right after sunset to eat and had asked for someplace with Middle Eastern food when he checked in. You could probably strike up a conversation at the restaurant. Maybe ask for food recommendations."

Seamus looked at his watch. Sunset was still hours away, and he had more important things to do between then and now.

"Okay. Maybe I'll come back about then."

Goymerac nodded. "Don't look for me. The next shift will have taken over. I think it'll be Schulz. Do you know him?"

Seamus shook his head.

"Shaved head. Built like a bull. He'll be driving an unmarked light grey sedan. By the way, don't ever arm wrestle with him, unless you like to be embarrassed. I think the guy could flip a car on its side with one hand."

Seamus laughed. "Thanks. I'll remember that. Gotta go."

He climbed out of her car and back into his own. He had some phone numbers to trace.

After a couple of phone calls, Lynch found Brad at home and rushed to the house. He and Mike had concluded that Brad would be the best offense they could mount. Besides, as Brad's chief of security, he would be remiss not to warn him of the danger facing him. He'd been targeted twice. Lynch didn't want the third time to be successful.

After their greetings, Brad ushered Lynch into his study and shut the door. Lynch noticed a large-screen TV on one wall, using picture-in-picture to display five news channels at one time.

"Drink?" asked Brad.

Lynch wondered what it was that made him look so thirsty today.

"Iced tea, if you have some. Otherwise, water is fine. Thanks."

"Be right back."

Brad left the room and Lynch wandered along the nearby wall. Photos of Brad and his family occupied spaces between those of Brad with this conservative celebrity or that politician. Lynch had been unaware of the extent of the connections Bradley Graham had made leading to this run for the Senate.

"Cara's getting drinks for us," Brad stated as he reentered the room. "Have a seat."

Once both were comfortably seated, Lynch on an

overstuffed couch and Brad in the adjacent upholstered chair, Brad looked at Lynch closely. Lynch felt as if the man's eyes could scan his vital organs.

"You look worried," Brad stated after a moment of silent scrutiny.

Lynch nodded. "I . . . we . . . have reason to be."

There was a knock at the door and Cara appeared with a serving tray. The tray held two glasses with ice, a small pitcher of tea, lemon slices, a bowl of sugar and a small plate of cookies. After setting it on the table in front of them, she stepped over to Lynch and reached for his hand.

"Lynch, I want to thank you. Your awareness and quick thinking saved my husband's life yesterday. I owe you more than you can imagine. Thank you."

Lynch felt a blush rise to his cheeks.

"Y-you're welcome. But, you don't owe me anything. I was just doing my job."

"And doing it well," she replied. "I *do* owe you. If I can help you with anything, you let me know."

She turned toward her husband.

"Dear, I need to run to the store. Is there anything you need me to get?"

Brad started to reply, but Lynch interrupted. "Mrs. Graham, um, Cara, you might want to hear what I have to say. It's going to affect you, too."

Brad raised his brow, looking curious. His wife looked at him and he nodded. Lynch scooted to one end of the couch and gave her room to sit down.

"So, what do you have for us?" asked Brad.

Lynch embarked on a detailed account of his

morning's discoveries, leaving out only the identity of the man who provided them. He would not jeopardize Mike Jurgesmeyer's life, nor break that trust. Besides, they might have a future need for his services.

"In the end, I came to you for two reasons. First, as your chief of security, I felt you needed to be warned. You've already been targeted twice. Second, the only way to fight this is to bring it into the light of day. You have the biggest platform to do that right now."

Brad folded his hands, closed his eyes, and looked upward. Lynch expected to see tears and worry on Cara's face. Instead, he saw a steely grit and determined-to-fight look.

After several minutes, Brad opened his eyes and looked first at Cara and then to Lynch.

"Do you have the recording and the phone numbers?"

"Yes."

"Do we have anything more on those numbers?"

"Seamus O'Connor is supposed to be working on it and alerting those police departments."

"Which is unlikely to stop anything. There are too many soft targets. Have we identified who possesses the phone?"

"We believe so, but we haven't confirmed it yet."

"And just how are you planning to do that?"

"O'Connor wants to hear him speak, maybe get him into an innocent conversation. We don't think he knows who O'Connor is. Anyway, if we can get an audio sample of his voice and put it together with the voice on the recording, we'll have him."

"Why not just try a frontal approach?" Cara spoke in

a calm, confident manner. "He's got to keep the phone on him. Approach him while ringing the number. If you witness him answering, and can identify the phone on him, you've got him, too."

Brad looked at his wife and smiled. "She's always been the direct one."

Lynch smiled. "That might work, *if* he has the phone on him. If it was me, I'd toss the phone after launching any big move and get a new one."

"But he's not you. He sounds like he thinks he's above the law. Maybe he's just cocky enough to think he can get away with it, without taking the precautions you or I might take."

Brad had a point. If Seamus succeeded in capturing an audio sample, it might take the crime lab days to compare the voice samples . . . *if* they would be willing to do so with an illegally taken sample. That was a huge "if."

With the direct route, they might have an immediate answer. If not, they could still fall back to the voice recognition route.

"You're right. It's worth a try."

"Good. While you're working on that, I'm going to set up a press conference for tomorrow morning. They've been expecting one since the bombing. We'll give 'em more than they bargained for."

Karolus had finished talking with several groups of guests as they arrived in scheduled waves for his welcome reception and luncheon. He had never before felt so energized. He had been groomed for the position he had assumed that morning. The world was at a crossroads, and he would help lead it down a new, enlightened path.

He felt privileged. Indeed, he *was* privileged. The man who had groomed him was someone he once had felt unworthy to stand before. *That* man would lead them to a higher state, a level of peace and co-existence men had only dreamt about in earlier centuries. And *that* man had chosen Karolus to assist him by leading the august body of diplomats who would help make it possible, the United Nations.

Based on his heritage, education, and intellect, Karolus had been chosen to initiate the peace process, to speak on that man's behalf, and to prepare the world for his leadership. Rome would become his home, and people across the globe would come to him for guidance, to hear his wisdom.

"Sir?"

Karolus turned to see his aide behind him.

"Yes, Francois."

"You asked to be notified about, you know."

Karolus appreciated the man's discretion. There were ears about them that didn't need to hear what his aide might say.

Karolus turned and walked to a corner of the room. Francois followed.

"Yes, proceed. Have things begun?"

"Yes, and no. I just received word that the first suicide bomber raised suspicion as he approached the Mall of America. A security guard ordered him to stand down, at which point he ran, fell, and prematurely detonated himself, causing no other injuries. Police departments around the country are on the alert and Homeland Security has been forced to raise the threat level, or risk looking incompetent. Or worse."

This was not the news Karolus expected. He frowned and began to rub his chin in contemplation.

"It appears several major police departments were warned of possible threats based on phone numbers tracked to their cities. I believe these might have been phone numbers used by Fawaz to initiate the attacks, but I cannot confirm that."

"And Fawaz?"

"He has become the prime suspect in St. Louis. Our friend, the assistant U.S. Attorney, called to inform us that a detective approached her for a search warrant and phone tap. He had no case, but she encouraged him in order to get the information. The number provided to her *is* Fawaz's, the phone we've used to contact him."

"Is our resource still in St. Louis?"

"Yes, sir."

"Have him remove Senior Analyst Fawaz from our employ."

Thirty-nine

Fawaz started to leave for dinner but upon reaching the outside door, he noticed a dead hawk in the parking lot. It appeared to have been struck by a vehicle. Perhaps it had been hungry and too focused upon its prey to see the threat coming toward it. No matter the circumstances, Fawaz saw it as an omen. He, too, had been focused. Did he need to be alert to a potential threat?

Well, Fawaz was hungry, but perhaps this would be a good night to eat in. He returned to his room and found the motel's amenities folder. Inside it, he found a list of restaurants that would deliver right to his room. There were several Chinese food and pizza establishments on the list. A sports bar by the name of Mattingly's would deliver its American fare.

"Ah, that is more to my liking," he said to himself as he saw a listing for Simply Thai. He checked to make sure he had adequate cash, which he did, and called the restaurant.

As he awaited his order of fresh spring rolls and salmon with teriyaki sauce, he turned on Headline News. He watched reruns of Karolus Karling's first address to the U.N., with clips from his welcome luncheon. Malaysia Flight 370 still had not been located, despite wreckage adrift in the south Indian Ocean that once appeared consistent with the plane.

The clock moved to the top of the hour, and he

watched the lead story with mounting anxiety. A suicide bomber had been foiled in his attempt to kill shoppers at the Mall of America. The security guard involved stated the man seemed unusually dressed and nervous. When asked to stop and show some ID, he turned to run, stumbled, and exploded upon hitting the ground. No one else was injured, and only minor damage had been done to the mall.

Thinking back to the dead hawk, Fawaz knew where his threat would come from. He would not be blinded or distracted.

Yet, this was not his fault. The attack had been planned for the next day, a busy weekend day with a new cold front coming through to make bulky clothing less conspicuous. The man had been overeager and emotionally ill prepared. His handler had not been equipped for that. Now, police departments across the country would be on high alert. Fawaz could not be blamed for that, but he would be.

The knock on the door startled him. He grabbed $30 from his wallet to cover the meal, tax, delivery, and tip, and approached the door. Caution surrounded him.

He didn't dare use the peephole. He'd seen that on television. As soon as the glass darkens, POP! The assassin shoots the viewer through the eye. Yet, he didn't want to open the door, even with the security chain. That, too, could result in a deadly shooting.

"Who is it?"

"Simply Thai with food order."

The voice and accent sounded right. He would chance it. He grabbed the amenities folder and held it up to the eyepiece. No bullet. He opened the door to the extent of the chain and saw a slight, Asian man, early twenties, holding a plastic bag with a foam food container inside. It smelled delightful.

He released the chain and opened the door wide enough to complete his transaction. The man held out the bag, and as Fawaz reached for it, the man's other hand reached behind his back and grabbed something black.

Fawaz flinched, his heart racing. As he thought about diving behind the door to avoid the coming bullet, he saw the man open a black vinyl folder and pull out his bill.

"Cost is $23.74."

Fawaz sighed in relief and handed the man the $30. "Keep the change."

"Hey, thanks, mister."

A smile filled the man's face and he sauntered off down the hall. Fawaz looked both ways down the hall and saw nothing suspicious.

He returned to the television and ate his meal. The food was good, he admitted to himself, but he'd lost his appetite. His mind kept returning to his predicament.

The next morning Fawaz awoke on the couch. He must have fallen asleep there somewhere around two a.m. despite the difficulty he'd had doing so. His mind revolved around a torrent of speculation and fear. That vortex had kept him awake and now filled his mind as he awoke.

The image of the dead hawk filled his consciousness again. His family's crest included the falcon and bow and arrow, symbols of the hunter. Was the hawk representing the falcon and foretelling his own demise? He tried to eliminate that thought, but the sign seemed obvious.

Taking extra precaution, he peered outside through his window. He half expected a bullet to shatter the glass and find its mark, but nothing happened. He did, however, notice a car in the adjacent parking lot. The small deli restaurant that had once operated there had closed months earlier according to the front desk staff.

As he watched, a second car pulled in behind the first, and a man, his arm in a sling, emerged to join the other driver, whom he saw now was a woman. He felt relief at that revelation. A man and a woman meeting in a closed parking lot might mean nothing more than a convenient place to meet. Perhaps something immoral would occur. He had come to expect as much in this decadent western society.

He felt confident, however, that they were not associated with The Assembly. Karolus Karling might have a man in St. Louis, and Fawaz knew to be cautious, but the Director never utilized women.

His gut grumbled. He hadn't eaten all of his dinner, and cold salmon held no appeal for breakfast. His habit since taking up residence in the motel had been to grab coffee and a muffin for breakfast at the adjacent Starbucks. He could not risk that today.

His intuition today told him to run. To head straight for the rental car return, go to the airport, and fly somewhere unexpected. If he could keep one step ahead of The Assembly, he might keep his head.

He took a quick shower, dressed, and packed his belongings. After checking out, he darted to his car, threw his belongings into the back seat to minimize his exposure outside, and climbed behind the wheel. He did not delay and moved toward the back of the parking lot. He would take the side street, past Starbucks, to exit the lot.

Fawaz could always grab a quick meal from a fast-food drive-through lane. Of more concern, he hadn't decided what to do with the manila envelope that now sat on the front passenger seat. He had applied adequate postage, but he had no address.

He didn't dare send it to a family member, which would place that person in jeopardy. He had considered Imam al-Bashara but had realized the man would only hand over its contents to the same people Fawaz wished to penalize for his death.

Perhaps he had no need to send it. Again, he analyzed the probabilities of staying a step ahead of The Assembly. And, again, he chose to ignore the poor odds.

Fawaz needed to eat. He could wait no longer, but he refused to eat at a McDonalds or similar place that fried its foods on the same griddle as they fried their pork sausages. He looked about for a St. Louis Bread Company. At home, he knew the company by its Panera title and enjoyed their food. Another advantage: the place would be crowded and public. He could safely eat there and then progress to the airport.

He had not risked turning on his phone, so he followed the GPS in his car. To his chagrin, he overshot the turn for the restaurant. He performed a quick U-turn at the first opportunity and headed back. As he drove, he spotted the same car that he'd seen near the motel, the car with the woman.

Coincidence? Perhaps. And maybe Allah was with him after all. Who was the woman who seemed to follow him? He would not have seen her had he made the correct turn. And who was the man who had met with her? Was he nearby?

He sat to the back, away from the windows, and took time to enjoy his breakfast. Rather than coffee, he savored a hot tea that reminded him of his parents. And the poppy seed muffin brought his grandmother to mind. All three had passed on into Paradise, and while at times he missed them, he felt no hurry to join them.

He pulled his phone out and began to scan the map for potential destinations. The Assembly had people everywhere, but he might find peace in a southern, conservative, and more rural area of the country. He decided to fly direct to Houston and move south from there. Maybe he'd settle in Victoria, or end up near the border in Brownsville.

While he had the phone out, he had one more thing to do. He composed a final text message to those groups on his list. As he completed it, a red-haired man entered the restaurant and looked his way before turning around and leaving.

The man's appearance was enough to spook him. He arose, paid his bill, and rushed outside. He would begin to drive, and at the first stop, he would review the message and send it.

As he neared the rental, he saw the man with the sling. He walked toward Fawaz with his cell phone held to his ear with his free arm. At that moment, Fawaz's cell began to ring. Confused, he stopped to glance at the number displayed by Caller ID. The number was local, and unknown to him.

At that moment, the red-haired man moved toward him from a different direction. He turned to flee, only to see a woman approaching. She had a badge on her pantsuit jacket and a handgun at the ready.

He fumbled with his phone to get back to the text message screen. He needed to send the message now or he'd not get the chance.

He never saw what hit him.

At Seamus' request, Lynch had met with Detective Pat Goymerac at the Myer Barn Deli lot soon after her arrival there to monitor their suspect. They were discussing his plan when the man bolted from the front doors, running for his car. The secondary car had spotted him leaving by the back lot and turning north.

Seamus was en route to the police department when Lynch called, and quickly picked up the tail. Lynch coordinated the effort, and, at the first major intersection, he had Seamus fall back to let Goymerac take the lead. He thought they had been detected when the man suddenly turned back. His concern turned to relief when the man drove into the Bread Company lot and entered the restaurant.

In the back lot, the three cars converged.

"Shay, good thing you were where you were. We might have lost him."

Seamus nodded. "Wouldn't want to miss out on the fun."

Goymerac joined them outside Seamus' car.

"So, what's our plan?"

Lynch knew this place like the lumps in his mattress. He could always find a comfortable spot.

"He parked in front, so no matter which door he tries to leave by, he has to come back there to get the car. Pat, you find a spot in the east side. Shay, you take the west. I'll come in the front while dialing the phone number. If the phone rings and he answers, move in on him and we'll have him."

The trio moved into position and waited. Twenty minutes later, Fawaz still hadn't emerged from the building.

Lynch's phone rang. Seamus.

"How long does it take to eat and drink some coffee?" He sounded impatient. "Could he have gone out the back to lose us? Maybe he had a second car."

Lynch didn't think so but couldn't discount the possibility. "You know what he looks like, right? Go on inside and see if you can flush him out."

Lynch watched his friend enter the building, only to exit a minute later, flashing a thumb up as he moved back into position. Whatever Seamus had done, it worked. Two minutes later, their subject rushed from the front door.

Lynch jumped from his car and started walking toward the man. He'd already entered the number into his phone and had only to press "Call" as he left the car. Seconds later, ring tones came from the man's phone.

Fawaz looked at his phone and appeared confused. The man looked about to see Goymerac and Seamus heading his way and started to fumble with his phone.

Lynch picked up his pace. He didn't know what the man was about to do, but he didn't want him to finish whatever it was. The trio was no more than ten feet away from Fawaz when blood spurted from his forehead and the back half of his head splashed across the car next to him.

Lynch pulled his own gun, dropped to one knee, and looked toward the direction of the bullet at the same time as Fawaz fell to the ground. Traffic on the main road appeared normal. He saw nothing unusual. At first. A moment later, a sense of movement in the sky caught his eye, and he focused on it to see a drone aircraft leaving the scene.

Forty

Colonel Andrews arrived first after Goymerac placed the call to dispatch. She, with the help of the two men, had cordoned off the area. As an officer of the local department, she also had taken control of the scene, to the dismay of the patrons and staff of the Bread Company.

"You say you saw a drone leaving the area after he was shot?" asked the police chief.

Lynch nodded. "Yes, sir, and this wasn't some Amazon delivery. No four-prop toy controlled by a smartphone. The thing had to have a wingspan of ten, 15 feet. I can only guess its altitude when I saw it, but it was clearly climbing." He offered the colonel an image on his cell phone. He had tried to capture the drone with his camera. "By the time I could switch to my camera, the thing was pretty far off. But I think you can still see it well enough to corroborate what I saw."

The colonel gazed at the image, nodded, and turned to an officer nearby. "Hester, check with Lambert air traffic control and see if they have anything on a drone aircraft in the area." The officer scrambled to his marked patrol car.

The two men moved closer to the body. Goymerac now had the assistance of two colleagues, and together they began processing the scene. Evidence markers and collection bags were sparse. Other than body parts and a dropped cell phone, little else in the area mattered. Even the photography of the scene took less than five minutes.

Lynch stared at the dead man and marveled how intact he looked, from the front. The man's suit seemed immaculate, expertly pressed, and untouched. He noted a small American flag lapel pin and felt incredulous at the hypocrisy of it.

The Death Investigator arrived within 15 minutes. The man took one look at the body and shook his head.

"I'd say the cause of death is obvious."

Lynch wanted to smack his forehead and say, "Duh," at the DI's comment, but he held his tongue. He had, after all, witnessed the whole thing. He, Seamus, and Goymerac would all have to provide written statements.

The DI continued, ". . . but look at the trajectory. Top of the forehead blowing out the brainstem and upper neck." He paused and looked around. "There's nothing around here high enough. Where did this shot come from?"

Lynch started to say where, but the colonel stopped him with a subtle shake of the head. He was correct. Restaurant patrons were slowly being excused from the building. They didn't need someone overhearing that the man was shot by a drone.

"Anyone see the bullet fragment? You can't tell the bullet size by the size of the entry wound, but this one was huge by our usual standards. Maybe 30-caliber range. Someone wanted to be sure this guy didn't survive."

The DI began checking the man's pockets. Technically, everything on the body fell into the jurisdiction of the Medical Examiner. His eyes bugged out as he discovered the man's Homeland Security credentials. He let out a low whistle as he handed them to the police chief. Those creds were followed by his driver's license.

"We know who he was."

Lynch saw Seamus walk back to them from the area around the street.

"Don't see anything of use in that direction, but if it was a dro—" Both the colonel and Lynch gave him a "shhh" and he caught himself. "Yeah, if that took him out, that shell casing could be far, far way.

Lynch's attention went to the cell phone on the ground. He had no authority to pick it up and inspect it, but he remembered that Fawaz was fumbling to do something on it before the shot came. In the commotion that followed, Lynch had forgotten that.

"Shay, the phone. He was trying to do something with it before he died."

Seamus consulted Goymerac first. She had finished photographing it and offered him an evidence bag. With gloved hands, he picked up the phone. "Another LG 221C. Seems to be the terrorists' phone of choice these days." The screen lit up and Seamus' eyes widened. "Whoa. Didn't want the guy dead, but I'm glad he didn't finish this."

He held up the phone for the colonel and Lynch to see. The screen revealed a draft text message to be sent to 12 numbers, numbers that seemed familiar to Lynch. He pulled a sheet of paper from his pocket, unfolded it, and compared the numbers on the screen with those on the paper. A match.

The screen read, "Power grid. One week. Send two teams to designated targets."

"Pat, did you get the screen?"

She shook her head and lifted her camera to her eye. With a click, the screenshot became evidence.

Seamus pressed the 'Home' button and navigated to "Settings." After a moment, he found the phone's ID settings and confirmed the number of the phone as that which had broadcast the text the day before. He looked at Lynch and nodded.

Lynch nodded back. Within the hour, Brad would be holding his press conference, and Colonel Andrews needed insertion into the loop.

Seamus faced the police chief. "Colonel, we've got more information on this. I was coming to brief you when I got diverted to help tail Fawaz. Since Lynch is here, I'll let him fill you in."

Lynch proceeded to tell the colonel what he had learned, followed by his and Seamus' discovery as to who was behind it. He again withheld *who* had provided the information. He played the recorded conversation for the colonel.

"I recognize Fawaz's voice there. And you say the top guy is the new Secretary General of the U.N.?" The police chief shook his head and took a breath. "Lynch, do you know what this implies?"

"I do, sir."

Seamus nodded in agreement.

"How do we even begin to go after someone like that?"

"We expose him, sir."

"And the President? And the head of DHS? I mean, who would we call to arrest them? What if all the chiefs—

FBI, CIA, ATF, Secret Service . . . who could we trust?" He paused for an answer no one there could give him. "And if they took out one of their own with a . . ." He looked about. ". . . a you-know-what, then none of *us* is safe either."

That comment hit Lynch hard.

"Brad Graham! Oh crap. I need to get to Brad." He bolted toward his car.

Forty-one

Under the watchful eye of his security detail, Brad welcomed the group of three into his home. Jim Collins and Sheila West had been here before, but this was a first for Cindy Dye. Few employees from his company had been guests in his home. *Maybe that should change*, he thought. Yet, he regretted that with his time constraints and the need for personal time, such a thing was unlikely to happen.

He led them into the front room, which had evolved into his strategy and conference room after the bomb blast. Cara had already set out coffee, foam cups, and a variety of morning treats.

"Beautiful home, sir. I could help you with the gardens, though. You could use something more than trees and shrubs."

"I've been telling him that for years," replied Cara. "You're Cindy, right? Brad tells me you have something to do with daylilies."

"Yes, ma'am. Y'all might say I'm a daylily addict. My husband, too. Our garden has over a thousand different cultivars of daylily and hundreds of other perennials. It's gorgeous in the summer."

"Well, come springtime, we might just have to sit down and talk about this place." Cara smiled.

Brad looked at them both and half rolled his eyes. "Sounds like I'm gonna need a full-time gardener." He paused to pour a cup of coffee. "Help yourselves." He pointed toward the refreshments and then faced the graphic artist. "So, Cindy, did you put together what I asked for?"

"Sure did. And I found a couple of extra aluminum easels to display them on. They're over by the front door."

"Would you bring them in here and set them up for me?"

As Cindy walked away to retrieve her work, he turned to Jim. He had found it necessary to take Jim and Sheila into his confidence because they were dealing with the audio clip Lynch had provided him.

"Are you sure you want to do this?" asked Sheila. "If even half of what you said, and a fraction of what that implies is true, you'll be painting a neon bulls-eye on your chest. Your family, too."

Brad nodded. "We've discussed it. The bulls-eye may only be fluorescent, but it's already there, remember? Look, if no one exposes them for this, what will happen then? Our nation can't afford that. If I have to be a martyr, so be it. But I'm convinced God has other plans for me, and if that's true, we'll be just fine."

"Done, sir," said Cindy.

Brad could tell she was eavesdropping as she set up the posters. He had not planned on telling her the full story of what he was about to do but now realized it would make little difference. In just over an hour, the whole world would know.

He perused the posters and put them in the order he desired. By themselves, they made no sense. With the revelation of the audio clip, though, they drove home the point. He nodded.

"Good work, Cindy."

"Jim, can you play the audio clip?"

As the clip ended, Brad looked at Cindy's questioning face. He began to explain when one of the security men interrupted.

"Sir, you might want to see this. On the TV."

As a group, they all walked into an adjacent room where a large screen television displayed a scene of carnage. Flashing lights of emergency vehicles bounced off buildings and personnel rushed about. The news anchor continued . . .

"Roughly ten minutes ago, eleven-thirty a.m. in New York City, a suicide bomber struck Times Square. The scene you see now is from our permanent camera overlooking the street. The first reports we have say that a man, in Arab headdress, walked down Broadway and stopped where a tour bus was releasing its passengers near the square. Members of the tour were to sightsee along the square before going to a matinee of *Jersey Boys*. The man walked along at the edge of the group, and as they joined the crowds already in Times Square, he yelled "*Allahu akbar*" and detonated a bomb vest he was wearing."

"These early reports state dozens are dead and over a hundred are wounded in a scene reminiscent of the bombing at the Boston Marathon last year."

Tears dropped from Brad's eyes. Although police departments had been alerted, they had been too late for these people. He glanced around the room to see similar expressions of horror, disbelief, and sadness. *What has happened to our country?* he wondered.

He saw Cindy gaze back toward the posters and point. Her hands trembled. "Th-that's what this is about?"

Brad took a deep breath and nodded. "We tried to alert the police. Now, we're about to alert the whole country and accuse some very powerful people of treason and murder."

Lynch had to maneuver his car carefully around the crime scene, and he counted every second. He also attempted to multi-task, trying to reach Brad by phone. Voice mail. He'd try again once he hit the interstate.

As he found his way clear, he saw Pat Goymerac running after him. She waved something in her hand and wanted him to stop. He complied and powered down his window. Huffing, she ran up to the door.

"You might want to take a gander at this before you go. Found it on the passenger seat of his car."

Lynch put the car into park and opened the manila envelope. His eyes widened as he examined its contents. In addition to papers, there were three flash drives. He had no way to check them in the car but speculated that they contained more than enough evidence to help them.

Leaning into the window, she added, "The colonel says take 'em. We're going to close this case, unless we can come up with that drone. And we both think that's highly unlikely. Anyway, he figures this thing is going to play out on a much larger scale than the St. Louis County Courts, so he thinks Brad Graham will need them more than us."

Lynch furrowed his brow. "Doesn't matter what court

hears it. There's still the chain-of-custody thing. It's evidence."

"Then I'll take them." Seamus walked up behind Goymerac. "Sign them out to me."

Lynch thought that might work, if they managed to get that far. He handed the materials back to Pat, who gave them to Seamus.

"Good luck." She turned and headed back to the crime scene.

"Wait a minute and follow me," said Seamus. "I'll give you a legal police escort." He grinned. "Besides, you might need some help."

Once upon a time, Lynch had been macho enough to believe he didn't need help. That attitude had led him into a death chamber he almost didn't escape. He had no problem accepting assistance now, especially when it had police authority attached to it. He missed having that authority.

"Thanks. Head to the county government center. Then I'll have to find out exactly where it is."

Moments later, with lights flashing and siren wailing on Seamus' car, the two vehicles took off like F-18s catapulting from an aircraft carrier's deck. In less than two minutes, they were on the interstate heading toward Clayton, the county center and location of the upcoming press conference.

Karolus sat in his penthouse overlooking Central Park from his favorite chair. Yes, he would miss this view and New York City. Unfortunately, the United States was about to become a most uncomfortable and inhospitable place to live. As he spoke, most ambassadors to the U.N. were already en route to their homes, their personal belongings and staffs to follow.

The new world government would set up temporary offices at the U.N. building in Geneva, while a new complex was built near Rome. Karolus saw it as fitting that they would return to the location of perhaps the world's greatest empire. Although Constantine had chosen his eastern capital instead of Rome, he had been shrewd enough to blend Christianity into their ancient mysteries and form a totalitarian state in which he had complete control. Centuries later, that power consolidated within the church in Rome.

Lost in thought, Karolus later saw that Francois had slipped in and laid some paperwork on the side table next to him. He picked up the half a dozen sheets and reviewed them.

On top, his schedule. He had but an hour remaining in this fine city. Perhaps, after the coming turmoil had been quelled, they would be able to rebuild here. They had no immediate plan to do so.

The remaining sheets brought a smile to his face. Fawaz no longer stood as a weak link in their plans. A series of aerial photographs showed the man leaving a restaurant, looking at his phone, a hole appearing in his forehead, and his collapsing to the ground. The man's death was confirmed.

He picked up a satellite phone from the table where the papers had been. He wouldn't risk using a landline or commercial cell phone for this call.

The phone on the other end rang once.

"One moment, sir. He's in a meeting. I'll retrieve him."

A minute later, "Hello, Karolus, or should I say, Mr. Secretary General? To what do I deserve this honor? Congratulations, by the way."

"Good morning, Mr. President, and thank you. The selection process was a rough one." Both men laughed. "I want you to know that everything has been set into motion and to confirm that the loose end known as Fawaz has been dealt with. When the time comes, I'm sure you'll have comforting words for his family about the service he gave his country."

"No doubt. We already have two storylines prepared about his death once it's picked up by the news services. I prefer the first where we have created a militant Christian group that will claim responsibility for his death, as retribution for the attack on the school. There are so many fringe groups in the Ozarks, that was an easy one."

Karolus chuckled. "Excellent."

If all went as planned, the afternoon's breaking news would be the fire bombings of two mosques—Detroit's Islamic Foundation, where Imam Al-Bashara would also cease to be a loose end, and the Masjid Usman Bin Affan here in the city, as the closest mosque to Times Square. Both, of course, would be reported as retaliation for the recent spate of Muslim terror attacks. Tomorrow, two churches, in Los Angeles and Dallas, would be bombed.

The ensuing holy war would bring civil unrest such as America has never seen on its shores since its Civil War. The resulting stock market plunge would create economic turmoil and embroil the globe. Calls for the government to intervene will increase. Yet, neither America, Russia, nor the European block would have the resources to succeed.

Emboldened and encouraged by The Assembly, Iran would form an alliance with its Islamic neighbors and allies, and move to remove Israel from the map. This time they would successfully remove the global scourge of Judaism.

At that time, as the world cried out for help, Karolus will step in with his plan, their "messiah" will appear, and a negotiated agreement will bring peace to those countries in turmoil, and ultimately, to the Middle East. The Assembly will introduce its global currency, and all nationalist governments will electively relinquish their sovereignty to the new global government.

Indeed, the end game was in sight. Check and checkmate.

"*Novus Ordo Seclorum*. Karolus, we are about to see the new world order our forebears dreamt to see in their lifetimes."

"Yes, we are, Mr. President. Yes, we are."

Forty-two

Lynch and Seamus raced through the late morning traffic to get to the location of the upcoming press release. Lynch had grave concerns about Brad's safety. He had stressed avoiding the outdoors because security was next to impossible. Yet, in the rush of setting up such a last minute event, had they been able to find an indoor venue?

For the third time while en route, he pressed the speed dial button for Brad's phone, only to go straight to voice mail. He realized he didn't have Eric's number, and in thinking about Eric, he remembered that they needed to have a "little chat." In desperation, he fumbled with his thumb trying to scroll through his contact list to find Stan's number.

He almost plowed into Seamus' rear bumper coming off the inner beltway. Despite the lights, the drive into Clayton's business district took longer than he hoped. Seamus pulled in front of the county police building and Lynch pulled in behind him.

Stan answered his phone on the third ring.

"Stan, it's Lynch. Where's the press conference this morning?"

"What press conference?"

"Brad didn't tell you?"

There was silence on the other end for a moment, followed by an audible sigh. "No. We didn't have anything planned for at least a week, thanks to the bomb, so I'm at my place on the Lake of the Ozarks. What's up?"

"I, uh, can't talk about it on the phone. Where would he be having one? You know, a press conference. He mentioned Clayton, but not exactly where, and I haven't been able to reach him."

"Well, we have a contract with the Ritz Carlton, but their facilities were tied up this weekend. Check there, and I'll try to get hold of Brad or Eric and call you. What time is it scheduled?"

"Eleven. I think."

"Okay. I'll be in touch."

The man sounded exasperated, but then this wasn't really a campaign speech or announcement. He could see where Brad might not have wished to disturb his campaign manager's weekend away at the lake.

Lynch pulled out and eased up next to Seamus' car while lowering the passenger window.

"Let's try the Ritz. Stan's trying to get me more info."

He pulled ahead and led the way to the Ritz. As he neared Carondelet Circle, in front of the hotel property, he could see activity within the small park-like plaza inside the circle. To his dismay, he found Eric there, marshaling the troops to set up sound equipment on top of a small platform. He rounded the circle and found the closest parking spot he could.

"Eric!" He waved as he ran toward the group. "Not outside! We can't do it outside!"

Eric waved back and stopped what he was doing to meet Lynch at the edge of the plaza. He removed a set of ear buds and let them drop over his shoulders.

"What?"

Lynch stepped up next to him. "We can't hold this outside. We have to find a more protected space."

Eric threw up his hands, shaking his head. "This is all I could do. This is the third time we've started setting stuff up. The Ritz has no room. None of the restaurants that are open this early have room. The April primaries are just a week away. Everyone is booked. We're gonna be lucky to get any reporters here at the last minute anyway. I just don't get why this is so important."

Obviously, Brad had not informed his staff about the nature of this press conference. Not that Lynch could blame him. Not only would they likely try to talk him out of it, the risk of a leak would be high. Lynch decided he would not be the one to tell them.

"Okay. I, uh, guess we'll have to live with this."

Eric smiled. "Hey, look, even God's favoring us. The sun's coming out. The temperature has warmed ten degrees since we got here. We're going to have a nice day for an outside press conference. A nice day, period, for a change. Enough of winter."

Eric returned to his work, and Lynch began scrutinizing the area, spinning from one direction to another. Seamus walked up as he did so.

"A security nightmare. Does it have to be outside?"

Lynch looked at him and frowned. "Guess so. Nowhere else to do it."

Lynch saw Seamus scanning the area and knew he was likely thinking the same things—tall towers from the east to southwest, with one narrow gap for an access road to the south. A shorter building to the north and northwest. All excellent vantage points for a shooter.

Then, there were wide gaps to the northeast and west, for Carondelet Plaza, the main thoroughfare.

How could he begin to protect Brad here?

Well, he knew he lacked the manpower to deal with the towers. He decided he needed to focus on a potential drone attack.

"Shay, I was thinking . . . how could a drone make such an expert head shot like it did?"

"Yeah, I was thinking about that, too."

"Okay, so the drone would have to come straight in on the target, identify the target, and shoot at just the right time."

Seamus nodded. "So, first thing, how does it identify the target? A camera, obviously."

"The technology's there. But the thing would have to come head on to the target, right? I mean, for an operator to see and identify a face, he's got to have a direct look at the face. What if he can't get that look?"

Seamus nodded. "So, we need to position Brad in a direction to minimize, if not eliminate that possibility."

Lynch nodded. "Go stand where Eric has the microphone, and pretend you're talking. Look to different directions as you talk and I'll check you out from the west and northeast. Those are the only two avenues where a drone could have a clear shot."

Ten minutes later, at Lynch's directions, Eric and his crew repositioned the platform and mic to face the south. That gave them the best protection from facial recognition.

Seamus walked back to his car, while two reporters, whom Lynch recognized, arrived and started to chat with

Eric. Lynch watched Brad's aide shrug his shoulders. The men looked at their watches and then at each other, as if deciding whether or not to stay. Lynch walked over to the group.

"Hey, it's Lynch Cully. Good to see you, Lynch."

Both men extended their hands.

"Trust me, fellas, you're gonna want to stay for this one and your colleagues who decide to skip it will be kicking themselves for a lifetime."

"What's—"

Lynch held up both hands. "Trust me."

As he said that, Seamus came running up and grabbed his shoulder, pulling him away from the men. He looked anxious.

"Hey, O'Connor, you're here, too?" One of the men tried to get his attention, but Seamus simply waved in recognition and continued to pull Lynch farther from the group.

Eric yelled, "Twenty minutes, folks. He'll be here in 20 minutes," and began corralling his volunteers and placing them in position. Two more reporters joined the group.

Lynch pulled away from Seamus. "Hey, I need to get back there. My security guys will be here before Brad, and I need to brief them."

"No, you need to see this first." He waved the manila envelope from Fawaz's car. In particular, he waved a sheet of paper with handwritten notes on it.

Lynch reviewed it and saw a list of places and buildings. Times Square had today's date and a time, 90 minutes ago.

"Did you hear what happened?"

Lynch shook his head. He'd been too focused on the "then and now" to wonder what was happening in the world.

"I had the radio on, on our way down here. Ten-thirty, eastern time, a suicide bomber hit Times Square. Dozens reported dead but nothing official yet."

Lynch's heart sank, but he gazed again at the paper. Two more places were tied to today's date but with times this afternoon. The first place leapt off the page at him— the Islamic Foundation in Detroit. He pointed to the name.

"Isn't that where you tracked down the school shooters?"

Seamus nodded. "And that second place is a second mosque, in Manhattan. I looked it up on my phone. It's just blocks away from Times Square."

Lynch began to see the pattern. Tomorrow's date listed two churches. Tit for tat. You strike us, we'll strike back. The population was already on edge. After more than a decade, the fall of the World Trade towers remained seared in many minds, and they weren't happy with the government's failure to eliminate Al Qaeda, despite the President's lies that the group was no longer a threat.

Add to the mix the failed presidential promise of finding those responsible for the attack on our Benghazi consulate, the President's repeated ignoring of laws on the books, distrust over the problem of illegal immigration, and unrest over a failed healthcare program. People weren't going to wait for a leaderless government to step in to bring justice. They would see these as attacks by an opposing faction, not as moves by a federal chess master using his pawns to bring down the country. They might just be on the verge of a religious civil war. Mike Southworth had been right.

"You've got to alert those police departments."

"I will, but I wanted you to see something else." Seamus pulled a second sheet from the envelope. "Do you know any Arabic or Farsi? I don't know which this is."

He pointed to a phrase at the top of the sheet: الله يبارك لك وله المحيطي سلام عليك.

Lynch shook his head. "No, I don't. They have different origins, but both are written in the Arabic alphabet. That's all I really know. Why?"

"See the numbers below it? More phone numbers and they're just a digit or two different than the ones used to launch these attacks."

Had they stumbled upon some kind of abort code? Or one to launch more terror cells?

The lead car arrived and members of Lynch's security squad emerged. Lynch turned to join them.

"I gotta go to work. These guys aren't going to believe what I'm about to tell them. Call your own Bureau or the county. I'm sure there's a translator somewhere on call to help."

"And then what?"

"Let's hope we have time after this press briefing to figure that out."

Lynch ran back to the plaza and began his briefing. As he'd expected, there were a lot of raised eyebrows, not to mention incredulous comments.

"Tony, go see if you can gain access to the roof of that residence building. It's our tallest vantage. Watch for roof shooters and a possible drone." He watched the man take off for the building to their south. "Alex, get four sets of binoculars from the car. You four will spot all directions, air and ground. Jim, you're with me by the platform."

Eric walked up to Lynch. "Five minutes."

Lynch nodded. The crowd had grown. He felt sure his comment had some role in that. The news was a highly competitive business. Just the fact that the two reporters he'd spoken with had decided to stay would lure others in, others afraid of missing out on something big. And *this* was something huge.

Brad's SUV rolled into the circle and several people got out. Lynch recognized Jim Collins and Sheila West. Each carried a box of press materials. A third woman carried easels, which she set up on both sides of the platform before placing large posters upon them. The top poster was covered. Then came Brad.

Lynch sighed in relief to see that Cara had not joined him. The pressure of protecting Brad alone weighed on him, without worrying about covering his family in an open space such as this.

Brad stepped up to the podium and tapped the microphone. He looked around at his audience and nodded to several individuals in greeting. "Good morning everyone." As if on cue, the sun came out and illuminated the circle. "Looks like I'm getting a vote of confidence from above." He laughed, along with about half of those present.

"I'm here for two reasons. First, and although this might seem important in itself, it's really the lesser reason I'm with you today. I know the 2016 elections are over two years away, but I am officially announcing that I will run for president under the American Party banner. The bomb that destroyed my offices and killed three people, three friends whom I valued, will not deter me. In fact, that act of cowardly treachery sealed the deal. Those involved in that act of terror will find me a formidable foe."

He paused and looked out across the crowd. Lynch scanned the crowd, the surrounding circle and all traffic lanes coming in and out of the circle. Nothing caught his attention, but he continued to watch.

"However, as I stated, that is the lesser reason for this conference. As you know, over the past week there have been a number of terrorist actions across the country, some successful, some thwarted. Just this morning, a suicide bomber struck Times Square."

He ticked off a list of those offenses and paused again. Lynch remained on edge. Seamus ran up to Lynch.

"Here, look at this."

Seamus handed him another sheet. Lynch's eyes widened.

"Interrupt him. Give it to him."

Lynch hesitated.

"Go!" Seamus whispered.

Lynch took a deep breath and walked toward the platform. He handed the paper to Brad and whispered, "This came from materials we found with Fawaz this morning."

As he left the platform. Lynch noticed Eric walking toward his car. The man opened the trunk and peered inside, but Lynch couldn't see what he was doing. A moment later, he closed the trunk and moved to sit down in the driver's seat, with the door open. Lynch wanted to run over there to see what he was doing, but duty called him to remain vigilant near the platform.

Brad showed no reaction as he read the papers provided by Lynch. He glanced heavenward and then continued, "My main reason for this briefing is to inform you, and the American public through you, that the President of the United States, the new Secretary General of the United Nations, the head of Homeland Security and other high-ranking officials in the federal government have been complicit in these actions in an effort to destroy American sovereignty and remove the U.S. as the last remaining superpower. In fact, the paper just handed to me reveals that National Security Advisor Roberta Faris initiated the chain of events that led to the recent school shooting here, as well as bombings and other terror acts that followed."

Hands shot up, cameras clicked, and video camcorders caught the frenzy that resulted. Brad nodded to the woman by the easel on his left.

"Before I answer questions, I wish to explain the evidence we have so far." Brad moved to the easel and began to lay out the evidence. Cameras continued to catch every phrase, every nod of his head. Even the most liberal of the news people in attendance hung on his every word. He had their attention.

"Lynch!" Tony's voice came through Lynch's earpiece. "Rooftops are clear and I don't see anything unusual in the windows and balconies I can spot. But there's something in the air, in the distance, coming from the northwest. I can't make it out yet, but it's low in altitude. And it's moving!"

Lynch heard growing anxiety in the man's voice.

"Holy crap! I didn't really believe you earlier, but it's a drone. It's really a drone!"

"Record it, Tony! Catch it all, everything it does."

Lynch didn't need to say anything to his men. They all had heard Tony's report, but they couldn't see anything or hear anything yet.

And why was it coming from the northwest? Was the operator using the lower building as cover? Still for facial recognition, the drone's camera would have to find Brad, who no longer stood at the microphones, and ID him. The drone would have to circle around to make that possible.

Unless.

Lynch knew that instant that his assumptions were wrong. He hadn't played the "what if" game to its logical conclusion. How did the earliest smart weapons find their targets? Someone on the ground had to tag them with a laser. Lynch ran to Brad.

"You're in danger, sir. We need to go!"

At that moment, the drone's engine buzzed above the usual traffic noise. Brad, reporters, volunteers, Lynch and his crew—everyone there focused on the direction of the strange noise they heard.

Lynch scanned his boss' body. No laser points. And then he saw the American flag lapel pin. It was identical to the one on Fawaz's jacket.

A GPS locator tag. The drone didn't need to be as sophisticated as he'd thought. The locator tagged the target and software on board used the camera simply to find the head. Then came the shot. They didn't need a face. They could come from any direction and pull off a fatal head shot.

Lynch grabbed the lapel pin and ran, looking around as he moved away from the crowd. To the northeast was open ground beyond the road. But how could he fool the computer? Then he saw it. A lamppost with a single globe for its lamp. Its head?

He dashed toward the pole and above them the drone changed course, angling toward him. He ran up to the pole. Would it work just to lay the locator at its base? On the sidewalk side, he found something better. Someone's lost cat poster, stuck to the pole with that ticky-tack stuff. He ripped off the paper, stuck the locator to the putty, and bolted back toward his crew.

Halfway into the circle, he heard the blast of the lamp's glass globe shattering. However, a sudden roaring noise overtook them all, and the bright light of flames caught his attention. A missile whizzed overhead and struck the lamppost at its base.

The percussion of the blast pushed Lynch five feet forward and onto the ground. Two nearby cars flipped to their sides as if some unseen hand had tossed them like toys. In fact, Lynch felt as if hands had cushioned his fall and surrounded him. As he climbed to his knees, he saw debris all around him but nothing within three feet of his body. Metal shrapnel, concrete chunks, and more lay around him, but something had protected him.

Lynch looked up to see everyone from the plaza scattering. His crew remained on site, and all had taken to shooting at the drone. Their chances of hitting it were nil, but then Lynch realized the odds of his finding that putty on that lamppost were equally as bad.

He said a quiet, "Lord, please" and as if guided by

another unseen hand, one bullet seemed to hit its mark. The drone sputtered and shook as it crashed to the ground 100 yards west on the main street.

Forty-three

For the second time that day, Lynch found himself surrounded by police. They had no trouble convincing the authorities of the validity of their claims. They had the drone. They had video footage from Tony's camera, as well as from those of several reporters on the ground. They had Fawaz's handwritten accounts, plus whatever they might find on those flash drives.

Miraculously again, no one had been hurt. Even Lynch's shoulder felt fine, despite landing on it again. Maybe he needed to practice diving to the *right*, not his left.

The press corps, although shaken, rushed to take on the story. They grabbed their copies of the materials produced by Jim and Sheila, which included copies of the sound clip between Fawaz and Karolus Karling. Experts would be called in to analyze and verify the voices on that clip, and Lynch suspected the naysayers would outnumber those who agreed it was Karling.

By the afternoon, press vans would be parked outside Roberta Faris' home, the White House, and other federal office buildings. Unfortunately, they'd be filling the street outside the Graham home, too. That could become a security nightmare, if Lynch hadn't already taken steps to move the family.

Lynch sat with Brad in the back of the SUV as they left the scene of the drone attack.

"That was quite the press conference, eh, Lynch?"

"Yes, sir. Most explosive I've ever been to." Unsure whether the humor would be appreciated, Lynch offered half a grin with it. "Sir, about that lapel pin . . ."

"Yeah, about that. How'd you know? I've worn that since we started campaigning for the Senate."

"Who gave it to you?"

Brad pursed his lips as he thought about that. "First, how did you know?"

"It was off. You know, just not right. And it was identical to the one on Fawaz's lapel."

"Okay, but off how?"

"It only had 12 stripes. I didn't expect all 50 stars on something so small, but there was plenty of room for the bottom red stripe. And did you notice the stars? They were the upside down stars of the Freemasons. I bet if we ever find the pin and count the stars, there will be only 33."

Brad sat there, staring out the window as the car moved past the Galleria Mall.

"Anyway, I thought it highly unusual that you had the same pin as Fawaz."

Brad turned toward him. "I'm sure glad you're observant. How could I have worn that pin for the past three months and not have noticed?" He shook his head. "To answer your question, Eric gave it to me. Well, he put it on the jacket anyway. I hate to think he's responsible."

Lynch nodded. Money had a way of talking to even the most loyal at times. As he thought back to the event, he tried to recall Eric's location as the drone approached. As best he could remember, the man had remained sitting in his car.

"Where is Eric, by the way?"

Brad frowned. "Good question. Maybe he's taking some of the volunteers home. I believe the two cars that overturned belonged to two of them."

Brad pulled out his cell phone and dialed.

"Eric, where are you?"

Lynch couldn't hear the man's reply.

"Thanks. Meet up with us at the Doubletree in Chesterfield when you're done." He put aside the phone and looked at Lynch. "I was right. He's taking those volunteers home. He's dropped off two and has one more to go."

Lynch thought about that for about one second before saying, "Change of plans, sir. *I'll* meet him at the Doubletree. You pick up your wife and son, take the other car, and go to this address." He wrote down an address on a business card. "I'll let the people who live there know you're coming. You'll be safe there."

Brad looked at the address. He gave no look of recognition.

"You'll like them. They have a great old house that Mike restored and Mary's a great cook."

"We can't impose on them."

"Don't worry, sir. They won't see it that way. They sure didn't when Danijela and I appeared on their doorstep without warning."

The thought of Danijela hit Lynch harder than he expected. Had it really been just four days since he saw her last? Had they made it home to Bosnia? Something inside wanted to deny she had gone. He shook his head to clear his thoughts.

"Is it okay if I let Stan know? He called to say he was on the road heading back from the lake. He wasn't real happy with me over the press conference. He started out as soon as you called him, so he should be here within the next 30 minutes."

Lynch thought about that. He didn't want *anyone* to know where Brad would be staying.

Brad must have read his thoughts. "Look, Stan and I go back to elementary school. I trust him with my life. You can't say anything to make me suspicious of him."

Lynch wanted to try but knew he'd get nowhere. "If I said 'no,' would you call him anyway?"

Brad chuckled. "You're getting to know me too well. Yes, I'd probably call him anyway. If I was risk adverse, I wouldn't have the company I own now, and I sure wouldn't be running for president."

Lynch took a deep breath. What could he say?

Lynch didn't have to wait long for Eric to show up. The SUV, decorated with campaign signs, appeared under the canopy outside the main doors. Only Eric emerged.

"Hey, Lynch. Is Brad inside?"

"Kinda. We need to talk."

Eric gave Lynch a skewed look. "Um, sure. What's up?" The young man crossed his arms over his chest and took a defensive stance.

"I've had some questions for you ever since the office bombing. "

Eric looked uncomfortable and did not relax.

"After I left to go to the conference room, did you

move either of the copiers? I'm trying to figure who put them where they ended up."

"I never touched them. The delivery guy brought them in, and all I did was fill out the paperwork."

Eric started to look more relaxed. He even uncrossed his arms. Maybe Lynch was wrong about him.

"So, the delivery guy was the last to touch them?"

"As far as I know. Stan came out from the back to find me. I preceded him to the conference room, so I honestly don't know if he ever touched them or not. Why? A bomb's a bomb, right? Did it really matter where they were in the room?"

"What about Brad's lapel pin?"

Eric's eyes widened. "Wow, wasn't that something. How in the world did you suspect that pin was involved?"

Eric continued to unwind. It seemed apparent now that he had no concern about a personal involvement in the assassination attempt.

"Brad says you gave it to him, put it on his coat yourself."

Suddenly, Eric's eyes widened and he looked aghast. "A-are you suggesting I-I had something to do with both events?" He shook his head. "That's crazy. I'd never ..." His brow furrowed. "Wait a minute; Stan gave me that pin, too. He's the one who asked me to use it on Brad's coats and jackets whenever we were out and about. I just followed orders and moved it from one jacket to the next." He shook his head again. "Not me. He's not gonna pin this on me."

"Eric, does Stan have a place at the lake?"

"I-I'm not sure."

Lynch felt like slapping himself on the head. He

should have been more insistent about Brad keeping his whereabouts secret. The odds were excellent that Stan had already arrived at the Southworth's home to meet Brad. Were they all in danger now?

In reflecting on Eric's statements, he now recalled that Stan had indeed come into the conference room last, after Eric. Although, he had no way of corroborating Eric's claim about being given the pin, the man's body language seemed to say he told the truth.

And Stan was absent from the press briefing. How could they verify that he was at the lake? Maybe he'd been not too far away, operating a drone. For that matter, he could control a drone from the lake. The Air Force controlled some drones in the Middle East from bases in the U.S.

"Does Stan have any hobbies, or past military experience?"

Eric shook his head. "No military background that I know of, and his only hobby is sticking it to political adversaries. He'll go for the jugular if that's what it takes." He paused and again his eyes widened. "You know, he once mentioned working for McDonnell-Douglas until shortly after Boeing bought them. He was involved in the Tomahawk cruise missile's avionics."

Lynch ran to the SUV Brad had left behind for him. He dialed Brad and his call went directly to voicemail. He tried Mike's cell with the same result. He had success with Seamus.

"Where are you, Shay?"

"Still in Clayton. Why?"

"I think there'll be another attempt on Graham's life,

and his family. I sent them to the Southworth's home. I think Stan is the man, and I'm not talking Stan Musial. He's probably there with them by now, but I can't get past anyone's voicemail."

"Okay, uh, I-I'm, uh . . . let me see what I can do. I doubt they'll let me take off right now. I'll call Ferguson PD and ask them to send a car over. I'll keep in touch."

Lynch wasted no time on the interstate, but the trip still required over 30 minutes. Seamus could have been there in ten, with lights and siren. Would the local department be able to handle things?

He pulled into the quiet neighborhood of century-old homes and felt relief to see a patrol car parked outside the Southworth home. A single patrol car. No EMS. No watch commander's SUV. Nothing to signify a problem. Also, no other car besides the one the Grahams had used to get here. Stan had not yet arrived.

He debated taking his gun inside and chose not to. After exiting the SUV, he walked over to the car and identified himself to the officer.

"No problems here, Mr. Cully. By the way, it's an honor to meet you. You've become like a legend in the local PDs."

Lynch smiled, unsure how to respond. To him, legends were myths, and every aching part of his body bore proof that he was very much real flesh and blood.

"Thanks for watching over them. I can take it from here. I'm sure you've got things to do."

"Not a problem. I know the Southworths. I'd sure hate to see anything bad happen here."

Lynch watched the patrol car pull away, and then

walked past Brad's car, up the driveway, and to the front door. As he walked, he saw signs of their gardens coming to life. Green poked through the old leaves everywhere. He'd been told that he needed to visit often in June and July because their gardens would be at their peak.

"Come in, Lynch," said Mary at the front door. "We're just about to have a late lunch."

Lynch greeted everyone inside. Cara sat on the same couch where Lynch had recuperated a month earlier. Mark sat in front of the aquarium, mesmerized by the fish.

"We just got wonderful news, Lynch," said Cara. "Harris Burke, Mark's principal, is awake and communicating with his family. God has answered a lot of people's prayers."

"That's great. I'm really glad to hear that." He truly was glad the man had pulled through, but he had other concerns at the moment. He motioned for Brad to join him on the front porch, out of earshot of the others.

"Where's Stan? I expected him to be here already."

"He had a flat. Might be another hour." Brad turned to look back inside. "You were right. This couple is great. We've made some new friends today."

"Eric checks out. He says Stan gave him the lapel pin, and that Stan was the last person in the front room before the bomb went off. Seems kind of convenient that Stan was out of town for both drone attacks and that he has a previous work history in avionics."

"Stan? No way. He was a poli-sci major in coll—"

The retort of a handgun, followed by splintering wood on a nearby porch column interrupted. Both men dove for the floor.

"Get inside. Call for help."

Lynch pushed Brad to move and shoved him through the front door just as another shot struck the house next to the front doors.

Lynch now regretted having no weapon. Accustomed to wearing a shoulder holster as a detective on the Ladue police force, his injury precluded wearing it. And he found a hip holster too uncomfortable to manage while driving. Why had he had left it secured in the car?

He lifted his head above the porch rail long enough to see a figure peering from behind the large walnut tree in the front yard. The person appeared to be male, with a dark grey hoodie covering his head and hiding his face.

The man stepped out from behind the tree. What was Lynch to do? With no answering gunfire, the man knew he had no direct opposition. Lynch wanted to move inside as well, but the gunman had him pinned down. He rose up again to see the gunman easing his way toward the house, gun extended and ready to shoot.

Could Lynch jump him as he came onto the porch? Doubtful. The man knew he was there. And with his bum shoulder and left arm in a sling, he had little chance of taking the assailant. He was a sitting duck.

The man was 20 feet from the porch when one side of the double front door opened.

"Lynch."

Lynch could hear Mike whisper from inside, but the retired Army colonel was hidden from view.

"Get ready. When I count to three, jump up and get behind the post."

Lynch wondered what that would accomplish, but the

wide post with its ornate woodwork would easily protect him from being shot. He moved onto one knee and prepared to do as instructed. The gunman was now just below him on the first step to the porch.

"One . . . two . . . three."

Lynch jumped to both feet and dashed behind the post. As he did, another shot reverberated through the neighborhood, and he heard the bullet whiz past his ear and embed itself in the side of the house somewhere behind him.

And that shot was answered from the doorway. Then there was silence.

Mike walked out the front doors just as two patrol cars pulled up in front of the house. He held his own 9mm S&W with both hands, prepared to shoot again.

In short order, two officers, one of whom was the man Lynch had seen earlier, converged on the downed gunman. One kicked the man's gun out of reach while the second stooped down to check the man. The officer spoke into his radio.

"Dispatch, we need EMS at our location. One victim with gunshot wound to the chest."

That officer began to apply first aid, while the other approached Mike for his gun. Mike relinquished it without complaint.

Lynch walked down the steps and stood over the man. Within the sweatshirt's hood, he saw a familiar face. Eric.

Forty-four

Amy couldn't believe what she saw on the evening news. Every channel she checked showed the drone coming in low over Carondelet Circle. The aircraft was small in comparison to something like the military's Predator, but its lethality was well displayed.

And Lynch. Running toward that lamppost with what was reported as a homing device, only to have the drone destroy the lamppost as he fled away. He had again saved numerous lives, and the press was calling him a hero.

Yet, the aftermath of that attack—the reports of collusion by officials at the highest level—would keep the news industry busy for months, even though CNN, NBC, and CBS were already siding with the White House. Plus, the FBI and every other law enforcement agency in the country would be investigating the claims. The Justice Department held jurisdiction. However, their track record and regard for the law under the current administration had been dismal. So it appeared they might be busier defending their lack of action, and state and local police authorities would do the lion's share of investigating while pressuring the Department to act.

The White House spin masters had already labeled the reports as false, fallacious, and felonious. The President had gone on the news to condemn Senior Analyst Abdul Aleem Malik Fawaz as an Iranian mole who had deceived the Department of Homeland Security and all involved so he could plot and unleash the heinous attacks witnessed across the country over the past week.

Conservative groups braced for an onslaught of attacks by those same powers, who took up Hillary Clinton's mantra of a huge right-wing conspiracy. They became galvanized in their grass-root efforts to remake the federal government, a government that had become so corrupt under the present administration that the President ignored the Constitution to pick and choose which laws to enforce and when.

Richard spoke up. "Hey, did you see—"

Amy's phone interrupted him. Caller ID displayed MedAir HQ, so Amy picked up. "Hello."

"Amy, it's Craig. Hey, you know that deal we made? Um, we have a slight emergency and could use your help tomorrow."

She still had the weekend to complete her medical leave, but that leave had not been her idea. It had been weeks since she'd been in the air. She was ready to go.

"Sure. I'm ready to fly. What's up?"

"We have a patient who needs to go to the Mayo Clinic from here. They couldn't get a fixed wing medevac, so we agreed to take her by one of our 407s."

The Bell 407 had an easy cruising range of 380 miles at a speed of 145 miles per hour. Amy did the calculations in her mind. Roughly 340 miles to the Mayo. That would be just over two hours up, refueling, and a bit longer back due to seasonal winds. Not much longer than flying by a twin turboprop airplane. Six hours seemed a reasonable time expectation. She didn't particularly like that it would tie up her Sunday, but the patient obviously needed the transfer, and Amy was well qualified to manage anything that might happen en route. She had only one reservation.

"Okay, I can do that, but aren't we expecting a weather front sometime tomorrow? Will that keep us from flying back?"

"We don't think so. We want to depart St. Luke's by six, so it's an early start. But that should get you back before any bad weather."

"Sign me up then. Where do we meet up?"

"The crew will pick you up here at the O'Fallon helipad at 0500."

Amy liked the sound of that. Their headquarters in O'Fallon was but ten minutes from her home.

"I'll be there."

Forty-five

Karolus needed no clock to awaken him. He sensed a change in the aircraft and knew they were approaching their destination, Rome's Ciampino Airport. The tailwinds had favored them, and their arrival would be 30 minutes earlier than planned. Still, dawn remained over two hours away, and his meeting with the Pope would not be until lunch, when he would dine with His Holiness in the vicar's private chamber.

As he sat upright, he noted a stack of papers awaiting him. He had not requested anything of Francois.

As he perused the material, anger rose within. Heads would roll. Mutineers would be hung from the tallest yardarm. Blindfolded rebels would face firing squads at dawn. Perhaps they needed to bring back the Persian's crucifixion, a form of execution perfected by the Roman Empire.

All of their plans for the United States now crumbled, instead of the nation's economy. Fawaz had betrayed them. Roberta Faris should have foreseen that potential. She should have completed the man's psychological profile instead of rushing ahead with the plan, although Karolus understood the administration's desire to remove Bradley Graham as a threat. Her resignation was expected. Then, an unfortunate accident would soon follow. They could not allow her to testify.

And their man in the Graham campaign? What of him?

He had failed as well, but he had paid for that failure.

He pressed the button next to his seat. Francois appeared within seconds.

"Yes, sir?"

"Thank you for this." Karolus held up the papers.

"Yes, sir. I knew you'd want to see them before landing. There are likely to be reporters at the airport, so I asked the pilot to reroute and land at Fiumicino instead. Perhaps we can avoid the reporters with the last minute change. The Vatican's car will meet us there."

Karolus smiled. "Always thinking ahead. I appreciate that, Francois. Now . . . I will need to speak to the Chinese Prime Minister sometime today. Please set it up."

"Yes, sir. Anything else?"

"Not at the moment."

Karolus returned to the papers in his hand. He had to give Fawaz credit. The man had been thorough in collecting data and documenting the involvement of the President's administration. If the President survived a potential impeachment, he would become the ultimate lame duck. Yet, he was expendable. There were more ways to skin the American cat.

"Sir?"

Karolus looked up.

"The Chinese Prime Minister wishes to talk with you right now if that is convenient."

Karolus nodded. They had yet to make their final approach to the airport. Now was a good time.

A minute later, the two leaders connected.

"Ah, Mr. Prime Minister, good day to you."

His Mandarin Chinese was a bit rusty, but it would

suffice. He listened to the man's reply.

"Yes, I am aware of what has happened in America. Our people failed to collapse the economy as planned, so we must now rely on you. I would like you to dump your dollars onto the market and publicly announce that you are abandoning the dollar in favor of the euro."

The Prime Minister protested.

"Yes, yes, I know what that will do to your economy as well, but it is necessary now, and you will be well compensated, as you know."

After further discussion and additional enticements, the man agreed to Karolus' request. The Chinese held so much American debt that it could do in one day what the failed plan would take a month to accomplish. The Chinese plan had always been Karolus' favorite, but they had protested because of the damage it would do to their own economy. Now, they had little choice.

Yes, one way or another, the American Goliath would be defeated so that *Novus Ordo Seclorum* could become the reality that fate held for it.

The Southworths invited Lynch, as well as Brad and his family, to join them at Destiny Church that Sunday morning. Brad and Lynch were recognized right away and swarmed by well-wishers. When Pastor Jim called them up for prayer, they welcomed it, for both realized that God had been protecting them.

Their plan for lunch became an impromptu pizza party at the Southworth's home where the Elite Eight of the NCAA Tournament dominated every television set in the house. Seamus and Sarah joined them, as did Jim Collins, Sheila West, Cindy Dye and their spouses. Lynch overheard Brad ask Mike if he could invite a few others to join them. To which Mike's answer was "the more the merrier."

Soon, the party's alternate purpose became evident to Lynch. Everyone who arrived had survived either the office bombing or the drone attack. Brad, with Mike's concurrence, wanted this to be a time of healing.

As the rooms of the first floor filled with conversation, laughter, and tears for those lost, the tinkling of metal on glass could be heard and everyone quieted. Brad pulled a chair to the wide doorway between the dining room and library, and stood upon it to address the gathering. The televisions were placed on mute.

"Friends, I would like to thank you for coming to this most impromptu get-together. I think, as you look around to see who is here, that you know *why* you were invited. We've gone through a horrendous last few days together."

Heads nodded and murmurs were heard throughout the two dozen or so people there.

"First, I'd like to thank Mike and Mary Southworth for sharing their absolutely gorgeous home with us."

Mike and Mary nodded and smiled as people clapped and several said "Here, here."

Brad continued, "I won't take long . . ." Several people laughed. ". . . I know, I'm a politician and long is a relative term. But seriously, I want to thank you for your work on my campaign, for supporting Cara and me, and for being honest people we can call friends. At this point, I'd like us to remember the three friends we lost three days ago.

Dominick had a passion for this country and a zeal to see it return to the bastion of freedom it once was, with the American Dream intact. Susan gave us her all. After losing her son in Afghanistan, she, too, was eager to see America return to the rule of law and to reclaim its heritage as a place where one was free to pursue his or her dreams without government intrusion. And Wanda, sweet Wanda, she wanted nothing more than to leave her grandchildren with the semblance of the country in which she grew up, without the mounting national debt that threatens to cripple us as a nation. For these three friends, let's have a moment of silence."

The rooms went silent as people bowed their heads and tears filled most eyes. After a minute, Brad continued.

"The events of these last days have galvanized the patriots in this great country and opened the eyes of many who stood on the sidelines. We've been given an opportunity to take our country back. We need to seize that opportunity and move forward. So, today, let's celebrate our friends. And tomorrow, let's get back to work and live up to their expectations."

With that, Brad stepped off the chair and joined into the conversation of the group nearest to him. Lynch scanned the room and was about to join Seamus when he saw Mary's face light up into a huge smile, and she rushed toward the front door.

A moment later, he heard a voice over the jumble of conversations around him.

"I think I go home, I am make big mistake. My family apply for asylum, too."

He didn't need to hear any more. He pushed through

the people around him toward the front door. Danijela!

He grabbed her from behind and pulled her to him. She laughed and turned into his arms.

"Hi there. I see on news where you about to get blowed up by missile and I—"

He didn't let her finish. His lips met hers, and he knew she had about a 100% chance of getting that immigrant's visa. He wasn't letting her go this time.

Mike stepped up to say hello, followed by Brad. Lynch introduced her to his boss. Danijela took his hand into both of hers and a tear rose in her eye.

"Thank you."

Brad replied with a subtle shrug and a smile. "I thought it to be the right thing to do."

Lynch furrowed his brow. What were they talking about? Did they already know each other? His confusion must have been obvious.

"Mr. Graham—"

"Please, call me Brad."

"Brad, he . . . I don't know word . . . he come to help my family."

Again, Brad shrugged, as if saying "No big deal."

"I was impressed by the way you folks took down that human trafficker, and when I heard that ICE was deporting everyone involved, I didn't think it was right to treat the victims that way. I may not be a senator or the president yet, but I still have friends in high places. I made a few calls and twisted a few arms. I think they're all going to get to stay and be allowed to become citizens, if they want to."

"Oh yes. Is dream of all the women there. Again, thank you, thank you." Danijela kissed Brad on the cheek.

As Brad introduced Danijela to Cara, Lynch heard a knock at the front door. Mike walked to the door, opened it, and stepped back.

"Richard? What . . .?"

Richard Nichols stood in the doorway, looking shaken and upset. He stepped inside but appeared lost in thought. Brad and Lynch approached him together.

"Richard, what's wrong?" asked Brad.

"I-It's Amy. She flew with a lady who needed to go to the Mayo Clinic this morning. They were supposed to return an hour ago. I just got a call. The storm front moved in faster than expected and her helicopter went down. They've not been able to reach any of the crew."

Sneak Preview:
WRONGFULLY REMOVED

One

ა❖ა

"Uh-oh!"

Amy Gibbs' head jumped to attention from its half-napping position, their helicopter sliding through the sky as if a giant heavenly hand had swept them aside, like brushing crumbs off a tabletop. Those were not words you wanted to hear from your helicopter pilot.

They had left St. Louis early that morning to transport a patient to the Mayo Clinic, eager to outrun a promised weather front that would move into the region that afternoon. All had been going smoothly and she tried to take advantage of the trip home to take a much-needed nap, as best she could manage on the Bell 407 where she attended as the flight nurse.

"Oh crap!"

Kent Howard had the reputation for being easy-going, calm, and methodical as a pilot, so even the mild expletive emerging from his lips gave Amy cause for concern. "What's wro—?"

A thump, loud enough to hear over the engine, arose from the rear of the aircraft, followed by a wobbly, slow uncontrolled spinning of the chopper, a spin that began to accelerate.

"Hang on!" yelled Kent into the intercom. "That storm cell popped up out of nowhere and something just took out our tail rotor."

Amy had seen training films about tail rotor failure. The tail rotor countered the torque of the main blades and kept a helicopter from spinning around. Without it, safe flight was no longer a possibility and most flight instructors trained their pilots to perform an autorotation to the earth. Under the best of conditions, that would be like careening down from the tallest peak of a roller coaster and hitting soft sand at the bottom. Under the usual circumstances, autorotation was more like a rock falling out of the sky. With this wind, well . . . the odds were strongly in favor of their hitting the ground, hard, and rolling.

There was a word for that, crashing.

A tear emerged from her eye at the thought. She'd become engaged to the man of her dreams less than a week ago. This wasn't fair.

"No trees, please," murmured Amy in a short, quiet prayer. "Lord, please help us safely to the ground." She donned her helmet, brushing her shoulder-length, dirty blonde hair back inside the headgear to keep it out of her eyes. She took a deep breath, but refused to close her eyes. She needed to be alert to everything happening around her.

Kent struggled with the aircraft, but managed to minimize its spin. "I can't autorotate with the winds we have now. I need to attempt a running landing."

Amy saw that he had managed to align the chopper so that it had a left crosswind, which helped to reduce the spin and compensate for the tail rotor's failure. But his airspeed remained high. A running landing at even 10 knots could seriously injure them all.

Rain and hail now pelted the windshield and made visibility impossible for those in the back. The darkened skies, making it seem as if they were flying at dusk and not late morning, didn't help that visibility. She hoped *he* could see what loomed ahead in the trajectory he had chosen. Again, she asked for no trees. Landing in trees would kill them all.

A flash of lightning gave her a sense they were nearing the ground. Kent had managed to slow the aircraft. She felt him flare the main blades and watched him temper the cyclic to bring their ground speed to zero. Hopefully.

A sudden gust of wind caused the 407 to shudder and in an instant, Amy felt the right skid hit the ground and dig in. Before she could blink, she was on her side, then upside down, her five-point restraint keeping her in the seat. They continued to roll, as she lost consciousness.

Sinead O'Malley criticized herself inwardly. Why had she told the man that she knew how to operate this blasted tiller? The April air had warmed and she was anxious to prepare the little garden plot she had so carefully laid out in her mind over the previous couple of weeks. She couldn't afford to waste time in a town that was over an hour away from the house. *How hard could it be to operate a tiller?* she thought. *Isn't it just like a lawn mower?*

Besides, the man at the rental store seemed so patronizing. She couldn't ever recall being called "little lady" before, despite her petite stature.

She again adjusted the choke and pulled the cord for what seemed like the hundredth time. This time it caught short and about yanked her arm off. She massaged her right shoulder and took a deep breath. After a moment, she grabbed the pull cord in her left hand and placed her right foot on the edge of the machine to stabilize it. She pulled and the old Briggs & Stratton™ engine sputtered for a few seconds. Encouraged, she eased off the choke and tried again. This time the engine roared to life.

She let it run, to allow the engine time to warm up, as well as to refresh her memory on how to engage the tines. Satisfied that the tiller wouldn't die on her, she eased the lever forward and startled as the machine began "walking" forward without her. She quickly grasped the handles and fought to maintain a straight line as she worked down the twenty feet of the first row.

At the end of the row, she stopped the tines and turned back to see what she had accomplished. Nothing more than scraping off the tops of the newly emerging weeds.

"This is going to take more work that I thought," she muttered. If the town wasn't so far away and her funds so limited, she'd almost consider giving up this fantasy she hoped would become a vegetable garden. What business did she, a New England city girl, have trying to become a farmer in rural Illinois?

Suddenly, a gust of wind slapped her like a Boston Bruins player checking her into the glass. She caught her hat as it tried to escape her head, and looked up expecting to see a tornado carrying off the house, as her old nemesis peddled into the clouds with Sinead's daughter strapped onto the back of the bicycle. She shook her head at the thought. Her Technicolor™ world devolved into black and white as the ominous clouds fomented toward her and seemed to swallow the sun.

The weather forecast had called for a storm front to move into the area that afternoon, but God apparently saw humor in making those weather people look foolish most of the time. How did that scripture go? "For the wisdom of this world is foolishness before God."

No, that wasn't the precise one she searched for. Mentally, she stepped ahead one verse. "The Lord knows the reasonings of the wise, that they are useless." Well, that fit most politicians, maybe weathermen, too, but it still wasn't the verse she strove to recall.

The first few drops of rain began to pelt her face. She saw that she would not have time to move the tiller out of the weather, if she wished to remain dry. So, she dashed for the back door of the house, holding tightly to her hat. She heard the noise as she reached the door.

The sound, like two cars slamming into each other head-on at high speed, came from above, but with the wind and escalating rain she couldn't tell exactly from where. She searched the sky, wiping more and more drops from her eyes as she did so. About to give up and go inside, she saw it. A helicopter spinning, in trouble, and falling.

"Mom!"

Her daughter's cry reached above the wind to catch her ears. At fourteen years of age, the girl still anguished over thunderstorms. She dashed through the door, into the kitchen.

"It's okay, Ruth. It's just a storm. Why don't you go

into the safe room? I need to go back outside."

The girl started to move from the kitchen, but turned her head back and reached toward Sinead with her right arm. "Come with me."

Sinead walked over to her daughter and cradled Ruth's hand in both of her hands. "I will. Soon as I can. Someone's in trouble out there and I need to see if I can help." She leaned over and gave the girl a kiss on the forehead. "Go on. You'll be safe in that room. Don't come out until I come get you."

The girl pleaded with her eyes, but Sinead knew she'd argue no more. Ruth knew her mother's grit and determination well. Once Sinead's mind was set, little could change it.

"Go on." She watched Ruth leave the room, and mentally thanked her friend, Adriana, yet again for the use of the old family home. Even more, that there was a room prepared which could withstand all but the most powerful tornadoes. That reassurance had proven critical for dealing with Ruth's fear. Yet, it wasn't a fear of the storm that lay at the bottom of the girl's anxiety, but fear of being separated from her parents again. Sinead sighed. The year and a half struggle to regain her daughter from foster care had been draining on them all. But the persecution wasn't over. Her husband, Jameson, sat in a Massachusetts jail cell on contempt charges, charges that the judge would drop if she and the girl would return to the state. In agreement, the couple vehemently refused to do that.

Another blast of wind caused the house to shudder. Sinead wrapped her arms across her chest and wondered what good she could do, even if she found the helicopter.

Still, her parents hadn't raised her that way. She knew she would offer what aid she could, even if that jeopardized being discovered by the authorities. There were other states in which to hide.

She grabbed a poncho from a coat hook near the back door, slid it over her head, and pushed through the back door into the storm. Small pebbles of hail, mixed with cold, heavy drops of rain made her pause. She shook her head and moved into the yard where the house no longer provided a modicum of protection from the wind. She looked toward where she had seen the aircraft, not expecting to see it there, of course. Yet, it had been on a course toward the northeast. The farm on which the home sat extended that direction. The fields had been leased to neighboring farmers, but an old tractor path had been maintained to allow movement between the fields. She decided to follow that rutted road, to find whatever she might discover. If she had found no crash site by the time she reached the end of the road, she would return to the house, her conscience satisfied that she had done what she could.

A quick note from Braxton . . .

I hope you enjoyed *The Silenced Shooter* and thank you for purchasing it. Please consider writing a review at Amazon, Barnes & Nobel, iTunes, Goodreads, or elsewhere. Reviews are crucial to Indie authors. It doesn't have to be lengthy. Just a couple of sentences will do.

Also, if you'd like to stay informed about my new books, book signings, and more, please sign up for my newsletter. You can do that at my website: **www.braxtondegarmo.com**. As a thank-you for signing up, you can get the eBook *And Then One Day*, a prequel to the MedAir Series. It's the story of how Lynch and Amy met . . . and how their relationship fell apart.

And did you know you can purchase signed copies of my paperbacks at my website? With shipping included in the price, ordering them directly from me is typically cheaper than ordering them online.

ABOUT THE AUTHOR

Braxton can't lay claim to wanting to be a writer all his life, although his mother and seventh grade English teacher were convinced he had what it would take. A bachelor's degree in Bio-Medical Engineering led to medical school and a residency in Emergency Medicine. He served for a decade in the U.S. Army Medical Corps with tours such as the Chief, Emergency Medical Services at Fort Campbell, KY, and as a research Flight Surgeon at Fort Rucker, AL. Who had time to write?

By the 1990s, as a civilian, his professional and family life had settled down, somewhat, and his mother once again took up her mantra, "Write a book. You're a good writer." In 1997, a Valentine's Day writing contest convinced him that maybe he could write fiction. He spent the next fifteen years learning the craft of writing.

Now, twenty-plus years after that first hesitant start, he has sixteen novels published, as well as non-fiction books and a children's book, and can't find enough time to write. As a Christian, he writes "true-life" Christian fiction (suspense and thrillers) that many call "cutting edge," as he's not afraid to take on such issues as human trafficking, racism, and more. His characters are real-life as well, with all the flaws and blemishes real people have. As such, his books are never likely to gain acceptance by the Christian Bookseller Association. But then, he never intended to tell stories just to the choir.

Books by Braxton DeGarmo:

<u>Still Here Series:</u>
The End Begins - 1
The Shaking - 2
The Beasts – 3
The Trumpets – 4
The Mark - 5

<u>Non-fiction Study Guides:</u>
Still Here! Surviving the End Times
Still Here! The Apocalypse is Now
Still Here! Countdown Revelation

<u>MedAir Series:</u>
Looks that Deceive – 1
Rescued and Remembered – 2
The Silenced Shooter – 3
Wrongfully Removed – 4
A Zealot's Destiny – 5
Kidnapped Nation - 6
The Khmer Connection - 7
Resurrected Trouble - 8

<u>Seamus O'Connor Thrillers:</u>
The Militant Genome
Ten Seconds 'Til

<u>Other Books:</u>
Indebted

<u>Children's Books:</u>
The Toucan Who Can Can-can

www.ingramcontent.com/pod-product-compliance
Lightning Source LLC
Chambersburg PA
CBHW051003180726
48291CB00006B/1957